JIM MORGAN

and

THE PIRATES

OF THE

BLACK SKULL

BY

JAMES MATLACK RANEY

J
RANEY

ISBN: 0985835931
ISBN 13: 9780985835934

Books in the Jim Morgan series:
Jim Morgan and the King of Thieves
Jim Morgan and the Pirates of the Black Skull

To COL James P. Holley, USA Retired,
one of the best men I've ever known.

TABLE OF CONTENTS

BOOK II: On the Shores of the Veiled Isle

Magic, Monsters, and Doom Beyond this Door.

Ye Have Been Warned...

O n dark nights, when the wind grows cold and the rain falls hard in London, the old pirates at the Inn of the Wet Rock spin tales as black as the weather. They tell of ghosts, devils, monsters, and magic by the light of a roaring fire.

There is one story darker than all the rest. It is the legend of the Pirates of the Black Skull, and the finding of the Treasure of the Ocean.

Many years ago, four friends vowed to seek out a long lost treasure from time out of legend. The four called themselves the Pirates of the Black Skull. Beyond the farthest islands they sailed. Into the deepest oceans they ventured. They uncovered ancient and dangerous secrets - secrets of magic and power not meant for mortal men. At long last, in the safekeeping of a kingdom under the sea, the pirates found the Treasure of the Ocean. It was a treasure worth more than silver and gold.

The Pirates of the Black Skull stole the Treasure. They bore it away to a ruined temple upon the shores of a forgotten island. There, beneath a stormy sky, they sought to unlock the Treasure's power. But men's greed and the Treasure's magic were both beyond the pirates' reckoning.

The pirates' lust for power corrupted their friendship. Within the walls of the temple they turned on each other and fought until one of the four was struck down dead. The Treasure's magic turned the dying man's blood into an enchanted cloud, a Crimson Storm bent upon fury and revenge. The remaining pirates barely escaped each other and the red storm with their lives. But the Treasure of the Ocean was lost once more.

Some say the story ends there. They say that the Treasure of the Ocean is gone forever and the wise should leave it so. But others have heard rumors, tales, and hints that the Treasure was found again. They've heard that the Crimson Storm still haunts the sea. They say those that remain of the Pirates of the Black Skull still seek to regain that which was lost...and will kill whoever stands in their way.

JIM MORGAN

and

THE PIRATES

OF THE

BLACK SKULL

BOOK I

DANGER AND DOOM ON THE HIGH SEAS

ONE

AT THE LIGHTHOUSE BY THE SEA

T he pirate captain drew his sword as he crossed the ship's deck. His cheek twitched with wicked glee beneath a grungy eyepatch. Through the sun's harsh glare he leered at his prisoner with his one good eye, holding her at bay with the point of his blade.

"Prepare yer soul for Saint Peter, and yer body for Davy Jones' locker, young lass. Ye've crossed us fer the last time and now me and me scurvy crew'll be seein' ya to sleep with the fishies o' the deep. Walk the plank, ye dog!"

The prisoner, her arms bound in rope, backed down the plank. A hint of fear swirled in her eyes. Her auburn curls drifted in the ocean wind. Her name was Lacey. Once she had roamed the streets of London

3

with a small clan of thieves. But now she cowered at end of a pirate's plank, just above the threat of the ocean deep.

"Tis the end of the road for ye, little Lacey," the pirate captain growled. He jabbed his sword once more in the girl's direction, intent on seeing her drop like a stone into the sea. "Swimmin' time!" All seemed lost for Lacey, when, from nowhere, a lone figure swung in on the rigging, sword gripped between his teeth. He landed with a flourish between the pirate and his prey, taking his blade in hand.

Jim Morgan had come to the rescue, ready to battle his old foe to the bitter end.

"Think again, Thick Beard, you poltroon!" Jim leveled his sword at the captain's chest. "If you wish to hurl Lacey into the ocean to swim with the sharks, you shall do so over my dead body!"

"Morgan!" Thick Beard rasped. Surprise flashed for a moment in his lone eye - but only for a moment. A slow, sly smile curved at the edges of the pirate's mouth. "What you don't know, Morgan, is that over yer dead body was exactly me plan! Haha! Ye've walked into me trap, set by me...and me entire crew!" On cue a battle cry erupted from the ship's deck. A second pirate, cutlass in hand, leapt to the captain's side, teeth bared and growling.

An epic sea battle for the ages was about to begin...

...only, something was not quite right.

Something was missing.

Captain Thick Beard paused to survey the deck with his one eye. An irritated grumble slipped through his gritted teeth.

"I said: me and me *entire crew!*" Thick Beard bellowed.

A third howl pierced the air and another figure swung on deck. But instead of landing beside Captain Thick Beard, he fell in at Jim's side, producing a sword from between his own teeth.

"Surprise, Thick Beard, you cur!" the new pirate shouted. "You're the one who's walked into a trap! Now you shall face not only the wrath of Jim Morgan, but the extra wrath of me: One-Eyed Pete!"

Jim turned and indeed found his good friend, Peter Ratt, quite unexpectedly at his side. Some sort of sock was wrapped about his head, half-covering his left eye. Jim shrugged and was about to go along with it when Thick Beard's wooden sword tumbled with an angry clatter on the deck at Jim's feet.

"Peter?" said Thick Beard. "Just what do you think you're doin'? We said at the beginnin' that you was gonna be part of the crew!"

"I'm tired of bein' part of the crew, George," Peter said. "I want to be a pirate with me own nickname. So I switched sides and joined Jim while your back was turned! No rule against that, now is there?"

"You can't DO THAT, Peter!" George, who had only a moment ago been playing the pirate captain, shrieked. "I'm Thick Beard, you and Paul are the crew, Jim's the navy cap'n, and Lacey's the damsel in the dress!"

"That would be damsel in *dis*tress, George," Jim offered. But when he turned toward the plank, Lacey's binds lay in a pile on the board and she sat lazily on the edge with her back to the boys. Her feet dangled in the water as she happily read her favorite book, looking anything but distressed at all.

George screamed again and kicked his wooden sword for good measure. Paul, who had been growling for the better part of five minutes, finally burst into laughter, which marked with certainty the end of playing pirates for the day. Jim laughed himself and sheathed his wooden sword in his belt.

The three brothers, George, Peter, and Paul Ratt, may not have been very good pretend pirates, but they were marvelous friends. They were also as close to famous as a trio of orphaned boys from London could be in those days. In their own words they were: "the princes of pocket picks," "the counts of the con," and "the barons of breaking and entering." Of course, those were their own words. But as it happened, they were nearly as talented as they thought themselves to be. There was not a more skilled pickpocket in all of England than George Ratt. Peter was equally renowned as an incomparable lockpick, and Paul was a natural-born con man. Then there was Lacey. She may have been the only person Jim knew who could coral all three Ratts at once. More importantly, the three brothers were Jim Morgan's best friends in the whole world, along with Lacey. She was as tough as George and as smart as Jim, and could always be counted on in a pinch.

As the Ratts argued amongst themselves on the little boat, Jim breathed deeply of the salty ocean air and stole a glance toward the shore. A tall lighthouse stood like a castle tower, looking over the bay. A field of green grass ran over the hills beyond, waving and whispering in the sea breeze. For the better part of a year that lighthouse had been home for Jim and his friends, where old MacGuffy, the retired pirate, kept watch over them.

A sandy beach and a crooked pier led up to the lighthouse's front door. It was at the end of this pier that just over one year ago, Dread Steele, the most famous pirate on the Seven Seas, had dropped off Jim and his friends after a harrowing escape from the streets of London. Dread Steele's former first mate, MacGuffy, had been quite surprised to find five orphaned children on his doorstep that night. But the gruff pirate had a kinder spirit than he would ever admit, and took the children into his home. The old salt was especially fond of Lacey, and had even given her one of his own books, which she read constantly and took with her everywhere. In fact, it was the very same book she was reading on the plank, about the stars in the sky and the stories of how they took their names, and of how they could predict men's futures.

The Ratts, on the other hand, had nearly driven poor MacGuffy mad. They spent most of their days arguing with Lacey, or wrestling each other one against two, or stealing MacGuffy's underclothes from the drying line to use as pirate flags, which they had done that very morning. All this sort of activity would turn MacGuffy's wrinkled face as purple as the scar that ran down from his old eyepatch. Of course, George was the worst of them all, dreaming up adventures and trying to live them out – often with catastrophic results. He was bottled up lightning just bursting to break free. In fact, Jim noted, George was causing a bit of trouble even now.

"You can't just untie yourself, Lacey," George complained. He made sure to put an additional dose of nastiness on Lacey's name and flipped up his eyepatch to glare at her with both eyes for good measure. "That's stupid!"

"Well I think this entire game is stupid, George!" Lacey retorted, climbing back to her feet and slamming the book down on the plank. "And why do I always have to be the damsel in distress? I wouldn't mind playing so much if I could be a pirate every once in a while."

"How many times do I have to tell you, Lacey?" said George, rolling his eyes. His brothers joined in to form a Ratt Brothers' chorus in reply. "There are no girl pirates!"

"Yes there are!" Lacey said. She threw her hands on her hips and her eyes flashed like blue lightning. "Dread Steele even said so himself."

"He was just bein' nice to you, Lacey, 'cause you were obviously terrified for your life."

"I was NOT, George! And if you're so sure, why don't you give me one of those swords and you and I have a go? Then we'll see, won't we?"

"Oh, come off it, Lacey," Jim said. He stepped up onto the plank to calm things down before his two best friends unleashed a real corker of an argument. "You know what George means. He just wouldn't want to fight you because it wouldn't be fair and all that. He's trying to be polite."

This was, as Jim was about to learn, the absolutely worst thing he could have said. He should have remembered the time Lacey knocked Big Red, a rather burly bully from London, flat on his rear end. But boys have rather short memories, especially boys who are nearly thirteen years old and absolutely full of confidence they can do anything.

"Wouldn't be fair?" Lacey balled up her fists and raised her foot to stomp, as she often did when dealing with the "usual boy stupidity," as she put it. But at the last moment her face surprisingly transformed into a sweet smile and she gently folded her arms across her chest. "Well," she said in an overly calm voice. "That is so chivalrous of you and George, Jim. Really, it is. But let's just say if I wanted, out of curiosity of course, to *try* to swordfight you - as silly as that would be - how far would you go to make it easy on poor little me? Would you fight me with one hand behind your back?"

"Of course, Lacey," Jim said. He thrust one arm behind his back and threw a wink to the Ratts behind him.

"Very kind of you, Jim. But I'm still not sure I could win, even then. You are *so* strong, after all. What about standing on one foot?"

"On one foot?" Jim asked. George and his brothers began to heckle Jim at his back, as though they had not been the very ones to start this argument in the first place.

"Fine then," said Jim, and he lifted his right foot.

"Perfect," said Lacey. Her little smirk twisted into a full-blown smile and she finally stomped her foot on the plank. The slim wooden board wobbled like a saw blade and Jim, on only one foot, tipped over backwards, his sword-bearing arm whirling like a windmill.

"Lacey, you—!" Jim shouted as he tumbled into the bay. George, Peter, and Paul's uproarious laughter accompanied him the entire way down.

Jim was far more aggrieved at having been so easily tricked than he was about falling into the water. He was by far the best swimmer of all his friends. "Swim like a fish ye do, Jimmy," old MacGuffy had said. In fact, Jim was planning on using that talent to sneak up beneath the plank and pull Lacey down with him, when something gave him a sharp tug. Jim looked beside and beneath him in the clear water, afraid he was under attack from an unfriendly fish. But the waters about Jim were empty, save for a few stalks of wavering seaweed.

Jim felt the tug again. This time it was a rough jerk. It not so much grabbed at Jim's ankle or wrist, but rather seemed to pull at his very soul. On the third tug, stronger and harder than the first two by far, Jim closed his eyes – and in the darkness saw a shape materialize before him.

An image flashed in Jim's mind - sudden, loud, and violent. Jim saw a roiling, crimson cloud. In the cloud was a face, eyes lit by purple lightning – eyes in the face of a black skull.

Jim tried to scream, but all he accomplished was swallowing a lung full of bay water. His plan of surprising Lacey completely forgotten, Jim surged back to the surface and came up coughing and spitting. Lacey pulled him up by the collar, helping him sit on the plank. She patted him hard on the back to force out the water, her cheeks quite pink and concern etched in her eyes.

"Oh, Jim, I'm so sorry! That was an awful trick! You were down there so long, I thought I would have to come in after you." As apologetic as Lacey appeared, the Ratt brothers were still howling like monkeys and pointing at Jim from the side of the ship. In spite of himself, the Ratts' laughter almost always made Jim smile. He laughed along as he pulled his feet all the way out of the bay and spit the rest of the water from his mouth.

"What happened down there, Jim?" Lacey asked. Jim was about to tell her exactly what he had seen, but looking down in the clear water, where there was nothing larger than a minnow and nothing deadlier than seaweed, he decided just to keep it to himself. It had been a rather frightening and confusing moment, one most difficult to explain without sounding quite mad.

"It was nothing," Jim said.

He had never been so wrong in his life.

Grizzled old MacGuffy was waiting for Jim and the others on the pier when they returned. His wispy white hair was tossed in the wind. He squinted his good eye as he whittled away on a piece of wood, which was only slightly less gnarled and twisted than the fingers carving it. Even as a retired pirate, he was the roughest looking salt Jim had ever seen.

"What have I told ye' lads and lass about sailin' on the bay alone? Or about bein' out there this late in the day? It be nearly nighttime! A storm or wave'll likely come up out o' nowhere's and smash yer skiff to matchsticks, and leave ye to be shark food in the meantime."

"I'm not afraid of storms or waves, MacGuffy!" Jim shouted back with an impossibly confident smile. He pulled the little boat to a stop at the pier and moored it to the post with the same ropes he and George had used to tie up Lacey. "She's a beautiful ship and besides, I'm your best sailing student ever. You said so yourself!"

"Not afraid o' storms or waves, says he," MacGuffy snorted. He shook his mangy head and held his hands up to the sky for mercy. "Those be the most foolish words ever I heard, ya sea pup!" MacGuffy was just about to expound the very same lesson on sailors and storms he had preached nearly every day since he had begun teaching Jim how to sail, when he caught sight of the buccaneer banner tied just above the skiff's sail.

"Are those me underclothes again, ya' blasted sea-Ratts? I told ye 'afore I would take the three of ye at once and knock yer senseless heads together like the brainless stones they be! Poseidon be merciful!" MacGuffy roared. His old, wrinkly face screwed up like a furious toad's. Jim almost felt sorry for the former pirate, but he couldn't help laugh as his friends scampered off the boat and passed MacGuffy on the pier, chortling and shouting at the top of their lungs.

"Only one more day, MacGuffy," Jim said happily, hopping off the boat. "Then you can go back to peace and quiet again, I promise."

"Aye, I'd almost forgotten what peace and quiet be like!" MacGuffy replied, his hands on his hips, glaring wickedly at the boys taunting him from the lighthouse steps. "Tired of me old lighthouse are ye, young Morgan?" MacGuffy said. Jim thought he heard a trace of sadness on the old man's voice. He even felt a bit of it in his own chest.

Jim's favorite part about living at the lighthouse had been the days MacGuffy spent teaching him how to sail the little boat in the bay. But Jim's time there was finally drawing to a close. Only a few days before, a letter had arrived from the town of Rye. Jim's wicked Aunt Margarita was finally to be arrested for her crimes. Ever since she betrayed Jim's father to his enemies, the Cromiers, Aunt Margarita had been living opulently off of the Morgan family fortune. But no longer. Morgan Manor was to be returned to Jim. At long last he was going home. Jim smiled at the thought. Even so, he would miss the lighthouse. He would miss MacGuffy.

"You know I love the lighthouse, MacGuffy." Jim said. "You never really had to let us stay, did you? But you did. You taught us how to swim and how to fish and how to sail. I'll never forget any of it. I promise."

"Well, what kind o' pirate'd I be if I'd let the old Count Cromier have ye, eh? Asides, twas good for old MacGuffy to have some company for a time, it was."

"You could still come with us," Jim said. The day the message had come, Jim had offered MacGuffy to come live at Morgan Manor, to continue teaching him about the sea and sailing and the stars. But the old man had declined then and declined again now.

"Nay, lad," MacGuffy said, looking past Jim and out over the sea. "Truth be told, this lighthouse ain't my home neither and it never were. The sea is my home, boy, the only home I'll ever have. Remember this, young Morgan." MacGuffy's good eye never left the ocean. "Lands and titles'll all pass on to others the very day a man dies – but his scars, his tales, and his great deeds in the storms o' the sea belong to him forever. Aye, they do."

Jim regarded the old man for a long moment, still staring over the waves and perhaps daydreaming of some long forgotten adventure. Jim felt sorry for MacGuffy at times like this, for the old man had never had a place to which he belonged. But Jim knew for himself that he belonged at Morgan Manor. He was certain that he was meant to be the next Lord Morgan, like his father before him.

But for the second time that day, Jim was more wrong than he could possibly know.

TWO

A FACE IN THE STORM

Night fell over the grassy hill, where the lighthouse stood watch over the bay. Inside the tall white tower, Jim Morgan was climbing the stairs for bed. His room, if it could even be called such, was barely a closet with a hammock stretched between two walls. Small as the room was, it at least had a little window that faced the sea. On warm nights, Jim would leave it open and let the ocean breeze and the rhythm of rushing waves lull him to sleep. Those nights he would dream of the day he would go home – dream of tomorrow. So it was that evening, and Jim opened his window to lean out into the moonlight.

From the floor below he heard the Ratts getting ready for bed. George was delivering his nightly sermon to his brothers. He railed on about how they would lose their pickpocketing skills if they gave up taking some real practice. He also added that the nice thing about having lived in a cellar beneath a shoe factory had been that they were never forced to do laundry or scrub floors all afternoon, which had been their punishment for getting into MacGuffy's underthings.

After a long moment at the window, Jim retreated back into his room and sat on the edge of his hammock. From under his pillow he withdrew a small, wooden box, an ornate drawing of a trident and a pearl carved upon the lid. Jim pushed with his toes on the rough floorboards to swing slowly back and forth on the hammock. Then he opened the box.

Beneath the lid was a delicate necklace, charmed with a silver shell, and also a folded piece of yellowed parchment. In all the world, the contents within the box were Jim's most valued possessions. They were all that was left to him of his father, who had been poisoned by the treacherous Cromiers, and his mother, who had died when Jim was but a baby. He ran his fingers over the smooth rounds and perfect ridges of the shell charm. Then he withdrew the parchment and took it back to the window where he knelt down beside the sill.

Jim unfolded the page slowly and carefully so as not to tear the paper, and found the letters of his father's script faint and faded on the page. As he did each night before bed, Jim held the page out beneath the moonlight. Like a sharp breath on dying coals, blue light sparked to life through each and every pen stroke, the words waking as though only just written in their enchanted ink beneath his father's quill. Jim read the letter, pretending to hear his father's voice as he did.

"Does the letter say the same thing every time?" Lacey's voice said from the stairs. Jim turned to find her standing at the entry to his little room in her nightgown, the worn leather book of stars in her hands.

"The way you read your book, you would think *it* certainly didn't, wouldn't you?" Jim said, hastily standing. He quickly folded the letter and jammed it back into the box. His ears were burning just a little at the edges.

"I wasn't making fun, Jim," Lacey replied, her own cheeks flushing a bit. "I'm quite serious, you know." She stepped inside the room and came to sit on the hammock, where Jim joined her, reopening the box just a bit to peek once more at the letter inside.

"Of course it never says anything different, Lacey. My father only wrote the one note. It was all he had time to do."

"But it is a magic letter, isn't it?" Lacey asked in a whisper. She peered warily at the box, as though some sorcery may even have been at work that very moment. "I would think a magic letter could do all sorts of things if it wanted to - and have all sorts of secrets - don't you?"

"I suppose it might," Jim replied with a shrug. To Jim, words that hid in his father's note from all but moonlight were magic enough.

"Is your necklace magic as well?"

"I don't think so." Jim took it out of the box and handed it to Lacey, who turned it over carefully in her fingers. "My father used to wear it all the time. He said it belonged to my mother."

"Why don't you wear it, Jim? I think it would look fetching on you." Lacey opened the chain and moved to loop it around Jim's neck. But Jim caught it in his hand and simply laid it back in the box, shutting the lid with a soft tap.

"Not yet, Lacey. Maybe never. I don't know." Lacey nodded slowly, looking down and playing with the tattered cover of her book. After a moment though, she smiled again and straightened herself up on the hammock, putting on her best, noble airs. "I think you shall make a fine Lord," she said. Then she laughed at Jim's blushing ears. "Lord Jim Morgan, greatest Lord of them all. And do you know how I know for certain? The stars tell me so!" Lacey held up her book before her face and peered over the cover mysteriously at Jim. "They tell me that tomorrow is the start of a new adventure for us!"

"Oh really?" Jim said. "Do they tell you how long it will take for George and the others to ruin their new clothes?"

Lacey, who was smart enough to know when the boys were teasing, shook her head and gave Jim a light punch on his shoulder. "Goodnight Jim Morgan," she said. "You'll see tomorrow. A great journey will begin." Then Lacey tiptoed out of the room and went down the stairs to her little room across from the Ratts'.

"Goodnight, Lacey," Jim called after her.

Jim was hardly sure that stars and constellations meant anything more than lights and pictures in the sky. In any event, tomorrow was indeed going to be the best day of his life. He smiled at the thought and breathed deeply of the ocean air. In only a matter of hours his little box would sit on a proper nightstand beside a proper bed in a proper home, where he, his friends, and his remaining possessions truly belonged. Avoiding the bother of changing into nightclothes, Jim simply kicked off his shoes, hung his jacket and hat on a rusty nail, and blew out his lantern. He leaned back into his hammock and in a few gentle swings fell effortlessly to sleep.

The wind and the waves rushed the little sailboat toward the pristine shores of a white sand beach. Jim Morgan stood at the prow, breeches rolled up over his knees. His hands were full with a wooden sword and a rope for the sail, tools for dream adventures too glorious and epic to exist anywhere but a young boy's mind. Jim's smile stretched wide over his face and he crowed at the top of his lungs.

Standing tall on the green hill beyond the beach, Morgan Manor came into view. Her tall iron gates were stanchioned with the bold letter M. Her orchards and gardens stretched all the way to the dark forest beyond. Home, Jim thought. He was finally sailing home. He raised his wooden sword once more and shouted with joy into the air. But no sooner had his call faded than the warm sea breeze turned cold. It stole the cry from Jim's lips and pricked his cheeks with icy needles. A shiver crawled down his back as he turned to look behind him.

Dark clouds, blacker than burnt paper, boiled on the horizon. They bled across the sky like a spreading stain. Lightning flicked forked tongues at the cloud's edges, bursting in purple flashes. Crimson tendrils wormed through the cracks and folds, rivulets of burning red in the dark.

It was a storm - yet this was no mere summer squall. As Jim watched the unfolding thunderheads roll toward the bay, he knew in his heart that there was something unnatural about them. Jim had seen too much magic to miss its smell, or its feel.

Thunder clapped like a door blown open by the wind, and Jim flinched in his boat. The sea quaked and frothed. Black clouds, rimmed with red, devoured the sky and the sun, swallowing them whole. Darkness descended upon the bay and a cold wind chilled Jim to the bone. But a cold, icier still, gripped him when he turned about in his boat. He found himself no longer alone.

A man's form melted from the shadows at the back of the boat. A black coat flapped in the rising wind. A pitch hat hid the man's face in darkness. A steel cutlass, glowing red as the storm clouds above, burned in the man's hand. Jim's heart beat like a hammer in his chest. His legs quivered beneath him. The dark man raised his blade and leveled it at Jim's chest. Then he swung it out over the raging sea, toward the storm. Jim followed the sword to the clouds. A flurry of lightning bolts blazed within the tempest. The lightning formed a face in the blackness.

The face of a skull in the storm.

"Jim Morgan," the face called with a voice of thunder. "Jim Morgan!"

Jim flew awake. Cold sweat had beaded upon his brow. His shirt clung tight to his damp chest. Stuck for a moment in the tight space between awake and asleep, Jim frantically searched the room for the man in black and the crimson storm. Yet all he found was his small space in the lighthouse, window open, and hammock swaying back and forth beneath him.

Footfalls on the wooden steps outside Jim's door creaked into his room and MacGuffy appeared. He held a candleholder in one gnarled finger. The whispering flame cast a wavering yellow over his old, scarred face.

"Heard ya moanin' and groanin' from all the way down the stairs, lad," MacGuffy said shortly, searching the room with his lone eye. "Be ye all right, young Morgan?" Jim sat up and wiped the sweat from his face with the back of his hand.

"I think so, MacGuffy. Just a bad dream, that's all."

"Yer too old for nightmares, boy," MacGuffy replied gruffly. He shook his head and lowered the candle a bit, as if a bit disappointed no real danger lurked about to confront. "Conquer yer wakin' fears and ye'll conquer the sleepin' ones as well, or so me pappy told me once. Now what was it ye were dreamin'? Spiders? Dragons? Ghosts? Girls?" MacGuffy laughed with a gravelly sound more akin to coughing or barking. But Jim only furrowed his brow, licking the sweat from his upper lip, trying with great effort to hold the dream in his mind like water in his hands.

"It was a storm. A crimson storm. It covered the sky and had a face…a skull face in the clouds." MacGuffy's rough chortle caught in his throat. His ruined smile faltered. For a long moment the old pirate stood silent and still in the doorway, looking at Jim over the whispering candle flame with his one remaining eye.

"A red storm?"

"Yes, a crimson storm. And the storm knew my name."

MacGuffy stood like a statue for a long time, studying Jim intently. But after a while the pirate's smile once more found its way back onto his face, forced though it seemed to Jim.

"Well, twas only a dream, my boy. Mayhaps brought about by me stern lesson on sailin', now that I be thinkin' about it."

"Perhaps," Jim said. He hardly thought that was the case at all, especially not after what he had seen in the waters that afternoon. But MacGuffy carried on as though the matter had been settled.

"Well then, to sleep with you, lad. Tomorrow be a long day and we be settin' out bright and early with the dawn." MacGuffy nodded sharply and turned to climb the stairs to the lamphouse. Jim lay back in his hammock to try and return to sleep when the candlelight brightened once more in the doorway and MacGuffy reappeared. The old salt seemed suddenly so much older and worn to Jim. The flame-drawn shadows carved deep into the crevices on MacGuffy's face.

"Jim, I know I be not much more than an old salt o' the sea. And I know youth ne'er listens to age, nor never has. It was so even with me and me pappy when I was but a sea pup like yerself. But hear me this one time if ye've heard me at all. Storms come in this life, boy. Sure as the sun n' the moon, n' birth n' death, storms'll come. Not all of them be made o' wind and rain. Me old sailin' master used to say to me that ye don't know if a swabby be a sailor or no till ye see him handle the wheel in a storm. He was right about that. But I say that ye don't know if a boy be a man or no til ye see him handle hisself in the storms o' this life. Do ye understand me, Jim?"

Jim stared at MacGuffy through the candle flame. "I think so, MacGuffy."

"Good," said the old pirate. "Then we'll be seein' ye in the mornin' to take ye back home, and a joyous day I'm sure 'twill be. Goodnight, young Morgan."

"Goodnight, MacGuffy," Jim replied. This time he heard the old man creak his way all the way up the steps to the lamp room above. Jim closed his eyes, but it was a long time before he fell asleep again.

THREE

To Morgan Manor

The next morning, Jim woke before anyone else in the house, even old MacGuffy, who rarely rose after the sun. Jim leapt from the hammock, his nightmare forgotten for the moment and the joy of this long-awaited day bursting within his chest. Down the stairs he rushed to boil a few pots of water, enough for him and even the Ratts to have a bath in the tub behind the lighthouse.

After scrubbing himself cleaner than he had been in at least a year, Jim ran back to his room, dripping wet. He tugged on a pair of breeches and socks, and pulled on a bright white shirt with a cream-colored waistcoat. He also slid on a pair of new shoes and finished dressing with a blue riding coat and tricorn hat. These were nothing like the costly fashions from Austria and France that Aunt Margarita used to have tailored for Jim, but they were the best clothes he had worn since running away from home that stormy night so long ago. They would more than do for this most marvelous of days.

The Brothers Ratt were waiting for Jim in the kitchen as he came down the stairs. They stood all in a row, hands on their lapels and looking every bit the dapper, noble-born boys they were absolutely not. The devilish smirks upon their faces told Jim at once how obscenely taken the three thieves were with their new look.

"Ah, Lord Morgan, you've arrived at last," George said tiredly. He sauntered forward, arching one eyebrow and yawning into the back of his hand in a perfect imitation of the nobles whose pockets he'd once picked in London. "In honor of this glorious occasion, sire, we, the humble Clan of the Ratt, bid you good day."

The three brothers turned as one on their heels, flipped up the tails of their coats, and bowed with their nobly dressed rears in a perfect row toward Jim. Together they shouted in unison: "We salute you, sire!"

"Knock that off, you blockheads!" Jim shouted. He laughed out loud and leapt from the stairs to deliver a swift punt to the seat of George's upturned pants.

"Oy! That was a bit unlordly of you, don't you think, Jim?" George said, gingerly rubbing one set of cheeks and the irrepressible Ratt smile still stretched across the others.

"And to have leapt down the stairs in such a manner?" Peter added, shaking his head and clucking his tongue in feigned shock and dismay. "You may have twisted your noble ankle, milord!"

"My lord!" Paul shouted, falling to his knees before Jim. "I postulate myself at your feet!"

"No you don't!" Jim smushed Paul's hat down over his head and slugged Peter in the shoulder. "And besides..." he was about to correct Paul, but Peter cut him off.

"The word is *prostrate*, Paul," Peter said, shaking his head as though quite disappointed.

"Well done, Peter," Jim said, impressed.

"Well, I have been doin' a bit of readin', haven't I?"

"Yes, we know," Paul and George replied together, giving Peter the snootiest of looks they could muster.

"It's so BO-ring," George added. "And keep gettin' your nose stuck in all them books all day, you'll forget your lock pickin', Peter, which is the really the only thing you know of any use, innit?"

"Readin' is useful, George," Peter replied. "For civilized men like meself, that is. Readin' is like pickin' a lock in your mind." Peter paused to sneak a self-impressed wink at Jim. "And besides, George, I could still out lockpick you in my sleep."

"You'd be surprised what I can do in me sleep, Peter," George said, emphasizing his brother's name as nastily as possible.

"Too true, Georgie, too true," Paul said seriously. "You're an absolute master at peeing yourself in your sleep. A genius really, and I'm not just saying that, I swear."

"THAT...WAS...NOT...ME!" George shrieked, snatching his new hat from his head and slamming it on the ground. "That was PETER!" Peter, of course, remembered events differently and the three of them were about to descend into a brotherly brawl when a stern shout came from the stairs behind them.

"Boys!" Lacey's voice rang down into the kitchen. "You promised no fighting today. You'll ruin your new clothes before we even step out the door!"

Jim turned to remind Lacey that the brothers were destined to ruin their clothes eventually, but the words caught in his throat. Instead, his mouth dropped open as though the hinge to his jaw had broken.

Lacey stood on the stairs looking down at the boys, a long yellow dress flowing in ruffles all the way down to her feet. White lace frosted her skirt like a dusting of snow on the first day of winter. A broad-brimmed hat framed her auburn curls and blue-eyed face like an angel from a painting. Somehow, Jim thought, Lacey suddenly seemed a great deal taller and older than she had ever seemed before. He had no idea why, but Jim felt irresistibly compelled to remove his hat. When he looked over at the brothers Ratt, they had stopped wrestling each other and held their hats in their hands as well.

"Lacey," Jim said, scrunching up his face, which felt suddenly itchy. "You look like, like…well you look like, like a girl, don't you?"

"Right," George added, as though he'd just come to that brilliant epiphany at the same moment. "Like a girl, alright! Like a real girl!"

Lacey, who had been blushing fiercely while her four friends stared at her, suddenly mustered a familiar, fierce glare and her hands flew to her hips. "Well what do I normally look like then?"

"Well…you know, I…" Jim stammered. He looked to the Ratts for help – which even Jim knew in a situation like this would have been the last place to find any.

"Which is how you always look," Peter managed first. "I think."

"Right, always… you know, that's what I meant: you always look like a girl, Lacey," George said. "I mean, maybe not as much as right now…right?"

Paul was even less help than George and Peter. He simply stared at Lacey with a furrowed brow and an open mouth, as though still trying very hard to figure out whether or not she was even the same person. But it was MacGuffy, hobbling from down the hallway, who set Lacey's concerns to rest.

"Ye look ever the graceful beauty, lass," he said, limping gamely across the room and holding out his gnarled hand to guide Lacey down the stairs. The former pirate had done his best to tame his wild, white hair. His finest gold loops hung from his ears, and he wore his best and newest coat, which was probably only twenty years old and had been through merely a handful of storms and sea battles.

"You must forgive 'em, ma'am. All boys be born fools, and only one man in ten ever manages to grow from his foolery a'tall. Ye look no lov'lier today than yesterday, lassie, but it is a fine dress, if ye let an old man say so."

"Thank you, MacGuffy," Lacey said. She leaned up and kissed the old man's wrinkled face on the cheek, just beneath his eye patch. Then she stormed out the front door, leaving the boys with only an irritated snort on her way.

"What was that for?" Jim said, slamming his hat back on his head.

"It be the charm ye lack, lads," MacGuffy said, a smile as roguish as the Ratts' stretched over his cracked lips. "And I could out charm the four of ye in *my* sleep, and that be a fact, young pups." MacGuffy winked his one good eye at the Ratts and followed Lacey out the door.

"You know," George said thoughtfully, adjusting his own hat on his head. "If it weren't for all the preachy lessons about the ocean and gettin' into trouble, and scrubbin' the floors all the time, I might actually miss that old blighter."

"Fortunately, George, I don't think it'll be so long before he comes to visit us at Morgan Manor," said Peter.

"Why's that?" Jim asked.

"Well, unless he can figure out where we hid all the underwear he made us wash yesterday, he'll need to ask us where we put it, won't he?" answered Paul. The three brothers sniggered naughtily, nodding to each and then to Jim before marching out the front door themselves.

Jim followed his friends, pausing at the threshold to take one last look around the old lighthouse. No more cellars or attics or closets for Jim Morgan and the Clan of the Ratt, he thought. Tonight they would sleep in the comfort of Morgan Manor — warm beds and hot dinners. Without doubt, this was going to be the first of many good days to come, Jim knew. He stepped out into the sunshine with a smile on his face, shutting the lighthouse door behind him for the last time.

For the better part of the day the carriage bounced down the road, winding along the southern coast of England toward the town of Rye. Jim and his friends pointed and stared at the cliffs and beaches they passed, and at the waves and the gulls floating on the winds above the waters. At one point Peter attempted to read a book he'd borrowed (most likely without permission) from MacGuffy's library. The road was so bumpy that Peter was forced to grip the book quite tightly and hold his face close to the pages in order to make out the words. It was too choice an opportunity for George and Paul to miss. George produced a good-sized rock from his pocket, the availability of which should come as no surprise to anyone who's ever known a young boy or two, and hurled it with perfect timing from the window before one of the wheels. The carriage took such a start that the book snapped up and smacked Peter right in the face, sending George into the most impolite howling and cackling.

"George!" Peter yelped, holding his nose with one hand and slamming his book down with the other.

"It was just a bump in the road, Peter," Paul said, without a trace of guilt in his face (he was a born con after all). George, of course, hollered like a monkey, pointing shamelessly in Peter's face. This led to Peter falling on his brother with fists flailing and Jim and Lacey had to pull the three of them apart, as usual.

"Can the three of you not keep out of trouble for even one hour?" Lacey shouted, clearly agitated. "Not even on a day like today?"

"Have to stay on our toes, Lacey," George replied matter-of-factly. "If you have a gift, not to use it is a crime. And that's even in the Bible, in't it? It just so happens that our gift is trouble!" At this, Lacey threw up her hands and refused even an attempt at arguing. But Peter, who was still rubbing his nose, nodded as if that made total sense.

"True, George, true," Peter said in a quite nasally voice. "You caught me off guard on that one – but not the next time! I'll be ready!"

"I'll even sleep with one eye open," Paul said, his arms folded over his chest. "Got used to doing it at St. Anne's. Never knew when George was gonna wet the bed. One must stay on his toes indeed."

"That wasn't me!" George raged. "IT WAS PETER!"

The remainder of the journey passed without incident. As the afternoon stretched toward evening the Ratts and Lacey drifted off into naps and dreams of their own. Jim, however, stayed awake the entire time, wringing his hands and shifting back and forth in his seat.

The closer and closer the little carriage drew to Rye, the more and more anxious and restless he became. What would he say to the staff when he arrived? The house would surely be in an uproar over Aunt Margarita's recent eviction, Jim imagined. It was also quite possible that many of them still had no idea Jim was even alive after that night Cromier's soldiers had chased him into the dark forest.

Jim thought back to that day his father had returned from his mysterious sea voyage. He remembered the way the former Lord Morgan had greeted each of the servants by name, shaking their hands and smiling. That was the way Jim would do it, he decided. That was the way he would do everything – just like his father. It would be as though Lindsay Morgan had never died.

Jim rehearsed his arrival over and over again until the carriage rounded a bend and the town of Rye came into view. The red sun edged down to where the sea met the sky. The failing light painted the buildings with rust, and blue shadows leaned long into the streets. The carriage rattled down the main street to the edge of town. There the road turned to dirt and wound over a hill, beyond which stood Morgan Manor.

Jim leaned out the window to catch the first glimpse of the north tower beyond the hill. But as he took in a deep breath of evening air, a thick stream of smoke swept into his face, stinging his nose and burning his eyes. Jim heard MacGuffy growl an order to the driver from the top seat, and the carriage picked up speed. A dark haze had settled over the hill, drifting like a black fog toward the edges of town. Like a cold gust of wind on a warm day, a pang of dread caught Jim by surprise. It snatched his breath away and turned his stomach into knots.

"Are we almost there?" George asked in a yawning voice, groaning as he stretched awake from his nap. Lacey, Peter, and Paul all came to as well and looked sleepily at Jim.

"Something's wrong," was Jim's only reply.

A column of black smoke climbed into view like a writhing serpent rising into the evening sky. It snaked its way into the red dusk, blowing out over the sea from the place where the road ended...from a place Jim knew well. Jim hardly breathed until the carriage crested the hill.

What little air remained within Jim's chest escaped in a gasp.

"Oh, Jim," Lacey said quietly, looking out the window at his side. But Jim said nothing. His tongue refused to speak what his heart refused to believe.

Morgan Manor, every brick and every beam, was burned to the ground.

FOUR

FIRE, ASH, AND MOONWATER

J im climbed down from the carriage on numb legs. Needling stings crawled over his body. The charred stink of burnt earth stung his nose. A dark fog choked the air over the blackened corpse of Morgan Manor. Tears fell onto Jim's cheeks. They would have fallen even without the smoke in his eyes.

Jim wandered toward the remains of the building. The Manor was now little more than an ashy heap, robbed of all colors but black and gray. Small flames flickered amongst the piles of burnt stone - where the kitchen once stood and along the stretch that had once been the great hall. Through his bleary vision Jim could still place every tower and every wall where it had once stood. He could remember every room and every hallway, where there now lay only rubble and ruin.

Lacey and MacGuffy called for Jim to come back, but Jim's legs mechanically carried him through the drifting smoke. He walked until he came to a place where the walls and roof had burned so cleanly away that only the floors remained, covered in ash. Even so, Jim knew this spot and knew it well.

It was the hallway that once led to Lindsay Morgan's study.

Jim stepped over the ruined wall and walked the length of the corridor's remains until he reached the place where the great oak doors had once barred the way to his father's library. He remembered standing in that very place over a year ago, preparing to barge in and give his father a piece of his mind. But the oak door was now gone and Jim stepped directly into the room beyond. The great bookshelves and the voluminous library they once held lay in blackened piles upon the floor. Only the stone fireplace, over which the picture of Lord Morgan and his three friends had once hung, remained whole.

Jim stood there, searching for any piece of the past that survived the flames, until an ashy scrap lying on the fireplace's brick hearth caught his eye. Jim kicked at it with the tip of his shoe. Beneath a layer of soot he discovered a pair of eyes staring back from the ash. The remains of his father's painting, edges eaten away by the fire, lay at his feet. Jim picked up the canvas. The likenesses of his father, Dread Steele, Count Cromier, and an unknown, fourth man were still visible, though scorched by the heat.

The ruined painting began to fall apart in Jim's hand. He turned it over to let the wind take the ashes away, but as he did, Jim found yet one more figure on the back of the canvas. For a moment he thought it was only a trick of the light upon the burnt cloth. But before the painting disintegrated entirely, he was sure that a fifth face had been drawn on the back. It was a painting of a large, black skull, a bolt of lightning gripped in its teeth. Jim saw the face for only a moment before the canvas turned to dust and crumbled to pieces in his fingers.

Jim watched the burnt flakes drift off like black flower petals when a sudden gust from the sea chased away the smoke in the study. Like a ghost in the dark, a man appeared, standing in the place Lindsay

Morgan's desk once sat. Jim sucked in a startled breath and fell back from the shape. The man's clothes were so black and his ash laden hair so red in the setting sun that for a moment Jim saw the form of Count Cromier, gloating over the fall of the house of Morgan.

When the man came further into the light, though, old, sad eyes glistened beneath bushy eyebrows on a familiar, wrinkled face.

"Phineus," Jim said. Soot covered the man from head to toe. The old tutor looked more aged and bent than ever before.

"If you've come to loot, young man," the old tutor shouted with a shaking voice, "Take your time and take what you will. All that remains here is ash and sorrow and forgotten dreams. Steal as much of that as you wish and be gone with you!"

"I'm not here to steal anything, Phineus," Jim said. He took a step closer to the old man in the failing daylight. "I've come home. I didn't send a letter – it was going to be a surprise." Phineus stared vacantly at James for what seemed like an age, until slowly, a glimmer of recognition lit his eyes.

"Master James?"

Jim drew closer still. As though not daring to trust his eyes alone, Phineus reached out and touched Jim on the shoulders and face and hair until he finally accepted that the boy he once knew stood before him. The old man fell down on his knees and took Jim in his arms, weeping furiously.

"Oh, Master James! All that was your father's and his great house has been lost. I'm sorry I was not able to stop this – I'm so sorry, my boy."

"No, Phineus," Jim said, fiercely hugging the old man back. "I'm the one who should be sorry. I am sorry."

After Jim had let poor Phineus shed tears until none remained, the pair of them abandoned the pit of rubble that had once been a great mansion. MacGuffy, the Ratts, and Lacey met them on the grassy hill between the blackened grounds and the white sand beach that stretched to the ocean's shore. Nothing remained of Morgan Manor save for one of the stables and the iron gates at the entrance to the main road, the bold letter Ms darkened with soot.

The Ratts stood all in a row, heads held low and hands in their pockets. Even MacGuffy, so full of pirate wisdom and earthy proverbs, had nothing to say. He but stood shaking his head, glaring at the destruction with his one good eye. It was finally Lacey who found the words to speak.

"You must be Phineus," she said. Her voice was thick, but she managed a polite smile and a curtsy. "Jim told us all about you. He said you were a great teacher, the greatest teacher."

"Once perhaps I was," Phineus said. He bowed his old head and did his best to return Lacey's smile. "And who might be you be, young lady?"

"I'm Lacey. I'm Jim's friend. And this is George, Peter, and Paul Ratt. They're Jim's friends as well, from London, sir."

"What evil befell this place, Master Teacher?" asked MacGuffy. "In a house as rich and fancee as this'un, there'd of been servants and men aplenty to stamp out any kitchen fire gone out o' control, I warrant."

"This was no kitchen fire, sir." Bitterness seeped into Phineus's voice. "And yes, in the days of Lindsay Morgan there would have been servants aplenty, had not that witch squandered the wealth and pride of this once great house!"

"A witch did this?" Paul cried in dismay, shivering a little in the cool evening air.

"Not a real witch, Paul." Jim gritted his teeth and clenched his fists at his sides. "But close enough to one. You mean Aunt Margarita, don't you, Phineus?"

Phineus nodded. His old lips twisted upon his face.

"She spent every last piece of gold on parties and opulence until hardly a farthing was left. I was the last of the staff to remain, and only that for the memory of Lord Lindsay and Master James, for I thought you too were dead, milord. Madness took hold of her, Master James. When the constable arrived with a letter for the Dame, announcing her reign over this house had finally and mercifully ended, the madness overwhelmed her completely. She flew into a rage, spouting all manner of strange words - of curses and treasures and storms that would devour the world. First she burned the letter. Then she burned the house. Then she ran away."

"So it's all gone, Phineus," Jim said, staring out over the smoke-drowned hills and ruined gardens. "It's all been for nothing. Everything my father built and fought and—" Jim's throat grew suddenly sticky. "—and died for—all of it is gone forever."

"Perhaps not all, young master." Phineus cleared his throat and stood up straight, summoning his scholarly dignity once more. "I was able to save but a single item. Your father entrusted it to me long ago. I never trusted it to any safe or cabinet, locked or no. I carried it on my person, always. Now you are the Lord Morgan, and it is yours." The old tutor reached inside his filthy jacket and withdrew his hand, closed in a fist.

Phineus unfurled his bony fingers one at a time until a bright blue glow shone from his palm in the darkening evening. The brilliant flame all but blinded Jim for a moment. But as the light dimmed he found a glass vial, filled to the stopper with a thick blue liquid, lying in Phineus's open hand. Lacey gasped. The Ratts and old MacGuffy huddled close to Jim. They craned their necks over his shoulder to see the wonder Phineus had produced. The blue light threw swimming glimmers and curling shadows over their curious faces.

"It's called moonwater, Master James," Phineus said. "It is one of the rarest and most precious liquids in the world, worth one hundred times its weight in gold. Now, the night you fled, I believe your father must have given you an old, weathered parchment, perhaps with a note written upon it. Did he do so Jim? For try as I might, I could not find the parchment in the house no matter how long I searched."

"He did, Phineus!" Jim reached into his pocket for his box. Opening it, he carefully withdrew his father's letter. "When he was poisoned, father spent his last moments writing me this letter." Jim held the folded page forth to his former teacher with a trembling hand.

"I thought he might have, for your father was a man of many secrets, Master James. Not all of them did he share with me." A wise smile stretched over Phineus's soot and tear-stained face. "He never told me of his secret journey at sea, nor how he came to possess that parchment or this vial of moonwater. Those tales he shared only with Hudson, his faithful valet, God rest that man's soul. But before he entrusted me with the moonwater, he gave me a hint as to its purpose. Open the letter, young Master."

Jim unfolded the parchment. As always, the newly rising moon lit the letters of his father's note fresh upon the page. Though they had seen this before, Lacey and the Ratts caught their breath in awe and George gave a low whistle. This was magic, and it tingled their blood and prickled their skin.

"Your father was wise to hide his words in such enchanted ink," Phineus continued. "Moonwater is concentrated light of the full moon itself. I believe it has the power to unlock even deeper mysteries still." Phineus took Jim by the hand and turned the letter over. When the old man held the vial in his bent fingers between the moon and the page, a thin, blue beam lit upon the yellowed parchment. Like light shimmering off water, shapes and letters appeared on the paper, illuminating the dark and flinging their glowing forms on the faces of the small group gathered round. Jim could not be sure, but it seemed to be the faint outline of a map drawn on the aged paper. Phineus passed the light over the parchment from top to bottom then once more curled his fingers over the vial, extinguishing the blue glow and the enchanted glamour on the back of Jim's letter.

"I never asked your father what secret the parchment held, nor did I ever surrender to the temptation to use it myself, though the desire was great, especially for an old tutor who values wisdom and knowledge above all else. Those things were not meant for me to know, young Master. But they are meant for you." Phineus pressed the vial into Jim's empty hand and closed Jim's fingers into a fist. "Wait awhile until your head and your heart clear from this loss, then perhaps this will guide you on your way."

"Thank you, Phineus," Jim said quietly. He took both the vial and the letter and tucked them into his box, which he then placed into his pocket.

"Speakin' o' makin' our ways," MacGuffy interjected from the back of the group. "It be far too late for travellin' tonight, and the carriage we brought be already gone back to town. There be not enough gold amongst the lot o' us to buy a room for even a single evenin'. So perhaps we shall rest in yonder stable, if there be even a little straw for our beds. Then tomorrow, to the lighthouse we shall return."

"Will you come with us, Phineus?" Jim asked. But only a look at his old tutor's face gave Jim the answer.

"No, Master James. I shall always be your servant and your teacher, but my frail body is too old for such adventures. I shall go to Kent to stay with my sister for a time. Perhaps I shall find another family to teach before I grow too old and too frail to carry out my duties with honor. But never will I find another house as great as the house of Morgan."

"I'll get it back, Phineus," Jim swore then. He swore it with all the heat and fury of a young boy's heart caught afire. "I don't know how, but I will. I'll find treasure like my father did. I'll do whatever it takes. I'll get back at the Cromiers for this and I'll rebuild our house and I'll make it an honorable family again. I swear it."

Phineus pulled Jim close and held him there for a moment. Then he stood again with a groan, one hand on his old back. Phineus shook the hands of the Ratts and MacGuffy and bowed his head politely to Lacey. Then lastly and again, he took Jim's hand in his own.

"Farewell, Lord Morgan. I have no doubt I shall hear your name again, attached to the beginning and end of a great adventure, I'm sure. If I am still alive on that day, I trust you shall call on me if needed, and I will come." Then the old tutor walked away, disappearing over the hill and into the night.

Jim and his friends watched old Phineus hobble away. They were about to walk down to the stables when the rattle of wagon wheels and the clang of bells on reins came from the road. A prisoner's carriage rounded the bend. Next to the driver sat a constable of Rye, a blue cloak over his shoulders, blue tricorn hat on his head, and the badge of the King's Men on his breast.

"Good evenin', sires," the constable said, tipping his hat to the clan and MacGuffy, who stood beside Jim near the road. "Tis an evil night indeed. Though I know it will do little to bring back what's been lost, we've a prisoner we believe wrought this misfortune on Morgan Manor. Caught her screamin' and rantin' in the haunted forest. Thought at first she was one of the ghoulies herself! We're takin' her to London for justice."

"Nonsense!" A shrill voice screamed from the back of the wagon. George, Lacey, Peter, and Paul, jumped at the sound – all except for Jim.

Jim knew that voice.

He knew it from his childhood.

"You shall refer to me as DAME, you common dog! For it was I who gave grace to the wretched name of Morgan and I who gave that pile of rocks even a touch of nobility. For I am still as noble as…as a queen!" The voice cackled from the black bowels of the wagon, from the shadows behind the bars.

But shadows or no, Jim knew to what villain this voice belonged.

FIVE

Dame Margarita Morgan

Jim's teeth clamped so hard that he heard them grind together in his ears. He squeezed his fists so tight that his fingernails bit half-moon cuts into the palms of his hands.

"You're no Dame, Aunt Margarita!" Jim shouted, his voice hoarse and raspy. "My father threw you out of his house for being a liar!" A sharp gasp echoed from the blackness behind the bars of the prisoner's carriage.

"I know that voice," the mad cackle said. "But it cannot be, can it? It could not possibly be my dear little friend, James Francis Morgan, could it? This I must see with my own eyes."

From the shadows, two hands reached through the bars. The pale fingers were ringed with diamond and gold that glistened in the rising moonlight. Finger by finger the bejeweled hands gripped the bars tight, and with a fierce tug, yanked Aunt Margarita's face into view.

Paul and Lacey leapt back from the wagon and George and Peter braced themselves at the sight. But who could blame them? The old woman had become more ghoul than flesh and blood. No longer as round and pale as the full moon, her madness had sucked the life from her, a bit at a time. Dame Margarita's body was as drained as her mind and her soul. Her wrinkles folded deeply. Black bags hung low beneath her eyes, open wide and unblinking. Even her platinum blonde wig was gone. Only thinning wisps of gray remained, dead and lifeless as the gypsy witch's that once cursed Jim's box.

Aunt Margarita's wide, watery eyes passed over each of the clan until they reached Jim's face. It was then she reared back her head, erupting in laughter, deep and throaty like a hungry wolf's howl.

"Well, well, well, so you survived after all," Margarita said gleefully. "Old Cromie thought you might have. I was certain, oh so certain, that you were too soft to survive beyond the manor walls - without your servants, your playthings, or your chocolates. But perhaps I was wrong about you, my boy."

"It'll take more than you and the Cromiers to finish me off, hag!"

"Mind your tongue and mind your words!" Margarita pressed her face close to the bars. With bulging eyes she glared down on Jim. "You eluded Bartholomew in London. Well done! And I can tell you that his father was none too pleased with him at that. But by your company and those hopeless rags you now wear, you failed to find your father's treasure, didn't you? And now look!" Aunt Margarita jabbed at the blackened ruins before her with a crooked finger, a bent smile upon her face. "All that was the house of Morgan is gone." Jim shook from head to toe at his Aunt's taunts. All the hurt and disappointment of his broken dreams bubbled up within him.

"You poisoned my father, the greatest captain on the seas! You tried to kill me, and now you've burnt down my home. I hope they throw you in a dark hole at the end of some forgotten corridor in a forgotten prison, so long that you never see the light of day again!"

Dame Margarita squeezed the bars until her knuckles rose up on her hands. The sinews in her arms and neck drew taut as straining ropes. Her face trembled and her eyes bulged in their sockets.

"You think you know it all, don't you, you fool? You think Lindsay Morgan was some great man of honor? That he was some unblemished image of nobility and goodness? You don't know half of what you think you know. If you knew what I knew … if you knew what Count Cromier told me. If you knew what that Treasure of the Ocean really was and what Lindsay Morgan's thievery truly cost, you would not speak so boldly to me." Aunt Margarita pulled one fist from her bars and leveled a finger at Jim's face.

"If you knew who you were, James Morgan, Son of Earth and Son of Sea. If you knew what fate lay in store for you, you would wish the soldiers had caught you in the forest that night. Mark my words, boy, you shall come to curse the day you were born." Aunt Margarita began to wag her finger back and forth, cackling laughter once more lacing her words. What little reason left in her eyes slipped away. "You'll see! You'll see, you'll see!" Margarita released her bars, sinking back into the shadows of the box until only her echoing laughter remained.

"That will be enough of that," the Constable said. He nodded his head toward Jim and his friends. "I'm sorry for your loss. Have no fear, though, we shall see her to justice." Then the driver flicked the reins and the carriage jerked down the road. But before it turned round the hill and out of sight, Aunt Margarita's shrill voice cried out once more.

"You'll see, Jim Morgan! You'll see!"

"Be givin' no mind to a mad witch's words, lad," MacGuffy began to say. But Jim hardly heard the old pirate. The weight of all the sorrow and sadness broke the dam in his heart. All by themselves Jim's legs began to run. Hot tears burned in his eyes as he ran over the hill toward the stables, which was all that remained of the great house. Smoke from Morgan Manor stung his nose and singed his throat as he ran, but the pain in his heart ached far worse than any heat.

"Come back, Jim!" Lacey and George called from the top of the hill. Their words never reached Jim's ears. He ran alone in a bubble of hurt, with all the rest of the world on the other side. As he ran, his little box rattled against his side in his pocket. It was once again his only possession in all the world.

SIX

PHILUS PHILONIUS

J im ran as hard and fast as he could, churning up sand and ocean water as he pounded down the beach. He struggled to hold back his tears and slapped away the few drops that spilled onto his cheeks. On and on Jim ran until night fell like a blanket over the coast and the stars appeared in the darkened sky.

When Jim had run until his burning legs were finally ready to give out, he slowed to a walk, coughing for air with his head hung low. He looked around with stinging eyes to find himself on an unfamiliar, rocky stretch of beach. No homes or houses lit the nearby hills and Jim cursed himself a fool for running so far on his own. He shoved his hands deep into his pockets with a defeated sigh and turned to walk back in the direction from which he'd come.

As Jim trudged through the sand he kicked at stones and cursed the Cromiers and Aunt Margarita for all the evil they had inflicted upon him. Along the way, and as angry young men often do, Jim began to formulate fantastic and impossible ways to get back at those fiends. He grew so distracted by his miserable plotting that he reared back to kick a particularly large stone without realizing that it was quite a bit bigger than he suspected. He struck the stone square and very nearly shattered his toe, which sent him yelping like a pup and hopping up and down on one foot. Jim was about to swear retribution upon all the bloody stones in England in addition to his enemies when the sound of pipes playing a sad song caught his attention from just up ahead.

Jim ceased hopping around immediately and bit his upper lip to keep from howling. His cheeks burned at the thought of being seen breaking his own foot on a rock, so he tried to walk casually down the beach. This was nearly impossible, however, with a smashed toe, tired legs, and an aching head. But instead of letting him limp away with even a shred of his dignity intact, the pipes grew louder the further Jim walked. In only ten yards or so, he found a man sitting cross-legged upon a large stone, facing the sea and playing a strange flute with twin pipes. Jim furrowed his brow and approached the man slowly. It seemed strange to so plainly see this fellow on the rock, and to so clearly hear his sad song, Jim thought. For not a few moments before, when he had run past this very place, he had seen no man nor heard any song.

Jim finally drew up to the rock and his curiosity only deepened. The flute-player was perhaps the smallest man Jim had ever seen. Even perched upon his rock the gentleman came up only as far as Jim's shoulders. He wore a tiny suit of green breeches with a brown waistcoat and cream shirt - clothes, Jim was quite sure, that could have been fitted for a small child. Yet the man's bald head shone in the moonlight and a neatly trimmed gray beard hung from his chin. Jim thought by the man's face that he was perhaps only a few years younger than old MacGuffy.

The little man kept on playing his song as though he never saw Jim at all. His fingers danced along the pipes and his eyes remained fixed upon the sea. It was as though he was hypnotized by the waves. Jim was about to clear his throat or say hello, if nothing else but to see if the man might reply, when the diminutive musician blew a final, wavering note and at last pulled the flute from his lips.

"Lovely night for a stroll," said the flute-player with a voice not nearly as small as the man himself. "Lovely night for even as angry and woeful a stroll as yours, I'd say."

"I'm sorry?" Jim said. He was taken aback by the man's blunt words and felt once more ashamed that a total stranger might have seen him muttering to himself and kicking huge rocks like a fool. "Just so you know, I wasn't even crying or anything," Jim threw in with a ridiculous measure of indignation. "There's nothing wrong with me at all!" One eyebrow arched high upon the old man's bald head, and his eyes flicked for the first time from ocean to Jim's face.

"A young man, racing like the wind down a dark beach with tears so thick in eyes that he nearly runs over a poor fellow playing his flute, without even knowing he did so, obviously has something wrong with him indeed! In fact, I would go so far as to say such a young man is in desperate need of a drastic change in fortune. It is quite clear to me, young sir, that you are afflicted - afflicted with an affliction as plain as the nose on your face."

"Afflicted?" Jim said, a bit of bitterness trickling into his voice. "What would you know about it?" Yet in spite of Jim's irritability, he could hardly tear his eyes from the pipe player upon the rock. The old gentleman's eyes were clear as glass and green as leaves in spring. They struck Jim as being somehow very old, older than even the hills and the rocks on the beach. Jim felt the gaze of those eyes cut through his flesh and bone down to his soul, as a cold wind cuts through clothes to sting the skin.

"You, my boy," the man said, those unnerving eyes fixed on Jim's face. "Are afflicted with a broken heart."

Jim thought of denying it, but what was the use? The truth was written all over his face and it would not be tucked away. Jim's heart was utterly and completely broken and there were no two ways about it. The old man seemingly took Jim's silence as an admission and reached out to tap him sharply on the top of the head with his flute.

"So," he said. "Perhaps you and I should discuss this broken heart and these unfortunate circumstances in which you find yourself. Then, just maybe, we shall see if we might not be able to procure you a remedy."

"No offense," Jim replied. "But you hardly know a thing about me or my problems, sir. Even if you did, I'm not so sure there's much you could do about any of it at all." The moment those words left Jim's mouth the old man clucked his tongue and threw up his hands as though Jim had just uttered the most ridiculous words he had ever heard.

"Youths these days - never thinking things through. Don't you suppose that a fragile old man, especially one as tiny and defenseless as this one, sitting here on this rock all by his lonesome in the middle of the night, with god knows what manner of thieves and scoundrels lurking about, would not have at least one or two tricks up his sleeve?"

The little man snapped the flute to his lips and ripped off a trill that sent a spark through Jim's arms and legs. He then flicked his sharp eyes over Jim's shoulder with a wink and a nod. Jim looked back in that direction and nearly shouted in startled surprise. A wooden carriage sat on a patch of grass just beyond the sand. A bright fire burned beside the camp, crackling over a pile of large, cut logs.

Jim's mouth fell open and his brow furrowed deep. He could understand how he might have missed the small man, alone on a rock in the dark. But there was no way Jim would have missed an entire camp, burning fire and all, just sitting on the edge of the beach. No horse or mule tracks of any sort led toward or from the inviting campsite. It seemed to Jim as though it had all simply appeared out of thin air.

"Does even a little magic startle you, my boy?" the old man said, clucking his tongue again. "As I said, youths these days - no respect for the older things in the world."

"I wasn't startled," Jim said. "I've seen magic before!" But this was half a lie, for the magic had been so sudden and so unexpected that it had taken Jim quite by surprise. Perhaps, he admitted to himself, it even frightened him a little.

"Well then," said the man, offering Jim a friendly smile and motioning up toward his magically produced camp with an open hand. "If it bothers you not, good sir, come sit with an old man for a time, and let us have a chat."

"Actually, I really should be going, sir," Jim managed, his heart beating wildly in his chest. If he had learned but one thing over the course of all his adventures it was this: magic was not a thing to be taken lightly. More often than not, it was a doorway leading straight to danger and trouble. But the old man was not so easily deterred.

"Then go you must, and on my word of honor I shall not stop you. But perhaps, oh broken-hearted one, it would be wise if you spared me only a moment, just one, even if only to hear what I have to offer. Would even a chance to mend your current predicament not be worth a few minutes of your time?"

Jim hesitated on the beach, just beyond the firelight's reach. His chest ached and his throat was still tight. Tears yet threatened and nothing but a scorched piece of earth that used to be his home awaited him at the end of the beach. He cast one last glance toward a turn in the shore, where the beach led back to the stables on the manor grounds, where his friends waited for him. But curiosity - curiosity and perhaps even a touch of hope, pulled Jim's eyes back toward the camp.

"Only a moment," Jim finally said, starting up the beach toward the little camp as the old man cackled with delight.

The tiny pipe player blew a joyful tune as he and Jim approached the fire. He danced a spry jig around the flames in a circle or two before making his way up to his wagon. There he came to a prancing stop and loosed another trill on his flute, finishing with a deep bow.

"Philus Philonius, purveyor of magical goods, remedies, relics, and potions, at your service, my boy. A pleasure and honor to meet you, young sire! And who, may I ask, might you be?"

"I'm Jim Morgan," Jim said. He gave the old man a quick bow himself before checking nervously over his shoulder toward the beach, as though a small part of him was afraid he might be magicked away by Mister Philonius at any moment.

"Well, Jim Morgan, let us see what soothing balm I might offer to cure your affliction!" Philus seized the side panel of his wagon and with a flick of his wrist popped it open like a shopkeeper's window. Row upon row of shelves revealed themselves there, lined from side to side and top to bottom with an assortment of vials, baskets, cauldrons, boxes, colored crystals, shiny stones, and even a polished skull or two. As nervous as Jim felt, that small flame of curiosity burned a bit brighter and pulled him nearer still to the wagon, his eyes poring over the goods there within.

Philus Philonius rubbed his hands together and giggled with anticipatory delight. With a dancing shuffle he kicked the lower edge of his wagon, releasing a step upon which he leapt. This made the small man just tall enough to reach his shelves, and also to look Jim in the eye.

"Now, we can hardly just give you anything, can we? Only the proper remedy will cure the proper malady, eh?" Jim opened his mouth to say something, but the small man held up his hand and shook his head. "No, no, no, master Jim – I am a professional, a craftsman at my trade, I am, I am, so no hints, no hints!" Philus ran his finger down one of the shelves, pausing when he came to a small pot, teeming with bright green, four leaf clovers.

"A pinch of Irish Luck to do the trick, perhaps?" Philus blew a note on his flute and a rainbow leapt from the pot, flitting into the air like a brilliant butterfly. But no sooner had the rainbow flown in two circles than Philus swatted it from the air with his flute, bursting it like a soap bubble and shaking his head with a distasteful frown. "No, no, no, not nearly enough, is it? Not nearly enough!"

Further down the shelf the old man searched until he came to a tall vial of pink glass, which he plucked gingerly off the shelf with two fingers, a bright smile upon his face.

"Now here's a little beauty: Perfume of Summer's Love!" Philus pulled the cork with a slight pop and a tendril of pink mist rose into the air followed by the unmistakable scent of strawberries and cinnamon, with just a hint of hot chocolate. But after a long, deep breath of the delicious odor, the little merchant's nose suddenly twitched and he unleashed an enormous sneeze, blasting away the pink fumes and leaving only an annoyed wrinkle on his brow. "No, no, no," he said, corking the vial and tossing it back on the shelf. "Too young, too young! Perhaps in a few years, eh, my boy? We need something bolder for you, don't we? That I can tell!"

Philus grabbed a small box next, holding it tight with both hands, and for good reason. The box shook so violently in his grip that the small man was nearly thrown to the ground. Jim took a step or two back in fear of his safety.

"These little beauties are a pair of Bulgarian Boxing Rocks!" Philus announced, his voice herking and jerking. "Hold one of these stones in each hand and you're guaranteed to knock any foe into the dirt, regardless how big or how strong he may be!" Jim arched one eyebrow at the Boxing Rocks, thinking for a pleasant moment of using them on Bartholomew Cromier. But the old man snorted again and all but threw the box into the back of his wagon, breathing heavily and wiping sweat from his brow with the back of his sleeve.

"No, no, no!" Philus repeated once more, stomping a foot on his little wooden step. "Hardly proper for a gentleman such as yourself. Besides, they're a devil to get back in the box, believe you me."

The old man sighed and his shoulders slumped. He hung his head and tapped his flute on his bald crown as though on the verge of surrender. Again Jim looked back over his shoulder to the beach. He very nearly thanked Philus for his efforts and insisted he should be going, when the little man suddenly shrieked as though struck by a bolt of lightning. Mister Philonius threw back his head and laughed a long, how-could-I-be-so-foolish laugh. When his cackling laughter finally subsided, Philus snuck a long, sideways glance at Jim, as though measuring and weighing him with those old, green eyes. Then he slowly, slowly turned his shrewd, bearded face back toward the shelf.

"There is one other possibility, isn't there? It could be just the thing." Philus rose up on his tiptoes and reached to the very top shelf, taking down a square, glass bottle, red as blood and capped with a burnt black cork. Stepping down from the wagon, Philus crept slowly and purposefully over to Jim and handed the bottle over.

"This is the number, isn't it, my boy?" he whispered.

Jim took the bottle and nearly dropped it immediately. It was surprisingly warm, no, almost hot to the touch, as though it had just been heated over an open flame. Jim turned the bottle over in his fingers until he came around to the label, bearing but a single word, written on the side. When Jim read this one word, a desire as hot as the liquid in the bottle began to burn in his chest. The one word was written in black letters on a white label, and the word was this:

REVENGE.

SEVEN

THE POTION AND THE BLACK ROSE

J im looked up at Philus and found the old man staring back. The eager gleam in Jim's eyes and the white knuckles with which he gripped the bottle seemed to be answer enough for the magician. The old man smiled from ear to ear. The fire danced like coals in his clear, green eyes.

"Rare stuff that is, young master Morgan," Philus said. His voice grew low and urgent. "Won't bother telling you what it is or from whence I got it. You'd hardly believe me if I did, and I'm not sure you really want to know. All you need to know is this: one administration of a potion made from this elixir, and you are guaranteed to turn the tables on your foes."

Jim closed his eyes. The hot fire crackled behind him. The warm bottle sent waves of heat up his arm. He pictured himself holding

Bartholomew Cromier at sword point - the very way the pale captain had once held him, back in his father's study so long ago. In Jim's mind, Bartholomew's father, Count Cromier, was there too, on his knees and begging for mercy. Jim imagined locking them up with Aunt Margarita, sorrowful misery dripping from their faces. Jim's friends would then cheer him on as he rebuilt Morgan Manor with the reclaimed wealth of pirate treasure.

"Yes," Jim said, his voice hungry. "This is what I need."

"Indeed it is, Master Morgan. Now, how much would something like that be worth to you, my boy?"

Jim's shoulders slumped. The glorious fantasy burning a hole in his mind evaporated like smoke off a match. The fact that all Jim had ever owned was now burned to a blackened crisp rolled over him like a wave. He had nothing, not a farthing to his name. Now even this one chance to set it all straight, to get even with the Cromiers, was about to slip through his fingers.

"I don't have any money. I can't afford it, sir." Jim held the bottle out to Philus, his chin drooping toward his chest. But the old man grabbed both Jim's hand and the bottle and held them tight together. For a small man, his grasp was uncannily strong.

"Easy, lad," Philus said. He clucked his tongue and shook his head, the smile still fixed upon his face. "Empty pockets and broken hearts often walk hand in hand, don't they? But I told you I was here to ease your ills, did I not? I'm here to help you, not rob you, my boy. Yet nothing worth anything in this life is free, is it? However, being the reasonable merchant I am, I would be willing to come to a trade for a single dose of revenge. Surely you have a little something to trade for this golden opportunity."

"I have nothing," Jim said. A lump formed in his throat. Philus chuckled slowly, though, and let his sly smile stretch a bit further.

"Trust an old salesman, Jim Morgan. Nobody has nothing. We've all got something we can trade. It just depends on how badly we want whatever it is that we want. Now, think hard! Are you absolutely sure have you nothing to trade?" For a brief second - Jim could not even be entirely sure he saw it - Philus's eyes flicked down to his coat. As though an invisible hand had dropped a rock in his pocket, Jim remembered the square shape that jabbed him in the side every now and again.

His father's box.

A sudden hope surged through Jim's mind. All his fantasies of plunging those wretched Cromiers into prison and restoring the house of Morgan roared back to possibility. Without thinking, Jim pulled the box from his pocket. Handing the bottle of Revenge back to Philus, he flipped open the box and looked inside.

The letter, the moonwater, and the necklace all lay within, safe and sound. One by one Jim considered them all.

The letter, lying folded beneath the vial of moonwater, had turned out to be more than just a letter. It held a secret from Jim's father – possibly even a map to buried treasure. Jim could never part with it. Of course, in order to read whatever was hidden upon the letter he would need the vial of moonwater lying on top of it. But, just peeking out from under one edge of the tattered parchment, a coil of fine silver chain glimmered in the firelight – Jim's mother's necklace.

Swallowing so hard it hurt, Jim withdrew the necklace. He closed the lid behind it with a soft tap and put the box back in his pocket. The shell charm dangled at the end of the chain, spinning slowly before Jim's eyes. Philus Philonius let out a low whistle at the sight of it.

"Well, I say, Master Morgan, that is a lovely necklace, indeed. Fairly small, not much silver really, but quite, quite lovely."

"It was my mother's," Jim said, his eyes fixed on the silver shell, all but glowing in the moonlight. A pair of strong, invisible bands squeezed Jim's chest. *Don't do it,* a voice whispered in his mind. The voice could have belonged to Lacey, or Phineus, or even Jim's father.

"Not much silver, really," Philus repeated. He leaned his little face so close to the necklace that his nose nearly tapped the shell. His fingers were reaching for it, though they never touched the charm. "But for you, my boy – for you it would be just enough - just enough to take a crack at those who have taken everything from you. It would be just enough for a chance to reverse your fortunes. You have only to say the word."

Jim stared at the necklace. His insides churned and he felt as though he would be sick. It seemed as though his arm wanted to shove the necklace back into his pocket and his legs wanted to run away. But in Jim's mind, all he could see was a world put right – a world with the Cromiers locked up like animals and Morgan Manor built anew, a proper home for Jim and all his friends. He could build a room, Jim told himself, a whole wing of the new house to honor his father and his mother. Surely that would make up for the cost of this one necklace, would it not?

Jim slowly extended his arm and offered the necklace to Philus. At the last moment he nearly yanked the necklace back and ran away, but Philus pushed the bottle of warm Revenge into Jim's other hand. Jim felt the heat in one palm and the cool metal in the other.

He let go of the cold silver chain.

"Aha!" Philus announced with a whoop. "Then it is done! A well-struck bargain my boy, and I do believe you came away with the better end of the deal, I do say, I do say. But now, to prepare your concoction!"

Philus leapt from the step, flute to his lips. A rollicking, raucous tune, wild and dangerous, spilled into the night. All by itself the fire whipped into a burning whirlpool of orange and yellow tongues, so bright and so hot that Jim covered his face with his arm and fell back on his seat in the sand. When he dared to look again, he found a black cauldron, perhaps summoned from the dark night itself, hovering above the fire. Water steamed within, frothing and bubbling over the sides.

Philus danced around the cauldron, his fingers flying over the twin-piped flute. Even when the old man stole the enchanted instrument into some hidden pocket, the melody continued to thrum in Jim's ears, like wind through the trees. From other unseen pockets the tiny man withdrew the potion's ingredients, chanting their names as he dropped them into his magic brew.

"Three drops of venom, squeezed from a scorpion's sting!"

"Four yellow petals, torn from Birdsfoot Trefoil!"

"Two black feathers, fallen from Nemesis's wings!"

"And one rose, cut from Brutus's garden!"

Every item dipped into the cauldron's depths sparked the enchanted tincture with thick smoke and flashing color. First came a sickly yellow, then a fiery orange. After that was a bruised purple, and lastly an emerald green. The colors dazzled Jim's eyes. They were not quite natural colors in the potion, nor quite earthly scents upon the smoke. This was real magic. Jim knew it in his gut and felt it in his bones. It was as real as the Pirate Vault of Treasures or the Amulet of Portunes, both of which Jim had faced during his time in London.

"Now boy, the final touch to bend all the others toward your noble purpose." Philus danced over to Jim, wrapping his small, strong fingers around Jim's wrist. Pulling Jim over to the cauldron, Philus unstopped the vial and drew Jim's hand over the boiling concoction. The heat burned against Jim's skin and he wanted to snatch his hand away. But Philus was stronger than his small frame belied. He held Jim's arm firmly in place and carefully, oh so carefully, let slip one perfectly measured drop from the bottle of Revenge into the cauldron's brew.

The moment the liquid splashed into the potion, smoke and magic erupted in a column of red fire. The explosion threw Jim back from the cauldron and into the sand, his eyes closed tight with fear. When Jim found the courage to open them again, all was calm once more. The fire had died to a lazy burn, the smoke had drifted off in a strong sea breeze, and the potion in the cauldron had settled into a bubbling simmer, glowing a dim, blood red. The faint scent of burnt honey hung in the air.

Philus produced a pair of long, wooden tongs and reached into the red brew. He swirled the mixture with the tongs once, twice, and then on the third, delicately squeezed the tongs shut and withdrew what remained of the rose cut from Brutus's garden. The red petals, still full and blossomed and curled, had turned to ashy gray, and the stem to solid black. On one side, just beneath the color-drained flower, protruding and glistening with potion, sat a single curved thorn. Philus held the rose stem toward Jim from between the tongs.

"Here, my boy, take it. Take it if you will, but do be careful! Mind the thorn." Jim reached out with a trembling hand and took the rose stem from Philus, pinching it between two fingers below the wicked sticker. "Now, listen to me close, lad, and listen well, for I will say these words only once. This potion will grant you but one chance to strike revenge against your foes and reverse your fortunes. Do you understand?"

"Yes," Jim said. The rose stem was hot in his hand from the fire. It stung his fingers, but he refused to drop it into the sand.

"There is but one ingredient that yet remains to spark the spell: a single drop of your blood. You must wait for your enemies to be close, boy. Even if it means waiting until fortune, fate, and foes have you under their boot. You must hold your enemies in your gaze when you ignite the spell. That is of paramount importance! Hold them in your gaze, boy! Then prick your finger with the thorn. Do not prick lightly! You must dab the thorn in blood. Do this and the road of time will lead you inevitably to your revenge. Do you understand?

"Yes," Jim said. He could hardly wait for the chance to put this magic to work and undo those horrible murderers and thieves.

"Good," said Philus. "Then be on with you. It has gotten late and you should be home. Doing magic has drained me of my strength and soured my mood. I must rest and regain my vigor."

Jim took a good, long look at the old man, and found that he indeed seemed to have aged some years in but the last few moments. All but ignoring Jim, Philus Philonius trudged to his wagon and dropped down on the little step. He withdrew his flute once more and began to play that same sad song he'd been playing when Jim had first stumbled upon him.

"Thank you, Mr. Philonius," Jim said. But the old man's eyes were now closed and Jim's words fell on deaf ears. So Jim pulled his box from his pocket and gently set the blackened rose stem on top of his father's letter for safekeeping. Then he strode off down the beach, the flute song playing softly as he went. Jim had gone but a few paces, when a last pang of guilt or regret struck him. He thought back to his silver necklace. He turned about to ask Philus to at least take good care of it for him, as it was special, or perhaps to hold it for him to buy back once he'd regained his fortune. But when Jim spun around, the wagon, the fire, and the little man were gone. Only the song lingered in the air for a few more lonely notes before it too faded away.

Jim took a deep breath, knowing now for certain that what was done was done. There was no turning back. As he made his way down the shore, the moon shining on the restless ocean waves, his thoughts dwelt on his forthcoming chance at justice. He thought on the rose stem in his father's box, which felt heavier in his pocket than it ever had before.

Hot-blooded dreams of revenge bubbled over in Jim's mind nearly the entire, long walk down the beach. It was only when the stables came in view that a small sting pricked Jim's heart, like a bothersome splinter in his thumb. There would be no way he could properly explain the rose to his friends just yet. The Ratts would probably love the idea of vengeance, Jim thought, but MacGuffy and Lacey would most certainly disapprove, especially of his trading away his mother's necklace.

So Jim concocted a slight bending of the truth as he stepped from the sand onto the grassy hill leading up to the stables. He came up with a story about how he lost the necklace while running down the beach, and how he failed to find it in the dark no matter how hard he searched. He loathed the idea of lying outright, but there was no other way. Jim had just formulated the right words when he pushed open the stable doors.

Lacey, MacGuffy, and the Ratts all sat on the dirt floor in a half circle about an old lantern. Jim knew from the looks on their faces that he was in for a rough reception. MacGuffy furiously squinted his one good eye beneath a furrowed brow, tears glistened on Lacey's cheeks, and not one roguish smile stretched across a Ratt Brother's face. Jim sighed deeply. He expected his friends to be none too pleased with him for running off the way he did, but he hardly thought it would be this harsh.

"I'm sorry," Jim began. "I know I shouldn't have run off like that. I just needed to get away for a few moments. But I'm back now and there's no need to worry."

"Oh, but we were worried, young Morgan," a voice replied – but this voice belonged to none of Jim's friends sitting on the floor. It came from a shadow on the wall. "We are so, so glad, that you have finally returned. In fact, you're just in time." Jim's heart froze in his chest. His arms and legs turned to stone. He knew that voice. It often times echoed in the depths of his worst memories from the night he lost his father.

From behind the stable, in the farthest corner of the room, the owner of the voice stepped into the lamplight. His black coat and black hat oozed from the shadows. A crimson wig fell in long curls about a pale face and a purple scar ran the length of his left cheek. Jim trembled where he stood. An anguished cry froze in his throat.

Count Cromier had returned to finish what he started. He had returned to kill Jim Morgan.

EIGHT

RETURN OF THE RED COUNT

ount Cromier emerged from the back of the stables, hand on the pommel of his sword. An eager, cruel smile played upon his mouth. It took Jim a moment too long to remember his new weapon against these villains, the enchanted rose thorn hidden in the box in his pocket. Before Jim could even reach for it, a cold, sharp point tapped him beneath the chin. Jim followed the slender blade at his throat to a black-gloved hand, to a red-coated arm, and to a pale face beneath crow black hair. Bartholomew Cromier stood above Jim. His blue eyes quivered with so much hate that Jim's knees shook beneath him.

"Do you remember that night on the docks, Jim Morgan? When you ran away and I swore to you this was not over? I always keep my promises."

From behind the stable dividers, ten men or more ambled into the light. These were no soldiers with torches and bayonetted muskets as had chased Jim from his home the first time. They were unshaven, swarthy sailors - bandanas, eye patches, and unkempt, wild hair curling about their faces. To a man, each had pistols shoved into cracked leather belts and naked knives at the ready, dried blood from their latest dark deeds still fresh on the blades. Pirates – and of the worst sort, Jim knew.

"Thought you'd made a joke of me back in London, didn't you, Morgan?" Bartholomew growled. He gripped his sword so tightly that the blade trembled beneath Jim's chin, stinging his skin. "Thought you'd seen the last of me when you sailed away that night? Thought I'd fall for all of Dread Steele's lies and chase him round the globe for the rest of my days while you took your dead father's place and became Lord of the Manor? Well, welcome home Lord Morgan."

"Still yer tongue, ye wretched, raven-headed blackguard!" MacGuffy shouted, twisting and fighting the bonds about his wrists. "Leave these pups be and let an old salt teach ye a lesson!" Bartholomew's eyes flicked to where MacGuffy knelt. His mouth folded into a cruel sneer and gave a quick nod to a burly pirate from the crew. The pirate, scars like dreadful tally marks running down his arms, stepped forth and viciously kicked MacGuffy in the ribs. He then cracked the old salt on the back of the head with a pistol butt. MacGuffy slumped into the dirt with a weak groan.

"Still *your* tongue old man, and perhaps I'll allow you to keep your remaining eye a little longer!"

"Leave him alone!" Lacey cried, her eyes wet with tears for poor MacGuffy. But the pirates only laughed, gleeful and loud. Even Bartholomew's sneer melted into a wolfish grin to match his father's. Jim balled up his hands into fists. He wanted desperately to say something – or better yet to do something. His hands itched to take hold of the magic rose, but Bartholomew's cold blade left him nothing to do but tremble in anger. Hot tears welled up in Jim's eyes.

"Tears?" Bartholomew mocked, his voice cracking in mirthless in-dignation. "We've taken everything from you, Jim Morgan! Everything! And you can do no more than weep? At least your father had courage. You should be glad he never saw the coward his son became!"

"Jim's not a coward!" Lacey cried. "He went into the Pirate Vault of Treasures all by himself and defeated that awful place. Then he beat the King of Thieves and rescued us. He's the bravest person I've ever met! You're the coward! What did he ever do to you to deserve this?"

"Oh, but he *does* deserve this." Bartholomew's ice-cold eyes latched onto Jim's face. His voice burned at the edge of every word. "He has taken more from me than he knows, more than I have ever taken from him. I'll show you what he deserves. I'll show you what I'm not afraid to do!" Bartholomew pressed his sword point against Jim's throat so firmly that it drew a trickle of blood from his neck.

"Bartholomew!" Count Cromier barked from the shadows, lashing his son with such a brutal stare that it seemed to startle Bartholomew nearly as much as it did Jim and Lacey. The Count stormed across the stables and slapped away his son's blade as a mother would slap a child's hand. "Not now, boy. Not yet!"

Bartholomew's eyes opened wide at his father's command. Jim could not tell if it was from hurt or anger, but nevertheless the pale captain eased his hold on his sword. He withdrew the point from Jim's throat, the tip touched with a red drop of Jim's blood. Count Cromier ran his gloved hand down the length of his son's sword until he wiped clean the red spot. He rubbed it between his thumb and forefinger, glancing back and forth between Jim and the blood on his fingertips.

"Young James - or is it Jim now? I would never have allowed my son to disrespect his heritage by taking such a common moniker. Jim? So low and beneath your class. But alas, you have no father to keep such rules, do you?" Jim stiffened at Cromier's harsh reminder, but the Count had only just begun.

"Nevertheless, you did indeed show courage and resourcefulness after our last meeting. You escaped my soldiers. You outwitted a great

London thief. You navigated the Vault of Treasures. And..." The Count's eyes flashed at Bartholomew. "You even managed to escape my son."

A quiet rage brewed just behind Bartholomew's face. Jim could all but see the hate growing within the younger Cromier – and he knew that hate burned for him.

"I see you forgot to bring soldiers along with you this time," Jim finally managed, his voice shaking as he tried to steer the conversation from Bartholomew's failure in London. "Or perhaps they just weren't up for hunting down children anymore?"

Cromier laughed, shaking his head so hard that his curls bounced on the sides of his face. "Oh, but you have your father's haughty cheek, don't you? It's as though I'm speaking to Lindsay himself! No, it was less the soldiers' moral quibbles than the fact that for this particular adventure, we shall be doing some travelling, young Morgan. Oh, the places we'll go and the things we'll do!" The Count laughed. "These sort of quests require a different sort of man, Jim. Wouldn't you agree, Splitbeard?"

At the sound of his name, another pirate swaggered through the stable doors. He was not a terribly large man, nor overwhelmingly powerful, but one look told Jim this was a true pirate of the seas – and a dangerous one at that. Long years beneath the sun had burned his skin dark as smelted bronze. Two daggers and a pistol leaned ready against his hips, tucked into a dirty sash about his waist. From beneath a blood red bandana about his head fell a single lock of black hair. Black also was the beard from which Splitbeard drew his name. It fell in two braids like a forked dragon's tongue over his chest, tied off at the ends with jagged shark's teeth. When the man spoke, a thick accent from somewhere far to the south of England drenched each and every word.

"You speak the truth, oh magnificent Red Count. Dangerous work requires dangerous men, yes? And the sea is very dangerous. But only Splitbeard the Pirate and the Corsairs of the *Sea Spider* have faced more than flesh and blood or earth and water and lived to tell the tale."

"Where have you been, pirate?" Bartholomew snapped, apparently quite unimpressed with Splitbeard's boast. "We pay you well for your services and your men, not to wander around like a useless lay-about!" But Splitbeard only smiled and laughed as though the insults were jokes.

"Alas, I was but surveying these once most beautiful grounds, oh great son of the Red Count. It was furthest from my desires to insult your graces by suggesting you needed my aid corralling such…fearsome quarry as this." Splitbeard slapped Jim hard on his shoulder and squeezed him tight, drawing a wince on Jim's face. "I assure you all is well, oh pale Bartholomew." Splitbeard finally released Jim with a small push and wandered over to his men. He leaned casually against a stable wall as though he were quite bored. "When the time comes, you shall see all that Splitbeard is, and will know that he has been worth every piece of gold he will be paid."

"And you shall be paid handsomely," the Count said. "Once we find what we came for."

"What have ye come for, eh, Cromier?" MacGuffy said stiffly. He forced himself back to his knees, still bent over from the kick to his ribs. "Can ye not see that ye've left the boy nothin'? He's as penniless as I am, with naught but the clothes on his back left to him, ye vile sea serpent!"

"Oh, please – do you really think you can play dumb with me, MacGuffy?" said Cromier. "You know perfectly well why we're here. And so do you, don't you, Jim?" Cromier came to stand directly in front of Jim, looking down on him with a knowing smile on his face.

"You're still looking for the Treasure of the Ocean." Jim whispered. His thoughts flashed back to that night so long ago. With Aunt Margarita's help, Count Cromier had killed Jim's father for the secret to the Treasure of the Ocean. Bartholomew would have done the same to Jim if he had not escaped on his pony, Destroyer.

"Right you are! And you are going to help me find it."

"I don't know where it is! I promise you that's the truth! It disappeared. I saw it for just a moment in the Pirate Vault of Treasures. But then it all disappeared like smoke. It's gone. Gone forever, just like everything else that was ever my father's or mine. You've won, alright. So just leave us alone." A lone, burning tear dripped onto Jim's cheek. It ran fast down to his chin and fell like a raindrop onto the earthen floor between his feet.

"Oh, Jim, Jim, Jim," the Count said. His tender voice hardly masked the mocking cruelty beneath it. "You are such a clever, clever boy - as clever as you are courageous, to be sure. So do not play the fool with me." The Count snapped his fingers and a pirate brought him a stool from one of the stables. Flipping the tails of his black coat behind him, Cromier sat down and looked Jim in the face.

"As much as I hated your father and as much as I hate him still, he was never a fool. He was a brilliant strategist - a planner of plans and plans within plans. He would have protected this Treasure in a web of schemes to rival the Minotaur's maze! He would have done everything in his power to ensure it was you, you and only you, young Jim, to whom the Treasure would eventually fall. Now, before he died, he must have told you something, or given you something, yes?"

On the streets in London Jim had learned to be a very good liar, and he did his best to keep his face stony and still. But all of Jim's anger and all of his hurt were too much to fight at once, and the Count read Jim's face like an open book.

"Yes! He gave you something, I can tell!" The Count rubbed his gloved hands together. He leaned in close to Jim, his eyes wide and greedy. The Count looked him over from head to toe until his eyes came to rest on the square bulge in his jacket pocket. Panic nearly overwhelmed Jim as the Count reached into his pocket and withdrew his father's box. Cromier held it in his hands, trembling with an uncontainable excitement.

"The symbol!" The Count cried, stomping his feet up and down like a spoiled child. "The treasure's symbol is carved onto the lid of this box! How long, how long I've waited to see this symbol again."

"All this time and all this gold you've spent on soldiers and pirates and fighting my father," Jim said with a thick voice. "Will the treasure even be worth it by the time you find it?"

Cromier stared at Jim for a long moment, as though not quite sure whether or not Jim was serious. Then the Count erupted in laughter. He threw his head back so that his blood red curls shook like a lion's mane. Bartholomew and all the pirates in the room joined in the Count's laughter, shamelessly heaping their derision on Jim – all that was, save for Splitbeard. The pirate captain silently leaned against the stable walls, staring hard at the box in Cromier's hands.

"My boy, I already have more gold than I could ever spend! I am a Count after all and they don't just make anyone a Count, do they?"

"Then what do you want?" George demanded. "What are you doin' all this for?" But Cromier never turned around. His eyes glazed over and he stared into some far away time and place in his memories. His gloved hand went to his face and slowly began to trace the purple scar that ran from his left eye to his jaw.

"Your father never had the chance to tell you what the Treasure of the Ocean really is, did he? You see, all the other gold, gems, treasures, and baubles you saw in the Vault were merely window dressing, decoration lying in heaps around the true Treasure of the Ocean. They are nothing in comparison – dust and shadows. Amongst all that wealth there is but one item, one talisman of ancient magic older than you can possibly imagine." The Count's finger stopped halfway down his scar and pressed hard into his cheek. The lamplight in the stables glowed in the watery pools that became the Count's eyes until it seemed to Jim that Cromier had gone quite mad. "The one who possesses the Treasure of the Ocean, the one who knows its secret, will gain the only possession on earth more valuable than gold. Tell me, Jim. When you hear the waves crash against the beach, do you fear the ocean?"

"No," Jim whispered. But he did fear the madness swimming in the Count's face.

"That's because you are young," said the Count. "When you've seen what the ocean can do when it runs wild - the waves, the wind, the lightning, and the thunder. The ocean is the most frightening thing in all the earth. Imagine all that might under your control. The Treasure is as its name suggests, boy. It is the *Power* of the Ocean."

"Even magic power fades with time and tide, oh magnificent red one," Splitbeard interrupted from where he leaned on the wall. "But gold is always gold." The pirate's words finally brought Cromier back to where he sat in the stables and he blinked his eyes free of the reverie that had gripped them.

"You shall have as much of it as you like, Splitbeard. Once I unlock the power of the Treasure of the Ocean, I shall have surpassed the need for such trivialities as wealth and riches." The Count opened the box. The moment his eyes fell on the letter and the vial of moonwater, his scarred face lit up with dark joy. "Here it is," he said. He withdrew the parchment and the vial and tossed the box down on the floor by Jim's feet, the rose thorn still resting inside.

NINE

THE MAP OF BLUE FIRE

"If nothing else, Lindsay was brilliant to the end," Cromier said. He held up the vial, admiring the shimmering blue liquid within. "Moonwater – ingenious! You love gold, Splitbeard? The substance in this one bottle is worth more gold than you and ten men could carry at once."

"We are strong, oh glorious one. Our arms can carry much," Splitbeard replied. In spite of the carefree grin on his face, the pirate leader's eyes, along with those of his men, remained fixed on the mysterious vial. The Count unfolded the letter and quickly read the words. He snorted with disgust when he reached the end and shook his head with a sad sneer.

"This letter reeks of sentiment. That is what destroyed your father, Jim Morgan. Sentiment makes a man weak, but it will never undo me!" With that, Cromier snapped his fingers. Another corsair pirate grabbed Jim by his collar and shoved him down on the floor beside his friends.

Bartholomew seized the lantern and hoisted it high before his father. The Count, all but shaking with anticipation, held the vial up to the flame. The lamplight shone through the moonwater and onto the page. Blue shapes and letters once more leapt from the yellowed parchment. The glowing reflections danced on Cromier's greedy face. Laughing aloud and licking his lips, he dropped to one knee and flattened the parchment on the stool beside him. He uncorked the vial and slowly dripped the iridescent liquid from one end of the parchment to the other, until dark splotches soaked the page through. For the span of breath, nothing happened – until the Count blew lightly upon the sheet to dry it.

Blue flame blazed from the page. The once soft lines and shapes seared themselves upon the parchment in lightning strokes. The pirates uttered oaths and curses of dismay in their own tongues. They covered their eyes in fear, as though even the sight of such magic could damn them for life. The stable about Jim and his friends seemed to fall into deeper shadow, muted beneath the luminous display of islands, cities, symbols, and a star-filled sky. The secret to his father's letter was indeed revealed to be a map, drawn in the same fiery blue strokes as his last words to Jim.

"At last!" Cromier shouted. He held the empty vial of moonwater above his head as his trophy. "So many fruitless years and so many near misses were all worth this moment! Now I have a map drawn by Lindsay Morgan himself. The Treasure is at last within my grasp! We've not a moment to lose! We begin our journey this very night!" The Count folded the parchment, snuffing out the blue light and leaving only dazzles in Jim's eyes.

But as the pirates readied to leave, Bartholomew stalked to the center of the stables, where Jim knelt beside his friends. He drew his sword from its scabbard, letting a glimmer catch Jim's eye and the steel ring in his ears. Once more, the pale captain held the blade to

Jim's face, the sharp point not an inch from his nose. Bartholomew leaned close, as though to whisper a secret to Jim.

"My father will soon have what's he's waited a lifetime for, won't he? And who is left to stop him? I suppose it wouldn't hurt to let me have a share in the good fortune. I too have waited long for something denied to me. Say hello to your father for me, Jim Morgan. Let him know his failure is now complete!" Bartholomew raised his sword to strike. But a sharp word from Count Cromier stayed Bartholomew's hand for the second time that night.

"Bartholomew, no!"

"But father!" Bartholomew shrieked, sword still held above his head, quivering as though it ached to strike. "We have the map. You don't need him anymore! Not when you have me!"

"There are many dangers that lie ahead, my son," Cromier said. "And the boy did escape the Pirate Vault - no simple trick, I tell you. He may yet prove useful. As for his friends — well, he'll have five chances to see what happens if he won't cooperate, won't he? Bring them with us!"

The Count turned on his heel and marched from the stables. But the matter seemed far from settled for Bartholomew. To Jim's surprise, the raven-haired captain's blue eyes brimmed with tears – tears of dark, trembling rage. Bartholomew muttered a curse beneath his breath and finally sheathed his sword.

One of Splitbeard's men bound Jim to his friends with ropes and dragged them from the stables into the moonlit night. Once outside and wrapped in the cold air off the ocean, Cromier shouted a final command to his pirate thugs.

"Burn the stables. Let there be no trace that the house of Morgan ever stood. Leave no hope that it shall ever stand again." The pirates hurled their lanterns onto the stable's roof, where they shattered and broke. Flames spread over the tiles like yellow water, devouring the last pieces of what was once Jim's home.

"Oh, Jim," Lacey said. She rested her head on his shoulder and wiped her tears away with the back of her hand. "I'm so sorry."

"Me too, mate," added George with a shaky voice.

For his part, Jim said nothing. He could only watch the fire burn. He remembered the day he tried to ride his father's horse, Thunderbold, before this very building. Memories were all that remained. After a moment, Splitbeard the pirate came to stand beside the crestfallen clan, his sun-darkened skin aglow in the firelight.

"Even I, pirate of the Seven Seas, might have pity on one who has lost all, oh desolate one. So it was with me, before I became a prince of the waves. So here, let it not be said you have nothing, oh young lord – lord of a box!" With that the Pirate stuck Jim's box into his pocket and slapped him so hard on the back that it forced the air from Jim's lungs. He walked off to join his men, laughing heartily. Yet not the sting on Jim's back, nor the pirate's cruel laughter, counted for anything against the desire that sprang up in his heart. For little did Splitbeard know that he had just handed Jim his one and only chance to turn all the blackness to light.

But before a plot to wriggle his hands free and seize the box took shape in Jim's mind, from nowhere a weight settled quite unexpectedly upon his shoulder. Jim turned to face this surprise and bumped his nose into a rather sharp beak – a beak belonging to a very familiar raven's face.

"Cornelius!" Jim whispered. He was so surprised for a moment that he forgot even his plans to employ the rose thorn in his pocket. After blinking his eyes several times to be sure, Jim found that indeed the talking raven was once more perched upon his shoulder. It was the very place the bird had sat when the two of them braved the Pirate Vault of Treasure's deadly traps, not much more than a year gone past. "What are you doing here?"

"What am I doing here?" said Cornelius. "Why, I've come to rescue you, naturally. Did you really think we would allow you to meet your end at the hands of these trolls, Jim Morgan? Speaking of trolls, remind me to tell you about the lot we ran into this past fall on Gibraltar - nasty business that was, and the stench! Good lord!

"Mister Cornelius!" Lacey squealed as quietly as possible beside Jim. "Oh, I'm so happy to see you! But where did you come from?"

"Indeed, it is I, Cornelius Darkfeather, once again at your service, Miss Lacey," Cornelius said. He bowed low on Jim's shoulder, one wing outstretched in a feathered flourish. "And in answer to your question, my dear, I came from there."

Cornelius pointed his wing toward the ocean. When Jim followed the feathers his mouth opened in a surprised "O". A massive rush of fog, roiling and churning like a storm cloud, crawled over the ocean waves toward the white sand shore. This was no ordinary fog drift, Jim thought. It surged forward like a galloping horse, moving fast over the waters. It came straight for the beach and the hill beyond, where Jim and his friends stood captives of Count Cromier's pirate thugs.

TEN

RESCUE IN THE FOG

"Good of ye to finally drop in, Darkfeather," MacGuffy growled. He forced a smile on his ruined face, though he was still hobbled from the vicious beating he had taken in the stables.

"Good to see you again as well, old friend," replied Cornelius with a nod of his head. The Ratts however, forgot entirely to greet the raven. Their wide eyes were fixed past the bird and onto the frothing fog that neared the beach.

"Jim!" George exclaimed, obviously trying to come to grips with what he was seeing. "What in blazes is that?" But it was Cornelius who answered, smiling proudly at the corners of his beak.

"That, young Master Ratt, is a proper rescue!"

The mist rushed toward the shore, frightening Jim and his friends more than a little. They gathered together in a huddle, holding each other close. At just that moment, the burly pirate, who seemed to take an obscene delight in the fear of children, overheard their whisperings and stalked over. He drew back his heavy hand with the intent to silence Jim and the others with a rap of his knuckles. Yet before he loosed the blow, he realized the small clan was ignoring him completely and followed their eyes to the shores of the beach.

A terrified squeak, not unlike a mouse's at the mercy of cat's claws, burst from the burly pirate's mouth. The hand once meant to slap Jim silly suddenly pointed wildly toward the waters and the big fellow shrieked in the most unmanly fashion.

"Cap'n Splitbeard, Cap'n Splitbeard! Somethin' comin' over the waters! Somethin' comin' for us!" The twin-bearded pirate, Count Cromier, Bartholomew, and the rest of the pirates came running at the alarm. All of them, though, skidded to a halt the moment they saw the fog. In the light of the stable fire a pale shade of fear passed over the Cromiers' faces. The Count turned on Jim as if to curse his very existence, until his dark eyes came to rest on Cornelius Darkfeather, perched upon Jim's shoulder. The scar on the Count's face writhed and twisted. He managed to rasp but one, enraged word:

"Steele!"

The fog struck the shore. It rushed over the sand and onto the grass like a passing shadow. Jim and his friends squeezed together, shutting their eyes tight as the mist rolled over them. The fog shocked them with a cold bite like a splash of frosty water.

When Jim opened his eyes again he found the world masked beneath the mist. The moon and the stars were hidden completely. Even the raging firelight from the burning stable was reduced to nothing more than a muted red glow. Bartholomew and his father drew their swords and prepared for battle. Their pirate thugs backed together in a tighter knot than Jim and his friends, weapons and courage forgotten, quaking with fear. Only Splitbeard, crafty scalawag that he was, slowly backed away from the shore, keeping his men between him and whatever terror was about to emerge from this unnatural fog.

Silence fell over the hill. Besides the slamming of his heart in his chest, all Jim heard was the faint crackle of his burning stable and the steady thrum of the waves upon the beach.

Until music chimed in the dark.

The wheezy, tired collection of whistles and hoots slowly and steadily rose as they drew closer and closer – a dread tune cranked at the hands of an organ grinder. A rogue's smile crept onto one corner of Jim's mouth. He'd heard that tune before – only a year ago on the deck of an old sloop.

Shapes appeared in the mist, the darkened shades of men. One by one they came into view and threw the fog from their shoulders and faces like cloaks and hoods of mist. The red-bearded organ grinder faithfully turned his crank. A bright smile carved a path along the dark face of huge Mufwalme. Black-bearded Murdock, long-mustached Wang Chi, and even sleepy Mister Gilly, bulbous nose still as red as ever, appeared as well. Those and a dozen more stepped from the fog, faces lit with gleeful eyes, hungry for battle.

Last of all, a shadow darker than those before melted from the gray. His eyes were hidden beneath the edge of a tricorn hat and his face behind the upturned collar of his great cloak. But Jim knew the man in spite of his disguise. His face was darkened by the sun and lined with a black and silver beard. He was Dread Steele, Lord of the Pirates. He drew his sword and leveled the blade at the Cromiers.

"I told you once, Bartholomew, never to harm this boy or anything that was his again. But I see now you've gone a step beyond and brought with you the truest of villains. Long has it been since I've seen your cowardly face, Cromier, you devil."

"A long time indeed, Steele. But even old memories cut deep, do they not?" Cromier drew one gloved finger down the purple scar on his face. "Yet now the numbers are on my side. You've lost your old comrade, Lindsay Morgan, while I've gained a new one." Cromier pointed his sword toward Splitbeard, who wisely kept his distance from Steele and the *Spectre's* crew.

"Splitbeard," Steele spat. "Deceitful snake! Lord of Liars! I always knew you to be a poltroon – but I thought even you stood above scum of Cromier's ilk."

"I go where gold may be found, oh lord of the pirates," Splitbeard said, that clever, unflappable smile creeping over his fork-braided beard. "And gold buys the favor of many men!" The roar of at least thirty more voices rose up from the direction of the town of Rye – followed by the pounding of at least sixty boots on the pathway behind the hill. The rest of Splitbeard's crew had come to join the fight.

Without even a trace of fear, the Lord of the Pirates raised his voice in command to his men. "Free the prisoners! Escape to the sea! Charge!"

Steele's crew rushed forward to clash with Splitbeard's men. The shouting and ringing swords redoubled at the arrival of the Corsair pirate's thirty extra men. Chaos erupted in the fog. From out of the mist, sleepy Mister Gilly appeared before Jim and his friends, plump belly poking out from his striped sailor's shirt. He bowed clumsily, a lazy smile spread across his stubbled face, as though fog-shrouded rescues were hardly a thing out of the ordinary.

"Hullo, friends. Not certain if you'd remember old Gilly or not, as most people don't you see. But here I am to undo your bindin's if you please."

"No time or need for introductions now, Gilly, old chum!" Cornelius cawed with shrill impatience. "Untie them already! Untie them and let's be off!"

But Lacey, who Jim knew had always felt sorry for poor Mister Gilly because all the other pirates seemed to laugh at him all the time, smiled back and even managed to curtsey in spite of the ropes. "Of course we remember you, Mister Gilly, and your help would be most appreciated!"

Mister Gilly's smile widened and his cheeks turned as red as his nose. He tipped his sailor's hat and rushed forward to cut Jim and his friends loose. "Most certainly, ma'am! It should be my pleasure of course!" Mister Gilly made short work of the ropes with his knife, careful to not so much as nick a wrist or finger. Once they had all been freed, Cornelius flapped up to Gilly's shoulder to lead the escape.

"Stay close together, my young friends. Hold hands tightly and don't lose your way in the mist. Gilly, take MacGuffy on your shoulder. It's not far to the beach, so keep small and close to the ground. The fog will conceal us from Splitbeard's cronies and aid in our escape."

"Don't worry about us, Cornelius," said George, thumbing over at his brothers. "We been escapin' all kinds of grown-ups since before we could walk!"

"Indeed you have, Master Ratt," said Cornelius. He leaned over on Gilly's shoulder to look directly into George's face with his midnight eyes. "But the Corsairs of the *Sea Spider* do not usually seek to catch their enemies. They have the horrible tendency to slit their throats. So you will stick together now, won't you?"

"Right," said George quietly, swallowing hard and feeling at his throat with a pale hand. "Stick together - best way to be safe, or so our father always said." With that settled, the little party set off through the fog. All the while the battle raged about them.

Jim heard more of the fighting than saw it. The sounds of shouting men echoed over the hill and the ring of clashing swords carried on the fog. The warring pirates were little more than silhouetted shades, lit by the glowing red fire that burned in the mist. The small rescue party had been going for some time, though, and Jim thought they surely must be near the beach. But before they cleared the fog's edge, four figures appeared in the murk.

Steele must have knocked Bartholomew over his head with the bell of his sword, Jim thought, for the raven-haired sea captain lay still in the grass. Meanwhile, Dread Steele fought Count Cromier and Splitbeard at once, a sword in one hand and a rapier in the other. Jim watched in awe for half a moment, his mouth cracked open in an amazed smile as he followed the shadow pirate's whirling blades, parrying and striking in flawless rhythm. There was no one who could beat Dread Steele, Jim thought, no one ever save for perhaps Jim's own father.

But as Jim watched, another sound rose over the din of battle. It was soft at first, but it grew so quickly in the back of Jim's mind that it soon became the only sound – the song of a flute playing a sad, sad song. A voice whispered within the pipe's tune. *Now is your chance to strike, Jim Morgan!* The box in Jim's pocket became suddenly heavy; so heavy that it slowed Jim's pace. Jim's thoughts fell to the rose hidden there within, and to the rose's enchanted purpose.

Jim let go of his friends' hands.

He wandered into the fog toward the thick of the fight. It seemed to him as though he was in a dream, and he could not be hurt, for none of what he saw was really happening. He was only watching it from the safety of his sleep. Jim drew the box from his pocket. He flipped open the lid and took the rose thorn in hand. Old Philus Philonius's instructions played over in the back of Jim's mind to the tune of the magic flute. Jim readied himself for a brief moment a pain – a pain worth the price of revenge. He fixed the Cromiers in his sights, his eyes opened wide so as not to even blink and risk foiling the spell.

Slowly, he pulled back the thorn to prick himself on the thumb.

Yet before Jim could strike, a dark shape burst from the mist, barreling between Jim and the Cromiers. With his enemies hidden from sight, Jim came to his senses and found himself face to face with the burly pirate. The scoundrel held a drawn cutlass in his hand and raised up to strike Jim Morgan from the world forever. As his mind cleared, fear welled up within Jim like a fountain. But just when he thought this would be the end, a cawing, flapping, black shadow careened over Jim's shoulder. It flew into the pirate's face, beating the man with his wings and scratching at his eyes with his claws.

"Get back, poltroon! Young Morgan is under the protection of true men of the sea, you dog!" Cornelius drove the big man back. At that same moment a strong hand seized Jim by the collar, jerking him so hard that he had to scramble backwards to keep from being dragged. Jim was suddenly yanked free from the mist and tossed onto the beach, his hat falling from his head and the box and the rose tumbling from his hand.

"Jim Morgan!" Lacey screamed, stomping one foot on the sandy beach as Jim picked himself up. The last cobweb traces of the spell finally fell from his head as he focused on the sound of Lacey's voice. "Just what in the world do you think you were doing? If it weren't for Mister Gilly and Cornelius you would have been killed!"

"You just wandered off, mate," added George, he and his brothers looking at Jim with concern on their faces. "For a second there we thought you was a goner!"

"Apologies for tossing you down in the sand so rough, Mister Morgan, sir," said Mister Gilly, smiling sleepily. "But there were some rather scurrilous cutthroats and villains about and we did need to move quite quickly, didn't we?"

"Ye should've dumped the fool on his head to knock some sense into 'im, Gilly!" MacGuffy raged. "What in blazes were ye doin' wanderin' off in a fight that way, young Morgan?" With the eyes of all his friends so heavy upon him, for a moment Jim considered telling them of the rose and its magic. But when he opened his mouth, a little lie came out instead.

"I don't know what happened, really. I saw Dread Steele fighting Cromier and Splitbeard at the same time and I...I thought maybe I could help."

"Dread Steele needs no help, my boy!" squawked Cornelius. He flapped out of the fog and landed on Jim's shoulder, delivering him a sharp peck on the side of the head in the process. "He is Lord of the Pirates, is he not? He came here to rescue you, not the other way around."

"Sorry about that," said Jim. He did really mean his apology, for he had not entirely been himself for those few moments in the fog. He certainly had not meant to endanger any of his friends.

"Well, no matter, now," said Cornelius, ruffling his feathers and seeming to have taken all of his anger out in the one, fierce peck to Jim's temple. His small bird smile appeared once more at the edges of his beak. "After all, what is a rescue without at least a little danger and excitement? Even better than that, we flee to no sloop moored to a London dock this time, my friends. We've brought another surprise along with us! Cornelius pointed toward the sea, and the sight there stole the guilt from Jim's heart and swept wonder into the eyes of him and his friends.

It sat on the white-capped waves, aglow in the moonlight, bobbing in the tide - the *Spectre*, mighty ship of the seas. Her mainmast rose higher than a tall tree. Her bowsprit reached for the horizon. Bold lettering glimmered her name proudly along the deep green hull. The sight of her drew a slow smile across Jim's face that glowed with a light all its own

Jim could have stared all night, but the small moment of quiet on the beach was quickly shattered. The *Spectre's* pirate crew poured out of the fog, hollering to one another to make haste - Mufwalme, Murdoch, Wang-Chi, the Organ Grinder, and all the rest. Dread Steele came last, striding toward the ocean.

"To the ship! Get to the ship you men! Hoist up anchor and bend every sheet to the wind for your lives depend upon it!" When Steele reached the place where Jim stood, he came to a sudden halt. He turned upon his heel and faced the fog once more. Holding up his hands toward the churning cloud, the Captain whispered a few quiet words into the air. At his magical command the billowing mist began to swirl. Faster and faster it turned until it became a misty cyclone, trapping the Cromiers and their bewildered men inside the cloudy whirlpool. The spell cast, Steele lowered his hands and turned to Jim and his friends.

"The enchantment will not last long, young ones. The fighting for tonight is done. Now is the time for flight. Cornelius, take wing to the ship and command the men to set course for the open sea."

"Aye, Captain, aye!" Cornelius cawed, flapping off toward the *Spectre*. "To the sea, to the sea!"

"Let us be off then, shall we?" Steele said. A half smile curled on his sun-darkened mouth and a dangerous gleam twinkled in his black eyes. "Bid farewell to England for the time being, my young friends. You now shall sail upon the *Spectre*, and our mighty ship is bound for the deep ocean and far-off adventure."

Jim's smile widened at this thought, and he moved to follow George, Lacey, Peter, and Paul, who were already running pell-mell down the beach to three rowboats run upon the shore. Yet only a step or two toward the water, Jim stopped and turned back for his hat, fallen in the sand. As he leaned over to pick it up, he found beneath it his father's box and the blackened rose protruding from the sand. For a whole heartbeat and a half Jim considered abandoning the magical item there, for he was ashamed of how recklessly he had abandoned his friends in the fog. But at the back of Jim's mind the quiet sound of the flute song began to play once more. An image blazed to life in Jim's thoughts of Count Cromier, Bartholomew, and Aunt Margarita laughing together as Morgan Manor burned to ash. A prickling heat burned to life in Jim's heart.

Jim seized the stem from the sand and set it in his box. He slid the box back into his pocket and finally dashed off to join his friends.

ELEVEN

IN THE CAPTAIN'S QUARTERS ABOARD THE *SPECTRE*

W hen the English coast had shrunk to a dark line in the distance, Dread Steele ushered the children and MacGuffy into his quarters aboard the *Spectre*. The Captain sat MacGuffy in his own chair and Mister Gilly tended to the old pirate's injuries. As Jim and his friends gathered about the old salt, Jim could not help but sneak a look about the Captain's quarters.

An oak desk, battered and scarred from what appeared to be everything from knife gouges to shark bites, stood at the back of the room by the aft windows. Upon it sat a single quill, leaned within an inkwell, beside a tattered book, which Jim assumed was the Captain's log.

Jim wished he could steal but a single glance into those pages and the adventures of Dread Steele and his pirate crew kept within.

An odd bell hung from a hook on the desk's corner, though it seemed to Jim far too big and too old to serve as a simple dinner bell. He wondered what purpose it could possibly serve other than a useful perch for Cornelius. The raven sat on the hook at that very moment, pecking at his wings and ruffling his feathers. There was also a tall shelf, stuffed full of books so old that most of the covers had fallen off, and a modest bed with a dusty, wooden locker at its foot. Last of all the same map that had hung in the captain's quarters onboard the little sloop in London was there on the portside wall. As before it was covered end to end with drawings of mythical creatures, mysterious landmarks, and arcane symbols.

For all the legends and tales Jim had heard of Dread Steele, Lord of the Pirates, he had fully expected this room to be piled high with the spoils of battles and raids, jewels and riches from the world over. But the quarters were practically bare. Jim suddenly imagined that Dread Steele's pockets were lined more with secrets than they were with silver and gold.

"How do you feel, my friend?" Steele asked MacGuffy. He handed the old man a glass of brandy from a bottle kept within one of the desk drawers.

"Old and useless as a sock with a hole in the toe, Cap'n," MacGuffy grumbled. "In the old days MacGuffy the pirate would ne'er o' 'llowed himself to be taken unawares nor find hisself unable to defend his charges, neither." The poor man hung his head. His lips fell into a deep frown upon his scarred face. But Lacey, who cared very much for the retired pirate, put a gentle hand on his shoulder to comfort him.

"MacGuffy, please don't say such things. You did your best. You've taken such good care of us for all this time, haven't you? Besides, there were ten of them after all, and that's not even figuring the Count, that horrible Bartholomew, and that wicked pirate, Splitbeard."

"Too right, Lacey," George agreed. His brothers flanked him on either side and all three of them gave MacGuffy their winningest smiles.

"And I say, you took that wallop to the back of the head like a true champion, MacGuffy! That blow would have killed a lesser man, no doubt about it!"

"Your head is hard as a rock, MacGuffy!" Peter added.

"Solid as an oak, sir," Paul concluded. He clenched both fists before his face for added effect. "Solid as an oak!" Jim thought those might have been the worst compliments he had ever heard, especially given the circumstances. But they were genuine and so even MacGuffy managed a laugh, which had him wincing with pain all the more.

"Rascally sea pups! Ye have good hearts after all, don't ye? I thank ye for it, I do. But I think that'll be enough dawdlin' o'er an old man's bumps and bruises, Cap'n. I'll live, I will. Per'aps we should be gettin' down to business and tellin' the lad why ye was sailin' to Morgan Manor this night in the first place."

"You are right, MacGuffy, for our arrival was not by chance." Dread Steele said. The lantern light in the cabin cast a hard shadow on the Captain's face, so much so that it seemed to Jim that darkness was drawn to the pirate lord.

"You were coming anyway?" Jim asked. But he quickly realized that Dread Steele could not possibly have known the evil goings on at Morgan Manor. Even if he had, the *Spectre* could hardly sail to the coast of England in a single night. "You were coming to talk to me about something. You were coming to ask me about the Treasure of the Ocean, weren't you?"

Steele nodded in reply to Jim's question, his mouth drawn into a thin line. "Indeed, I was, Jim. For little more than a year now Cornelius and I have sailed the *Spectre* to the very world's edge and back. At every port and isle did we lay a false trail of bread crumbs for Cromier and his dark son to follow."

"We did have some fun with it all along the way though, did we not Captain?" Cornelius said. He laughed with a caw and hopped down from the hook onto the desk, twisting his wings this way and that as he spoke. "Told old Shark-Tooth Tim we'd buried the entire treasure beneath the Inn of the Wet Rock. Largest overbite you've ever seen has old Shark-Tooth. Could very nearly nip the bottom edge of his own chin with his incisors, I'd wager. Ha! Anyway, never expected Tim to actually believe that one, really. Thought he caught the winks I was giving him the whole way, if you know what I mean. King's men captured the poor bloke the next week breaking in after midnight. He was pulling up the floorboards, using his teeth to draw out the nails, no less. Had the fool in stockades for half a month. Left the most wicked splinters in his lips too, or so I heard."

"How awful!" Lacey said with a gasp. But Dread Steele cleared his throat loudly and frowned in Cornelius's direction. Cornelius squawked irritably, tucking his wings down to his sides and keeping quiet.

"Nevertheless," Steele continued. "Certain were we that the Cromiers had set themselves upon our winding path. Thought we that finally you would be safe to return home, Jim. So we came to meet you in hopes of divining some clue as to the Treasure of the Ocean's true whereabouts."

"You knew about the map, then?" Jim asked. A sudden pinprick of suspicion stuck him in his heart. It seemed that everyone wanted the Treasure. Though only the Count had given Jim any hint that the desires were for far more than simple wealth. "You were coming for the map?"

"Map? What map?" Steele exclaimed. His dark face sparked with such surprise that Jim and his friends flinched at the growl in the pirate captain's voice. Though Dread Steele had been Jim's rescuer twice over, he was still the most dangerous of all pirates to sail the Seven Seas.

"It was a magic map, sir. I never even knew I had it until tonight. When we arrived at Morgan Manor, the house was already burnt. Phineus was there, and the one thing he had been able to save from the fire was a vial of moonwater. We had only to shine light through the vial to see that something more than words were written on my father's letter. When the Count poured the moonwater on the page, a map burned on the letter, as though it was writ with fire, blue fire. It lit up the entire room. The Count said it was a map to the Treasure of the Ocean."

For a long moment, Dread Steele said nothing. His eyes drifted from Jim's face into nowhere, as though a thousand thoughts flew through his mind all at once. Finally Steele's mouth twisted into a bitter frown and he swore aloud.

"Confound Lindsay and his infernal cleverness! Did the man trust no one but himself? The loss of this map is a brutal blow indeed!"

"Captain," Cornelius cawed. "While I am no great master of the magical arts myself, it seems highly doubtful to me that Lindsay Morgan would have known exactly to where the Treasure of the Ocean would have disappeared from the Vault. Magic that powerful is unpredictable at best, unknowable at worst. For that matter, Lindsay could not have known for certain the Treasure's fate at all after he left it in the Vault."

"Argh," MacGuffy harrumphed from his chair. "Then what good be the map, Cornelius? Why draw it at'all?"

Cornelius placed one feathered wing beneath his beak, as though thinking quite hard on the matter. "The map must lead to some other magical object, some talisman of a sort. Lindsay may have wanted to ensure Jim could find the Treasure at any time, if ever it was lost or wherever it might be hidden."

"You mean like a seeker?" Jim suddenly asked. "When the King of Thieves wanted to find the Pirate Vault, he used a silver dragonfly that could find any hidden or secret place, as long as the person looking knew the place to be there—"

"But not the where of the there!" Lacey finished for Jim. A spark of excitement lit in her voice, for Lacey was a very clever girl indeed and enjoyed solving riddles and mysteries a great deal. Steele paced back and forth before his desk. He cast his dark eyes to the floor and rubbed his hand furiously along his unshaven jaw. When he spoke it was as much to himself as to the others gathered about him.

"Indeed, this may be so. But if Cornelius is right, and if the Cromiers find whatever magical item is buried at the end of the map's path, they shall be one step closer to possessing the Treasure of the Ocean. If Cromier finds that…if he and Bartholomew hold it in their grasp…"

Steele never finished the thought. MacGuffy whistled long and low and shook his white-haired head in distress. Jim remembered the mad look in the Count's eyes as he had spoken of the vast power to be his once he obtained the treasure. Jim's stomach clenched in his gut and frosty tendrils climbed through his veins.

"We must not allow Cromier and Bartholomew to take this prize. But we are at great risk of losing the race before it has even begun," Steele continued, shaking his head. "Count Cromier has the map, and with it, the only clue as to this mystery's hidden location."

Despair took hold of all in the cabin. Even Dread Steele ceased his pacing and stared hard at the wall in silence. But Lacey, whose eyes had been sparkling with adventure since Jim had reminded her of the seeker, suddenly spoke up.

"There may be one clue, left, Captain Steele," she said. "We could use the stars."

"Stars?" Cornelius squawked, flapping his wings and ruffling his feathers. "What know you of stars, fair Lacey?" Lacey reached into the handbag she had worn with her new dress and produced her tattered and faded volume.

"Well, Mister Cornelius, I know about all the stars in this book. MacGuffy gave it to me. Even though it was only for a moment or two, I'm sure I saw some that I recognized on the ceiling at the stables. Somehow I think they can give us a clue!"

"Oh no!" George said, shaking his head. "Not your stupid star book again!"

"It's not stupid, George!" Lacey snapped. George took a wise step backward for Lacey seemed quite ready to club him with the volume if he opened his mouth again. "It's full of special constellations, ones that regular sailors don't even use. And those were the ones on the map, I'm certain of it!"

Dread Steele raised a curious eyebrow at this and stepped slowly over to Lacey. He held out his hand to take the book and leafed through the pages. After a moment the Captain furrowed his brow in ever deepening wrinkles of concentration.

"Lacey," he finally said, "show me the stars you saw."

TWELVE

LACEY'S STARS AND A TALISMAN LOST

S teele wasted no time and spun on his heel toward the desk. He shooed Cornelius from the hook with a swat of his hand and motioned everyone closer.

"Lacey, is there a page in this book that shows the full night sky in one picture?"

"Yes," Lacey said. Nervous excitement bubbled over in her voice. "On page number sixty-two, almost at the back of the book."

Steele flipped to the proper page and pulled it up from the book with two fingers. He held the single leaf before the lantern's light. The slender flame shone through the page and onto the strange map on the wall. After a few adjustments the Captain lined it just perfectly, so that a sky full of lamp-lit stars hung over the painted world upon the map. Lacey and Jim, and even the Ratts, took quick startled glances at one another, squeezing a little closer to the wall to get a better look. Before them on the map was now a duller, yellower image of the magic blue shapes thrown on the stable walls and ceiling.

"Show me the stars, Lacey," Steele asked.

Lacey stepped over to where the Captain held the page. Careful not to place her shadow between the lantern and the wall she used her small finger to trace the shapes of the constellations on the glowing map.

"There were three that I remember for certain. The Sea Horse was here, and next to him was The Giant Squid. And last was The Mighty Hunter." The three shapes faced one another in a triangle over the ocean.

"Those stars lie o'er the deep ocean, me cap'n," MacGuffy said from the chair, squinting his one good eye hard at the map. "There be monsters and merpeople beneath those waves, I fear."

"Merpeople?" Jim asked. "Monsters?"

"Indeed, Mister Morgan. The deep ocean is full of old mysteries. But we are faced with a new one this day that is more puzzling still." Captain Steele closed the book and rushed over to the map, placing his finger on the spot that lay beneath the center of the constellations. "No island lies in that spot upon the ocean."

Disappointment fell over the party in the room and Jim's shoulders slumped.

"However," Steele continued. "Perhaps there is another possibility. These stars are not stars used by modern men of the sea. They are old constellations, old as sailing itself - symbols used by the ancient folk. It is possible they lead to as ancient a place, or even a place somehow hidden by magic. If that is true, it is beyond even my knowledge. Yet I know of one who might have the answers we seek."

"Captain," Cornelius said with a rather loathsome groan. "You can't possibly mean who I think you might possibly mean, can you?

That old loon is as likely to put us all to sleep for a hundred years or accidentally roast us where we stand with one of his blasted magical discoveries than do us any good. He nearly captured my voice in some Far Eastern jar the last time! Imagine the tragedy that would have been for us all!"

George snorted a stifled laugh and was about to say something before Lacey elbowed him sharply in the ribs. But not even a trace of a smile crossed Dread Steele's mouth, for he seemed lost in thoughts of plans and action.

"Egidio knows more of magic than any of us here. We will need such wisdom, and not only for the map, I think. It may be that we still have some powerful enchantments on our side. Magic Count Cromier has no idea we yet possess, and that few know is tied to the very Treasure of the Ocean itself. Jim, bring forth your mother's locket, the one given to you by your father."

Jim's heart froze solid in his chest. His mind raced for an answer, for some solution to the tragic quandary he now knew he had caused. He'd always known the locket was special, if for no other reason than the fact that it reminded him of his father and of the mother he never knew. But how could he have known the locket was enchanted? How could he know that it possessed magic that could aid him in such a time as this?

Jim looked around at the group about him, who were waiting for him to bring out a locket he no longer had. Jim wished a hole would break open in the floor beneath him and swallow him whole, rescuing him from the expectant eyes of his friends and Dread Steele. A great lump formed in his throat. For a brief moment he considered telling the truth, the entire story, but three words alone escaped his lips.

"I...I lost it."

"Oh, Jim," Lacey gasped. For a moment longer, not another word was spoken. Dread Steele's face trembled. His dark eyes locked upon Jim. A prickling in Jim's skin warned him a storm was about to break loose.

"You...lost it?"

"Y...yes, sir," Jim let his eyes fall to the tops of his shoes, for it was too painful to meet Dread Steele's gaze. Whether he meant to or not, he told yet another lie to escape the hurt. "When...when I ran off after we saw the burnt house and Aunt Margarita tonight. It...it must have...fallen out of my pocket in the sand." Jim risked a glance at Steele, but wished he had not, for the dam broke and the pirate captain's fury poured forth.

"How could you lose it? It was your mother's! It was a great gift and you could not keep even that one thing safe! A curse on all you Morgans and your confounded talent for losing or breaking all things precious in the world!" Jim's shoulders slumped and the pain in his heart from all that day's darkness redoubled in his heart.

"Captain," Cornelius cawed softly. "The boy has lost more than just that necklace this day, sir."

Steele noticed that all the children had taken two steps back from him, and that Jim stood completely crestfallen. He straightened his waistcoat and took a deep breath, burying his anger back into some hidden place within himself.

"What's done is done. It cannot be helped now," the Captain said. "We are at a disadvantage, but we are not out of the race yet. We have at least a chance. Perhaps what we need now is rest. To bed with all of you, for we have much work to do in the days to come. Mister Gilley will show you to your quarters. Cornelius, fly to the quarterdeck and order our course altered. West by southwest - we sail for Spire Island and Shelltown this very night."

"Aye, Captain, aye, west by southwest," Cornelius cawed. "Spire Island it is." Mister Gilly led the way from the cabin, Cornelius flying out into the night over his shoulder. Jim shuffled behind his friends, anger and hurt and miserable shame rolling about in his chest.

THIRTEEN

JANUS BLACKTAIL

J im stood once more on the deck of his sailboat as it skipped across the waves toward the white sand shore. The sun shone on his face and the wind pushed at his back. When Jim looked to his hands, however, his wooden sword was gone. His fingers and palms were black, smudged with soot and ash. Jim looked everywhere in his boat for his lost plaything, but it was nowhere to be found.

As Jim searched, a bright glow flared up before him from the beach. When he looked to the shore, Morgan Manor was awash in flames and burning to the ground. The fire took the shape of Count Cromier's face, and the smoke the likeness of his son, Bartholomew. The two faces floated into the sky and there they mocked Jim and all his pain with horrible laughter. Worse still, with no sword in hand,

Jim had nothing with which to defend himself from the Cromiers' vicious hate. He had no way to save his home.

But the worst was yet to come. The Crimson Storm came again.

The shadow man returned as well, waving his red sword over the sea in warning. But there was no escape. The black-skull face formed in the red-rimmed clouds. It called Jim's name with a voice like a hundred firing cannons until Jim lurched from his sleep, gasping for air and wiping cold sweat from his brow.

Midnight had long since come and gone. In the darkest hours before dawn, five hammocks in a little cabin below decks swung in time to the roll of the ship. There, Jim sat awake, slowly regaining his senses after the dream. When Jim finally calmed himself enough to attempt a return to sleep, he turned to find Lacey swinging in the hammock next to his, her blue eyes open and staring back at him.

"Jim?" she whispered. "Are you alright? You were saying things in your sleep, groaning even. You were saying a storm was coming. A red storm. It sounded so frightening."

"It was nothing," Jim said. "It was just a dream." Lacey seemed less than convinced, but Jim felt too tired to argue. He wanted nothing more than to forget his nightmare and his lost locket, the stolen map and his burnt home, and all the other people and things he'd lost that day and all the days before. "Just go back to sleep, Lacey." Jim lay back in his hammock and turned over, pulling his blanket up over his shoulders and wishing that Lacey might just leave it at that. But after a pause Jim heard her whisper to him again.

"Jim?"

"What?"

"What really happened to your mother's necklace?"

A hot bite stung Jim in his chest. He curled up tighter in his hammock, sinking a little lower beneath his blanket.

"What do you mean? I lost it on the beach when I ran away. I told you already, didn't I?"

Lacey was quiet for another moment, and Jim risked a little hope that she might let it go. Of course, he knew better because he knew Lacey. The maddeningly clever girl had probably been turning the whole thing over in her mind ever since Jim had told the story in the captain's quarters.

"There was something new in your box when you came back to the stables. You dropped it on the beach after we ran from the fog. You picked it back up and put it in your box again before we got on the boats. What was it, Jim?"

Jim wished his hammock and blanket would just swallow him whole and spare him the merciless needling that pricked his insides. He sat up in his hammock and glared hotly at Lacey.

"It was nothing! Alright? Nothing! I lost my house. I lost all that I own. Now I lost the necklace, too. It's gone, so just let it go! Why do you always have to think so much about everything, Lacey? It's so infuriating!" Jim had naturally expected Lacey to sit right up in her own hammock and shoot bolts from her eyes, as she often did when Jim or George was being particularly rash. But what happened instead was worse. Lacey's face filled up with hurt. It passed over her cheeks and her mouth and pooled up in her eyes. Jim realized Lacey knew he had just lied to her. He wanted to take it back, to say he was sorry, but there was no turning back from his lie. Worse still, Lacey knew that her hurt had showed, and to cover it up she obliged Jim with what he had first expected. She clenched her jaw and shot Jim a glare cold enough to freeze running water.

"Well fine, Jim Morgan! Just be that way! But I know what I saw. Whatever it is, it's going to lead to trouble for all of us, just like in that fog! It's going to get us all into deep, deep trouble. You mark my words!"

Jim felt so miserable then, that without so much as a word of explanation, he tossed off his blanket and rolled from his hammock to stomp out of the cabin and up the stairs to the main deck above. He threw but a single, angry retort over his shoulder as he went.

"Consider them marked!"

Jim stormed across the *Spectre's* main deck. He thrust his chin all the way down to his chest in an effort to avoid the eyes of the crew, working by moonlight to guide the ship over the waves. The ocean whispered to the ship as she passed, and the *Spectre* groaned in quiet reply.

When Jim reached the prow he had not nearly walked off all his wretched feelings. He paced back and forth in the dark, muttering to himself about how Lacey didn't understand and how he had every right to do what he wanted with his own things – what little of them remained. At the thought of the Count and Bartholomew's sneering faces, Jim reared back and slammed his fist down on the ship's railing. Of course, this left him with nothing but a nasty cut on the side of his hand, which gave him just one more thing about which to be miserable.

"Why is this happening to me?" Jim asked the darkness, as though it would know. "What did I do to deserve this?" The darkness however, had a surprise in store, for it decided to answer back.

"You could go round and round in circles for an age with that question, young sir. But if you're looking for someone to blame, I might be able to point you in the right direction." Jim took quite a start at this voice, for he thought he had been sulking all on his own at the prow. So he turned to tell whoever it was barging in on his pacing and muttering that he was perfectly fine, thank you, and that he preferred to perform such activities alone. But when Jim opened his mouth to give his little speech, he found only the night's dark behind him.

"Who's there?" Jim demanded, searching for the owner of the voice in the shadows.

"No one to fear, Mr. Jim Morgan – no, no, not little old me," the voice continued, deep and throaty. It held each syllable upon its tongue as if to savor the taste of every word. "I'm simply an old sea traveler looking to make the acquaintance of the famous Jim Morgan."

With that, from the blackness above a barrel lashed to the starboard railing, two emerald orbs burned to life in the night.

Jim strangled a gasp in his throat. He had seen such eyes in the dark before. The beast that had owned them had once hunted Jim and very nearly eaten him for dinner. But the voice belonging to this pair of floating eyes only laughed at Jim's fear. The orbs bobbed and bounced lightly until the bushy-tailed frame of a large black cat slunk into the moon's pale blue light.

"Greetings," purred the cat, dipping his black head low. He smiled with bright white teeth that all but shone against his midnight fur. "Janus Blacktail, at your service, Master Morgan."

"You're a talking cat?" Jim asked, eyeing the dark feline with skeptical curiosity.

"An astute observation, young sir," said Janus, laughing again with a coughing purr. "Nothing gets past you, does it?" Even in his surprise at running into yet another talking animal, Jim still knew when he was being made fun of. He found himself in no mood for teasing.

"It's not very nice to make fun of someone you've just met, is it? And what are you doing lurking around here anyway? Cornelius never mentioned you. I thought he was the only talking animal on this ship." At the sound of Cornelius's name, the black cat scratched his claws on the barrel's lid and rolled his green eyes.

"Cornelius Darkfeather? That old stick in the mud and I have crossed paths many times. It comes as no great surprise he has not bothered to mention me. As I'm sure you know, Mr. Morgan, birds and cats do not exactly make best friends." Janus ran his tongue over his sharp teeth, laughing aloud. He leapt from the barrel onto the railing and slowly slunk his way up beside Jim. "Besides all that, I'm not really what you might call an official member of the crew, if you know what I mean. I'm something of a stowaway, and I tend to stick to the shadows. I'm a homeless, lost soul, my boy - very much like yourself from what I hear." That last part stung Jim. He bit his lip, forcing the image of his burning house from his mind. "But don't think of me as a freeloader, please," the cat continued. "Oh no, no, no, not in the least! The lads on the ships tolerate me hitching a ride every now and again because I provide the most valuable service of catching mice and rats."

"I see," said Jim warily, taking a step or two back. He was not very sure he liked this Mr. Blacktail very much at all. In fact, he was thinking it wise to head back to bed, and be sure to let Dread Steele and Cornelius know they had a magical stowaway on board first thing in the morning.

"Well, anyway, as I was saying in regards to your woeful query to the night sky," Janus said, turning a slow circle on the railing and stretching his back into a high arch. "I, nor anyone else I know, has any idea at all why all the horrors you so lament have happened to you. But, as I said, if you're looking for someone to blame, you could start with the Pirates of the Black Skull."

"Pirates of the Black Skull?" Jim asked. In two quick flashes he remembered both the dark image on the back of his father's painting and the terrifying face in the crimson cloud of his nightmares. "I've never heard of them before."

"Ah yes, it is a fascinating tale indeed! You know, I will say this about old Darkfeather and I - we both share an affinity for storytelling, though for entirely different reasons. Cornelius loves to make people laugh or teach young sailors important lessons. How dull! I like stories because stories hold secrets. You see, secrets are ever more decadent, ever more filling, and ever more satisfying than even rats and mice - and they leave no fur stuck in my teeth. I expect you understand the value of secrets at least a little, boy. After all, I doubt you've told anyone *everything* you saw and heard and did in the Pirate Vault of Treasures, when you so gallantly won the Amulet of Portunes."

"How do you know about that?" Jim asked, freezing where he stood and not intending his surprise to leap so obviously onto his face.

"Haha!" Janus laughed. "You see? Secrets are so much fun! There are so many fools out there running around, digging in the sand for buried gold or diving beneath the waves for sunken treasure. A whispered secret is worth more than a thousand pieces of eight and can buy you more than a hundred crown jewels. The hint of a good secret gets at men's minds. It tickles their souls and gets just under their skin like an itch that needs to be scratched." As if to demonstrate his point, the black cat reached out with a deft paw and left a small claw scratch on the back of Jim's hand.

"Ouch!" Jim yelped. He drew back his hand as much from surprise as pain. The little cut was hardly deep enough to draw blood, but the urge to grab the stupid cat by the tail and hurl him overboard suddenly burned in Jim's chest. But once again, the cat spoke before Jim could lose his temper

"Fear not and be not offended – I but jest! I will give you the secret of the Pirates of the Black Skull in its entirety, and for my very best price, Jim Morgan. I will trade you a secret for a secret."

"I'm not giving you any sort of secret, cat," Jim said. But Janus Blacktail only laughed his purring chuckle, sauntering back and forth along the railing. "Besides, I don't have any that are any good to begin with."

"We shall see, my young friend, we shall see. I can be very purrrsua-sive, you know," the cat laughed at his own pun and swished his tail back and forth. "I'm sure one of these days you'll know something worth knowing, and then we shall speak again. But for now, relax. You'll see I'm not such a bad chap. Listen closely and I shall spin you a secret, Jim Morgan." The cat turned from Jim and stared off to the moon, which hung low over the horizon. His green eyes sparkled like flames in the pale light. Slowly and lyrically, as a master storyteller should, the cat began his tale.

"To begin this story, we travel back in time, when men who are now old were still young - young and brave...and foolish..."

FOURTEEN

THE CAT'S TALE

"Once there were four friends. They were young, gifted, and full of dreams to change the world. Each was a master of his own, unique set of skills. There was the Sailor, the Schemer, the Warrior, and the Thief. The four first met at university, though the Schemer and the Warrior were older than the Sailor and the Thief. But all four shared this in common: they all believed they would change the world and the world would be better for it."

"After the Schemer and the Warrior had left school, the Thief and the Sailor became the best of friends. They competed with each other in all things, but with no loss nor victory stronger than their bond. Over the course of the next few, happy years, the two of them all but forgot about their dreams to change the world. Instead they spoke of

101

nothing but becoming captains of great ships and sailing the sea, finding wives, and growing rich and old. Time passed. The two friends left school to chase these new ambitions. But one night, under a full moon in autumn, when the air first turned cold, the Schemer and the Warrior returned. Together they sought out the Sailor and the Thief."

Immediately, the Thief, who was perhaps even more clever than the Schemer himself, knew some great change had come over his old friends."

"My friends," said the Thief. "What has happened since last we met? You seem different. It shows in your very faces."

"Our eyes have been opened," said the Schemer. "We have seen magic, old friend. Real magic, with the power to truly change the world."

"Magic?" said the Sailor. He was a very practical man and also knew the Schemer to be prone to lies and exaggerations. "There's no such thing as magic."

"He speaks the truth!" cried the Warrior, who was quick to anger but always spoke plainly to all men, for he had no fear. So the Thief and the Sailor finally believed.

"My good, good friends," the Schemer continued. "Do you not remember all our dreams and all our talks of changing the world? Of making it a better place and a truer place if only men like ourselves could rule it? When we were boys, it was but a dream, but I have found a way to make it reality."

The Sailor remained skeptical, but the Thief's mind was taken with the idea. His heart quickly remembered all his youthful dreams. So he convinced his best friend, the Sailor, to come along, if nothing else but to lay eyes on this fantastic magic of which the Schemer spoke. Together the four friends left England and traveled to far off places, joined by an infamous pirate crew that sailed under a black flag."

Many adventures did the four friends share, and many dangers they did face, until they finally came to a distant island. There the Schemer led his comrades to a series of stones, engraved with an ancient tale of magic and power. There was a Treasure, the Schemer explained, a

Treasure that was the key to the power that would change the world. When found, the Treasure must be taken to an ancient temple upon a rock, and only there could the magic be unleashed. And only then by a Son of Earth and a Son of Sea."

Jim's heart skipped a beat in his chest and he nearly opened his mouth to interrupt the cat's tale. He had heard those words before: Son of Earth and Son of Sea. He'd heard them long ago in the back of a gypsy wagon from an old gypsy witch named Baba Yaga. The witch had called Jim the Son of Earth and Son of Sea. But Jim kept that to himself, for he did not fully trust the black cat.

"Now the Thief's eyes were as opened as the Schemer's and the Warrior's. His heart burned with desire for magic and power. Only the Sailor, the most practical man of the sea, remained concerned. He did not fully trust the Schemer's intentions. He tried to convince the others, especially his good friend, the Thief, to abandon this foolish quest. But once the seed of power is planted in a man's heart, the roots grow quickly and take deep hold.

"Who or what is this Son of Earth and Son of Sea?" the Sailor asked. "For if this plan is to work, we shall need such a man, will we not?"

"Leave that to me," said the Schemer, but he would say no more.

"It was only because of his great love for his friend, the Thief, that the Sailor agreed to go along. So the four men made a pact, a pact to find this Treasure of the Ocean, and to use it to change the world – to rid it of all its injustices and wrongs. Or so the Thief and the Sailor thought. They sealed the pact and called themselves the Pirates of the Black Skull.

"Together the four men travelled to the far away Kingdom of the Sea, ruled by a powerful King called Nemus. It was Nemus who possessed the ancient talisman, the Treasure of the Ocean. The Warrior suggested they storm Nemus's keep and take the treasure by force. The Schemer conceived an elaborate plan to pit the King of the Sea against the Kings of the Earth, and by that way come away with the Treasure. The Sailor more and more wanted nothing but to quit this adventure and return home. But the Thief was cleverer than them all. He convinced them of a plan to earn Nemus's trust by accomplishing three impossible tasks for Nemus – each bringing the King of the Sea a great reward."

"With each task the four friends completed, and with each reward they brought Nemus, the King allowed them deeper into his circle. When the third task was complete, he called the men Friends of the Sea, which made them as close to him as sons."

"It was then that the Thief struck, and a masterstroke it was. In the middle of the night he stole from Nemus not just one treasure, but three. Three treasures, said the Thief, one for each great task the four friends had completed in Nemus's name."

"It is not known what treasures the three were. One of them was certainly the Treasure of the Ocean, the great power told of in the engravings upon the stones. But it is whispered on certain ships on certain nights, that it was not that loss that hurt old King Nemus the worst. It was the theft of another treasure: one called simply the Flower of Nemus, which cut him deepest. No one knows what such a treasure was, nor how great was its worth."

Nevertheless, the betrayal drove Nemus nearly mad. He called out his armies to hunt down the Pirates of the Black Skull. He threatened to slaughter them for their crimes. But the Sailor was indeed one of the greatest men of the sea, and from Nemus's own lips had learnt some magic of the ocean. He guided his friends safely away, though his heart was sore ashamed of the thing which he and his friends had done."

"But now, at its very climax, the story grows cloudy and not quite clear," Janus said, his green eyes still aglow in the moonlight. "The final truth has eluded even me, skilled catcher of deep secrets. This alone I have discerned for certain - the Pirates of the Black Skull escaped Nemus and his armies by the skin of their teeth. Chased them Nemus did, round the world and back again, but catch them he could not. When the four friends finally reached the temple where the Treasure of the Ocean might be unleashed, something quite unexpected occurred. Just when all their well-laid plans were to be brought to fruition, and the great magic put to purpose, the Thief betrayed his own friends and broke the pact."

"Some say he was driven mad, though I hardly believe this to be true. Others say he grew suddenly afraid of the magic, though I doubt that as well. What I believe is that the Thief decided such power was too great to be shared by four, and he wanted it all for himself. So he betrayed his friends in very walls of the temple. The Warrior was killed, the Schemer was forced to flee, and the Sailor's friendship was lost forever, until the two of them became the greatest of foes the sea has ever known."

Even now, it is not fully known what the Thief did with the great Treasure. But many seek it still, and perhaps will until the end of time."

Janus finished his tale and twisted into a tight curl upon the railing, as though the telling of the epic adventure had been just as exhausting as the living of it. But Jim was not nearly satisfied by the ending. He jabbed an angry finger in the cat's face.

"What are you trying to pull here, cat? You said you were going to tell me a secret, not a fairy tale!"

"Indeed I did, young Morgan," Janus said, his emerald-green eyes sparkling with glee. "I don't recall saying, 'the end' yet, did I, oh most impatient of listeners? Truthfully, I thought I might not need to tell you the end at all, you being such a clever boy and all. But it seems you haven't quite figured it out, have you?"

"Figured what out?" Jim asked. But a slimy sensation already began to crawl up his arms and legs, that feeling that he was about to be told something he did not want to hear.

"Why, the best part of the story, of course," Janus said happily, smiling so that his teeth glinted in the dim light. "The names of the Pirates of the Black Skull! For I have found them all out! The Warrior's name was Lord Winter, a most angry and dangerous swordsman, a beast of a man. The Schemer's name was Vilius Cromier, now the man called Count Cromier, a villain to his bones. The Sailor is on this very ship. His name was Robert North, but now they call him Dread Steele, Lord of the Pirates, master of disguise and magic."

The slippery feeling crawled into Jim's stomach. He was already shaking his head in denial as the cat finally came to the secret he so gleefully meant to share.

"And the Thief – the one who betrayed all and stole all and broke all - he became a great captain in the King's Navy and even a friend of the King himself. His name was Lindsay Morgan."

"It's a lie!" Jim shouted. Without thinking he swatted at the cat with an open hand. But he struck nothing but air, for the cat was nimble as a shadow and leapt down from the rail, scurrying beyond Jim's reach. "My father was no thief! He was a man of honor! It was Dread Steele who betrayed him when he left the navy and became a pirate. My father was never a pirate! He was the best man in the world!" Heat bloomed in Jim's face, but not all of it was born of Jim's fury at Janus Blacktail. Some measure of it came from a small tickle at the back of Jim's mind – a small tickle of doubt.

"I am a teller of secrets, Jim Morgan," replied the cat, his voice once again a disembodied sound from the night. Only his emerald-flame eyes floated in the black. "How they make a man feel is not my concern."

"Well I don't care. That's a lie no matter what you say, and you can forget about getting any secrets from me!" But no sooner had the words left Jim's mouth did a burning pain ignite the back of his right hand, where Janus had scratched him. Jim cried out and grabbed his hand at the wrist in surprise, nearly falling back into the barrel.

"Secrets are what secrets are, Jim Morgan," said the voice, now coming from nowhere and everywhere, as even Janus's eyes disappeared. "I have given you a secret. Like it or not, you now owe me one in return! We shall meet again, and when we do, it will be when I come to collect!"

"You can forget it, Blacktail!" Jim shouted, but this time there was no response, for the cat was gone.

Leaning over the railing in the dark, Jim fought the urge to weep. He gripped the wooden rail so hard he could feel it cutting his fingers. He mourned the loss of Morgan Manor and cursed his wicked Aunt Margarita and the blasted Cromiers. He mourned his life on the run, homeless and penniless and directionless. But most of all Jim mourned for his father. If Lord Morgan was still alive, Jim thought, if he were here, Jim could ask him what had happened so long ago. He could ask his father for the truth. Then he could be sure again – he could be certain again. But for now Jim was certain only of his hurt – his hurt and his anger.

There on the prow Jim stood, still as a statue, thinking dark thoughts until the sun came up in the western sky and cut a thin line of gold over the white caps and gray rises of the ocean. He stood there until Mister Gilly, whose eyes must have been as sharp as an eagle's, called "land ho!" over the deck. A black speck appeared on the horizon up ahead – Spire Island.

FIFTEEN

THROUGH THE WINDOW

A few hours after dawn, the *Spectre* made berth at a ruined pier that shambled into the heart of Shelltown. Jim had hardly moved an inch since his run in with Janus Blacktail. He still stood firmly in place at the ship's railing, where he now looked over the teeming seaport before him. Tiled roofs ran from the beach all the way up to the base of the rocky spire that rose from the island's center. Gulls and albatrosses lazily circled the peak on the morning breeze, cawing, shrieking, and enjoying the rising sun's warmth upon their wings. In every street and every square, Shelltown bustled from end to end with rough-necked and roguish sailors, pirates, and privateers.

Jim's head ached and his eyes were still red and itchy. He had hardly slept a wink since the night before last, when he and his friends left the lighthouse for Morgan Manor. Every time Jim blinked he saw his home, burnt to ash, in his mind's eye. Yet there was one sliver of hope to which Jim still clung - the blackened rose in his father's box. Jim knew he should want to find the Cromiers to keep them from possessing the Treasure of the Ocean. That's what his father would have done, Jim thought. But in his heart he could not fight the hope to catch sight of those fiends long enough to employ the enchanted thorn. In either case, however, in order to find the Cromiers, the mystery of his father's map had to be solved.

When the *Spectre* was docked, Dread Steele emerged from his quarters, shrouded in his black cloak. Cornelius Darkfeather sat perched upon his shoulder. Even on his own ship the Captain hid his face in shadow beneath his tricorn hat. Jim opened his mouth to ask Steele to where they would be going today, but the Lord of the Pirates brushed passed him without so much as a sideways glance. Jim moved to follow the Captain down the gangplank when old MacGuffy blocked his way to the ramp.

"Captain Steele, wait!" Jim shouted. He tried to skirt around the old salt, but MacGuffy stayed Jim with a gnarled hand upon his shoulder.

"Shelltown be no place for a sea pup, Jimmy," MacGuffy growled, holding Jim put. "Yonder streets be full o' pirates o' the worst kind. They don't take kindly to children if ye know what I mean. The Cap'n'll find out what we need to know from the old shopkeeper, Egidio Quattrochi as he's called, and we shall be off again 'afore noon."

"I'm no child, MacGuffy! You know that and so does the captain. I went into the Vault of Treasures and came out again, didn't I? I outsmarted the King of Thieves. It was my house that the Cromiers burnt to the ground and it's my map that they stole!" Jim was about to go on listing all the reasons he should be accompanying Steele into Shelltown, when MacGuffy cut him off with a rough bark.

"Twas also yer mother's necklace that ye lost, lad. Or have ye forgotten that already?" The words stilled Jim's tongue like a slap to the face. MacGuffy must have seen the hurt in Jim's eyes, for his purple scar quivered on his cheeks and he clucked his tongue. "Forgive an old salt, Jim. Twas not me own words but the Capn's. He's a hard man, lad - as hard as yer own father ever was and that be the truth of it. But nevertheless, ye'll be stayin' aboard. Cap'ns orders. I go to follow the Cap'n, but stand ye fast on the ship and we shall be returnin' shortly."

"Well what if I just decide to go into town on my own?" Jim said as defiantly as he could. But the moment the words left his mouth he felt himself rise off the deck, lifted by the scruff of his collar as easily as a puppy in its mother's jaws. He looked over his shoulder and found himself eye-to-eye with the fierce face of giant Mufwalme.

"Which is why, little man, the Captain gave orders to have you locked in his quarters until he returns. In truth, he told me you would say exactly the words you only just now spoke. He ordered me, upon you speaking them, to place you under lock and key." A bright smile split Mufwalme's face and he erupted in a rumbling laugh like a peal of thunder. "You are most clever, young one. But Dread Steele is more clever by far!" Mufwalme carried Jim over to the captain's door and tossed him inside as effortlessly as a coat into a closet. Jim had time enough to turn and see Mufwalme cross his enormous arms over his chest before the door slammed in his face.

"This is bollocks!" Jim shouted. "How are we supposed to help if we don't even get to know what we're up against?" Jim kicked the door as hard as he could to go along with his shouting, but earned himself nothing but a set of smashed toes for his efforts.

"Exactly what I said, Jim," said the voice of George Ratt. "Actually that's exactly what I did too." Jim turned to find his four friends already locked in the captain's quarters along with him. George was indeed limping on his own stubbed toes, he and his brothers sporting expressions as dark and furious as Jim's. More than anything in the world, the Ratt's, much like Jim, hated being told what they could not do or where they could not go. Lacey, meanwhile, turned her chin up and whirled around on her heel the moment her eyes met Jim's. She was obviously still furious with him for storming out on her the night before.

"MacGuffy said we couldn't be trusted to run loose on the ship with no supervision," George continued. He threw his hands on his hips and shook his head. "Can you believe that rot? Us? Untrustworthy?" George and his brothers furrowed their brows in a united expression of deepest indignation. Of course, Jim thought, though he dared not say, MacGuffy was probably right.

"It's all a bit familiar, in't it, Georgie?" said Peter. He stepped over to the quarter's door and peered through lock with an expert eye. "Sorta like on that sloop in London last year. I could pick this lock in a breeze if I wanted. But there's no pickin' that huge bloke with the sword on the other side, is there?"

"We could try the old boy-who-cried-wolf routine, Pete," suggested Paul. "Worked wonders when we was still in St. Anne's."

"Mufwalme won't fall for that trick, or any other hair-brained scheme you three dream up," said Lacey without bothering even a glance over her shoulder. She had wandered over to Captain Steele's bookshelves and was trying very hard to pretend as if she hadn't been listening to the boys' entire conversation. "They're under Dread Steele's orders, you know, which they would never disobey. And besides that, they're all far cleverer than any of the nuns or constables back in London."

"Well, we wouldn't be the great thieves we are with that attitude, now would we, Lacey?" said George. "The proper spirit of things is to say what our father always used to say: when life – or pirates – shuts a door, look for a window."

George looked at Jim.

Jim looked at George.

They both looked to the window at the back of the captain's quarters. In spite of everything, the corners of Jim's mouth curved into a grin. He knew he and George were both thinking the same thing. No matter what Jim had lost, he still had the best friends a boy could have.

"You didn't know our father, George," said Peter and Paul in unison. But they came to stand beside their brother with eyes fixed upon the window and fingertips tapping before a devious set of smiles. All four boys then turned to Lacey. She let out a long sigh, slumped her shoulders, and put the book in her hand back on the shelf.

"Oh for goodness' sake," was all she said.

Out the window the five friends crept, quiet as mice. Just below the windowsill a narrow ledge, barely as wide as a man's open hand, ran along the *Spectre's* hull. But the Clan of the Ratt had cut their teeth leaping from rooftops and sneaking through windows in London. They pressed themselves tight against the hull and tiptoed to the ship's aft corner. There they found a mooring line stretched from the ship down to the pier below.

Jim took the lead and leapt from the ledge to the rope. He swung his feet over the line and scooted his way over the water. That old rogue's smile spread across Jim's lips. For better or for worse, he had grown tired of just letting horrible things happen to him. It felt leagues better to really do something about them. But half way down the line, a shadow crossed over his face. To his surprise, Jim looked up to see Janus Blacktail balancing on the rope above him.

"Something wrong with the gangplank, young Jim?" asked Janus. The black cat smiled and winked knowingly with one green eye.

"Get away, you blasted cat!" Jim whispered as harshly as he dared. "You'll get us all caught!"

"Oh, I would never betray a fellow sneaker, my boy. Thieves honor and all that. In fact, I'm doing a bit of sneaking myself. The *Spectre* is just about dried up of good secrets, I think. So I'm off for more interesting fare. I just wanted to take a moment to remind you that I'll be finding you some time in the not-too-distant future to collect that secret you owe me."

"I don't owe you anything," Jim snapped. He let go of the rope with one hand to shoo the cat away, but the moment he did, the scratch Janus had given him ignited in pain like a lit match. It burned so fiercely that Jim nearly lost his grip and dropped into the water.

Janus Blacktail laughed his purring chuckle and leaned his face close to Jim's.

"You see, young Morgan, secrets really are like an itch you just can't scratch. Toodle-oo for now, my friend. Don't forget about me though, for I shall be seeing you again one day soon." The cat scampered down the rope and onto the pier, where he disappeared into the bustling streets of Shelltown. Janus's reappearance nearly spoiled Jim's improving mood. But once all four of his friends joined him on the pier, without raising even the hint of an alarm, Jim's spirit of adventure caught up once more in his blood. He, the Ratts, and Lacey wasted no time and stole off down the streets of Shelltown, in search of Egidio Quattrochi's shop.

Jim hated to admit it, but MacGuffy had been right - Shelltown was no place for children. Every sailor on the streets walked armed to the teeth, outfitted with curved knives, loaded pistols, and deadly cutlasses. All their blades were far too sharp, and their pistol grips far too worn, to have gone unused for any length of time. There were turbaned Corsairs like those that followed Splitbeard, round hatted sailors from the Far East with long braided mustaches like Wang-Chi's, and seamen with peg legs, hook hands, earrings, tattoos, and cold eyes that warned of foul moods and dark deeds.

Of course, all this meant that George and his brothers were having the time of their lives.

"That's right, mind your business, mates," George announced, strutting with his chest stuck out ridiculously far, and his thumbs jammed in his lapels. "Dread Steele's crew comin' through 'ere. Mind your distance and no harm shall come to ya!" Peter and Paul followed suit, lined up behind their brother. They sauntered down the street in their best imitations of the bow-legged sea walks of the brutish sailors they saw, greeting the passing buccaneers with hearty "Arrghs!"

"Keep quiet, George," Lacey said. She was quite fed up and walked as far away from the Ratts as possible, both to minimize her mortification and to keep her eyes peeled for trouble. "You have to be an actual pirate to be a part of Dread Steele's crew, anyway – which…you…are… not!"

"Well, good thing for us we're startin' up our trainin' today, in't it?" George replied. "With our thievin' skills, we probably already have a leg up I'd wager. But I 'magine Dread Steele can show us at least a thing or two, can't he? We even already came up with our pirate names." At this, Lacey rolled her eyes and looked as though she wanted to cover her ears with her hands. The threat alone of the forthcoming announcement was more than she could bear.

"Here we go!" George announced. "I be One-Eyed George!"

"And I'm One-Eyed Pete!"

"And they be callin' me Paul of the One-Eye! ARGH!"

"The Pirates Ratt!" Peter and Paul shouted at the top of their lungs, hooting, hollering, and laughing so hard they nearly fell over each other. Jim could not help but laugh himself, but George ripped his hat from his head and waved it about emphatically, stomping his foot on the cobblestone street.

"Did I not just say, only last night, to pick different names from me?" George yelled. He rolled his eyes as if the chore of being an older brother had finally reached a mind-boggling level of suffering. "We can't *all* be one-eyed somethin' or other – that's stupid!"

"Actually, George, if you listened, I said Paul *of the one-eye*," Paul corrected. "Which is completely different."

"It's not different at all, Paul!"

"Well, I picked one-eyed first, George! Back when we was at the lighthouse. So really, you're the one stealing my name!" Peter roared.

"Besides, you have two eyes!" Paul yelled. This little spat was simply the last straw for Lacey, who suddenly exploded. She stomped her own feet quite loudly and turned nearly purple at the cheeks.

"You all have two eyes!" She thundered at the brothers. "And two arms and two legs! On top of all that, Dread Steele is *not* going to train you to be pirates! He has far more important things to do, like helping Jim stop the Cromiers from getting the Treasure of the Ocean. So for goodness' sake, shut it before you get us all caught!"

"How do you know, Lacey?" George asked quite snottily, his brothers nodding right along with him, as though they had not just nearly come to blows a moment ago. "And what's the worry? We just escaped from Dread Steele's own ship with a huge man armed with a giant sword standin' guard. If that can't hold us, nothin' can!"

"I wonder what they even call an orphanage in a pirate town?" Paul said, cleaning his nails on his shirt. "I guess they don't have Saint in the front of many of them, do they?"

"Pirates don't use orphanages, young one," a crackly voice wheezed from beside the boys. They simultaneously whirled on the speaker, who was a homeless beggar lying in the shadows of a nearby alley. The beggar leaned against a barrel outside a broken door, seeking shelter from the morning sun. "Nor do pirates use prisons. Those be the ways of more civilized folk."

"If they don't put you in an orphanage or a prison, then what do they do with you?" Peter asked, a small smirk playing on his lips. But the beggar just laughed - a sandy, choking, and mirthless laugh. He looked the boys over with a chapped and wind-burnt smile on his wrinkled face. "In Shelltown, when they catch a thief, they cut off his hands."

The Ratts considered this for a moment, trying to determine whether or not it was just another lie adults tell children to coerce them into such-and-such a behavior. They decided it was, and burst into laughter.

"Cut off your hands?" Paul said. "If you lie do they cut out your tongue?"

"He's cracked," George said, shaking his head with pity at the old man. "I've heard it all now."

"Have you?" The old beggar shrieked, staring the boys right in their laughing faces with his crazed eyes. "Have you seen it all as well?" The ragged man threw his arms up onto the edge of the barrel, revealing two stumps that had once been hands, wrapped in dirty, ragged bandages. The boys ceased laughing immediately and gaped at the empty places where the beggar's hands should have been.

"Right then," Jim finally managed. He nudged his friends farther down the path, never taking his eyes off the old man. "Sorry about that. We'll just be going now."

"Mind where ye walk and how ye talk, ya sea babes!" the beggar screamed after them. "Ye are no longer in the world! Ye are headed toward the deep ocean, where the laws and manners of men hold no sway!"

The rest of the way through Shelltown the Ratts uttered not a single word, nor did Lacey even bother to say that she'd told them so. All five members of the clan had gone quite pale. If Jim had forgotten it, he remembered then that the pirates and villains he now faced did not play at games, nor did they fool about. They were very real, and they dealt in vile and deadly deeds.

Fortunately for Jim and his friends, not every pirate in Shelltown was a complete scalawag. There was a merchant selling parrots of all shapes, sizes, and colors, who was helpful enough to point them in the direction of Egidio Quattrochi's shop. All the merchant's birds cawed the name "Egidio Quattrochi" over and over again in a squawking chorus as the small company walked down the street.

They found the shop not a few moments later, tucked beneath the remains of a derelict pier. The old walkway extended only so far as the rocky beach before coming to an abrupt, broken end. The rest of the boardwalk looked as though it had been smashed by a giant's hand and tossed out to sea. But it was the shop itself that caught Jim by surprise and furrowed his brow so deeply. The red wooden door and quaint shingled walls upheld a roof built from the biggest tortoise shell Jim had ever seen - green and brown and easily as large as MacGuffy's home beneath the lighthouse by the bay. It was the shell of an ancient monster of the deep.

SIXTEEN

THE SHOP OF EGIDIO QUATTROCCHI

A lone shingle, laced in spiderwebs and dust, hung over the red wooden door. The sign read: *Egidio Quattrocchi's Magical Books and Artifacts*. Taking care not to be seen, the clan snuck around to the side of the shop. George and Peter laced their hands together and hoisted Jim up by a foot to peek through a round window, placed in the hole through which the giant tortoise would have once stuck an arm or leg. It was dark inside the shop, and while Jim could make out a counter and a few shelves, he saw not a trace of Dread Steele or the man, Egidio. However, toward the back of the storefront, Jim found a short hallway. At the end of the hallway was a door, cracked ajar. Bright, flickering light snuck out from around the doorway's edges.

"Can't see them from here," Jim said, hopping down from his friends' hands. "I think they're in a room in the back. I can see the firelight from behind the door. It looks like we'll need to head inside."

"Say no more, say no more," said Peter, a devious smile breaking over his face. It had been a long time since Peter Ratt had employed his most valued possessions, a set of beautiful, silver pins he'd won from the ex-greatest lock pick in London. He cracked his knuckles and withdrew the leather pouch from a pocket inside his jacket.

Quick as a flash, Peter went to work. In less than three twists the door popped open, swinging into the shop with a low creak. Jim cringed at the groaning door. The hairs on the back of his neck stood on end and his teeth set on edge. The five former thieves leapt aside of the door, pressing themselves close to the building to avoid discovery. But when not so much as a ghost stirred inside the shop, Jim risked a peek. He saw nothing but shadows, and so he waved his friends inside.

Cluttered tables and shelves lined the walls from end to end within the shop. They were covered and stacked with clay pots and jars, labeled in Italian, Arabic, and nearly every other language of which Jim had ever heard. Glass vials and bottles, rolled scrolls, bound leather books, and various bones and skulls from strange animals (only some of which seemed entirely natural to Jim) filled the spaces between. Wicker baskets of all shapes and sizes stood in corners or in random stacks about the floor. Jim and the Ratts soon discovered that some of them rattled and moved all on their own.

The clan tiptoed to the hallway at the back of the shop and toward the door to the lit room. Bizarre paintings of mythical animals — unicorns, griffins, dragons and others of which not even Jim knew names or stories lined the corridor. The pictures seemed so real that the images all but stood out from the canvases. Paul nearly fell into a trance meeting eyes with a many-headed hydra. He leaned so close to the picture that he almost walked right into the wall before Jim caught him at the last moment.

Don't touch, Jim mouthed. Paul nodded in agreement, but he threw another mystified look at the painting before moving on. Finally, the children reached the door. Muffled sounds rumbled from the other side. The light creeping around the open crack flashed and changed colors from red to blue to green. Some magic was at work just beyond the doorway, Jim knew. His heart beat hard and his upper lip began to sweat. But curiosity provided Jim some measure of courage. He crept to the doorway, and carefully as possible, stuck his head around the corner to look inside.

Brilliant flashes of light blinded Jim as he glimpsed the room beyond the door. He closed his eyes tight and tried to blink the dazzles away. For a moment, however, all he could do was listen.

"These are difficult questions you have brought to my shop, Dread Steele," Jim heard a man with a thick accent say. "But I fear the answers may be more daunting and deadly still." The man speaking must be Egidio Quattrochi, Jim imagined. But as Jim's vision cleared, he quickly became far more interested in what he saw than what he heard.

A squat, round man stood in the center of the room, surrounded by several bowls, cauldrons, and baskets. He wore a shopkeeper's apron and his white hair trailed off his head like wispy bird wings. Beneath a set of long, feathery eyebrows, a pair of the largest and roundest spectacles Jim had ever seen rested on the man's pug nose, giving his eyes a most owlish appearance. Light and smoke in all manner of colors drifted from each of the containers at the shopkeeper's feet. Into these vessels he reached with both hands, casting the enchanted contents onto the floor and into the air above his head. He threw a handful of sparkles at the roof, where they hung like stars in the sky. He tossed a fistful of dirt at his feet, which rose up like rocks from the earth. Out of the largest cauldron the shopkeeper fanned blue smoke over the floor, where it rippled and rolled like ocean waves.

"It's a map," Lacey whispered over Jim's shoulder. The glowing lights from the room danced over her face, and George's as well, as they stared into the room with Jim. So much magic, Jim thought to himself, and how much more to come? But off to one corner of the room, Dread Steele stood still as black stone, wrapped in his cloak. Cornelius rested upon his shoulder and MacGuffy stood at his side. The pirates gazed upon the sorcerous goings-on with urgent intent.

"You were right to say that no island lies beneath the stars from Lindsay Morgan's map, my old friend," Egidio continued. "At least no island that can be seen. Look here!" Egidio knelt down in the enchanted mist about his feet and pointed to a pair of rocks in the water. They curved up from the ocean and nearly touched each other at the top, forming almost a complete circle. "The Devil's Horns," Egidio whispered. "Gateway to the Veiled Isle. I might have known!"

"The Veiled Isle?" Cornelius crowed, ruffling his feathers. "There are few enough islands these eyes have not seen, old man. But even this isle's name has never fallen upon my ears. Has magic masked it from the world?"

"Yes, master raven, yes. The gateway opens but one time a day, at sunset. It remains this way only from the moment the sun's disc touches the horizon's edge, and closes the instant it disappears below the sea. In that time alone might a ship, sailing into the face of the setting sun, reach the Veiled Isle. It is a magic place, Master Darkfeather, peopled by creatures both dark and light. It is said there is a mountain at the heart of the island. Beneath that mountain is a cave, a cavern full of paintings. In this cave is a chamber - home to an ancient terror. Lindsay would not have buried his artifact in the sand on the Veiled Isle. He would have hid it there, in the cave. Of this I am certain."

"We have faced such challenges before," uttered Dread Steele. "We shall overcome them again."

"Yet you must beware, Steele!" said Egidio. "The Veiled Isle is protected by more than the Devil's Horns and magical creatures. It is enchanted by a powerful curse. Any mortal that crosses the gate has but one day and one night upon the isle's shores. At sunrise on the following morn, if he has not returned through the Devil's Horns, he will be trapped there forever – prisoner of the Veiled Isle for all time."

"Is there a talisman you could give us to shield us from this curse?" the Captain asked. But Egidio shook his head in reply.

"There are few enough items in the world powerful enough to protect a man from magic this deep. Not even old Egidio possesses them. I do have more fog seeds, though. Came in handy, did they not?" Egidio chuckled and produced a leather pouch from his apron. He shook the bag and the contents rattled within.

"Fog seeds?" George whispered a little too loudly into Jim's ear. "So that's how he pulled that trick off on the beach! Brilliant that was...wonder if there's some of them seeds lyin' around in here?" But Jim just shushed his friend with a wave of his hand.

"Magic islands and curses be trouble enough, Egidio," MacGuffy grumbled. "But know ye what might lie at the end of our search? We think mayhaps it be not the Treasure of the Ocean itself. But if not that, then what?"

"Old Egidio may not know for certain, MacGuffy, but I do believe I have a very good guess. For it was I who told Lindsay Morgan of its existence." Egidio reached out his hands and murmured some spell into the air. All of the magical fog and dirt and sparkles answered his call. They swirled before him in a glowing cloud until they came together in the floating shape of a large shell. The light from the shell shone in Egidio's glasses, turning them to nothing but circles of molten color. "The Hunter's Shell – the most powerful seeker in all the world. One need but speak the words engraved upon the shell, and no matter how deeply buried or how far away, the shell will guide the one who holds it to whatever he seeks. I believe the map leads to the Hunter's Shell. I believe Lindsay made the map to ensure Jim could find the Treasure of the Ocean if ever he needed."

Egidio waved his hands once more and the luminous cloud before him whirled again. This time it formed a shape Jim had seen many times before: a trident with the circle of a pearl behind it. It was the symbol on the lid of his father's box - the symbol of the Treasure of the Ocean.

"Does the boy know, Steele?" Egidio asked. The shopkeeper's voice was low and grave. His glowing eyes were fixed upon the shape before him. "Does Jim know why he must be the one to find the Treasure? Does he even know what the Treasure is? What it does? Perhaps if he knew what it did to Bartholomew all those years ago, or if he learned of the storm that guards it, he would not be so eager to seek it out." Jim went cold where he crouched on the floor. His fingers and toes tingled and his mouth went dry. He strained his ears to hear what Dread Steele might answer to these questions he so longed to learn.

"The red storm," Steele whispered. The magic, shell-shaped cloud glimmered in his dark eyes. "It is our own fault that the storm even exists – Cromier's, Lindsay's, and mine. It was our tampering with the Treasure of the Ocean that unleashed it upon the world. It is a force of magic that even I fear. There is so much pain in the past, Egidio. Is it for me to tell a boy these things? These are things a father should tell a son. I am only a sailor - a pirate the boy hardly knows. I was his father's greatest enemy as far as he knows. I do not know how to speak to children. I know only the ocean. I know only the lonely life of the sea."

"The boy has no father, Steele. He has only himself, and his friends. He needs guidance and wisdom. The ocean you know so well is a wise teacher, is it not? He has the right to know, Dread. He has the right to know that—"

Egidio was about to say what Jim had the right to know, and Jim was nearly crawling through the wooden door to hear it. But a loud snap cracked in the hallway behind him, and a hissing noise rushed into his ears. Jim whirled around to find several things happening all at once.

Lacey and George were practically on top of him, just as eager to hear Egidio's next words as Jim. This, unfortunately, left Peter and Paul to their own devices. The two younger Ratts had wandered back to the paintings on the wall, where the brothers stood, frozen with fear, each with a finger on the canvas. Jim thought at first that one of them had broken the picture's frame. But just as he and the others were about to make a break for it, Jim realized that the snap had come not from the paintings, but from a small blue flame at the hallway's entrance. A column of smoke rose from the flame into the darkness – a column of smoke that took the shape of gray pirate, a smoky tendril of a cutlass in his hand.

With an ear-piercing howl, the floating pirate streaked down the hallway, pulling his smoky blade back to strike. Peter and Paul screamed at the tops of their lungs. Then Lacey and George shouted for Peter and Paul to stop screaming. Then all five of them, with nowhere left to go, stumbled backwards through the doorway and into the sitting room.

The gray pirate soared over the pile of children and faded away like a foggy ghost. But when Jim turned over, he found his nose not three inches from the very real boots of Dread Steele, who was glaring down on Jim and his friends with eyes so hot they could smelt iron.

"Welcome to my shop, Jim Morgan," said Egidio, an amused smile on the old man's face, and a spark of laughter in his enormous eyes. There was no such humor to be found on the hardened face of Dread Steele.

The walk to the *Spectre* through the streets of Shelltown was one of the longest and most miserable of Jim's life. Dread Steele surged ahead of the others, his black cloak trailing behind him and a dark storm raging in his eyes. When they reached the pier Dread Steele flowed onto the ship like an angry wraith. The Captain never even gave Mufwalme a chance to apologize for allowing the children to escape. He barked for the big man to take Lacey and the Ratts to scrub the decks for their disobedience. But when Jim moved to follow his friends, Steele stayed him with a black glare.

"As for Jim," the Captain said, the edge on his voice sharp as a blade. "Mister Darkfeather will escort him to my quarters, where he shall wait for my return. He and I have much to discuss. Mister Gilly, we shall set a new course if you please!"

As the Captain blew off to the quarterdeck and Mister Gilly's wheel, Jim's shoulders slumped and his stomach dropped nearly into his shoes. Lacey, George, Peter, and Paul gave Jim a horrified look before marching off to scrub the decks with Mister Mufwalme. Even

MacGuffy, hardened man that he was, wore a nervous frown. Jim slowly turned on his heel and made his way toward the captain's quarters with doom in his heart. When he got to the door, Cornelius patted him once with a soft wing on the back of the head.

"Good luck, my son," the raven said, then flew off to the mainmast. With a heavy sigh, Jim turned the handle and trudged into the captain's quarters to wait for Dread Steele.

SEVENTEEN

JIM MORGAN AND DREAD STEELE

J im dared not sit in Dread Steele's red leather chair, nor in fact, could he even bear to look at it. All he could imagine was the shadowy Captain sitting there in but a few moments, glaring at him with dark eyes. Neither did Jim wish to look out the window, which still hung open from his earlier escape. Everything in the cabin reminded Jim of some failure or warned him of some punishment to come.

So, not wanting to look at anything and not wanting to touch anything, Jim closed his and eyes and jammed his hands deep into his pockets. There, his fingers brushed the ridges of his father's box.

At but the feel of one sharp corner, an itching tingle brewed in the darkness behind Jim's eyes. The somber song of Philus Philonius's flute began to drift through Jim's mind. It pulled his thoughts inescapably to the enchanted rose beneath the wooden lid.

All by itself Jim's hand pulled the box from his pocket. When he held it in his hands, the flute song in his head grew so loud it was all Jim could hear. He held the box up before his eyes and pried the lid back with curious fingers. A violet glow lit his cheeks from within the box and a magical shimmer rippled from the blackened rose thorn. Jim stared at the burnt stem and petals, entranced by the shining glamour. The itch felt scratched just a little. Jim remembered that if he could get close enough, just close enough to see those wretched Cromiers, he could make all this pain and sorrow go away. All with just a prick of his thumb. Jim reached into the box, his fingertips passing over the ash-gray petals and blackened stem to the source of the violet flame – the glistening point of the rose's thorn. *Perhaps I could just test the sharpness now,* Jim thought to himself. He lifted his finger over the thorn, just to give it a tap.

"Mister Morgan," Dread Steele's voice suddenly called from behind Jim, accompanied by the slight creak of the door. The flute song in Jim's mind snuffed out like a candle. Jim slapped shut the box and shoved it back in his pocket at the same time. The sound of ocean waves returned to Jim's ears through the open window and the fog in his mind cleared. But Jim's heart still hammered. He felt cold and pale, yet sweat prickled on his forehead and upper lip.

Steele blew into the room and all but flew to his chair. He sat down in complete silence and placed his fingers against each other, pressing so hard that the tips turned white. Beneath the shadow of his hat, the pirate lord's dark eyes bored into Jim's face. Jim felt certain that the Captain knew - knew what was in his pocket. For a long, horrible second Jim was sure this conversation would be even worse than he had imagined. But after an awful silence, Steele reached up and pulled the hat from his head. It was as though a cloud passed from before the sun. The room seemed to brighten and the Captain appeared more a man and less a vengeful wraith.

"Get yourself a chair, boy, and sit down." Steele flicked his eyes to a corner by the door, where a wooden stool rested against the wall. Jim did as he was told without a word. His arms and legs trembled, and his insides were still furled into a nervous coil. Jim sat down and snuck a glance at Dread Steele. Even with the shadow removed from his face, the pirate captain seemed sterner than iron.

"Let us review this morning's activities, shall we?" Steele continued. "You have violated my commands, deceived a member of my crew, put yourself and your friends at risk, broken into my friend's shop, and eavesdropped on a conversation not intended for your ears. What have you to say for yourself?" With each point on the long list of Jim's misdeeds that day, his chin sunk a little lower to his chest. It all did sound rather awful when laid out that way, Jim thought. But the black rose thorn's itch yet tickled the back of his mind. It quickly unfolded into a hot bloom of anger.

"It's not fair!" Jim suddenly shouted. "You didn't lose your home. You didn't lose everything you had! The Cromiers have taken everything from me!"

"Not fair?" Steele replied. The Captain shook his head. "It's not fair. Those are the words of the weak. Do you think the fish of the sea look at the shark's teeth and powerful tail and say, 'it's not fair?' Life is a shark, Jim Morgan, and we but fish. No, it is not fair. But did the Cromiers force you to sneak off this ship? Did the Cromiers force you to break into Egidio's shop? Those deeds are yours and yours alone." Now that little bloom of heat grew quite a bit hotter in Jim's chest. This time he looked Steele right in the eye.

"I have a right to know why all this is happening to me. I have the right to get back what's mine and set things straight!" The moment the words escaped Jim's mouth, he immediately knew he should have left them there. Dread Steele was Lord of the Pirates. He was not accustomed to taking cheek from young men, or even grown ones at that. The cloud reformed over the Captain's face. His lips trembled and his voice rang sharp enough to cut through the itch in Jim's mind and freeze the fire in his chest.

"I have heard such words before, Jim Morgan, from men who made the world worse under the guise of making it right. You and your father are two of a kind! Fools too clever for their own good!" Those words caught Jim hard. He suddenly remembered the last time he had a conversation with an adult like this one. It had been on the beach outside the home that was now a pile of ashes. It had been with his father, some of the last words they had ever spoken to each other in this world.

"You would know better than I about my father, sir," Jim said, quite a bit more quietly. His throat grew tight and his cheeks grew warm. He felt incredibly alone just then, sitting before the Captain. No friend stood at his side and he had nowhere left to run or call home.

Jim expected no softness or mercy from the Lord of the Pirates. But when he finally dared to look again, he found the storm gone from Steele's face. For a brief instant, a sorrow for breaking something he only intended to bend passed through the pirate's eyes. Dread Steele rose from behind his desk and walked over to the open window. There he stood in silence. The breeze caught his cloak and ruffled it behind him. When the pirate captain spoke again, his voice was quiet and far away.

"Did you know that your father and I were in school together?"

"I'd heard that somewhere," Jim said, remembering the story Janus Blacktail had told him only the night before. Steele reached out and touched the windowsill, running his hand along the length of it. When he turned back, Jim was surprised to find a smile on his face. For a moment, Dread Steele seemed the younger, more carefree man he must have once been.

"There was a professor there named Toadswart. He was every bit as cheerful as his name suggested, if you can imagine. It was rumored that Toadswart never actually read any of the long, horrible papers he forced his miserable students to write. He simply counted the words to ensure you'd written every last letter he'd assigned. Yes, he was quite awful. Well, one day your father came to class and sat us both in the far back of the hall. Only a moment or two into the lecture, Lindsay produced two broom handles from beneath his cloak. We set our hats on the handles and our cloaks on the chairs. When old Toady turned to draw on the board we escaped through a window.

They nearly expelled us both for that, as I recall. But it is still one of the best days I can remember. Had you any clue that your father was such a rascal as that?"

"No," Jim said, shaking his head. He tried to picture that stern man on the beach, a little silver shell between his fingers, causing trouble like Jim and the Ratts. But another question splashed into the middle of those pleasant imaginations. "Captain Steele, was my father a thief?" Jim asked, his voice cracking. "Was he a pirate? Did he steal the Treasure of the Ocean?" Dread Steele stood silent for a long, long breath. His eyes lay fixed on the ocean beyond the window.

"Truth is a painting, Jim," the Captain said. "Moments captured in time. To know a man's whole life you would need a museum full of paintings – both the hideous, and the beautiful." Steele looked Jim in the face. Sadness had stolen into his eyes. "When we were young, your father was my friend. He was my best friend in all the world. That should say as much about him as anything else. We do not always end up becoming what we hoped to be. Come here, let me show you something."

Jim came to stand beside the Captain at the window. He breathed deeply of the salty air and followed Steele's gaze to the great blue expanse that lay behind the ship. The ocean stretched back to Spire Island and all the way to the edge of the world beyond. It made Jim feel so very small.

"Look out there," Steele said over the rhythm of the waves. "What do you see? The ocean is more than waves rolling beneath the wind and the clouds." Steele leaned onto the windowsill and nodded back toward the quickly shrinking island behind the ship. "Back there, on the land - in the world, roads run everywhere. Roads to the cities and roads to the country. Roads to your home and roads to your work. They are so well traveled and so well marked that we forget there is more to the earth than the pressed dirt between one place and the next. But on the water, every direction is its own road."

"Ten-thousand roads," Steele whispered. "On the open ocean, there is no one to choose your path but yourself. One day, ready or not, all of us must take our own road, and to any place we dare to venture. Learn to sail the seas, Jim, and you can go anywhere. You can be anything."

"Anywhere?"

"Yes, anywhere. But wherever that may be, Jim, know that there will be storms, and come they shall. The worst storms are not even those of rain and lightning and thunder. The worst storms are magic and monsters, pain and loss. It is in such storms that so many men lose their way. They let the gale and the waves toss the ship wherever they will. When you battle such storms, Jim, you must find the courage to turn into the great waves. You must face the lightning and the thunder. You must stay in command of your ship to sail through to the other side. If you don't, you'll be blown to wherever the wind takes you. Some men have lived their entire lives lost for fear of turning into the storm. Do you understand?"

"Yes, sir," Jim said quietly. "I think so." Jim waited another moment, to keep his voice from trembling. Then he said: "Captain Steele, what is the Treasure of the Ocean? Why is it that my father wanted me to have it so badly? Why does Count Cromier want it? And what did it do to his son?" Dread Steele took a deep breath. Any trace of the smile on his face faded away.

"These are the more difficult questions, Jim. But perhaps it is left to me to answer them after all. Your father collected many treasures. He was a master of such things, even more so than myself. But the Treasure of the Ocean was his crowning achievement. The Treasure is but one piece of the vast horde you saw in the Pirate Vault of Treasures – a golden Trident."

Jim's mind flashed to the box in his pocket – to the carved image upon the box's lid. The image of a trident and a pearl. The clue had been in his grasp since the beginning, but he had not known it for what it was.

"The Trident, which is the Treasure of the Ocean, is an ancient talisman of more powerful magic than any other on the face of the Earth. The one who wields it would hold sway over the very ocean itself – the winds, the clouds, the waves. Master over all of them he would be. Can you see now why the Cromiers must not possess it? As to why your father meant such a treasure to fall to you—"

A single tone of a ringing bell drowned out Steele's next words. The hairs on the back of Jim's neck prickled. The ringing note clanged in Jim's ears as loud as a church bell and scattered his thoughts. From the corner of his eye, he caught the briefest widening, like a hint of fear, passing through Dread Steele's eyes. The Pirate Lord was also more than surprised at the bell's alarm.

Dread Steele slowly turned his head over his shoulder to where the strange bell hung from the hook on the corner of the captain's desk. Jim and the Captain watched it for a long moment, holding their breaths. The bell hung silent and still long enough for Jim to hope that perhaps it had been nothing at all. He was about to risk saying so to the Captain, when he was interrupted by yet another echoing ring. After this second ring, Steele's voice turned hard as stone.

"Jim, go to the main deck. Find your friends there and take them below. Do not stop along the way or risk even tearing your eyes from the tops of your shoes. Below decks you will stay until MacGuffy or Cornelius comes to fetch you."

"Why?" Jim asked. Gooseflesh prickled up and down his arms and legs. "What's happening?"

"Do as I say, Jim!" Steele ordered with a growl, the bell gonging again as he spoke. "We are about come under attack."

"Attack? By who? The Cromiers? Splitbeard?" The bell was ringing over and over again, faster and faster, driving the terrified hammering of Jim's pulse.

"Not by who," Steele growled. "By what."

EIGHTEEN

THE SEA MONSTER'S ATTACK

Jim burst through the captain's door and scrambled to the quarterdeck. He pushed past Murdock and Mufwalme and ran by Mister Gilley, who was holding fast at the wheel. He could still hear the mysterious bell ringing over and over again behind him. When he came upon George, Peter, Paul, and Lacey, they had already abandoned their buckets and brushes, and were peering over the portside railing. Their mouths hung agape and the color had drained from their faces.

Jim was already too late.

He leaned over the railing beside George and Lacey. His arms and legs went cold and numb. A black shadow spread like a stain in the waters beneath the *Spectre*, growing in all directions under the ship.

"What is that, Jim?" George asked.

"We should get below," was all Jim could think to say. But before they had even a chance, a roaring fountain of water exploded beside the *Spectre*. Jim and the others fell back from the railing. Seawater rained down on their heads. A writhing monstrosity loomed above them and cast a dark shadow over the deck. The creature rose further and further into the air. It climbed as high as the mainmast and was thicker and stronger than a great tree trunk. Razor-sharp hooks glistened in a row along the length of the pale flesh. It was only then that Jim realized the enormity of the danger. The massive thing that now reared back to crush the *Spectre* was but one limb of a great beast beneath the waves.

The tentacle crashed across the main deck and smashed one of the cockboats to a thousand pieces with a single blow. The ship shook from aft to prow. The crew scattered in all directions, throwing themselves behind masts and barrels for protection. Jim and his friends rushed together on the quarterdeck as the arm reared back for a second blow. Jim feared the next blast would split the ship in two and throw the entire crew into the water with the creature. The awful question of what it would feel like to be dragged down into the depths with a tentacle wrapped about his waist snuck into Jim's mind.

But then Dread Steele melted onto the deck. He appeared in the heart of the fray, dark cloak flowing about him like a black flame. He stood with the splintered wound in the ship's deck beneath his feet and a gleaming cutlass in his hand. The Lord of the Pirates sneered at the creature's arm, as though it was the beast that should fear him.

The tentacle whipped back to strike. The crew of the *Spectre* - Mufwalme, Murdoch, Wang-Chi, and even old MacGuffy - flew to Steele's side. They raised their swords in the air as one and stabbed the creature's arm as it fell upon them. The tentacle jerked back as a burnt hand from a flame. Great drops of black blood fell to the deck from its wounds.

A dash of hope stole into Jim's heart when Steele and his men drove back the creature's tentacles. Yet it was quickly doused. From all sides of the ship, five more tentacles burst from the sea. But if Dread

Steele was surprised or frightened, not a trace of it showed upon his face. He raised his sword again and rallied his men once more.

"Do not forget your courage! Defend our ship! Defend the *Spectre!*" As the crew rushed to obey Steele's commands, the pirate captain locked eyes with Jim, who was huddled with his friends on the quarterdeck. "Cornelius!" Steele yelled. "Get the young ones below!"

"Yes, yes!" the raven shrieked. He flew to Jim's shoulder, pecking Jim mercilessly on the side of the head as he did. "Below, below, you fools! Are you mad?"

"What about courage and all that from before, Cornelius?" Jim shouted back.

"Yes, well, in your next lesson I shall endeavor to demonstrate to you the fine line between bravery and stupidity! Now let us get below decks at once before the lot of us are tossed beneath the waves or worse!"

Jim and the others leapt to their feet, but they only reached the stairs before a pale arm broke through the railing beside them. The tentacle knocked them all to their backs as it curled around a trio of pirates. The crewmen screamed and dropped their cutlasses point first into the deck as they were dragged overboard and into the sea.

"Come on, Jim!" Lacey shouted, her face white as a sheet. "George, Peter, Paul! We need to move!" She grabbed Peter and Paul by their shirt collars and yanked them to their feet. Jim and George finally came to their senses and followed close behind.

When the five of them reached the steps to the below decks, Jim breathed a sigh of relief a moment too soon. A tentacle lanced from behind them and seized poor Peter by the ankle. It hauled him into the air as he cried out at the top of his lungs. Paul, who had been holding his brother's hand in a vice grip, never let go, and thus two Ratts now dangled in the tentacle's grasp, screaming in terror.

"Peter! Paul!" George yelled. "No!" Lacey was shouting for someone to do something, but the pirates were fighting for their lives and could offer no aid. As Jim searched for help, his eyes lit upon the three cutlasses speared into the ship's deck behind them.

With no time for discussion, Jim grabbed Lacey and George by the arms and dragged them to his sides. "Cornelius, circle above and watch our backs for more of those tentacles. We're going to have to do this ourselves."

"Madness, madness!" Cornelius screeched. But the raven had been with Jim in dark places before, so off he flew in a low orbit above the children's heads.

"Do what by ourselves, Jim?" Lacey asked. Her question was answered as Jim pulled her and George to the three, fallen swords. The three of them yanked a cutlass each from the deck. As there was little time to think of something more memorable to say, Jim simply shouted as loud as he could:

"CHARGE!"

The three friends attacked the tentacle that held Peter and Paul, hacking and stabbing at it with all their might. The whipping arm pulled back from the Ratt Clan's attack, moving to escape and drag Peter and Paul to their doom beneath the water. But Jim leapt up and landed a well-timed jab directly into the heart of the tentacle's underside. The giant limb shuddered and reared up in pain. A loud roar reverberated through the waters below the ship.

The tentacle unspooled and dropped Peter and Paul just beyond the edge of the ship. Throwing down his sword, Jim rushed forward and dove between two rails. He caught Paul by the ankle at the last moment. But Paul still held Peter by the hand and the weight of two Ratts threatened to drag Jim into the water as well. Just when Jim tipped over the side, two pairs of hands gripped him by his legs. Lacey took hold of one ankle and George grabbed the other.

"Pull, pull, pull!" Cornelius cawed. The brave bird even flew down to seize Peter by his hair, flapping with all his strength to help. Of course, this simply made Peter scream louder and watered his eyes more than it aided in getting him to safety. But the entire clan finally managed themselves back aboard, where they collapsed in an exhausted heap.

"Are you two alright?" Lacey cried to Peter and Paul, tears welling up in her big eyes.

Neither brother said a word for a moment. Paul stared straight ahead, and then finally looked to his brother for confirmation. "Actually, I think we are."

"Yeah," Peter agreed, nodding. "You know, I think that may have been the most brilliant thing that's every happened to me. I just rode a sea monster, didn't I? I didn't even pee meself!" Then the two brothers unleashed as mighty hurrahs as they could and pumped their fists as though they'd meant to be picked up the entire time.

"Oh, you blockheads!" George cried, pulling his brothers into his arms.

"This is all rather touching," Cornelius shouted, dropping out of the sky and lighting upon Jim's shoulder. "And while I will, I assure you, be adding this little misadventure to my rather reputable collection of fascinating sea stories, perhaps we could handle all the formalities down below?"

Jim was about to agree when one more shadow fell over the deck. The giant squid was yet to be defeated. It snuck one of its arms through the crew's defenses, sweeping men aside and wrapping itself all the way around the *Spectre*. As the creature took hold, another roar split the air. The squid's massive face rose into view. Two dark orbs, lidless pools of black, stared over the deck. From the center of the six tentacles a sharp beak, large enough to swallow a grown man full, chomped and gnashed with ringing claps. The beast began to squeeze. The railings shattered beneath the creature's hold and the ship's hull groaned and trembled.

Neither Jim nor any member of the pirate crew spoke a word. Every voice had been robbed of sound until George dared a whisper from Jim's side.

"Well, there's somethin' we never woulda seen in London, now would we 'ave?"

"No George," Jim agreed. "We most certainly would not." Jim saw no hope for escape this time - until Dread Steele appeared at his side. The Captain's black hair, hat long lost in the battle, flew like a flag, and not a whisper of fear betrayed his stormy eyes.

"Find your way below, Mister Morgan," Steele growled, his eyes locked with the beast's, ready for the next attack. But Jim hesitated, not out of rebellion, but because some strange spirit had seized him by the heart. He had tasted action on the high seas for the first time, and had not yet had his fill. He scrambled to his feet and made for the cutlass he had dropped, bringing it back to stand beside Dread Steele. George, Peter, Paul, and Lacey gathered around him in a circle.

Jim fully expected to be spurned and sent down below decks with naught more than a dismissive bark. But Dread Steele glanced down at him, measuring him with his sea-gray eyes. Then he smiled. Not a hint of a smile, nor some simple curve at the corners of his mouth. No, this smile split the Captain's battle-hardened face like a ray of sunshine and he loosed a long laugh, full and joyous.

"Morgan and Steele," the pirate captain cried at the end of his laugh. "Together again at last! So be it, young Jim! But hang on tight to your sword and stay close to my side!"

"Attack that arm!" Steele shouted to the men who had fallen. "Force it to release the ship or we shall all be dragged into the deep!" Boards began to pop and break. Splinters and dust rained on the crew's head. Jim knew the *Spectre*, mighty as she was, could take little more of this.

"Stand fast!" Steele shouted.

But though the Captain and his crew, along with Jim and the Ratt Clan, did their worst to the squid's squeezing arm, the monster refused to surrender. Cracks and groans snapped from the ship's hull. Fears of falling into the grasp of the monster once again filled Jim's mind. All seemed lost, when from nowhere a spear flew through the air. It struck the creature in the side of the head and took the beast by surprise. Yet this was no pike from the *Spectre's* armory, nor was it even made of any wood from any tree upon the earth.

This spear was fashioned of the coral from the sea.

Another spear flew and another. A barrage of arrows rained down on the creature's head - arrows crafted of the same white coral. The squid bellowed in pain. Its grip on the *Spectre* loosened as it turned to face this new threat. Jim followed the creature's gaze, but it was Lacey who saw them first.

"Jim, George, look! There are people in the water...but...well, they aren't people at all!"

"Captain!" Cornelius called, circling overhead. "Sea folk off the port bow!"

"Merpeople!" Jim exclaimed as he craned his neck to see.

Floating in the water, some two lengths off the port bow, a handful of bearded men, hair long and tangled, skin bare to the sun, hurled spear after spear with deadly accuracy. They shouted battle cries in a tongue Jim had never before heard and charged the squid without fear.

"Look at that!" George shouted. He pointed just beyond the spearmen in the waters. Two hammerhead sharks surged from the waves. They were bridled like horses and pulled behind them some sort of chariot, encrusted with jewels that must only be found in mines at the bottom of the sea. A golden-haired mermaid guided the sharks with seaweed reins, until she released them to fire coral arrows from a bow fashioned from the jawbone of some great fish.

"Now men!" Steele shouted. "Do not lose the moment!" The Captain rushed to the tentacle wrapped about his ship and used the shattered remains of a board to pry the arm from the deck. Jim and his friends ran to Steele's side, helping as best they could. Slowly but surely the crew forced the behemoth to release the ship from its grasp.

The pirates reformed their ranks upon the deck. They fired their pistols and hurled wooden spears of their own at the squid. Under this assault the monster roared again, so loudly that Jim had to cover his ears. At last the creature fell back from the *Spectre* and dove beneath the waves. Storm clouds of black ink swirled in the waters to mask its escape.

The *Spectre's* pirate crew raised their spears and cutlasses and pistols into the air, filling the sky with shouts of victory. Jim, the Ratts, and

Lacey grabbed each other tight, jumping up and down with joy. Only Dread Steele remained calm. He sheathed his sword as though victory had been assured from the very start.

"Tend to the wounded," he said. "Search the waters for those fallen overboard. And extend the plank. I must break words with our rescuers."

NINETEEN

THE QUEEN OF THE MERPEOPLE

After the battle, the ocean around the battered *Spectre* calmed once more. The froth and ink from the monster's attack faded away, and the brilliant-blue waves sparkled again in the sun. Seawater and monster blood drenched Jim, the Ratts, and Lacey from head to toe. But other than a rather nasty cut over Peter's left eyebrow, along with a few other bumps and bruises, all were well and warmed by the sun and the ocean breeze.

The *Spectre*, on the other hand, came away far worse than the Ratt Clan. Overturned barrels, broken boards, and all manner of battle debris littered the deck. Pirates helped one another to their feet and formed a long line before Mister Gilley. The pot-bellied pirate seemed to be something of an expert at stitching up bloody wounds and setting broken bones, of which there were several amongst the crew. The rest of the pirates gathered at what was left of the portside railing, where Jim, the Ratts, and Lacey now stood. They watched Dread Steele step to the edge of the extended plank, where he bowed his head low to the clutch of mermen gathered in the waters before him.

"We are in your debt, Fulkern," Dread Steele said to the foremost merman, who seemed to Jim even larger and more powerful than giant Mufwalme. A brown beard covered Fulkern's grim face. A string of shark's teeth hung over his chest and blue and gold tattoos lined his arms and shoulders. Though the battle had ended, he still gripped a coral spear in his powerful fist.

"Payment in advance, Dread Steele," Fulkern replied. "For the keeping of your word given long ago. Had this been any other ship upon the sea, we would have stood by and watched the Kraken drag it down into the depths." The warrior scowled at the pirates behind Dread Steele, until a voice chimed over the waters to silence the enormous merman.

"Peace, Fulkern!" the voice said. The words rung in the air like a chorus of bells. "Dread Steele is a Friend of the Sea. He may be the last of them from the world of men. As such, he is like a brother to your King, and also to me." Fulkern bowed his head low and swam aside, as did the mermen with him. They cleared a path for the chariot, which rode up beneath the plank, pulled by the hammerhead sharks.

Without doubt, the mermaid in the chariot possessed the loveliest face Jim had ever seen. It was smooth and gentle as porcelain. Golden hair flowed from beneath a crown of pearls upon her head. Her ivory arms and shoulders were bared to the sun, but she wore a seaweed gown wrapped about her body. It was not dank, nasty seaweed that would wash upon the shore. Rather it was fresh and vibrant, as though still alive upon her skin, green as spring leaves upon a tree. A bejeweled necklace, laced with gold, hung about her neck. Where her green raiment ended, scales, sparkling blue in the sun, ran down to a bright white fin like a dolphin's tail.

"She's beautiful," said Lacey. Jim could not agree more. He could hardly look away from the mermaid as she spoke with Dread Steele, Lord of the Pirates.

"Dread Steele, it is good to see you again, especially after so many years."

"It is my honor, Queen Melodia. Forgive me that it has been so long."

"A Queen?" Peter asked from just behind George and Jim, where he and Paul stood on their tiptoes to see. "Queen of the Merpeople?"

"She looks like a Queen, don't she?" Paul said.

"I'm glad to see you safe from the wrath of the Kraken, Captain," the Queen continued. "Fulkern and I chased this beast all the way from the cold depths, below even our great city. It is a rare thing indeed for such a monster to swim to the warmer waters near the sun. But such things have been happening more and more often. It makes me afraid for us all. The tides speak of ill fortune, Dread Steele. They speak of the Trident - that which you call the Treasure of the Ocean - found again. They speak of the blood red storm stalking the skies. They speak of destruction and despair."

"If that is so, your majesty, then where is Nemus?" Dread Steele asked the queen of the Merpeople. "Where is the King?" The Queen paused for a long moment before answering. Jim thought he saw her brace for only an instant in her chariot and squeeze the seaweed reigns tight in her ivory hands.

"Nemus does sit upon the throne, Captain. But his heart is still broken, even after all this time. He has never been the same since the Flower...our Flower, was taken from us. He may have lost the will to take up his spear ever again. But those are our concerns. What business carries you and your men over our waters?"

"I still seek The Treasure of the Ocean, your majesty. I still chase Count Cromier and his son, the dark child, Bartholomew. They now sail with Splitbeard the pirate upon the *Sea Spider*, on a course to the rocks known as the Devil's Horns."

"You've been chasing the Treasure a long time, Captain, and much to our thanks," said the Queen. "But there is a renewed urgency in your voice and in your face. Something has changed, hasn't it? What is it, Dread Steel? What has happened?"

Dread Steele took a deep breath, so much so that his shoulders rose and fell. He stole a sideways glance in Jim's direction. Jim could see troubled thoughts churning behind the Captain's grey eyes.

"Something has changed indeed, your majesty. A new clue has been found," Dread Steele said. "A map was discovered – in part by young Jim there – Jim Morgan. He is Lindsay Morgan's son."

The weight of a hundred pairs of eyes descended upon Jim. A hush fell over the *Spectre's* deck. The mermen stared at him from the ocean waves – but there was no kindness in their eyes. Judging by their hardened glares, Jim thought more than a few of them wanted to skewer him alive with a coral spear. Even the pirates gathered around him took a step or two back, murmuring quietly amongst themselves. Only Jim's friends stuck by his side. But when he met the Queen's gaze, even Lacey and the Ratts' presence were of little comfort.

"I would meet the son of Lindsay Morgan," said the Queen. Her eyes, which were nearly as golden as her hair, were fixed upon Jim's face. Jim looked to Dread Steele for help, hoping the Captain would say no, or send him down below decks or into his quarters. But the Captain nodded for Jim to join him on the plank.

Jim slowly made his way across the deck. His face itched and his heart beat hard in his chest. He hated the way the merpeople glared at him so angrily. But worse still, he thought he knew why. If Janus Blacktail's story was true, it had been his father who had broken King Nemus's heart by stealing his treasure.

Jim stepped onto the plank, which was just wide enough for him circle around Dread Steele. When he came to the edge, he stood looking down into the eyes of the Merpeople's Queen. For a long moment Queen Melodia said nothing. She only held Jim in her unwavering gaze. When she finally spoke, her voice rang harder and colder than it had before.

"You are indeed the son of Morgan," she said. "I can see him in your face."

"Yes ma'am," Jim said. He felt Dread Steele flick him on the back of the neck to remind him he was speaking to a Queen. Jim remembered to bow his head, which he did rather clumsily. "Yes, your majesty," he corrected himself.

"You could not have known your father well, could you? Nor your mother, I imagine, if at all."

"No, your majesty."

"Did he ever show it to you, though? The Treasure of the Ocean? Did your father ever display it to you proudly and tell you what he planned to do with it – that which he took?" Jim gritted his teeth and put his hand behind his back to clench his fist. Queen or not, he loathed even the thought that his father was a thief.

"No, he did not." Jim replied, leaving off the 'your majesty' on purpose. "But I did see it once, in the Pirate Vault of Treasures. I stood in the same room with it. Close enough to touch it."

"But you did not even lay a hand upon it? Why did not take it for your own? I find this hard to believe. What foolish trinket lay in the Vault that would have distracted you from such magic as the Treasure of the Ocean?"

"It was just an amulet. An enchanted amulet I needed to rescue my friends."

"Rescue?" the Queen said. Jim thought he heard a hint of surprise in her voice. The Queen's eyes drifted then for the first time from Jim's face to his friends at the railing behind him. When she looked back to Jim, he thought her hard gaze might have softened ever so slightly. When she spoke, the bell chimes sounded faintly again behind her words.

"Your father's face does indeed live in yours, Jim Morgan. But perhaps that's not all that lives there. Perhaps you resemble another as well. We shall see. So I shall give you at least this warning. Beware the Veiled Isle, which lies behind the Devil's Horns. More than that beware the Treasure of the Ocean. Dark magic guards it. The path that leads to it is fraught with danger. And as for the Treasure itself…death and destruction surround it." The Queen pulled on the seaweed reins and the sharks began to pull the chariot away. At the last moment she turned over her shoulder and looked to Jim again.

"Be careful, Jim Morgan," she said. "Perhaps…perhaps it might be good to look upon your face again." Jim could not be sure, but for a moment, mixed with the ocean water, he thought there had been tears in the Queen's eyes.

The Queen and her warriors neither bade farewell nor waved good-bye. They dove silently beneath the waves and melted into the darkness of the deep. The Queen's caution rang in Jim's mind. He wondered at the anger and sadness that had welled up in her eyes. It was all so very confusing. But in spite of everything else, Queen Melodia had left Jim with a warning: danger and death lay ahead. Jim put his hand in his pocket to touch the box. He could feel the rose thorn's magic thrumming there within.

TWENTY

DARK SCHEMES ABOARD THE *SEA SPIDER*

Hanging in the sky above the high seas, like a great white eye, the pale moon lit a path for the black-hulled *Sea Spider*. Below and above decks, the Corsair Pirates laughed, cursed, sang songs, and boasted of the wicked ways they would soon spend their great wealth. Count Cromier - the Red Count, they called him - had already paid the pirates handsomely in advance. He had also promised them more gold than they could count once the deed was done. And the deed's completion was ever so close at hand. But the Corsairs were not the only ones burning with desire for glittering prizes just within reach.

Inside the captain's quarters, a rack of candles burned bright. The flickering flames threw wavering shadows over the faces of Bartholomew Cromier, the Count, and Splitbeard the sorcerous pirate. On the table beneath the candles, where great drops of wax fell like tears, sat Lindsay's Morgan's enchanted map. The drawings on the page still shimmered with blue magic. Bartholomew found himself entranced by the moonwater's light, still burning upon the parchment. But the glow twinkled brightest in the black eyes of his father, the Count.

"The quest for the Treasure of the Ocean is the quest of my life," said the Count, as much to himself as to the men beside him. "I was so close before. So close to total victory, before those fools, Morgan and Steele, intervened. But now, at long last, the end of my journey is at hand." The jagged purple scar on the Count's cheek twitched beneath his unblinking eye. "Soon, the power of the sea, and the sky above it, will be at my command. If a navy sails against me, I will send a wave to crush them to the ocean floor. If an army refuses to submit to my will, I shall smite them down with lightning. I will scatter them with the winds. The kings and queens of the world shall kneel before me and pay me homage, or I will cover their lands with a cold darkness that will last a hundred years. Can you even imagine, Splitbeard, what it will be like to hold such power in your hands?"

Bartholomew could. In truth, he could more than imagine it. He could remember it. It was a memory from a long time ago, when he was but a boy, younger even than Jim Morgan. Bartholomew tightened his hands into fists behind his back. Even so he could only lessen the shudder than trembled his body. The memory still terrified him – but he would never admit that to his father. Never.

"I am but a man of the sea, oh great red one," said Splitbeard. "What have I to do with such ambitions as yours? But is it this Treasure you seek that lies at the end of the map?" Splitbeard pulled at the shark's teeth braided into the split ends of his beard. The arrogant smile lingered on his face, but his black eyes were fixed upon the parchment.

"Not according to Lindsay's map," replied the Count. "But what awaits us in the cavern is the key to discovering the Treasure's final location. Once I have the Hunter's Shell, all else shall fall into place. The shell is a seeker more powerful than any other in the world. The Treasure of the Ocean's hiding spot will be revealed to my eyes. Whatever secret path leads to it will be uncovered in my mind. Such is the purpose and power of the Hunter's Shell. Lindsay was wise to retain such a tool. Soon, nothing will stand in my way."

"Not even Dread Steele, oh magnificent one?" said Splitbeard. At the sound of Steele's name, Count Cromier finally blinked and a sour grimace twisted on his face.

"A plague on that fool, Dread Steele! And a plague on Lindsay Morgan and his infernal scheming!" Cromier spat. "We shall reach the Devil's Horns in but a matter of hours, and beyond that the Veiled Isle. But we must wait an entire day for another sunset before we may pass through the gates. In such a time, with the *Spectre* at full speed, Steele may indeed catch us."

"But he does not have the map, father," Bartholomew said. "How could he possibly know where to find us?"

"Do not underestimate the Pirate Lord, boy," said the Count. The harsh emphasis he placed on the 'boy' caused Bartholomew to clench both his fist and his jaw. "Such a miscalculation could be the death of us all. Dread Steele has many friends upon the sea. Some of them are wise in the ways of magic. Not all of them are entirely…natural."

"Leave the Lord of the Pirates to me, my Count," said Splitbeard with a laugh. "Dread Steele may have many magical friends, but I, Splitbeard, am a master of magic itself. I shall set a trap for Steele at the rocks around the Devil's Horns." Splitbeard grabbed at the flames burning on the candlewicks. Three of the dancing tongues disappeared within his palm like captured fireflies. "If the *Spectre* does arrive – we shall be ready to spring the surprise!" Splitbeard opened his hand and the three flames burst to life again, all to the sound of the pirate's laughter.

"I, for one, hope that Steele arrives," Bartholomew growled. The candle flames glowed hot in his icy blue eyes. He could still feel the lump on the back of his head where Steele had clubbed him during the battle in the fog. He slowly wrapped his fingers around his sword's handle and squeezed. "More than that I hope he brings that fool Jim Morgan with him. I long to put him beneath my blade!"

"No!" Cromier all but shouted, snapping Bartholomew from his vengeful fantasy. "How many times must I tell you? I've decided we need Jim Morgan alive for as long as possible. He may be of some use before the end." A flash of heat rushed into Bartholomew's pale cheeks and he snapped back at his father before considering his words carefully enough.

"And how many times must I remind you that we don't need him, father? Not when you have –" Bartholomew never had the chance to finish. The gloved back of his father's knuckles rapped across his face. Bartholomew sucked in a startled breath. His cheek sang.

"Silence!" Cromier hissed. "You shall do as I say, *boy*. Do I make myself clear? If you wanted to kill the boy so badly you should not have failed so miserably in London. Jim Morgan must yet live. Especially should you fail – again, if you remember…"?

The memory surged once more to the front of Bartholomew's mind. If he were not so ashamed of it, he would admit that the memory haunted his nightmares. But nightmare or no, it was his failure that his father would never let him forget. His cheeks began to burn more from shame than from his father's blow.

"Yes, father," was all he said. Then he turned on his heel and stormed from the captain's quarters onto the main deck of the *Sea Spider*.

Out in the ocean air, beneath the stars and amidst the revelry and bravado of the Corsair pirates, Bartholomew Cromier marched to the railings. He drew his dagger from his belt and began jabbing at the railing's wood.

"I'll show him," Bartholomew vowed to himself in little more than a thick whisper. He drew his breaths sharply as he tried to calm himself. Even his whisper rasped at the edges. "We don't need that little fool. Not when we have me. I won't fail. Not this time. Not now that I'm a man." Bartholomew closed his eyes, trying to block out any thoughts of the long list of failures of which his father constantly reminded him. His father. Bartholomew thought then about Count Cromier. His father could not use the Treasure of the Ocean, could he? The Trident was nothing but gold in the old Count's had. He needed Bartholomew to wield it – because Bartholomew was special.

That thought curled a smile at last on Bartholomew's pale lips. He looked down at the railing beneath him. To his surprise he found that in all his heated stabbing he had carved a name into the black wood. MORGAN was scrawled across the dark grain. Bartholomew's smile faded away. He clenched his jaw tight. Once more he welcomed the hope that Dread Steele would catch them. He longed for Jim Morgan to be there too. He had his own vision of how the next meeting between the three of them would end. Bartholomew flipped his dagger in his hand and slashed a gouge through the Morgan name.

It was an ending he had envisioned for quite some time. One way or another, only one would live to see this adventure's end. Bartholomew would make sure of it.

TWENTY–ONE

AMBUSH AMONG THE ROCKS

The *Spectre* sailed into the deep ocean for another day and another night. The pirate crew grew ever more restless and grim with each passing hour. They no longer sang songs or told stories to pass the time. Instead, they sharpened their blades and set new flints in their pistols. Lacey and the Ratts did their best to keep spirits high, and even tried not to argue so much. But Jim stole away to be by himself more and more often, just to open his box and gaze on the rose thorn every now and again.

At last though, on the evening of the second day, the sturdy ship cut through the waves toward the Devil's Horns. Far away to the east, the sun glowed the orange of a hot coal. It lit the sky with purple flames and cast a golden glow over the waters. The Devil's Horns came into view. Boulders sprouted from the sea in circled rows like a massive maw piercing the waters, large enough to swallow an unsuspecting ship whole. In the middle of those jagged stones, the Devil's Horns rose above the rest, an open gate beckoning Jim to enter.

Dread Steele called to luff the sails and the *Spectre* slowed to a crawl over the waves. All hands gathered on deck. The pirate crew's sharp eyes searched the rocks for the *Sea Spider*, but not a sign of the Cromiers or Splitbeard's ship could be found. All lay quiet about the Devil's Horns.

Captain Steele approached the prow from the main deck. Cornelius sat perched upon his shoulder.

"Perhaps they already sailed through, Captain?" Cornelius suggested. "Perhaps last night?" But Dread Steele breathed in the ocean air and shook his head.

"No, they are still here. I smell a battle on the air – and dangerous men to wage it."

"The Cromiers?" Jim asked, gritting his teeth.

"Indeed," said the Captain.

"Well, I don't see nothin'," George said, squinting hard. "And me and me brothers are pretty good at sniffin' out a trap, Cap'n, I can tell you that!" Steele never took his eyes from the rocks ahead, but gave only a grim nod.

"I believe you, Master Ratt. But if there is one pirate with as great a knowledge of magic as my own, it is Splitbeard. He is a deceiver and master of illusion. When he is near, even your eyes and ears cannot be trusted. Thus you shall all stow yourselves away in my cabin. Cornelius will take you. When the *Sea Spider* appears, we shall wage a fierce fight indeed."

"Hide in the cabin?" Jim tore his eyes from the ever-nearing rocks ahead to glare at the Captain a bit more hotly than he first intended. "But we want to help! Steele and Morgan, isn't that what you said when we fought the Kraken?" Jim did want to help, that much was true. But even more so, that itch was still building up in the back of his mind. The thought of missing yet another chance to employ the rose thorn's magic nearly turned it into a maddening burn. A single, cutting flash of Steele's eyes, however, reminded Jim to whom he spoke.

"I remember what I said. And when we defeat these fiends and pass through the gates to the Veiled Isle, I shall permit you to come along. But until then you will lock yourselves in the cabin until you are instructed to come out. Do not disobey me again! The Corsairs of the *Sea Spider* will show no mercy when they attack!"

"Yes, sir," Jim replied. But he shoved his hands into his pockets and clenched his fists nevertheless.

"Come along now, my young friends," Cornelius said. "If we're not going to be in the battle, I can, at the very least, enthrall you with tales of many others - and there are several, I assure you! Perhaps we might start with the battle of Twelve Tree Island, which actually has hundreds of trees, really. There's a terribly fascinating tale of how it got its name, now that I think about it. It has everything to do with types of bananas. Bananas!"

"Good grief," George muttered. "Now I know I'd rather be in the battle."

Jim begrudgingly followed his friends when Dread Steele stayed him with a heavy hand upon his shoulder.

"Tarry here a moment longer, Jim." Jim took a deep breath, for he detected another lecture at the back of the Captain's tone. "Eager to face the Cromiers in battle, are you?" the Captain asked. He peered down on Jim through the dark gap between his hat's black brim and his cloak's dark collar. Jim looked down at the tops of his shoes. His hands were still in his pockets, and he felt the back of his neck warm just a little.

"They're robbers and murderers, Captain Steele. Shouldn't I be allowed to right their wrongs? Don't I have the right to take revenge?"

Dread Steele released Jim's shoulder. He turned to face the Devil's Horns once more, but his gaze reached far beyond the sharp rocks ahead.

"Do you remember what I said about the storms, Jim? Sometimes even patience can be a storm. There is no worse storm than the one we could have avoided, the one we sail into unprepared. Life is difficult enough without creating more trouble of our own. You have been through many storms already, have you not?"

Jim thought back through everything that had happened to him so far - losing his father, the dangers in London, losing his home. He nodded back to the Captain. "More than I ever wanted."

"Ask yourself this: to reach the shores you seek in your heart, how many storms would you weather? But a few? The best treasures are worth so many more. For myself, I would weather ten thousand storms to reach the far-off shores that I seek. I promise you that once again he names Morgan and Steele shall carry over the ocean waves. If you wish it, we will sail the seas together, seeking adventure and fortune until we find you a new home. But until then, your battle is with patience. Now, get to the cabin with your friends, and be quick about it."

Jim's throat began to ache and his nose began to sting. What good was patience when everything a person had was already gone, he thought to himself. But "Aye, Captain," was all he said, for there was little point in arguing with the Lord of Pirates.

Jim was about to turn on his heel and go when a wrinkle caught his eye - no more than a ripple one might see in the distance on a hot day. It glimmered not from behind or about a rock, but rather, Jim was quite sure, at the heart of one of the boulders themselves.

"What was it, Jim?" Dread Steele said, catching the startled look upon Jim's face. The Captain's quicksilver hand leapt to the hilt of his blade. "What did you see?"

"It was there," Jim said, pointing toward the rock where he had seen the shimmer. "It was like a wrinkle in the air."

"You saw it from behind that rock?"

"No, I...I thought I saw it in the rock itself."

The Captain tightened his grip on his sword. He leaned forward over the prow, staring hard at the rock. Stillness and quiet held over the waters. Beads of sweat prickled upon the back of Jim's neck and on his forehead. In the distance beyond the rocks, the bottom curve of the blood red sun touched the horizon beyond the rocks.

The rock shimmered again. The jagged edges of stone melted into a darkened shadow of mast and sails. The boulder twisted and turned and reformed into the hull of a ship, the iron letters of *Sea Spider* running along her flank. When the magical transformation was made complete, yellow light flashed and white smoke burst from the *Sea Spider's* hull. Thunderous cannon fire roared over the waters.

"Get down!" Steele cried. The Captain threw himself over Jim as the prow exploded in a shower of splinters. The entire ship shook and the mainmast trembled beneath the blows. "Turn us about Mister Gilley and return fire!" Steele roared again. He climbed back to his feet, leaving Jim on the deck with his ears still ringing. Yet even Mister Gilley, master of the wheel, could not turn the *Spectre* about fast enough. The *Sea Spider* had the jump on her and launched another volley over the deck. Barrels burst into bits and shudders shook the ship, throwing the pirate crew on their backs.

"A curse upon Splitbeard and his damnable magic!" Dread Steele cried. "A trickster and a coward he is. He never shows his true face until the last moment. Get us about now, Mister Gilley! Return fire!"

Finally the *Spectre* came about, blasting her cannons at Splitbeard's ship. But the shots had been rushed, and the cannonballs splashed into the waves or sailed over the deck. The *Sea Spider* was not even slowed, and she continued to lurch toward the Devil's Horns.

"Captain Steele!" Jim shouted over the din. "They're headed for the Horns! They've got us turned in the wrong direction and they're going to trap us out here when the sun sets!"

"Never count out Dread Steele and the *Spectre* until all is said and done, lad. Mister Mufwalme!" The Captain shouted. "Another volley if you please – slow them down!" The *Spectre* shook again with cannon fire. Thick, white smoke filled the air, but the blasts did little to impede the *Spider*, and the *Spectre* still sailed on the wrong side of the Devil's Horns. Old Egidio had said that the ship must sail east through the Horns in order to pass onto the Veiled Isle, facing the setting sun. But Jim saw there was no way the mighty ship, stalwart and fast as she may have been, could possibly sail around to the other side and beat the *Sea Spider* through.

"We're not going to make it!" Jim cried. He slammed his fist onto the railings. The Cromiers were going to beat him again. Jim gritted his teeth so hard he could hear them grind in his ears. His skin tingled with heat as though all the blood in his body caught fire at once. But Dread Steele still stood tall and undaunted on the deck.

"Take heart, young Morgan! I did not become Lord of the Pirates watching others perform feats of magic without learning a trick or two of my own. Follow me!" Steele sprinted to the quarterdeck, pausing only to kick aside smashed bits of wood blocking his path.

"Mister Gilly!" the Captain shouted to the portly pirate. Gilly was, as usual, standing tall at the wheel, steering as easily as if out for some fishing on a calm day. "Point us for the Horns, if you will."

"But Captain!" Jim protested. "We have to go through the Horns travelling east if we want to pass into the Veiled Isle!"

"True enough, Jim," Steele said, almost laughing. "But we aren't going to pass through to the Veiled Isle this night - and neither shall the *Sea Spider*. Watch and learn, my boy." From his pocket, Dread Steele withdrew a small pouch. From the pouch he produced a few white feathers, like those fallen from a gull's wings. The Captain rolled the feathers between his hands until the down crumbled to dust. Then he took a deep breath and blew the powder into the *Spectre's* sails.

"Hold on to something!" Steele commanded. "Hold on, all of you, for dear life!" Jim seized one of the few railings not blasted to bits by the *Sea Spider's* cannonball barrage and squeezed his eyes shut...and waited.

Nothing happened.

Jim peeked one eye open.

"Well," he said. "That was rather anticlimac-" The words had not even left his lips when the *Spectre* surged forward as though shoved in the back by a hurricane's hand. Jim's grip loosed from the railing and he tumbled backwards, head over heels as the great ship of the sea roared through the waves. Yet neither Dread Steele nor Mister Gilly so much as tipped backwards. Gilly steered back and forth, avoiding rocks as though they weren't even there while Dread Steele laughed at the top of his lungs. He only grew grim again when he drew his sword.

"Brace for impact! Prepare your hearts for battle, men! We shall take the *Sea Spider* for a prize!" Jim finally got to his feet again as the *Spectre* flew toward the horns. Mister Gilly aimed the ship to pass through the magic gate from the wrong direction and collide head on with *Sea Spider* as she attempted to enter.

"Perhaps you'll hold onto something a little tighter this time, eh, Lord Morgan?" Steele said over his shoulder to Jim. Jim took his advice to heart. He grabbed hold of the railing once more and shut his eyes tight. The two ships slammed into each other with a crack like thunder.

Jim pitched forward and nearly flipped over the railing. His hands burned on the rough wood as he held on for dear life. Dread Steele once again hardly wavered from where he stood, holding forth his sword.

"Draw blades!" the Captain commanded. The metallic ring of cutlasses, knives, and daggers leaping from scabbards echoed in the evening air. A howling battle cry erupted over the two decks and Splitbeard's rough-necked crew poured over the railings and onto the *Spectre*.

"CHARGE!" Steele bellowed. His pirate crew loosed their own cries and ran forward to meet the Corsairs. The clash of men and steel filled the air.

"Get below, Jim! Get below now!" Steele ordered. Then he was off. He leapt down onto the main deck and joined the fray. Jim was halfway down the steps to the captain's quarters when his eyes drifted above the melee and over the sea to the distant horizon. The sun, red as blood, sank deeper and deeper beneath the waves. With it, any chance of reaching the isle that night slowly slipped away.

As Jim shielded his eyes from the crimson glare, he caught sight of the *Sea Spider*, now nothing but a black shape against the burning light of the setting sun. A thought struck him. Jim had seen the Cromiers fight Dread Steele twice now. Both times Bartholomew had been first into battle. The pale captain was never afraid of a fight, not even against Dread Steele. Yet Bartholomew had not come charging over the rails with the other pirates – nor had his father, nor that fiend, Splitbeard.

They were not hiding, Jim suddenly realized. The Schemer - that's what Janus had called Count Cromier in his story. A Schemer would be doing more than cowering – he would be sneaking.

Jim squinted harder in the red sunlight. After a moment of searching, he saw the shadowy shape of a small boat slide into the water from beside the *Sea Spider*. Several silhouetted figures climbed silently aboard. Jim had no need to see their faces. He knew who they were and what they were attempting to do. He had to warn Dread Steele! The Cromiers had to be stopped before -

A desperate idea slipped into Jim's mind, like water running through his fingers. The flute song began to play again in Jim's head. The itch at the back of his mind became a burning whisper.

There is another way, the whisper said. *The Cromiers will row right past* the Spectre *on their way to the Horns. The Red Count and Bartholomew will be together, in the boat – right next to each other. You will be able to see them both together.*

For a moment, Jim tried to fight it. But the voice and the flute song grew too loud. He felt his fingers crawl to his jacket pocket. Before he even knew it had happened, his box found its way into his hands.

TWENTY-TWO

THE ROSE THORN'S MAGIC

Jim turned to climb the steps back to the quarterdeck. From there he would have the best vantage of the Cromiers' boat as they tried to slip past the *Spectre*. The battle raged about the main deck below. Cannon and pistol smoke hovered like a fog and there seemed to be no end to the Corsairs pouring through the smoky mist. Splitbeard's wild pirates shrieked and howled. Pistols cracked and swords clashed. In the center of them all Dread Steele held his ground. He fought four or five Corsairs at once, beating them soundly, until they fell back from him in terror. A squirming twist tied itself in Jim's stomach as watched the brave crew battle so desperately.

"I'm just helping," he told himself. He gritted his teeth and shook his head fiercely to rid himself of the lump in his gut. "Dread Steele and his men can take care of the Corsairs. I'll handle the Cromiers."

Jim slowly climbed the steps, determined to at last finish what he started in the enchanted fog on the beach near his burnt home. But just as Jim was about to reach the quarterdeck, a hand seized him by the shoulder and yanked him back. Jim whirled and raised his hands to fight off whoever it was attempting to stop him. But that someone turned out to be Lacey, and she seemed furious enough with Jim to wage a war of her very own against an army of Corsairs. Cornelius sat upon her shoulder and the Ratts stood behind her, their wide eyes fixed on the mad fight about them.

"Jim Morgan, just what do you think you're doing?" Lacey all but screamed. "I don't know if you noticed, but there's a war going on out here and you're going to get yourself, and all of us, killed! You were supposed to hide in the captain's quarters!"

"I agree, I agree!" Cornelius squawked. "It is madness for you to be out here! Do you not remember the Captain's orders? We must fly to the cabin immediately!"

"There's no time to explain. There's something I have to do!" Jim wrenched himself free from Lacey's grasp and charged back to the quarterdeck, where he could see more clearly over the clouds of white smoke.

"No time for what?" Lacey cried. Jim could hear her and the Ratts running up behind him.

"Get below, all of you!" Jim shouted over his shoulder. He was already scanning the waters below for any sign of the Cromiers. "Get to where it's safe. The Cromiers and Splitbeard are going to sneak through the Devil's Horns before the sun sets and I have to stop them!"

"The Captain! The Captain!" Cornelius cawed. He flapped his wings furiously and flew up to perch on Jim's shoulder. "We must tell the Captain!"

"Listen to him, Jim," Lacey cried. She reached up once more and pulled hard on Jim's sleeve to slow him down. "Tell Captain Steele. He'll know what to do!"

"He's in the middle of a battle, Lacey, in case you hadn't noticed." Jim snapped as he yanked his sleeve from Lacey's grasp. "Besides, I already know what to do. So get back to the cabin and let me do it!"

"We're with you, Jim," George cried, his brothers shouting their agreement beside him. "Tell us what to do, mate, and we'll help!"

But Jim was no longer paying any attention. His father's box had become so heavy in his hands that it was as though it pulled him toward the quarterdeck's railing. The hot fever in Jim's mind was now a runaway flame. All of Jim's thoughts were bent toward turning the tables on the Cromiers. *This is your chance*, the whisper said to him. *This is your chance to finally take something back - to set things right at last.*

Jim skidded to a halt at the quarterdeck's railing, nearly pitching himself into the water as he looked over the side. At first, he saw nothing but crawling tendrils of cannon smoke over the waves. But soft splashes soon slapped the water nearby. From the smoke, just below where Jim stood, came the rowboat, quiet as a ghost in the water as it sneaked past the battle. The light of the setting sun illuminated Count Cromier's crimson curls and Bartholomew's raven-wing hair.

Jim's face flushed so warm that sweat ran down his cheeks and onto his chin. He gripped his father's box tight. The sun was halfway dipped below the horizon's waters and the unsuspecting Cromiers were just below him, with no idea that Jim had spied them out. The moment to strike was now.

"Jim, please!" Lacey cried yet again. If Jim had been listening he would have heard the tears in her voice. "Cornelius can fly to the Captain and tell him! Let's go back down below, please!" Jim's friends pressed closer around him than ever, squeezing him against the railing. But Jim would not be deterred. He opened the lid of his box.

The violet glow cast itself into Jim's eyes from within once more.

An invisible bubble of magic around Jim muted the crashing of the battle and the cries of his friends. Only the whisper in the flute's song grew clearer. It urged Jim over and over to strike.

Jim took the blackened rose stem in his fingers. The heat from the rose surprised him. It burned his fingertips, but he refused to let it go. The Ratts and Lacey still pressed close about him, Lacey still pleading with Jim to listen. But all Jim could see was the glowing rose and the Cromiers in the boat beyond.

Jim fixed the Count and Bartholomew in his sights.

He dropped his father's box and took the rose stem in one hand, the black thorn aflame in violent light.

He pulled the rose back and pictured it all in his mind - he, the victorious hero, the Treasure of the Ocean in his grasp. The Cromiers defeated, locked behind bars with Aunt Margarita.

The flute song reached a crescendo and the rose's heat flared up Jim's arm and into his chest. There was nothing left to stop him.

Jim jabbed the thorn into his left thumb. Drops of blood flowed fast onto the thorn.

The violet light curled back into the rose like a drawn breath. In a great flash it then blasted back out again. The burst of magic left only a wisp of black smoke where the rose had been a moment ago. A white-hot needle of searing pain pierced Jim's hand and he cried out in agony.

"Oh, Jim, what have you done to yourself?" Lacey cried. Then a great many things happened at once.

A ferocious wind rose up over the sea and whipped across the deck. The Ratts and Lacey, who had already pressed tight up against the railing as they shrunk from the battle, were thrown against Jim harder still. The oak railings, weakened by the magical blast from the rose, cracked. The entire section broke away.

Jim and the others pitched overboard.

Down Jim fell, tumbling end over end toward the water. Lacey screamed somewhere to his right. The Ratts cried out somewhere to his left. Cornelius squawked all about his head. Yet all Jim felt was the blinding pain in his hand - even when his head hit the railing that had fallen before them. The water, whipped by the wind, rose over his face. Even as Jim's vision turned to black, the burning fire from the black rose thorn coursed through his body and blocked out all else in the world but pain.

BOOK II

ON THE SHORES
OF THE
VEILED ISLE

ONE

THROUGH THE DEVIL'S HORNS

Jim opened his eyes and found himself lying face first in a pile of wet sand. He coughed violently and spat out a lungful of water. The first thing Jim realized, other than that he was soaked from head to toe, was that his head ached terribly from a nasty bump at his temple. The second thing he realized was that he had no idea where on earth he was. Ocean waves washed onto a yellow sand beach. The shore ran up to a shelf of large boulders. Beyond the rocks, bright green hills rolled inland, dotted with bushes and trees.

Jim pushed himself onto to his hands and knees, wondering if he had just woken from some bizarre dream. He had been in a battle at sea, on a ship amongst a ring of jagged rocks. There had been a black rose, and a voice inside his head urging him to *strike now*. Then he remembered falling - down, down until he hit the water. That was when

169

he had woken. Jim was just guessing what such a dream might mean when a stabbing pain seared his left thumb. The burning spread into the palm of his hand, where it settled and throbbed.

It had not been a dream after all. The battle and the black rose had been real. The pain in Jim's hand would have been proof enough, but a few feet away, the broken railing upon which he had struck his head lay half-buried in the sand. Farther beyond the splintered wood, staring back at him with large, frightened eyes, sat Lacey and the Ratts, as soaked with water and caked in sand as Jim.

"Jim, are you alright?" Lacey asked. "Your head hit the rail so hard. I tried to reach you, but the wind was just blowing and blowing the waves. I thought I lost you."

"Your head sounded like a coconut, mate," George said, brushing sand out of his face.

"Right," Peter said. "An empty coconut!" He and Paul laughed between chokes and coughs of seawater.

"Your head must be as hard as George's to have survived that, Jim," added Paul.

"Hard as a rock!" George bragged. He smiled and wrapped his knuckles against the side of his noggin. "Me and Jim got heads hard as boulders, don't we Jim? The hardest heads there are!"

"It's not a compliment!" Lacey shouted. "Stop making jokes. This is serious." But George and his brothers were already head-butting each other to test George's boast and ignoring Lacey entirely.

"Where are we?" Jim asked.

"We, young Morgan, are on an island," came a caw from above. Cornelius flapped down on the sand between Lacey and Jim. "I've just circled it from above, and as far as I can tell, it is indeed the Veiled Island for which we came searching. And it is a much larger island than I thought it might be from the outset."

"We came through the Devil's Horns?" Jim asked. He turned on his knees in the sand and looked back at the ocean. Sure enough, sitting not a quarter-mile out in the water, two curved stones rose out of the sea to form the gate. But not a single other rock, nor the *Spectre* or *Sea Spider*, could be seen at all.

Jim touched the painful spot on the side of his head and furrowed his brow. "I must have been knocked out for hours and hours. The sun was nearly set and it was all but night when we fell overboard. Now it's early morning. One of you could have at least set me on my back for all that time. I might have drowned!"

"No, Jim," said Lacey. An anxious wrinkle creased her forehead. "It was morning the moment we came through the Devil's Horns. You were only unconscious for a moment or two."

"How is that possible?"

"If this island were simply invisible," said Cornelius. "The *Spectre* would have crashed into it before we even reached the Devil's Horns. But this island is at least ten miles across, filled with forests, rocks, fields, and hills. I think this isle is more than just hidden from the eyes of men. I believe it may be its own world entirely. A magic world."

"Speakin o' magic," said George, holding his head for all the head butting he had done with his brothers. "You used some, didn't you Jim? On the ship, right before we all went tumblin' down. There was this flash and smoke, and then that wind came up outta nowhere. How did you do that? You never told me you knew any magic! Was Dread Steele givin' you extra lessons or somethin'?"

"Magic?" Jim said, feigning surprise. But his throat went dry and Lacey and Cornelius's gazes were suddenly very heavy upon him. So, at last, Jim sighed and confessed the truth.

"I never lost my mother's necklace," he said. His eyes drifted down to the sand. He began drilling a hole in it with one of his fingers to keep from meeting his friends' eyes. "That night, when we came to Morgan Manor and found it all burned to the ground, when I ran away down the beach, there was this old man – a magician or something. He gave me a rose, a magic rose thorn in exchange for the necklace. He said that it would help...he said it would help me get back at the Cromiers for all they'd done to me...to us."

"Oh, Jim," Lacey said. Jim felt an unpleasant heat rush up into his face at the disappointment in her voice. Cornelius, however, refused to let Jim hide his eyes. The raven hopped right under Jim's nose and gave him a black gaze.

"Magic is a dangerous thing, young Morgan. You remember the Vault, do you not? It very nearly killed us both! Then there was the amulet – which tempted you to abandon your friends, and afterwards devoured the King of Thieves whole when it shattered! What possessed you to again take hold of such dark enchantments?"

"Now hold on a sec," George said, taking up for Jim. "It worked didn't it? I mean, those stinkers, the Cromiers and that blighter Splitbeard, woulda got on this island and done who knows what if Jim hadn't done that trick. I just wish you'd a told us, mate, that's all." There was a little hurt in George's voice, but Jim was glad enough to have at least one of his friends on his side.

"It's supposed to give me the chance to turn the tables on the Cromiers – to get revenge for what they've done."

"Perhaps," Cornelius said. "But at what cost? For good or for ill, my boy, magic always costs something, doesn't it? Let us take a look at your hand."

Jim hesitated, keeping his fist balled up by his side. He was partly afraid to show Cornelius and Lacey, but he even more terrified to look himself.

"Show us, Jim," Lacey said quietly. Jim pulled his aching hand up from the sand and slowly unfurled his fingers. George sucked in a sharp breath between his teeth. Lacey gasped. Cornelius let out a long caw and even Jim's stomach sank deep into his gut.

On Jim's thumb, where the thorn had struck, a deep blight darkened his skin - black as pitch. From the wound, dark tendrils crawled into his palm like vines on a wall.

"Does it hurt?" Lacey asked.

"It hurts something awful," Jim admitted. "Is it bad, Cornelius?" he asked. For the first time since Jim had known the bird, Cornelius

Darkfeather seemed at a loss for words. He shook his beaked head and ruffled his feathers.

"I don't know, lad. I don't know."

Jim stared hard at his hand with a queasy knot in his stomach. He was about to ask Cornelius if the bird knew any tricks to dull the pain, when loud shouting suddenly echoed down the beach. It was Peter and Paul. The wound momentarily forgotten, Jim, George, and Lacey leapt to their feet and ran toward the hollering. But drawing closer, they heard obnoxious laughter punctuating the shouts and found Peter and Paul leaping in circles around a row of grey rocks in the sand.

"Jim, George!" Peter shouted, laughing at the top of his lungs. "Let's have another head butting contest!"

"Right," said Paul. "You two go first and we can know for sure if your heads really are hard as rocks or not."

Jim had no idea what Peter and Paul were talking about until he approached the stones. The gray rocks were not rocks at all. They were statues - statues of five men running toward the water. Their mouths were stretched into frightened maws. Their eyes were open wide and staring.

"Oh, they're awful!" Lacey cried. She stepped back from the statues and dropped her gaze to her feet. "Their faces look so real. Who would make such horrible statues?"

"I'll tell you what's horrible," Paul said. "This one's got a hanger on his nose!" Paul pointed to a bit of moss growing inside one of the statue's nostrils. Peter, of course, pretended to pick it, which sent George and Paul into hysterics.

"That's disgusting, Peter!" Lacey shouted.

"It does seem strange, does it not?" Cornelius said, flapping down atop one of the statue's heads. "Five statues just planted here in the middle of the beach? As I surveyed the island from above I saw no building, temples, or signs of civilization at all. It's as though these sculptures were crafted, and with great skill I might add, then just left here on their own."

While the others joked and laughed, an appalling thought struck Jim. His heart dropped like a stone within him. "Stop playing with the statues, right now!" he shouted. "Don't touch them!"

"Oh, come off it, Jim!" George chided. "They're just statues."

"No, they're not. At least they weren't. I think...I think they were real people."

The three Ratts stopped laughing immediately. Peter yanked his hand away from the statue's nose as though his fingers had been burned. Even Cornelius leapt from statue's head and flapped to Jim's shoulder.

"When we were in Shelltown," Jim continued. "Do you remember what Egidio said about this island? He said it was protected by a curse. He said if you stay on the island for longer than one day and one night, you would be imprisoned here for all time. Don't you see? These were sailors." Jim's mouth went dry as the sand beneath his feet. "This is what happens when you don't leave the island in time. This is how the island imprisons you forever."

TWO

THE LIZARD'S WARNING

Jim and friends stood before the statues, silent as the grave.

"So," said George. "It's already mid-mornin' here on this magic island. And you're sayin' that if we don't get back through them Horns before it rises again, we'll be statues just like these poor blokes?"

Jim nodded. A cold shiver shook him in spite of the morning sun.

"And someone'll come and pick the moss bogeys from my nose?" Paul asked. He tried to smile, but his lips trembled.

"Well, as much as I hate to be the bearer of more bad news, my friends, our situation may yet be more dire." Cornelius cawed. "When I flew over the island I saw another boat set upon the shore a mile or so down the beach. Footprints led away from the vessel and up to the rocks." Jim gritted his teeth. Pain lanced through his hand. He knew to whom the boat belonged.

"The Cromiers and Splitbeard. They're on the island too. And they have the map!"

"What do we do?" Lacey asked, grabbing hold of Jim's arm. "Maybe we should wait here for Captain Steele to come through the Horns? Or go back through now and have the Captain come back with us. Surely he'll know what to do!"

"Hmm, all of those would seem like wonderful ideas, young lady," said a voice, crackly and dry as two stones rubbing together. "But you would be waiting a long, long, long time. All the way till the sun set and rose again, and the five of you turned to stone with a flash of light and a puff of smoke."

"Who was that?" Jim cried.

"Show yourself, giver of unasked advice!" Cornelius shrieked. "We are five who have come through magical barriers, deathly traps, and battles with monsters of the deep! We will not hesitate to face you if you prove yourself a villain!"

"Oh, I am no villain, sirs and lady," said the voice in its slow, grainy rhythm. "In fact, I do believe if you were to add up my virtues and subtract my faults, all that would remain would be a pair of eyes. And these eyes have seen much on the Veiled Isle. Step around those poor stone souls and see for yourselves."

Bundled up against one another, Jim and his friends crept down the beach toward the voice. Just beyond the five statues sat a wide, flat stone, and upon the stone rested a long, green-scaled lizard. It was bathing in the morning sun, saggy neck craned up toward the sky and spiny tail curled up behind him.

"A talking lizard!" Peter exclaimed. Seeing that the lizard seemed to move as slowly as it spoke, Jim and the others relaxed a little and even risked a few steps closer to the rock upon which the creature sat.

"How many talking animals are there?" said George, exasperated. "I never heard no animal speak until old Darkfeather here. Now they're poppin' up all over. It's just silly!"

"I know a great many enchanted beasts in our world," Cornelius said. "We run in the same circles, really. Once you've met one talking animal, you are bound to meet more in due time. Though I must say, I haven't had the pleasure of your acquaintance, Mr..."

"Hmm...there may be no word for my name in the human tongues, good sirs and lady," said the lizard. "And I doubt your rather short tongues could pronounce it in lizard-speak – as it is rather tricky. So for now, hmm, call me Twisttail, and it is a pleasure to meet you all." The lizard lifted one claw from the rock in an agonizingly slow wave. He then flicked his forked tongue twice, which seemed to be the only movement he could make with any speed at all. "Hmm, and I would say the reason you have not heard of me, master raven," continued Twisttail. "Is that I am not from your world. I am from this one, good sirs and lady."

"It would normally be good to meet you, Twisttail," said Jim, shoving his left hand in his pocket and trying to ignore the pulsing ache. "But my friends and I are here for something very important, and there are some very dangerous people that are here for that same something as well. Now, we were talking about waiting for more of our crew to come ashore, or going back to get them, but you said we'd be waiting a long time. What did you mean?"

"Hmm, I'm not sure I fully understand how it all works myself, good sirs, for I am no master of magic," replied Twisttail. "But if you crane your short, little necks back round toward the ocean and look closely at yonder stones, you will see red light shining through the Devil's Horns. Always it is this way when men pass through into our world. And always it remains until they leave again."

Jim and the others turned back toward the sea and stared hard at the Devil's Horns. Indeed Jim made out a faint reddish glow between the rocks, and a smattering of glittering crimson upon the waves. It was the red light of the setting sun from his world, Jim realized. His shoulders slumped as he worked out the implications in his head.

"The time on this island isn't the same as the time back in our world," Jim said, as much to himself as everyone else.

"Oh, yes, that makes total sense, Jim," George said. "To no one! What exactly are you sayin'?"

"I'm saying we're on our own, George!" Jim tried to hide the intense pain in his hand and clenching his teeth quite hard to bear it. "I think a whole day and night will pass on this island before the sun even sets in ours. When we cross back through the Devil's Horns, it will be just the same moment we left. Right in the middle of the battle. We have only that much time to find the cave before the Cromiers and Splitbeard do, and then to get back through the Devil's Horns."

"Or we'll be turned to stone!" Lacey cast a nervous glance at the five statues beside them on the beach.

"I'm afraid the odds of finding the shell in but a day and a night are stacked in our enemy's favor," Cornelius cawed, flapping his wings and shaking his head.

"Well," said George. "That all sounds pretty bad, don't it?" But even then that irrepressible, Ratt Brother's smile split his face. "Good thing we're here or you all'd be in a real pinch, wouldn't you? Me and Peter and Paul have gotten outta plenty of scrapes worse than this one back in London, I can tell you that!"

"What scrapes, exactly, threatened to turn you all into stone and involved ancient magical artifacts, George?" Lacey folded her arms and glared at the eldest Ratt.

George paused for a long moment. "Well, maybe not exactly like this one, Lacey...but close, really close. Just trust me, alright, there is nothing to worry about, at all."

"We're doomed," cried Lacey.

"Despair not, fair Lacey," said Cornelius. "We do have at least one clue, don't we? Old Egidio said that Lindsay Morgan would have most likely hidden the shell in a cave beneath the mountain at the center of the island. I am sure I saw this mountain when I was flying overhead. If we make it there, perhaps we might yet find this cave."

"Hmm...did you say a cave, good master raven?" the lizard interjected, having moved not one inch the entire breadth of the conversation. His tongue flicked rapidly in and out of his mouth. "I have lived on this island for many, many, many years, good sirs and lady. Hmm…and the majority of them spent on this very rock, now that I think about it. But when I was a younger lizard I traveled here and there across the island. There is only one cave that Twisttail knows lies beneath the mountain. But if you can avoid that place, good sirs and lady, you would be wise to do so. Hmmm…it is a dark and dangerous hole, home to some ancient evil, so lizards even older than I say."

Jim swallowed hard. His head still ached and the burning in his hand showed no signs of subsiding. But he hadn't pricked his finger with that blackened rose to come this far and fail. He would not give up this quest without a fight.

"We have no choice, Twisttail," said Jim. "We must find the cave. Do you know the way? A shortcut perhaps?"

"Hmm, I've not been to the black cave for many, many years, good sirs and lady," said the lizard. He shifted his long head ever so slightly as though thinking quite hard. His dragon-like tongue lanced in and out between his teeth. "Yet, I may be able to set you upon the right path. Hmm…walk down this beach for nearly a mile until you pass a hill topped by a dead and leafless tree. Beyond that hill lies the crags. There is a path through the crags that leads to a field called the Sea of Tall Grass. The tall grass will hide you all the way to the River of the Mountain's Tears. If you are able to ford the river, the Dark Forest waits for you on the other side. There is a trail through the forest that leads to the foot of the mountain. There will be found the entrance to the cave, good sirs and lady."

"That seems like a far way to go in one day and one night," Jim said. His heart sank a little further at the thought of all the places the lizard had listed between the beach and the mountain.

"It seems especially far, Master Lizard," Cornelius cawed loudly from Jim's shoulder. "When considering that I saw from the sky a vast stretch of rolling hills, just beyond these boulders. These fields would seem gentler travelling all the way to the mountain at center of the island, they would, they would."

"No, no, no!" roared the lizard. The green creature thrashed so suddenly upon the rock, that it took the clan quite by surprise. They jumped back in a protective knot, Peter and Paul sticking their heads between Jim and George's arms. "Go not through the Field of Lights!" cried Twisttail. His little chest heaved in and out from his brief exertion and his pink tongue flashed like lightning.

"Whatever happens, good sirs and lady," said the Lizard, slowly regaining his composure, "risk not that awful place. Hmm, many men have been lured by the easy path and ensnared by the beckoning glow. Evil spirits inhabit those fields! They live only to ensnare poor and hapless travelers like yourselves. You must go around, good sirs and lady. It is the only way!"

Jim looked at the lizard for a long moment, thinking hard. Twisttail's way seemed so long, and the cave so far away. But what choice did they have? The sun was already travelling quickly from morning to noon.

"We have no choice," said Jim, with a resigned sigh. "We take the lizard's path." The clan thanked Twisttail for his help and set off down the beach at once. But as they went, Jim snuck a glance at his aching hand. The black tendrils had already crawled a little farther down his thumb, slowly inching their way across his hand.

THREE

IN THE SHADOW OF THE CRAGS

"**A**nd so," pronounced Cornelius from Jim's shoulder, stretching his wings in the morning warmth. "That was how Frederick Nine Fingers became Freddy Sevens, and also how we escaped the Marauders of Malta. Hopefully I haven't done the old boy injustice in my story. Freddy really was a fairly decent pirate, you know, especially when it came to crossing blades with the enemy. But manning the cannons was obviously not his cup of tea, was it?" Cornelius cackled to himself. He held his belly with his wings as though his own story had been the funniest thing he had ever heard.

The children had been walking down the beach for nearly an hour. Rows of large boulders barred their way from the hills and fields Twisttail had warned them to avoid. The morning sun crept ever closer to noon. Cornelius had decided to pass the time telling some sea stories. This began as a charming idea, but many of the tales really were quite alarming and hardly did the clan's confidence any favors.

"Blimey, Darkfeather," George said tiredly, kicking at the sand with his toes. "How many stories do you know, anyway?"

"Oh, countless tales from countless adventures, Master Ratt! I could regale with you epics from each of the Seven Seas seven times over."

"Oh," said Peter as George groaned. "I was hoping you were going to say like eight or something…you know, like a more manageable number."

"I think he's told eight already, Pete," Paul said, picking up a stone and throwing into the water.

"Oh no, lads!" The raven cawed with delight, completely oblivious to the Ratts' apparent boredom. "I haven't even gotten to the really delectable ones yet. I was actually going to continue poor Frederick's saga and tell you how he went from being Freddy Sevens to simply Fred the Stump. Honestly he was probably the unluckiest bloke I ever knew."

"Oh dear," said Lacey. "That sounds awful!"

"If we become statues it's gonna look like I turned to stone from boredom," said George. This sentiment earned him a reproachful glare from Lacey and threatened to set off yet another argument between the two of them.

For those who have never walked a long way through sand, it sounds like a rather pleasant time, especially in the fair morning weather as was on the island that day. But it is exhausting work after a while, and the five friends were starting to grow grumpy with one another. Jim, however, was only paying half attention to either the raven's stories or the Ratts' wisecracks. Instead, he fixed his eyes straight down the beach. His thoughts were clamped as tightly on the coming day as his gaze upon the way ahead.

A mile or so behind them was the Cromiers' rowboat, run up onto the sand. The sight of it had set the clan's nerves on edge, but it had been worse by far for Jim. Every time he pictured Bartholomew

Cromier's pale face or Count Cromier's crimson curls, his jaw tightened and his left hand ignited in pain. The flute song would play in his thoughts and darkness would seize his mood.

Jim fought all this as best he could. Faced with the dangers of the Veiled Isle, he wanted only to see his friends safely from the shores of the cursed place. But as the black vines snaked their way onto Jim's hand, so black thoughts of revenge wound deeper into his mind. But just when George and Lacey nearly came to blows, and Cornelius kept trying to distract them with his story, Jim's unwavering stare finally fell upon the dead tree Twisttail had described.

"Look!" he cried. Only a half-mile down the beach, a hill had come into view. At its top stood a large oak, dead as a doornail. The leafless branches reached to the sky like boney fingers on a skeleton's hand.

The clan ran to the bottom of the hill and skirted around the base. On the far side, just as Twisttail promised, the grass and beach gave way to row upon row of gray stone ridges. These were the crags, a crisscrossing, winding knot of rock. Though not a single cloud marred the sapphire sky, as the company approached the entrance to the rocky maze, a shadow fell over the beach. A prickle of gooseflesh crawled over Jim's skin. The ache in his left hand began to reach into his arm, beyond his wrist. So Jim shoved his fist even deeper into his pocket, as though that might ease the pain.

"Just beyond these rocks should be the field of long grass Twisttail told us to follow," he said, though he could not help but frown at the grim look of the path between the rocks.

"Are we sure this is right?" asked Lacey. "I know Mister Twisttail was trying to help, but I don't know. There's something about this that feels wrong, Jim."

"Maybe it in't supposed to feel right, you know?" George offered. "Like in all them stories. The right way is supposed to be the hard way, right?"

"There is a difference, young Master Ratt," said Cornelius. "Between a way being challenging and difficult, and a way being dark and wrong."

The group stood there for a long moment. Jim felt his friends beginning to back away from the path between the hill and the crags. It did seem dark down that way, and cold, Jim thought. But the Cromiers were out there, ahead of him, and armed with the map. Perhaps they neared the cave even as he and his friends stood here, afraid to move forward. Between the ache in his hand and the dire thoughts in his head, Jim saw no other choice.

"Come on, you lot!" he called over his shoulder. "It's already noon and we used more than a whole hour coming down this beach. We only have the rest of today and tonight to find our way, so there's no turning back now."

"Are you sure, my boy? Are you sure?" Cornelius whispered into Jim's ear.

"Sure or not, we're wasting time just standing still. The Cromiers are out there, Cornelius. And I'm going to catch them." Jim took the first steps alone, but one at a time he heard Lacey and the Ratts fall in behind him. Together they entered the shadowy path beneath the crags.

The lifeless gray cliffs loomed like tall towers over the clan's heads. They warded off all sunlight and warmth, and allowed only a gray chill to settle and brew down in the deep ravines. The pathway between the rocks reminded Jim of the alleyways and backstreets of London - dark, dirty, and possessed of more than a hint of danger. Every once in a while, a few traces of blue snuck between the cracks above, but otherwise the shadows clung tight about Jim and his friends. Faces seemed to appear in the stony walls, laughing at the clan like gargoyles in the rock.

"Jim, I don't like this way," Lacey said at last. "I keep expecting the rocks to reach out and drag me into the shadows. I'd almost rather have dealt with those lights Mr. Twisttail told us about than risk losing our way down here."

"You heard what the lizard said about those lights," Jim answered. "They're evil spirits! In fact, I hope the Cromiers and Splitbeard did go that way, and I especially hope they all got snatched up by them!"

"Jim Morgan, how terrible!"

"It would be no more than they deserve, Lacey." Jim shivered as the words left his lips. As the day had worn on, an oppressive cold had begun to seep into his bones. His hand ached worse with each passing hour. Jim was afraid to pull his fist from his pocket. He could feel the black vines snaking their way toward his wrist.

"Well, I dunno about those lights or nothin'," said George, walking with his brothers in a tight knot just behind Jim and Lacey. "But as long as old Darkfeather keeps us straight, I'll be glad to get out of these rocks, that's for sure."

"You said it, Georgie," Peter agreed.

"I don't like dealin' with no trouble that you can't snatch, pick, or con your way out of," Paul added, staring warily about the stone walls. Nearly right on cue, a cawing came from above. Cornelius flapped down through the rocks and came to land on Jim's shoulder. With one black wing he pointed to a turn just up ahead on the path.

"This way, this way! Two lefts and three rights around the next few towers of stone should keep us moving in the right direction, my friends." Cornelius had been flying ahead and looking at the crags from above for the last two hours, guiding Jim and his friends to the other side.

"How far in are we in, Cornelius?" Jim asked the raven in a whisper. Whether he wanted to admit it to Lacey and George or not, he hoped more than anything that the end of this dark, twisting path drew close.

"Nearly halfway there, my boy. But be thankful you have my eyes and my wings. These crags are nothing short of a maze. Woe to the one who loses his way amongst them. A man could be lost for days and never come close to finding his way to the other side."

"What's that about being lost?" Lacey interrupted.

"We're not lost, Lacey, so stop eavesdropping on other people's conversations!" Jim snapped. Even as Jim heard his own voice, he wondered why it sounded so harsh. The heavy cold he'd begun to feel pressed upon him. He felt it in his chest and on his shoulders. Every time his hand burned anew, the cold deepened its hold on the rest of his body. It bit into his bones and made him so much more tired and dreary. Instead of apologizing for his harsh tone, Jim simply said: "Don't worry, Lacey, we just need to get through these ravines and then that forest. Once we get to that cave and find the shell, we'll get off this island and everything will be fine."

Cornelius harrumphed in Jim's ear, poking at him with his wing to encourage a bit more kindness than that to his friend. Then the raven flapped back and sat himself on Lacey's shoulder instead, to offer a few calming words and smooth over the moment of fear.

"I was saying nothing of the sort about being lost, sweet Lacey. I was actually just recalling the time that Dread Steele and I were forced to face the Minotaur's Maze on Crete...yes the very one from the old tales! It was no easy trick without a spool of string, I can tell you that!"

"Not another story," George whined under his breath.

"I like your stories, Mr. Cornelius," Lacey said. Jim could practically hear her glaring at George as she spoke. "They're the only cheerful things we have under these horrible rocks."

"George," Paul said, laughing to himself. "If we all turn to stone on this island, Cornelius has to have his mouth open and you've gotta be pluggin' your ears with your fingers, like this!" Paul demonstrated and Peter exploded into laughter at this suggestion. But Lacey stomped her foot on the ground and unloaded on the younger Ratts, bringing the small party to a halt.

"Stop talking about that! It's dreadful! And besides, we're not going to turn to stone, are we Mr. Cornelius?"

"Of course not," said the raven. "With me as your guide, we'll be out of these rocks in no time." Yet Jim could plainly hear a note of uncertainty in Cornelius's usually sure voice.

"Well, if we do turn to stone," said George, who never knew when to quit while he was ahead. "Lacey should make sure she freezes in mid-stomp with her finger up in the air so that everyone can see what a nag she was in real life!"

That was the last straw. Lacey balled up a fist. Her face lit up a bright red and her eyes flashed a furious blue. She was clearly ready to shut George up with a swing at his jaw. This was the last thing they needed now, Jim thought. His hand began to burn again and the cold shook him hard, getting him angrier and angrier the longer they dawdled in the ravines.

"Oh, would all of you just please shut it!" Jim hissed. He stalked back into the middle of his friends, hands on his hips. "I don't care if we tell stories or walk as quiet as ghosts. I also don't care if you lot want to make sure you're all standing on our heads when you turn to stone! I, for one, am not going to turn to stone. I'm going to find that shell in this cave and I'm going to use it to set things right and put those Cromiers in their place! So just be quiet for a few minutes, so I can think straight and get us out of here!"

Jim's friends stared at him with wide eyes, though that hardly bothered Jim just then. He was feeling quite good for having made his point so soundly, and was just in the process of spinning sharply about on his heel to march onward, when a loud voice echoed down the rocky corridor behind him.

"Well, that's got to be the worst idea I've ever heard! Doomed to failure it is!"

Jim stopped dead in his tracks. A dark scowl burrowed even deeper onto his face. He spun back around, one finger pointed into the air, ready to say something more to George, Lacey, or whoever had just—

Yet before Jim could begin his tirade, he noted the wide-eyed looks on his friends' faces were no longer directed at him. Rather, they were pointed in every other direction about the gloomy rocks.

The voice had belonged to someone else.

FOUR

THE SISTERS OF THE ISLE

"**O**cy, you're never wantin' to try anythin' new! Not never! If it were up to you, we'd do the same blasted nothins, talk about the same blasted nonsense, and eat the same blasted food until we died and turned to dust from boredom, you bossy old hen!"

A second voice had joined the first, and Jim and his friends frantically searched for any sign of their owners. Finding none, the clan threw themselves into a deep crack in one of the rock walls to hide. Yet, from one end of the stone corridor to the other, not a soul could be seen amongst the shadows, though the voices carried on as loudly as they from the start.

"Well it is up to me, Celia, you whiny old crow. Me and Ally like doin' the same thing every day, and don't get bored from it one bit,

189

do we, Ally? If were up to you, Celia, we'd probably end up dinner for some sea monster or rolled up on the beach, soakin' wet from some rogue wave, at the mercy of crabs and seagulls!"

"Ally does too get bored, don't you Ally?"

Anger shook in both of the voices. Jim could tell it was a corker of an argument, though it was somewhat muffled and echoed. The voices were bouncing off the walls from the other side of one of the crags. On top of that, there was something else about those voices, Jim thought - something not altogether right.

"Besides," continued the first voice, named Ocy, from what Jim had heard. "I'm not talkin' about movin' the whole bleedin' nest, for cryin' out loud! All I want to do is add some fish to our dinner, that's all! We could catch some easy, I know we could!"

"Hmm, fish would be nice, alright," said a third voice, though far less angry and a tad flightier that the others. "But I would just be happy if we could find some more glitteries for our collection. Haven't found any glitteries in what seems like forever, have we?"

"There ain't no more glitteries, Ally!" growled the second voice, who's name apparently, was Celia. "You found 'em all and there ain't no more to be found! And besides, me and Ocy wasn't even talkin' about glitteries, we was talkin' about dinner and the bone-headed idea Ocy has to go fishin'! Fishin', she says! We all remember what happened last time we tried that, don't we? Cause there was four of us at one point, now weren't there? You both know that wild boar and wild deer is what we got for huntin' on this island. So wild boar and wild deer is what we'll be gettin' for dinner!"

With that, something long and white came hurtling over a nearby crag and landed with a plop on the path in front of Jim and his friends. Lacey gasped. Paul's cheeks blew up like a puffer fish. Peter and George both went a shade of greenish-yellow. A queasy wave rose up the back of Jim's throat. A long bone, glistening wet and covered in ragged shreds of raw meat, lay not arm's length from where the clan hid.

Jim and George looked first at each other and then at Peter and Paul. At once, the four of them, without so much as a word, stole out

190

from the crack in the rocks and snuck toward the next turn in the path between the crags. Lacey all but tore the sleeves off Jim and George's shirts as she tugged to hold them back, and Cornelius waved his black wings in silent desperation. But curiosity had ensnared the boys' senses and there was no dissuading them.

If Jim's stomach had turned a circle at the sight of the first bone, it was now doing somersaults in his gut. Hundreds of skeletons littered the ground, picked clean of every scrap of meat and piled halfway up the crag walls. Boar husks and deer antlers protruded from skulls. Rib cages lay stacked one atop another. Worse still, amongst the bones, the empty eye sockets of men's skulls stared back at Jim. The scraps of what had once been their hats and clothes lay in heaps about them.

Another bone dropped down into the pile with a clatter. Jim followed its path up to a mound of sticks, twigs, and straw piled into a nest amongst the rocks. Hunkered there, three of the largest birds Jim had ever seen continued their argument.

But these were no birds. Dull blue feathers, nearly black at the tips, ran from their wings all the way to the end of their tail feathers. Black nails tipped their claws. At the top of their long, vulture-like necks, where there should have been beaked, bird snouts, sat the faces of three women. They were hideous and cruel, with teeth long as needles, matted hair the color of burnt straw, and golden eyes twice as wide across as any man's. Jim had only seen drawings of such creatures in Phineus's schoolbooks – harpies.

"Well I'm tired of boar and deer, Celia!" shrieked Ocy. She spread her wings and stamped her claws in the nest's straw. "I want somethin' new! I WANT SOME FISH!"

"WE AIN'T GOIN' FISHIN'!" Celia raked her claws along the rock wall. Sparks rained down into the pile of bones cobbled beneath the nest.

"I think," said Ally, the smallest of the harpies, "that if we all just go find some glitteries, we'll all be much happier today, don't you? It's been so long since we found any glitteries." She pointed with one wing to another ledge on the crag. An enormous collection of spyglasses, chains, cutlasses, pistols, coins, and jewels sat heaped in a massive pile, indeed glittering in the dim light.

"THERE AIN'T NO MORE GLITTERIES, ALLY!" both Celia and Ocy screamed at their friend, who shrank back even farther toward the crag wall.

"There ain't no more glitteries because there ain't no more men on this island, you dull bird," Celia added. "We ate them all that didn't turn to stone!" But at that thought, Ocy froze as though she had been struck by icy lightning. Her wings curled back toward her body and her eyes went round and distant.

"Oh, Celia, now that you've said it, I'll finally admit to what's been plaguin' me. I ain't really wantin' to go fishin' I ain't. I ain't even bored of doin' the same thing day after day, I ain't. What I miss...what I truly miss...is the taste of man flesh! We ain't had it in so long!"

"O-o-oh," replied Celia. She ruffled her feathers, the same dazed expression on her face. "The most delectable, raw, tasty dish I've ever had, ever, ever, ever! It 'as been *so* long, 'as it not, Ocy? Just right with a dash of sea salt, it is. You're right, you're right, you're right, I do miss it so, I do!"

Then all three harpies tittered and cackled and pranced about in their nest. They were all but watering at the mouths and crowing for just one taste of wayward pirate to satisfy their longing.

Well, that was all Lacey, Cornelius, and the Ratt Brothers needed to hear. Three giant harpies looking for a snack was too much for even their stouthearted courage. All four of them pulled Jim away from the crag's edge, pointing frantically back the way that had come.

Jim shook his head and jabbed his own thumb further down the path.

Lacey crossed her arms over her chest and absolutely burned holes in Jim's face with her eyes.

But Jim just gritted his teeth and felt his face flush. The cold in his arms and legs sank deeper and deeper into his bones. As he shook his head one more time, the piercing burn redoubled and stabbed the palm of his hand like a knife. Jim seized his wrist in agony. He dropped to his knees and watched helplessly as the black tendrils crested over his wrist.

Lacey and George caught Jim and supported him until the worst of the pain passed. When he finally came back to his senses, however, the first thing he noticed was how soundless the ravine had become. The harpies were no longer cackling and tittering.

The Ratt Clan waited with bated breath. One of the creatures finally spoke again.

"Ocy, do you smell that?"

"Yes, Celia, I do." Jim could hear Ocy licking her chops. "It came up all of the sudden. Not a pleasant odor, but on the back of it...just a hint...the smallest hint of...of..."

"Man flesh!" the three harpies cried together. The next sound Jim heard was the flapping of great wings lifting off from the nest. Three screams followed, echoing down the ravines like a thousand shattering windows.

"Run!" Jim cried from his knees.

The harpies erupted over the crag walls. Their wings darkened what little remained of the blue sky above Jim's head. Lacey and George yanked Jim onto his feet and tore after Peter and Paul, who were already racing through the ravines. They dashed left and right at random, using all the skills and tricks they'd learn from a life on the run from the law.

"This is like boltin' from the nuns at St. Anne's or the King's Men in London," Peter shouted, holding his hat on his head as he ran.

"Yes, Peter," George agreed, craning his neck to try and see where the harpies would dive from next. "But those blokes couldn't fly, could they?"

"I know," said Paul. "It's like a nightmare...only realer...and louder!"

"Oh, just shut it, you three, and run!" shouted Lacey.

"Cornelius," Jim said. He cradled his left hand in his right as the children dove and hit the dirt, only just avoiding a harpy's outstretched claws. The pain was digging deep inside his forearm now. It radiated all the way into his chest, mixing with the cold and stealing the breath from his lungs. Large drops of sweat rolled down Jim's face. "Do you remember the way out of here? Do you remember how far it is?" Jim's breaths grew ragged. He desperately hoped the raven would say not far. But Jim could tell by the Cornelius's face that the answer was not good.

"I don't know, I don't know! I looked only a little bit ahead each time! But we must keep going north! North is the way out!"

"I can barely tell right from left down here, Cornelius!" Jim cried, but there was no time for discussion. Two of the harpies barreled down the ravine, aiming right for the clan.

"Scatter!" George cried.

Jim, Lacey, and Cornelius rolled to the right while the Ratts dove to the left. All of them pressed against the crag walls as the harpies blew past. The outstretched wings dragged along the rocks. On one side they caught Lacey in the shoulder and threw her to the ground. On the other side they dumped George against the ravine wall, knocking the wind from his lungs.

"Lacey, George!" Jim did his best to help Lacey to her feet. She gripped her shoulder in pain and her face was white as a sheet.

"I'm alright," she managed. But Jim could tell right away that George would not be so quick to recover. His brothers had managed to sit him up, but his face was nearly purple as he fought for air.

Jim looked up between the cracks above his head. The harpies had regrouped in the sky. Gathered together, they circled back as one. This time there would be no escape.

"Remember, Jim Morgan," Cornelius whispered in Jim's ear, stretching out his wing and patting Jim on the back of the head. "You must weather the storms to reach the shore – but not all storms can be fought with anger. Head north through the crags. If you wish to reach the Sea of Tall Grass, head north!"

"Cornelius, what are you doing?" Jim asked. But the bird did not answer. He flapped his wings and launched himself into the air.

"Cornelius, no!" Jim called after the raven. A sick feeling roiled in his stomach as he heard his friend caw his avian war cry.

"Back you devils! I, Cornelius Darkfeather, wave rider and vault breaker flies to meet you! Preolium!"

"Mister Cornelius, come back!" Lacey screamed.

Jim knew Cornelius was buying them time to run. He also knew he needed to run if there was any hope of escape. But his legs grew suddenly numb and refused to obey his commands.

"Come on, come on!" Peter said. He pulled George to his feet, the eldest Ratt sucking in deep breaths.

"We gotta run, mates!" Paul added, taking Jim and Lacey both by the hand. They started to move, one step at a time, but Jim could not tear his eyes from the sky. One dark shape whirled and darted amongst the three harpies. But the battle in the air ended only moments after it began.

The children rounded two or three more corners. Jim and Lacey helped each other along and Peter and Paul supported George between them. The harpies were on top of them again in only a matter of seconds. The great wings pounded like wicked heartbeats just over their shoulders. The harpies' snapping teeth punctuated their hunting cries.

Jim held onto some hope of escape for as long as he could - until the five friends rounded a turn and ran straight into a dead end.

An iron grasp seized Jim from behind. Lacey screamed. Then Jim's breath was knocked from his lungs as he was hurled to the ground. A hideous face, jaws open wide and teeth glistening, leered at him from above.

FIVE

THE BROTHERS RATT VERSUS THE SISTERS THREE

Ocy, the biggest of the three harpies, pinned Jim beneath her. She grasped one arm in each talon and glared down on Jim with huge, hungry eyes. All Jim could do was cough and sputter where he lay, desperate to catch his breath.

Celia, the other large harpy, stood beside her smaller sister, Ally. Together they blocked Lacey and the Ratts in the dead-end ravine. A trio of red slashes decorated Celia's left cheek. Beneath her claw, one long nail pierced a small, black wing. There lay the still, mangy form of Cornelius Darkfeather.

"Mister Cornelius, say something! Mister Cornelius!" Lacey was crying now. Tears rolled down her cheeks as she pleaded with Cornelius to reply. But the raven neither moved nor spoke.

"Hard to catch, these ones," Ocy said from above Jim's face. A long slather of drool dangled from her teeth just above Jim's nose. "Fast and small and not givin' up as easily as the fat, old pirates from before."

"But less meat than the fat, old pirates from before," said Ally. Her head bobbed up and down on her long neck as she examined the Ratts and Lacey. "Though I will say that was fun, weren't it? Haven't had that much fun huntin' in years! It's a pity there's only a few of them... and so scrawny at that."

"Would have caught 'em faster if not for this disgusting flying traitor!" Celia spat. She pressed Cornelius's body hard to the ground with her claw, growling furiously. The bright red cuts on her face trickled with blood. "Helpin' the man-children and fightin' against us? Humans are liars and fools. They have no honor like the creatures of the sky. Meat or no meat, I will crush his bones betwixt me teeth!"

"No!" Lacey shrieked. "Leave him alone, please! Just leave him alone!"

"Silence!" Ocy roared. She squeezed tight and pinched Jim's arms in her talons. Jim winced beneath her iron grasp. For some reason, though, as the harpy squeezed his arm until it went numb, his mind cleared just a little. The faint sound of Philus Philonius's flute went quiet and the cold that so miserably gripped Jim lessened, if but a little. Jim looked at his friends and poor Cornelius. If only he'd followed them back the other way! Even if he had been forced to retreat back through the Devil's Horns and left the shell behind, it would have been better than this. What good was even the Treasure of the Ocean if he lost his friends?

"Let them go," Jim said. "You can have me but just let them go!" But Ocy just cackled over Jim's fallen form. She lowered her face until their noses nearly touched. The long string of drool pooled on Jim's cheek.

"We shall be lettin' none of those little tasties go, man-child. In truth, you are the only one we'll be settin' free this day."

"Letting me go?" Jim asked incredulously. "Why?"

"Your smell, man-child," Ocy said, puzzling over Jim with a wrinkled nose. "There is somethin' rotten in your smell. Tis this stink alone that dissuades me from eatin' you whole, man-child. It's the smell we caught in the air by our nest. Our noses may be gettin' old, they may, they may, but this smell is strong, strong, strong!" Ocy sniffed Jim's shoulder, down his arm, and all the way to his left hand, where the black tendrils crept from his thumb to his wrist. "It is the smell of poison, man-child. Poison runs through your veins. We will not be eatin' it, and we will not be killed by the blackness within you."

"Poison?" Jim shouted. "Killed?"

"Oh yes, man-child," Ocy said. "Our noses are very smart, aren't they, ladies? Our noses make no mistakes, do they? There's black-magic poison in your veins. Whether by turnin' to stone or the slow blackness in your blood, when dawn comes little man-child, you shall be dead."

Jim's head swam and hot tears rose up behind his eyes. He'd been tricked again – tricked by that scoundrel Philus Philonius. Now his friends were going to be eaten by harpies and Jim was going to die alone on this island, by poison or stone, whichever came first.

"There's four left then," Ally said happily from the dead end. "Not counting the little bird traitor. But I've heard woman-child is a rare delicacy, I did, I did! Which of us gets her? Or will we share a little bit of them each amongst ourselves?"

The last of Jim's hope abandoned him. Lacey's tears fell in great drops onto the ground. Even the irrepressible Ratt brother smiles were nowhere to be found. Jim realized this might be the end of the road for them all, when Ally said:

"It's only a shame none of them have any glitteries on 'em. I'd give up one share of tasty meat just for a glittery, I would, I would!"

From where Jim lay on the cold ground, he saw Paul's eyes light up with one last drop of courage.

"Ladies," Paul began. His voice trembled at first, but being one of the greatest con men to ever walk the streets of London, he coughed twice, straightened his shoulders and forced a smile back across his cheeks. "Excuse me, but I don't suppose you have much gamblin' on this island, do you?"

"Gamblin'?" said Ally, curiously. "Is gamblin' a type of glittery? Is it man-child, is it?"

"Well, no. Gamblin's a game, Madam Harpy. It's a type of game that always ends in a glittery. In fact, it could very well end with a glittery for you today."

"A glittery?" Ally cried. She hopped up and down on her claws, her head bouncing up and down on her long neck, tittering and cackling with glee. "A glittery and a game? Oh, Ocy and Celia – this has turned into the best day in years and years! We can play a game and get a glittery and eat man flesh all in one night!"

"A game and a glittery?" Celia said, looking up from Cornelius. Suspicion pooled at the edges of her voice and doubt was written all over her scratched and bloodied face.

"Sounds like a trick," Ocy added. "Sounds like a nasty human trick to me!"

"Oh, I wouldn't dream of trickin' such lovely ladies as yourselves," Paul said, putting on his best offended face. "As a matter of fact, I promise you this is no trick, 'cause in all honesty, there's no way you can lose! Now, am I mistaken, or did I happen to hear you say that huntin' us Brothers Ratt was the most fun you'd had in years?"

"Oh, but it was so much fun!" Ally said, cackling at the top of her lungs. "Ocy, wasn't you even sayin' it was a fun hunt, wasn't you?"

"Well," said Ocy hesitantly, but Jim could tell her curiosity was piqued. She dragged him to his feet and threw him against the wall with his friends. Then she stalked up beside Ally, scrutinizing little Paul with her bright yellow eyes. "It certainly was a bit of exercise now weren't it? Something new for a change, I will say that."

"How many years would you say it's been since you had that much fun, ladies?" Paul continued. "Be honest. A decade? Two?"

"Oh, fifty years at least!" cried Ally, clicking her needle teeth together and bobbing her head excitedly.

"Seventy, maybe," added Ocy.

"Seventy years?" Paul said, aghast. His brothers joined right in, shaking their heads sadly.

"Terrible," George added.

"A tragedy," said Peter.

"Well, we are five hundred years old each," said Ally.

"Five-hundred years? Why, I wouldn't have guessed you a decade over two hundred, would you, Peter?" said George.

"One seventy-five, Georgie. One seventy-five, tops."

Jim could hardly believe it, but he thought the harpies actually blushed as they cackled together.

"Well I certainly wasn't having any fun, now was I?" roared Celia, shoving her way amongst her sisters, little Cornelius clutched in one claw. "Look at my face!" She screeched, pointing one feathery wing tip at the claw marks on her cheek.

"Oh," said Paul, swallowing hard. "Well, I'm sure that was an accident. Old Cornelius wouldn't hurt a fly, milady."

"He said he wanted to peck me eyeballs out!" Celia raged.

"Oh, that," Paul replied, laughing spuriously and looking to his brothers for help.

"Oh, yes," said Peter. "That was...that was just a joke! It's sort of a go-to line for him, you know? Good morning, Pete, how 'bout if I peck out an eyeball this morning?"

"Told me he was going to peck my eyeballs out just an hour ago," said George, and on cue the three Ratt brothers looked at each other and burst into uproarious laughter.

"Oh, he's such a ham, that one!" said Peter.

"A regular court jester!" said George, tears forming on his cheeks.

"Well I didn't think it was very funny!" shouted Celia. As though flipping a lever, all three brothers stopped laughing on a dime and shook their heads, disgusted looks upon their faces.

"Terrible joke."

"Just awful."

"Not funny…at…all."

"But what is fun, ladies," continued Paul as quickly as he could. "Is the chance to win a glittery. And on top of even that, have a little more fun huntin' for your dinner. Now, me and me brothers know from our time in London that if you don't have to run for your dinner, it don't taste nearly as good, now do it, boys?"

George and Peter shook their heads convincingly. "Not nearly, Paulie!" they said together.

"Ladies, here is the deal and it's a one time deal only, for you and for you alone! I, Paul Ratt, will give you a chance to win a glittery by playin' my li'l game. If you win the game, you get to keep the glittery and eat us for dinner – and we are delicious, I can tell you that. Especially her!" Paul thumbed over to Lacey.

"Paul!" shrieked Lacey. But the harpies, even Celia, cackled and howled, all three of them ruffling their feathers and prancing about on their claws.

Celia even tossed poor Cornelius's limp form on the ground at Jim's feet. Jim bent down and gently lifted the poor bird into his arms. Putting his ear on Cornelius's chest, he detected the faintest heartbeat – the raven was still alive.

"And if you lose," Paul continued. "All you have to do is give us a head start, and then you can hunt us all over again – and then you still get to eat us!"

The three harpies now almost fell over on each other they were having so much fun. Jim looked over at Paul with concern all over his face. Paul had attempted a similar trick once before, at the Inn of the Wet Rock. Little had he known he was up against Dread Steele himself – until it was too late. But Paul threw Jim a wink and carried on.

"So ladies, do we have a deal?"

"Oh, yes, yes, yes!" said Ally, nearly hysterical with delight.

"Excellent!" said Paul. "Now, to present you with your potential prize, may I show you one of the rarest artifacts from all of England…"

Paul reached into his pocket and with an expert flourish of a circus ringmaster pulled out -"a marble!"

Paul held up the spherical trinket in his hand. It caught just a hint of the sunlight creeping down through the shadows and sparkled magnificently in his palm. Jim would have thought Paul had produced a chest full of gold the way the harpies shrieked and danced, flapping their wings and howling with delight.

"I ain't never seen anythin' like it!" Ally crooned. "It's so, so, ROUND!"

"Yes it is - the roundest of all marbles!" said Paul. Then, with three flicks of his wrist, he pulled the hats from Jim, Peter, and George's heads and dropped them on the ground at his feet. "Now, here's how the game works, ladies: I will put the oh-so-round marble beneath a hat, and then each of you gets a guess. Guess the right hat, and you find yourselves one marble richer and three bellies fuller, right? Now, 'ere we go!"

Paul rolled the marble over the back of his knuckles and tossed it beneath one of the hats so fast it was hard for Jim to tell under which one it supposedly went. Immediately the hats began to spin around on the ground beneath Paul's fingers. The harpies tried so hard to follow the marble that they nearly twisted their three necks into a single braid. Finally, Paul brought the hats to a sudden stop.

"Right then, ladies," Paul said, smiling. "Guessin' time! Choose your fate and choose wisely. For a whole, round marble and some savory, li'l man-children are on the line tonight!"

Ally, who could hardly contain herself and was half giggling and half screeching, shoved her sisters aside and snatched Jim's hat from the ground without a moment's thought. When she found nothing beneath the hat she let out a depressed sigh. Her neck drooped so low that Jim thought her head was going to drag along the ground. If the harpies had not just been threatening to eat them all, Jim thought he would have felt the slightest bit bad for Ally.

Ocy went next. In spite of her earlier suspicions, she was now very nearly as excited as Ally. But she was also more thoughtful. She looked back and forth between the hats and Paul with her enormous, yellow bird eyes, as though attempting to divine the location of the marble. But alas, when she plucked Peter's cap from the ground she found nothing but dirt underneath. Unlike her sister, however, Ocy took losing a bit less graciously. She squawked what could have been some ancient, harpy curse word, and kicked at the dust with her sharp talons.

Lastly came Celia. She laughed a dry chuckle and ran her long, purple tongue over her yellow, needle teeth. "You lost this li'l game before you started tiny man-child," said the harpy, leering at the children with the most horrible smile stretched across her grotesque face. She raised her claw over George's hat and let it linger there, as though she dangled the clan's fate from her talons. "You shoulda' used four hats, li'l man-child, for you gots only one left. Now I'm gonna get me a glittery and get me my fill o' man-flesh for dinner to boot. It's been a good day indeed. I'm gonna enjoy eatin' you clever li'l Ratt boys for dinner!" With that Celia seized George's hat, her yellow eyes never leaving Paul's face. But when both of her sisters gasped, Celia looked down to find no trace of the marble at her feet. Her freshly clawed face came up trembling with rage. More than hunger burned in her eyes then...now there was murder.

"This is a trick!" she screeched, rearing up on her claws with wings outstretched. The five friends backed up against the rock wall as far as they could go. "I knew you was playin' a nasty trick on us, lyin', man-child. Show us what's in your hand little trickster!" Celia reached out with her wing and seized Paul by the wrist.

Jim's heart dropped. Once more, he feared, Paul's con had been uncovered by his mark. This time, perhaps to their doom. But instead of fear, a smile slowly spread over Paul's face. He opened his hand one finger at a time. The palm was empty. It seemed, Jim realized, that the smallest Ratt had taken his brother's advice and been doing some practicing indeed.

"Sorry ladies, but there's been no cheatin' here," said Paul. "The marble really is under a hat." Paul reached up and removed his own hat. Underneath, balanced in Paul's tangle of brown hair, lay the marble, glittering in the dim light.

"Oh, very clever, very clever!" said Ally, who seemed ridiculously eager to play the game again. But Celia stretched out her long neck until her hideous face hung only inches from Jim and Paul's noses.

"Me still thinks this is some trick, man-children. I'm of a good mind to put you both outta me own misery right here and now!"

"Remember your promise!" said Jim, raising one shaking finger and doing his best to keep his voice from trembling. "Remember what you said about having bird honor and all that? Would be a shame to tarnish your reputation, wouldn't you say?"

Celia did not cackle nor screech. Only a smile crossed her face – a smile full of malice and hate.

"Oh, I'll be keepin' my word, little man-children. We'll give you your head start. But when we catches you again, there ain't gonna be no games and no guessin'…there'll only be gnashin' and mashin' of bones in me teeth! That be a promise."

"Well, that sounds fair I suppose," Paul replied weakly. Jim felt sweat bead up on his own forehead as well. "So, if you three will please so kindly close your eyes and count to ten—"

"Twenty," Jim interjected.

"Thirty," said Lacey.

"Right, thirty," agreed Paul. "We'll try and give you all a good hunt again."

Begrudgingly, eyes glistening with poisonous rage, Celia stepped aside, sweeping her sisters back with an outstretched wing.

"Run, little man-children," she growled. Her needle teeth clicked and clacked against one another and her talons scraped along the rocky path. "Run fast for I'll be seein' you soon, I will, I will!"

"Right then, thank you," said Paul, tipping his hat and scrambling out of the dead end.

"Remember not to count too fast or it's cheating!" added Peter as he followed his brother out.

"Lovely to meet you, Ally," said George, and the tittering harpy waved her wing to George before her sister slapped it down.

Lacey followed, wiping the tears from her cheeks and taking Cornelius's still form gently from Jim's arms, cradling the bird before dashing out. Jim came last. He backed out slowly, keeping his eyes fixed on the three sisters.

"Catch you or no, little man-child," Celia said, her lips trembling with rage. "That black poison runnin' through your veins is gonna 'ave you, even if I don't. Whether by my claws, the magic o' this island, or the black poison in your body…you ain't never gonna leave this place alive! Now…One," she roared. She and her sisters turned their backs and faced the rock wall. "Two!"

Jim did not wait for three. He turned and ran from the dead-end ravine. Celia's enraged prophecy followed him, ringing in his ears and filling his heart with dread. Once more Jim's hand began to throb and that cold chill climbed down his arms and legs.

SIX

UNDER COVER OF MAGIC FOG

The moment Jim rounded the corner out of the ravine, he ran smack into his four friends. They all stood in a circle, not running for their lives, as Jim was quite sure they needed to be doing.

"Why on earth are we just standing here?" Jim shouted. Celia's loud count was already at five and echoing through the crags.

"Paul, you were brilliant!" Lacey said, wrapping one arm around the smallest Ratt brother and squeezing him tight. "But right now I need all of you to trust me or we'll never make it out of these rocks alive. Will you follow me?"

Jim heard Celia hit seven and then eight. There was no time to argue. "Go, Lacey, go!" was all he said. Without another word the five friends bolted off, racing through the stone maze, darting around sharp corners, and leaping over small boulders fallen into the ravines. Jim had no idea whether they were running back the way they had come or toward the fields of tall grass Cornelius said lay north. Over the sound of their running feet and his own slamming heart, Jim could hear Celia's voice growing louder and louder, rumbling down the stone corridors.

"…Eleven…Twelve…Thirteen!"

"Lacey, where are you taking us?" Jim yelled in a hushed rasp. She was sprinting just ahead of him, with George and his brothers right behind. But as they skidded around one last corner, Jim found the answer. His heart froze in his chest. Bones littered the ground at their feet. Sticks and straw were piled in heaps upon the jagged edges of the crags above their heads.

They had run straight into the middle of the harpies' nest.

"The nest?" Jim cried, smacking himself in the head. "Lacey, of all the places you could have run, you chose here? Right in the place where those three birds are going to eat us for dinner?" Jim was aghast and a spike of pain lanced through his hand. "Why don't we just gather ourselves on a plate and sprinkle each other with salt and pepper for good measure?"

"Just shut it, Jim, and wait here!" Lacey snapped, thrusting Cornelius back into Jim's arms. With hardly a pause she plunged through the pile of bones, throwing them out of her way and leaping over the tusks and antlers, straight to the harpies' vast pile of glitteries.

"…Seventeen….Eighteen…Nineteen!"

"Lacey," said George, a little too matter of factly for Jim's taste in this particular situation. "Normally you know me and the boys are always in for a good burglin' – actually sort of miss it we do…but is now really the time? And do we really want to make that Celia bird any more furious than she already is?"

Lacey ignored them all, though, and was now hurling objects over her shoulder into the pile of bones. At last she found whatever it was for which she searched and ripped it from the pile. She stuck it beneath her arm and tore back through the bones to where Jim and the Ratts waited.

"Twenty-three...twenty-four...twenty-five!"

"Well, I'm glad we stopped for that!" Jim raged, throwing one hand in the air. "We have just enough time to baste ourselves in sauce for the main course!"

"Jim, just shut up!" Lacey shouted. Without a word as to what she was doing, she reached over and tore one of the sleeves right off Jim's jacket, cutting him off with an upheld finger before he could protest. "We're going to be alright as long as we use what George has in his pocket."

"What do you mean?" George asked.

"The fog seeds you stole from Egidio Quattrochi's shop."

"You stole from old Egidio?" Jim yelled at his friend.

"Twenty-eight!"

"You've had those the whole time, George?" Paul raged.

"I was savin' 'em!" George protested, pulling a handful of gray seeds from his pocket.

"Saving them for what, George? An emergency?" Peter cried, looking furious enough to slug his brother.

"Twenty-nine!"

While the boys had been yelling at George, Lacey had taken Jim's ripped sleeve and wrapped it snuggly about his left forearm, cinching it so tight that Jim winced from the pain.

Then came the last.

"Thirty!" Celia roared. With a clap like thunder the harpy sisters' wings beat down. Three dark shapes burst into the air, screaming with bone-rattling fury and hunger.

"Here they come!" Jim shouted. The three sisters circled tightly together, swinging back toward the nest, where the children stood entirely exposed.

"George, now!" Lacey screamed.

209

George poured a few of the seeds into one hand, reached high above his head and hurled them to the ground just as Celia shouted over her sister's screams.

"I see you, man-children!" She howled. But as the harpies streaked through the air toward the nest floor, a thick blanket of fog enveloped Jim and his friends. The mist hung so heavy Jim could feel it on his skin, like a cloak pulled over his shoulders, hiding him from all the eyes in the world. Stranger still, the mist became thinner in a small bubble just before them, allowing the five friends to make their way through the otherwise impenetrable mist.

"This way!" Lacey hissed. Jim and the Ratts followed her, just as three crashes shattered the bones in the pile behind them and Celia's infuriated roar rung in his ears.

"Curse you, you trickin' man-children! I'll taste you before this is all over! Me and me sisters is gonna hunt you til we either slices you up in our teeth and eats you, or watches you turn to stone, you trickin' man-children, you!"

"Does this mean the game is over?" Jim heard Ally say loudly behind them, followed by another roar from Celia and Ocy.

The five friends tore through the thick fog. As they went, Jim realized why Lacey had ripped the sleeve from his coat and wrapped it about his arm. The cloth concealed the rotten smell of his poisoned wound. Hidden from both sight and smell, the Clan of the Ratt would make their escape. More than even that, as it had been when Ocy had pinched Jim's arm beneath her claw, the tight knot of cloth slowed the spread of the poison. Jim felt his head clear for a few precious moments as he ran for his life.

"Looks like you saved the day, Lacey," Jim said a little sheepishly. "Sorry I yelled."

"How did you know I took them fog seeds, Lacey?" George asked. "Not even Dread Steele saw me nick those. That's how fast I was!"

"I never saw you take them, George," said Lacey. "But you knew you could not have them, and therefore I knew immediately that you took some."

"And what was it you took from the harpies' nest?" Jim asked.

"All of the glitteries in the nest were pirate gear that the harpies had taken from poor souls trapped on this island. So I knew one of *these* had to be among them." Lacey showed Jim and the Ratts a small box with a brass face in the center, and a needle moving about beneath the ring: a compass.

"With Cornelius hurt, I knew we would be lost in here forever if we couldn't figure out the direction in which we were going," Lacey continued. "So I took a chance and went back for one. Now, even if we make a wrong turn or two, as long as we keep heading in the same direction, we should be able to find our way out of this impossible maze."

"And which direction would that be?" Jim asked, licking his lips nervously.

"North," Lacey said with a long sigh. "We're going north."

"You're brilliant, Lacey," Jim said. Black poison or no flowing through his veins, he meant it. "Absolutely brilliant, you know that?"

"Thank you, Jim," Lacey replied. But when she looked back his way, Jim saw the worry in her eyes. They were on the run from three, merciless harpies and trapped in a maze of rock and stone. They had only until the next sunrise to make it to the hidden cave and back again. Worse still, Jim thought, swallowing hard and feeling the ache of his left hand beneath the wrappings, he may have even less time than that.

Travelling through the crags was tedious, frustrating work. Even with Lacey's compass dutifully pointing north, the small party wandered down several dead-end paths. More than a few of them were long and winding. Many times the clan was forced to double back and search out new corridors through the mist all over again.

Flapping wings clapped above their heads along the way. More than once the clatter of sharp-taloned claws sounded on the rocks above their heads. In those moments of nearest danger, Jim and his friends crouched as close to the ground as possible, where the magic fog was thickest. Jim would jam his poisoned arm deep in the crook of his other elbow to conceal the smell as much as possible, until more wing beats carried away whichever harpy lurked on the crags above.

The clan also took turns carrying Cornelius. The valiant raven had yet to regain consciousness and lay still as a stone in their arms. Lacey gave Jim a turn at the compass and made a little wrap for Cornelius's damaged wing from a strip torn off the hem of her lovely dress. She patted his little feathered head and whispered to him that it would be all right. Even George was kind enough to tell Lacey that he actually missed old Cornelius's stories and couldn't wait to hear one again as soon as the raven awoke.

But the long march through the ravines was especially cruel and draining for Jim. In spite of the tight bandage wrapped about his wrist, the pain sometimes tore through his hand and reached into his arm - sometimes even into his chest. The flute song faintly began to play again. Jim would shiver then, teeth chattering, as though caught by surprise in a winter wind.

SEVEN

THE SEA OF GRASS

After many miles the fog at last broke free from the crags. The billowing mist spilled into a vast field, thick with long brown grass that grew taller than a full-grown man.

"We made it!" Paul shouted. But Lacey and George immediately slapped their hands over his mouth and put their fingers to their lips. The harpies could still be near, they warned. As hard as it had been to avoid them in the ravines, it would be even worse in an open field.

Jim and his friends waded into the thick growth, keeping their heads low and creeping as quietly as possible. After a while, the enchanted fog thinned enough for Jim to take a look around.

"Well, the good news is that the harpies haven't guessed we would be this far away." He pointed to three small specks circling the sky a good distance away over the crags. "But I'd wager they could cover that space in pretty short order if they wanted to. So we better keep moving."

"What's the bad news, Jim?" George asked, peering at him through the grass. Jim looked toward the horizon. The sun hung low in the east, glowing orange as dying coals.

"It's already evening," Jim said. A throb grabbed at his hand and a wince crossed his face. "There'll only be a couple more hours of light. We were in the ravines for the entire afternoon."

"It'll still be alright won't it, Jim?" Peter asked hopefully, appearing in the grass beside his brother.

"Right," said Paul. "The cave can't be that far away now, can it?"

"I don't know," was all Jim said, gripping his aching wrist tight. "I don't know at all."

Jim and his friends pushed through the Sea of Tall Grass beneath the cool, purple sky. The fiery orange of the setting sun was just visible over the long blades. Dragonflies buzzed over the clan's heads and fireflies floated above the field. In some stretches the grass grew so thick that Jim all but swam through the brown stalks. He, Lacey, and the Ratts had to call out to each other, for they could see no further than their hands could reach. Other times, small paths weaved through the growth. Yet even in those clearings there was no seeing above the grass.

George, of course, took advantage of the situation and braided several strands of the tall grass into a sword, with which he attacked his brothers over and over. Peter eventually swore that if they all turned to stone he would jump on George's back at the last moment and pummel him, so that anyone who found them could see Peter punching his brother in the face for all eternity. But all the while, Jim feared that once the sun set and darkness fell, they would lose their way again - this time in a maze of grass instead of a maze of stone.

As the day's warmth died, the evening breeze bit deeper into Jim's skin. He was growing colder by the hour. Even beneath the makeshift bandage about his wrist, Jim could feel the source of that cold creeping farther and farther up his arm – toward the heart beating within his chest.

Jim sighed heavily and was adjusting his wrappings when the fading sunlight glimmered off something bright at his side. It was a spider's web. Within the shimmering strands, a firefly had become ensnared and was thrashing against its bonds – all to no avail. In spite of the dark cloud that had settled over Jim's heart, a brief tug of pity for the little bug pulled inside him. Jim was trapped in a web of sorts himself. One strand of the web was the Cromiers' wicked schemes and plots. But another part of the web holding Jim was crawling inside his veins. No matter how hard he kicked, it seemed there was no escape.

Jim reached out and, with a flick of his finger, set the firefly free. The little insect zipped into the air at once. It flew in an exuberant circle about Jim's head and came at it stop an inch in front of his nose. There it bobbed up and down, as though to say thank you, before flying off to the east, toward the Field of Lights. Jim managed a small smile before another pang gnawed at his hand and cut short even that small moment of levity.

"Does it hurt, Jim?" Lacey asked, pushing through the grass and appearing at Jim's shoulder.

"It's really not so bad." Jim said. But that was hardly the truth. He tried to sound strong even as a shiver shook his voice.

"Maybe if I tighten the bandage," Lacey offered, but Jim cut her off before she could finish.

"Just leave it alone, Lacey!" he snapped. "I don't want to talk about it, alright? I just want to get out of this fiendish grass so we can find our way to the cave." Jim was immediately sorry, but like the cold chills crawling up his arms, there was no escaping the angry thoughts crawling through his head. "They took everything from me, do you understand? It's not fair! I just want it back, Lacey! I want my life back!"

"You mean your old life?" Lacey said, glaring hotly at Jim. "You mean your old life before you met any of us, don't you?" Jim was about to yell something back when George interrupted their argument with a shout of his own.

"Oy, you two!" He called from what must have been only twenty or so paces away. "Quit makin' all that racket and get up here! I think you'll want to see this."

Jim and Lacey stomped through the grass into a small clearing. Before they could shout or argue with each other any further, their angry scowls fell from their faces. Standing in the clearing were two more statues that had once been pirates, imprisoned in stone forever on the Veiled Isle. Unlike the poor men on the beach, these two stood stock still, facing one another through the grass. They each gripped a pistol, and held their weapons at each other's chests, vile contempt chiseled upon their faces for all time.

"Looks like these two were about to have a duel, or somethin'," said George, staring at the two statues curiously. "Bad timin', eh? If the sun hadn't come up, I wonder who would have won."

"Can't you see what happened here?" Lacey said, looking back and forth between the two statues that had once been men. "They weren't having a duel. I think these two men came here together, almost like we've come looking for this shell. But when they finally found what they were looking for, they couldn't agree on how to share it. They both lost everything in the end."

"Treasure has torn more than a few friendships asunder," said a weak voice. "If I know my history right. And I usually do."

"Mister Cornelius, you're alive!" Lacey cried. The injured raven stirred in her arms, letting out one miserable croak.

"It will take more than harpies to finish off Cornelius Darkfeather," the raven managed, sounding very tired and very worn. "But I don't think I'll be flying anytime soon." Cornelius held out his wing, wrapped in the bandage made from Lacey's dress and spotted with crimson drops.

"Glad you're back, Cornelius," said Jim.

"You were so brave, Mister Cornelius," Lacey said to him, tears forming in her eyes. "I'll carry you the rest of the way until we get off this awful island. Don't you worry."

"Well, duel or argument or whatever it was," said Jim, stepping over to the taller of the two statues. "If Cornelius can't fly, then I think these gentlemen can at least give us a hand with our current predicament." With that, he used the statue as a ladder and climbed up to take a look around.

"Oh, Jim, how terrible," said Lacey. But Jim was already standing on the statue's shoulders, trying not to think about whether or not the stone man could feel or think anything at this point. George was quick to join him atop the other stone pirate.

"What do you see?" asked Lacey.

"Almost the whole island," said Jim, using the last of the setting sun's glow to survey the landscape. "This grass sea reaches out perhaps another mile or two north from the crags. Beyond that is the forest that Twisttail told us about, I think. It looks like the trees grow right up to the foot of the mountain."

"What about the cave?" asked Lacey, a fair bit of desperation chiming in her voice. "Can you see the cave?"

"No," Jim admitted. "But Twisttail said it was at the base of the mountain after the forest, so that's the way we'll go."

"But we could spend hours walking around a whole mountain looking for a cave, Jim!" Lacey all but shouted. Jim suddenly found himself wishing he had something close at hand to throw at her.

"I know that, Lacey!"

"Oy, you two," said George excitedly, holding his hat on his head as a sharp breeze blew south across the island. He pointed his other hand east toward the sunset, where the sky was bright pink and the wisps of clouds painted blue and gold. "Lookie there!"

"What is it, Georgie?" George's brothers asked from below.

"It's them lights. Them lights that that Twisttail the lizard was tellin' us about."

True to George's words, beyond where the grass sea faded out to the east, on a great field of rolling hills, lights, more lights than Jim could count, danced over the grass. They zipped and darted about, sometimes on their own, other times swirling into great clouds and sparkling across the landscape. They dazzled Jim's eyes in colors of blue and pink and green and gold.

"There's hundreds of them," Jim said quietly. "Thousands of them, aren't there?"

"It's funny," added George. "They don't look all that bad from up here, do they Jim? Actually…if I were a girl, I'd say they was actually the prettiest things I ever saw. If I were a girl."

"Because only girls think things are pretty?" Lacey said. Peter and Paul giggled at their brother from the foot of his statue.

"Looks can be deceiving, George," Jim cautioned, though he too was having a hard time pulling his eyes away from the shimmering sight.

"On that count you would be correct, young Morgan," growled a voice, breaking into the clearing, accompanied by the rustle of tall grass. "Not all that glitters is gold, and those cursed lights upon yonder hill indeed hide murderous intent."

Jim turned atop his statue's shoulders, just in time to see Count Cromier burst into the clearing. Bartholomew pushed through to his right and Splitbeard the Pirate to his left. Two members of Splitbeard's crew appeared behind them as well. All five gripped drawn swords in hand.

EIGHT

OLD ENEMIES ON NEW SHORES

L acey screamed at the sight of Count Cromier. She stumbled back with Peter and Paul to crouch between the statues, where George had jumped down beside them. Yet when Jim laid eyes on the Count and Bartholomew, a fire hot as a blacksmith's bellows raged up his arm. Lacey's bandages or no, the black rose's poison was sill winding its way through Jim's blood, and the dark magic through his thoughts. Jim never considered running. He thought only of launching himself from the statue straight into the pack of buccaneers, scratching, clawing, and biting, for lack of a sword. But the pain bit his arm so deeply that Jim's strength failed him. He managed to pitch forward, but landed hard on his back in the dirt, rolling to a stop at the Red Count's feet.

"Temper, temper, young Morgan," said the Count, smiling down at Jim. "This island is deadly enough without diving headlong into a fight you cannot possibly win. Besides, running across old friends on enemy shores is considered a good omen, is it not?"

Jim rolled off his back and onto his hands and knees, coughing and gasping for air. He scrambled away from the Count and Bartholomew as Splitbeard and his Corsairs slowly surrounded him and his friends in the clearing.

"You're not my friend," Jim shouted between gasping breaths. "You've taken everything! But I promise you this, one day I'm going to take it all back!"

"You shall find taking from the Cromiers a bit more difficult with my sword through your heart!" Bartholomew raged. He dashed forward with his blade raised to strike. Lacey screamed again and Jim did his best to seem brave as he waited for the blow to finish him forever. But once more, the Red Count stopped his son's deadly intentions with a sharp command.

"Bartholomew! Sheath your sword!"

"Father!" Bartholomew shrieked. His sword's razor sharp point had stopped only inches from Jim's chest. "This is the son of your sworn enemy. The only heir of the man who stole our glory all those years ago. Every breath he draws is an insult to you...and to me." A further dose of venom seeped into Bartholomew's eyes. Murder glinted in his bared teeth.

Jim's heart pounded. There was no way out of this trap. The pirates, including the grinning Splitbeard, had them surrounded. Jim was not entirely sure that even Bartholomew's father could stop him from killing Jim for much longer. The poison in his veins from the blackened rose had all been for nothing. He and his friends were about to die on the Veiled Isle.

The south wind blew again and rustled the grass.

Somewhere behind the flute song in Jim's head, which had been steadily gaining strength as the day wore on, a tiny idea pricked the back of Jim's mind. There was a chance, he thought, still one small chance at the revenge he had been promised in the blackened rose – or if not that, at least hope for escape.

"I took my revenge on Lindsay Morgan, Bartholomew - if you recall," said the Count. He walked up behind his son and once more swatted the sword down with a gloved hand. "And we would not have needed to set foot on this wretched island were it not for *other* failings."

Bartholomew's face went as dark crimson as his father's curled wig. His sword shook in his hand. If the young Cromier's eyes had been blades themselves, Jim thought, he would have run Jim through that very moment. But Bartholomew, his face trembling as violently as his sword, turned away from both Jim and his father and stalked off into the tall grass. He sliced at the brown stalks as he went, mowing them down until he disappeared into the field.

"You see, Jim, I'm not such a bad fellow, am I?" The Count forced a stiff smile across his face, but his scar quivered upon his cheek. "This is the third time I've saved your life from my own son, is it not? Now, that must count for something, don't you think?"

"Should I say thank you?" Jim tried as best he could to ignore the gnawing ache in his arm. But the pain only grew worse as he undid his wrappings behind his back, exposing the wound to the open air. "If you're keeping me alive just so you can steal something else, I think you'll be disappointed. There's nothing left to take."

"Oh, my dear boy." The Count leaned down to look Jim in the eye. The fake smile slipped from his lips. His voice coiled into a snarl. "There's always something left to take. This time I shall take you and your friends as shields from the devilry of this cursed island! Your father's map has led us along dangerous paths, and the number of our hired hands has begun to dwindle."

Jim looked the Count and his men over. Indeed, at least six or seven corsairs had been in the little boat with the Count, Bartholomew, and Splitbeard when they had slipped by the *Spectre*. Yet now there remained only two. Bruises, welts, and cuts to spare covered them both. All save for Splitbeard that was. The sinewy captain of the *Sea Spider* seemed as fresh and cheerful as when Jim had first laid eyes upon him.

"The Lord Lindsay Morgan was nothing if not a most clever man, oh great Count," said Splitbeard in his thick accent. "To have drawn a map through which even the holder would struggle to follow was a stroke of genius. And, most honorable one, does his son not seem equally as clever, to have come so far with no weapons and no map of his own? A great surprise indeed."

"Yes, a great surprise," the Count replied. He narrowed his eyes at Jim and a smile once more curled on his powdered face. "How ironic it is, young Morgan, that the two of us shall now finish what your father and I began? It is inspiring really. Cromier and Morgan, joining forces once more!"

"I've heard that before!" said Lacey, cradling the weary and injured Cornelius in her arms. "Joining forces is just a lie that means hiding behind children and sending them into traps and dangers first, so that we get hurt or killed while you get your treasure. No offense, mister Count, but we've heard better liars than you tell the same story."

"Oh, my, my, my, what a bold little girl." The Count glared nastily at Lacey. "So much wit and spirit amongst the five of you! I should have known there would be no reasoning. Fine then, let us forget joining forces." The Count leveled his sword at the clan and slowly passed the blade before each of their faces. "When I say join forces, what I mean is to march you through every door, over every barrier, and into every hole we cross until I find the cave on this map. Then I will take what I came here to find! And if there are none of you left when I am finished, I shall consider myself blessed with but a little more peace and quiet!" The Count then rested the cold point of his sword upon Jim's throat - the steel touch was cold as ice.

"All save for you, young Morgan. You shall watch your friends test the waters for us again and again. I will save you for last. For there is an even greater task in which you will yet serve me, to make amends for your father's treachery. Now, Splitbeard," ordered the Count, sheathing his sword with a flourish. "Bind our friends' hands and march them north. We have miles to go and little time in which to cover them."

Jim shook with anger at the Count. The more furious he became the hotter the poison burned in his hand. The black tendrils had worked their way farther up Jim's arm. The only relief came from the cool, evening wind...

...the cool wind blowing south toward the crags.

Jim strained his ears over the rustling grass. A small smile fought its way onto his quivering lips. He finally heard the sound for which he'd been waiting.

"Sorry, Count." Jim forced himself to his feet. "But we've already made some new friends on this island. In fact, I'd like you to meet them!" Jim thrust his poisoned hand into the sky, further into the wind. "Let me introduce you to Ocy, Celia, and Ally!"

A piercing scream split the darkening sky. The harpy sisters plummeted through the air, talons gleaming in the last traces of sunlight.

"Man-flesh!" shrieked Celia, bolting into the clearing.

"Harpies!" Splitbeard cried, diving into the dirt. The arrogant smile finally fell from his face.

The Count and his pirates scattered, waving their swords skyward as though they might offer some protection against the fury of the harpy sisters. Two pairs of arms seized Jim from behind and jerked him backward. It was Lacey and George, dragging him beneath the crossed, pistol-bearing arms of the stone pirates, where Peter and Paul already cowered.

But the stone pirates provided little protection for the clan. Ocy and Celia descended upon them. The harpies' claws shattered the statue heads into white dust. Two winged sisters perched upon what remained of the stone pirates, leering down on the children. They licked their lips and chomped their needle teeth. Ally came in behind her sisters and landed on the ground beside the clan, waving a wing at the Ratts. Jim thought he even saw her give Paul a wink, as though they were old friends.

"Thought you could escape us, did ya, ya scrawny runts? Thought you could run and hide forever from we three sisters of the island?"

Celia glared at Jim, the scratch on the side of her face still fresh and red.

"Actually," Jim said, holding his left wrist tight in his hand, for it throbbed and burned worse than ever before. "We felt really bad about that little incident back there, didn't we? So, we decided to make it up to you."

"Yes, indeed, Jim," said Paul immediately. "Absolutely terrible form. You should know that I, for one, felt deeply ashamed of myself the moment we left. But, we said to ourselves, we *are* awfully scrawny – just as you said, madam. And even if we were to do you right, and walk all the way back to the crags and offer ourselves up to you, which we actually thought about doin', well, we'd be no more than a snack! And that would just make things worse, wouldn't it?"

"What you ladies need, is a full-blown feast!" said Peter. He pointed to the Count and the three pirates, still picking themselves off the ground and beginning to run for their lives. "And we just happen to have a walking, talking feast waiting for you right over there."

"'Specially that red-haired chap," said George, thumbing toward the Count, who was stumbling backward into the grass. "Savory lookin', in't he?"

"And Ally," Lacey added. "We didn't forget about you, did we? Look at what all the tasty pirates are holding."

Ally's yellow eyes lifted to the pirates…then to their swords. If it were possible, her big, bird eyes went wider than they already were. They sparkled with some sort of madness and a greedy smile stretched across her hideous face.

"Glitteries!" Ally released a tooth-rattling shriek and launched herself between her sisters to chase down the Count and his men. She tackled one of the Corsairs to the ground before he reached the tall grass. Ally's two sisters were quick to follow, but not before Celia shouted over her shoulder:

"Just remember little man-children," she squawked. "There'll still be room for desert!"

"Run!" Lacey cried. But Jim and the others were already on their feet. The Clan of the Ratt scurried to the edge of the clearing in the direction of the forest. The sound of screaming and cursing men, screeching harpies, and flapping wings roared behind them.

"You know, I'm beginning to like them bird-ladies," George said, wiping his brow with a free hand. "Rather helpful in a pinch, ain't they?" Jim was about to tell George that he was an idiot, but before he could open his mouth, Peter and Paul parted a wall of tall grass like a brown curtain. Behind the stalks, appeared the dirty, sweat-stained red coat of Captain Bartholomew Cromier, his teeth clenched in hate.

Jim's eyes went to Bartholomew's gloved hand. It squeezed the handle of his captain's sword in a shaking grasp. The pale man's raven-black hair hung in sweaty strands around his face. Red circles rimmed his icy eyes. He had been crying, Jim realized, crying from the way his father had shamed him. For the first time, Jim saw how young Bartholomew really was.

"You have no idea what it's like, do you?" Bartholomew asked Jim, his voice tight and thick. "Not with your father, did you? Not with the perfect and honorable, Lord Lindsay Morgan. No idea at all." Bartholomew spat the name of Jim's father.

"No," Jim said quietly. "I do know."

"Know it all then, do you? Think you're better than me too, do you?"

Jim's heart hammered in his chest. Not the Count, not Splitbeard, not Hudson, not anyone else he had ever known was near enough to stop what was about to happen. Jim's poisoned arm burned hot and he fell to one knee from the pain.

"On your knees again then, eh, Morgan?" Bartholomew seethed, raising his sword. "The way it is destined to end between us! One on his knees and the other with sword in hand!" Bartholomew raised his blade over his head.

But before Bartholomew could strike, a howl split Jim's ears. The thumping beat of feathered wings clapped over his head and slammed into Bartholomew. The younger Cromier was suddenly rolling head over heels back through the tall grass, tossed aside like a rag doll. The spread wings of a harpy landed between Bartholomew and Jim. The flying hunter slowly turned to face the clan. For one terrifying heartbeat, Jim was sure it would be Celia's scarred face before him, ready to make good on her promise to devour them all for desert. Instead though, the face that greeted them was decorated with a deranged smile and googly yellow eyes.

"Hullo, ya li'l devils!" said Ally. "Couldn't be havin' my game-playin' friends skewered by that bully, now could I? Who would we chase after dinner? Now, run along with you and I'll make me sisters count to one hundreds before we come chasin' ya again! Harpy's honor!"

"Thank you, Miss Ally," Lacey said. The children wasted no time and ran off again through the tall grass. Paul, however, stopped for a moment, reached into his pocket, and flicked something at Ally's feet.

"You're a real sport, Miss Ally!" he said, tipping his hat and bowing low. "A real sport, indeed!" As the children made their escape, Jim could hear Ally cackling and laughing at the top of her lungs about owning the roundest, most-glitteriest marble in the entire world.

NINE

Fording the Tears of the Mountain

The sun had disappeared in the east and a pale moon risen in its place by the time the clan waded through the last wall of grass. The sounds of battle between the flying sisters and the Count's men had lasted for quite a while as they had fled. Celia and Ocy made off with at least two pirates for dinner (which Lacey said was awful, just awful, even for such rotten men as those pirates).

"At least the harpies will be busy for a while," Jim said. "But if the Cromiers and Splitbeard are still out there, they're most likely headed in the same direction as we are, so let's get on with it."

On they went, up a sloping hill beneath the rising blue moon. Try as Jim did to fight it, his teeth chattered when he spoke and he shivered in every breath of wind. With the wrappings gone, the chill had strengthened its grip on Jim's body – all except for his arm. The poison flowing there crackled like fire beneath his skin.

"How long do you think we got til mornin'?" George asked, nervously glancing at the moon.

"Long enough if we quit yapping and keep walking!" Jim snapped. The hard edge of his own voice stunned him. He had not meant to sound so heartless. But the flute song played louder in his thoughts and the black tendrils wound their way like ivy all the way past the crook of his elbow. The poison was on the move.

"We still have plenty of time, George," Lacey said. She put a comforting hand on George's back and pulled Peter and Paul along beside her. "Let's just keep moving. I think we'll go much faster back to the beach than we came to this point, don't you think, Jim?" Lacey looked with some hope at him, but Jim said nothing in return. He fought to keep his teeth from chattering, as though he were walking in winter's grasp.

The little band crested the hill where they paused to survey the way before them. A vast forest spilled out beneath the moonlight. Countless trees stretched for miles, all the way to the rocky mountain at the isle's center. The forest seemed black from where Jim and his friends stood - shadowed and thick. It was a maze of trees even longer and more winding than the crags or the Sea of Grass.

"Seems like a long way to the mountain," said Peter, whistling low and shaking his head. "And hard to keep headin' the right direction without Mister Cornelius bein' able to fly, ain't it?"

"We still got the compass, Peter," offered Paul, who had been carrying it for Lacey ever since they'd left the crags. "And it really is sort of like London, isn't it? If you look at the trees like buildin's, from here to that mountain can't be any farther from the cellar to the town square where we used to lift breakfast, could it?"

"Too right, Paul!" added George, sounding a bit brighter. "We used to run that whole way back, too, thanks to Butterstreet and his lot chasin' us. You know, if we make it out of this, I may just have to thank that old bloke for puttin' us in such tremendous shape, eh?"

"Before we even start worrying about the forest," Jim said, his chin quivering as he pointed to the bottom of the hill with his poisoned hand. "We have to find a way over that." By 'that', Jim meant the rushing river winding its way around the curve of the hill and along the edge of the dark forest. It was the Tears of the Mountain, the river of which Twisttail had told them.

When the clan came down the hill to the river's banks, their shoulders slumped and they all fell into silent dismay. Any hope that Peter or Paul had inspired at the top of the hill vanished. Lacey kept her eyes fixed on the river, risking not even a glance in Jim's direction.

"We should look for some rocks or something to cross upon at least, don't you think?" she said. This was a perfectly sensible plan, but Jim hardly heard her. When he looked at the river, all he saw was another obstacle thrown in his way by cruel fate. What little hope or goodwill stood in his heart against the rose thorn's magic crumbled. The black poison in his veins was quick to seize the moment.

"There's no time for that," Jim snapped. He seized Lacey by the elbow, for Cornelius was in one arm and her handbag still in the other. "Grab ahold, everyone, and come on. The only way across this river is straight through! I won't let a little trickle of water slow me down!"

"Jim, wait!" Lacey tried to say, but it was too late. Jim yanked her into the river. The Ratts barely had time to grab onto Lacey's other elbow and complete the chain.

The river struck Jim like an icy fist and shocked the breath from him. Ripples and waves smacked him first in the chest and then in the shoulders. Soon the water was cresting his face. Behind him, Jim heard Lacey and the Ratts coughing and sputtering as the water covered their heads. Lacey was fighting desperately to hold poor Cornelius above the surface and keep the raven from drowning.

Before they crossed the river's middle, poor Paul, who was the shortest of all the clan, could no longer touch the bottom with his feet. He must have swallowed a lungful of water, for he suddenly shouted with choking gasps that vaguely sounded like "Help! Help!"

Jim heard the desperate splashing and flailing in the water behind him. The last bits of his thoughts that were still free of the poison wanted so badly to turn back around and help, or give up crossing this river altogether. But the dark magic in his veins was far too strong by then. Jim squeezed harder on Lacey's arm and pulled with all his strength.

Whether by blind luck or fate, Paul managed to hang onto Peter's hand, and the entire group made it to the far side of the river. They dragged themselves onto the bank, drenched to the bone and exhausted from fighting the strength of the waters. George, Lacey, and the Ratts shivered in the cool night air. Lacey frantically rubbed Cornelius's wings with her hands to try and keep him warm, while George and Peter slapped Paul's back over and over again to beat the water from his lungs.

"Alright," Jim said, shaking so violently he had to clench his teeth to keep them from chattering. "No time to rest. Let's get through that forest and onto that blasted cave."

"Give us a moment!" George snapped. For the first time he sounded cross and irritated with Jim. "We're half drowned here, and Paul is mostly drowned! He almost drifted off down the river in case you didn't notice, you prat!"

"Well, he didn't drown, though, did he? You saved him! So unless you all want to turn to stone looking like wet, miserable sods, then I suggest we pull ourselves together and get moving again. Now, who has the compass?"

Silence followed for a moment. Paul coughed up the last of the water he had swallowed and looked up meekly at Jim and his brothers. "I had it," he said miserably, as though he were about to burst into tears.

"What do you mean, *had* it?" Jim demanded, the pain in his arm redoubling again.

"When the water rushed over my head in the river, I panicked." Paul's chin quivered and his voice grew thick. "I reached out for Peter and George. I...I didn't mean to, but I must have let go of the compass. I lost it."

"Lost it?" Jim asked. The black tendrils crossed from Jim's shoulder into his chest. His words were no longer his own. "You lost the compass? How could you do that, Paul?"

"He did it because he nearly drowned, Jim!" said George, standing up for his brother, who began to cry on the riverbank. "Because we couldn't take even one blasted moment to look around for some rocks to cross! Because you dragged us into that river without even thinking if we could make it across, mate! We could have all drowned!"

"Maybe it would have been better if we *had* drowned, George," Jim raged, taking off his soaking hat and throwing it on the ground. "Because now we have no way to navigate through the forest, do we? We might as well just sit here and wait to turn to stone!"

"Now, young Morgan, that is quite enough, I think," Cornelius cawed weakly, trying to restore some order. But Jim was far too furious to listen to the raven's words.

"Quite enough?" Jim snarled. "Will it be quite enough for everyone when we all turn into statues because we can't find our way through this bloody forest?"

"There might still be a way," said Lacey, trying desperately to calm the group down. She pointed up to the sky and opened her book in one hand. "The stars!" she cried. "Jim, George, the stars in the sky here match the ones from my book. They make constellations just like the ones that were in your father's map, remember? I'm sure they can help us find the way." Lacey pulled the wet book from her handbag and held out the open pages to show them. "There's still a chance that we can find the cave!"

"You and your stupid stars and your stupid book, Lacey!" Jim thundered. "The lizard, who is from this island, I might add, told us the right way to go. So that's the way we're going! The mountain, where the cave is, where the cave has to be – is right on the other side of these trees. We're not turning back now, not when we're so close!"

"Oh, Jim," cried Lacey, shutting her book with a thump. She stormed up beside George and glared at Jim with enough fire in her eyes to dry his soaked clothes and set the forest behind him ablaze. "This isn't you talking, can't you tell that? It's that poison in your arm. That poison from that horrible rose is making you do things you know you shouldn't, and say things I know you wouldn't. Come back to us, Jim! Help us, because if you don't, we're not going to make it. All of us are going to turn to stone on this island or worse. Listen to yourself. This isn't you...this isn't our friend talking. Please let us try to follow the stars, please!"

"There's no time, Lacey! We're not following the stars in your stupid book. If you want to follow them then here," Jim ripped the book from Lacey's hands. Without so much as a second thought, he hurled it into the river. It splashed into the deepest part of the waters and quickly drifted away. "Follow the book wherever it takes you! But I'm going through the forest, even if I have to go myself."

Lacey gasped - a shocked and sudden gasp like a blast of cold air that snatches the breath from one's lungs. Two teardrops trickled down her cheeks, so bright and glistening that they stood out from the river water still clinging to her face. But Jim was already turning on his heel and marching toward the forest edge, shaking from head to toe as though he was freezing. When he reached the tree line, he turned back over his shoulder and said:

"Are you lot coming or not?"

Peter and Paul looked at each other, then to George. George looked to Lacey, whose head was bowed so low her chin was on her chest. With a great sniffle, Lacey trudged forward. Peter helped Paul to his feet, and along with George, the three Ratts followed.

Jim said not a word of thanks or appreciation. He but turned to the forest and strode into the pitch-black darkness between the trees.

TEN

THE DARK FOREST

Jim, the Ratts, and Lacey trudged through the darkness beneath the black trees. The branches grabbed at them like clawing fingers, scratching their faces and tangling their hair. Mist clung to their legs like cold, damp spiderwebs. The crawling fog denied their shivering bones even the slightest hint of warmth. The ground itself seemed to fight against them. Roots, holes, and fallen branches bit at their ankles from beneath the milky fog. On occasion, a lone beam of blue moonlight found its way through the dense forest canopy. Blackness hid most of the sky and the stars, though it would have made little difference, for Lacey's book was lost to the river along with the compass.

Paul still sniffled occasionally. He whispered to Jim or to George or perhaps to himself how sorry he still was. But for the most part, they walked in silence. As the time dragged on, Jim shivered more and more violently. His teeth clattered and his legs shook. His left arm hung limp and dead at his side. The black tendrils from the wound in his hand were crawling over his chest. Yet he kept on, one foot after the other through the dark.

Whether the poison running through Jim's blood would allow him to admit it or not, somewhere in his heart he knew he and his friends were lost. Dawn was but several hours away. Doom would be close behind.

Yet, just when all hope seemed lost, a low rush penetrated the silence. A wall of blue moonlight appeared between the trees in the near distance. A surge of vindication swelled up inside Jim. He began to run as fast as his sickened body would carry him.

"See!" he shouted, his voice strained and shaking. "I told you! It's the end of the forest! We've reached the mountain and soon we'll be at the—"

Jim never finished. When he, the Ratts, and Lacey broke through the trees, they all staggered to a halt at the bank of the river called the Mountain's Tears. The water flowed fast and hard. On the other side was the hill that led back to the Sea of Tall Grass. They had walked in a complete circle.

None of the clan said anything. A flash of heat erupted in Jim's hand and the pain burned out of control. The agony brought him to one knee, but when George moved to help him to his feet, Jim slapped his friend's hand away and forced himself to stand.

"We must go back through!" Jim shouted. His voice was broken and gravelly. "There's still time! There's still time to beat the Cromiers to the cave!"

"Jim," Lacey said, her voice trembling. "We've been walking for hours and hours in a circle. We're not going to find the cave. We must go back. We should try and go back to the beach while there's still a chance to make it though the Devil's Horns."

"A chance?" Jim screamed. "I can't let them do it! I won't! They've taken everything. I won't let them take any more! I will have my revenge!"

"Can you even hear yourself, mate?" George walked over to Jim and shook him by the shoulders. "I wanted you get your stuff back just as much as anyone, I swear I did. But look what it's doin' to you! Can't you just let it go?"

"Let it go?" Jim staggered back from George. "You don't understand! You don't know what it's like to have lost your father and everything he gave you. You never even knew your father, George!"

George stood still in the moonlight by the river, as though morning had already come and turned him to stone. Silence like death fell over the children, so quiet that the lone tear that fell from George's cheek could almost be heard as it landed in the grass. Neither Peter nor Paul tried to make a joke or smile. There was no cheer left in any of their faces. In the end, it was Lacey who finally spoke. Her voice shook as she spoke.

"We do too know what it's like to lose, Jim Morgan," Lacey said. "Now we know what it's like to lose a friend. We have to turn back or we're going to turn to stone on this island."

"There is no way back!" Jim raged. "The only way is forward! To the cave!"

"I'm sorry, Jim," Lacey replied, and she finally turned away.

"Fine then! Go back! I don't need you! I'm glad you're going. I'm going to find the shell and the treasure for myself. Do you hear me? All mine and nobody else's! I'll show those Cromiers…I'll show you! I don't need anybody!"

Paul and Peter hung their heads. Cornelius lacked the strength to argue with Jim or give him the tongue-lashing he deserved. But as the others began to shuffle along, George alone stepped to the riverbank beside Jim, his hat in his hand.

"I still remember the day you gave me this hat, Jim," George mumbled, looking down at his hands. "I was gonna give up on everythin', remember? I was gonna quit thievin' and give up helpin' you and me own brothers, even. I said some rotten things and made Lacey cry. But you didn't give up on me then, did you? You bought me this hat on Christmas. It's the only present I ever got from anybody. That's the truth and you know it. So, please don't tell me to give up on you now."

George's words stung some hidden place within Jim - some deep chamber in the depths of his heart. But even then the black poison and the wretched cold that held Jim in their grasp refused to let him speak. The dark magic held his chattering teeth shut, and all Jim could do was look away from his best friend.

"Come on, George," Lacey said. "We have to go."

George lingered another moment longer, as if hoping Jim might still change his mind. But Jim refused to meet his friend's eye. Yet it was that moment, as George sadly put his hat back on his head, that saved them all from complete disaster.

Just as Lacey, Peter, and Paul began to search for a river crossing, a loud crack snapped from the forest edge. Leaves fluttered down from the braches into the thick mist. The clan froze where they stood. None of them dared draw a breath. For what seemed like an eternity, the five friends and the raven stood in complete silence. Four orbs, wide as boulders and glowing green, opened in the darkness beyond the trees.

Lacey and the Ratts scurried away, but hardly fast enough. At the sound of another crack, the two pairs of flaming green orbs dropped down from the trees. With a hammering like thundering war drums the shadowy creatures burst into the moonlight to the beating of great wings.

The mists curled away like parting curtains to reveal great owls - old feathers of brown and gray bristling like armor. Gnarled beaks and claws snapped and grabbed at the air. The owls rose up into the night, talons outstretched and their deep green eyes fixed upon the clan, who cowered like frightened mice beneath their claws.

Lacey screamed and fell back toward the river, but the owl's screech drowned out her cries. The winged hunters descended upon them. Jim watched in a trance as one of the mighty birds came for him. But before the owl's outstretched claws seized him, George leapt and tackled them both into the wet mud at the River's edge. The owl's talons sliced through the air just above their heads.

Sliding in the mud, George dragged Jim between two rocks, safe from the owl's clutches. George screamed for Lacey and his brothers, but the others had not been nearly quick enough. It was only moments before the owls had them in their grasp. Lacey, still clinging to Cornelius in one arm, was taken by the first, Peter and Paul by the second, hanging on to each other for dear life. All three of their mouths were open wide as though they were screaming, but to Jim the world was silent and numb. He could no longer feel even the pain in his arm or the cold wracking his body. He watched the owls soar off into the moonlight. Lacey stretched her arm back to George and Jim, as though they could reach out and pull her back to safety.

George screamed again for his brothers, but the silence entombing Jim would not be broken. He closed his eyes and let the darkness swallow him whole at last.

ELEVEN

GEORGE RATT AND THE QUEEN OF THE FAERIES

J im dreamt of a time long ago. He was racing his old pony, Destroyer, through the forbidden forest that stretched from the borders of Morgan Manor. In the dream, Jim was running for his life, but a danger worse than soldiers on horseback chased him this time.

It was the Crimson Storm.

It came quickly for Jim. Blood red rolled in the shadows of its dark crevices. Lightning burned white-hot eyes into the black skull within the storm clouds. The face shouted Jim's name as it descended upon him, blasting trees from its path with fiery bolts. Fast through the forest Jim fled, as he had over a year ago. He pushed Destroyer harder and harder until he came to the river into which he had fallen during his first escape – but this time there would be no such fortune. The river's waters had turned black as pitch, black as the poison tendrils in Jim's arm.

The poisonous river was alive.

It reached out beyond the banks and seized Jim by the arm. The black water pulled him from Destroyer's back and dragged him beneath the surface.

Down the river Jim floated, whisked away by the dark rapids. He tried to escape, but again and again he was yanked beneath the waves. Rocks and branches bruised and battered his body along the way. The river refused to release Jim, and Jim failed to break its hold. Finally he surrendered and let the current take him where it would. Down Jim sank into the depths.

But before Jim fell all the way to the riverbed, a flame bloomed to life above the surface. It was bright as the morning sun. Glowing tendrils broke through the waters. They reached out and surrounded Jim. They kept him from falling even deeper in the murk - but they did not pull him to the surface. A voice spoke to him from the light.

"Jim Morgan, you have very nearly sunk beyond even my reach."

"Will you help me?" Jim asked. He reached for the cords of light, but they lay beyond his grasp.

"Why should I rescue you? What cause of yours is so noble and true? Was it not by your own hand that you pricked your finger with the rose thorn and poisoned your blood?"

"I'm looking for the shell, the shell my father left me. It leads to the Treasure of the Ocean."

"Many have sought the shell – and many more have sought the Treasure of the Ocean. Many have perished on their quests. I did not help any of them."

"But I never wanted the shell in the first place. I just wanted to go home. The Cromiers – they're the ones! They burnt it to the ground. They killed my father and burnt my home to the ground. There's nothing left now but the shell. I have to stop them. I have to beat them to the shell!"

"It is true, the Cromiers burnt down your house. But your home was not wholly lost until this very day, nor was it truly destroyed by the Count or his son. If the only answer you have for destruction is more destruction, or pain for more pain, how will anything good ever grow in your life? Think about your home, Jim Morgan. What do you see?"

"I see a blackened pile of ashes lying in ruins on the coast of England!" Jim cried.

"Are bricks and beams all there is to a home for you?" The light replied, flashing brighter and hotter in the gloom of the river. "If so, then I shall leave you here and call it a mercy, for you shall never know joy in this life. Now, think of home. What do you see?"

Jim closed his eyes and searched his memories. At first, he thought only of Morgan Manor, before it had been burned to nothing. But then he thought of the cellar beneath the shoe factory, the lighthouse by the sea, and even the cabin below the *Spectre's* decks. Yet there was something more beneath the surface of those memories. It was his father's strong hand on his shoulder, MacGuffy's grumbling lessons, Lacey's flashing blue eyes, Peter and Paul's laughter, and George's arm over his shoulder. Another thought occurred to Jim then. It cut him more deeply than all the other pains put together.

"I burnt my home down," Jim said. The image of Lacey reaching out to him from the clutches of the owl flashed in his thoughts and broke his heart through and through. "I burnt it down in just one day. Maybe you should let me go."

"What would you go through to rebuild that home, Jim Morgan? What would you endure?" Jim thought about it for a moment, but he found his answer inwardly, spoken by the most unlikely of teachers.

"I would weather ten-thousand storms," Jim said. There was quiet for a breath, but then the light flared so brightly it broke the darkness. The brilliant flash blinded Jim, even in the dream.

"So be it, Jim Morgan! But know that you shall bear a scar, and there shall be great pain." One tendril of light reached out and took Jim by his poisoned hand. It seared Jim's arm to the bone. It burned so badly that Jim screamed aloud and wished he would die. But as it scorched his arm, the light also pulled Jim up through the pitch waters.

"Now," said the voice. "Wake up, Jim."

Jim broke the surface of the river. He gasped in the warm night air and the light enveloped his entire body.

"Jim, you must wake up!"

"Jim, wake up!"

Jim sucked in the startled breath of a broken dream. He kicked and thrashed about until his eyes fluttered open. He shouted aloud and swung at the air as though still in danger of drowning. After a moment, though, Jim realized he was free of the waters. He took a deep breath, his heart still pounding.

Jim found himself beneath the branches of a great tree planted beside the river. A fine coat of spring flowers dressed the branches, red and white and bursting into bloom. The mist that had been crawling on the forest floor, grabbing at his ankles, was gone, replaced by a soft bed of grass. In that grass beside him sat George Ratt, and Jim realized it had been George calling for him to wake.

"You're awake," George said. He was a bit pale in the moonlight and let out a long, slow breath, as though he had been holding it for a very long time. "Are you alright? Is your...is your arm alright?

"My arm?" Jim asked. The cobwebs of the nightmare were still clearing from his mind, but it struck him suddenly. The pain, that gnawing agony that had been clawing at his arm from the inside ever since he'd pricked his thumb, was gone. The ice-cold chills that had wracked his body had disappeared as well. The evening air felt warm once again. Even the whispering voice at the back of his mind and the song of Philus Philonius's flute were silent. In fact, the only sensation

Jim felt on his hand was a gentle scratching, for his arm up to his elbow was wrapped in bandages.

Jim took another deep breath. He felt alive and refreshed, like waking up after a long sleep or climbing out of bed the first morning after a fever has broken. But it took only another moment for Jim to remember what he had lost. He had said things – awful things to his friends. He had cut them to the bone with his words. He could still see Lacey reaching for him from beneath the shadow of great wings, her mouth open in a silent scream.

"Oh, George! Oh, George, they're gone! It's all my fault…it's all my fault. I'm sorry. I'm so sorry." A great knot tied itself in the center of Jim's throat and his chin quivered uncontrollably. "Those things I said to you. If I were you I would have let those owls take me instead of your brothers."

"It wasn't you, Jim," George said softly. "It was that poison inside of you talkin', not the real you. I know that."

"I think some of it was me, George," Jim whispered. "Maybe the poison just let that part out. You should have just left me there, George. You should have left me for those owls." George said nothing for a moment, as though thinking very hard about whether or not he wanted to say anything or not. Then he cleared his throat and told Jim something he'd never told him before.

"I really did know my father, Jim." George stared into the grass beneath them without blinking. "I don't remember much of 'im, you know, just one memory, really. I guess I'm actually more like a couple of years older than Peter and Paul, not just one – 'cause I remember standin' there, on the steps of St. Anne's. Peter and Paul were sittin' there at me feet, and they was cryin' and everythin' cause it was cold. And there was me da' and me ma'. Me ma' didn't say nothin', but me da' patted me on the shoulder and he said to me, he said: "George, you're the oldest, so take care of yer little brothers until me and your ma' get back. But we'll be back, he said. We'll be back. But they never came back. They lied.

"So I took care of me brothers the best I could. Was always makin' up stories about things our father had said and things he'd done, just to make 'em laugh. Then, one day, you come along." Finally George looked at Jim. His eyes glistened in the gray light. "At first I had to look out fer ya, just like me brothers. You was an awful thief at first, Jim, if you remember the incident with the apples and all." George snorted a snuffly laugh.

"But then all the sudden you got good, as good as me and Lacey. And we was stuck, stuck in that cabin with Dread Steele. I though then, just like me da', that'd be the last time I ever saw you. But you come back, didn't you? That's when I knew...that's when I knew you was more than me friend. You was me brother, too."

Jim stared at George, his eyes and his nose and his throat all stinging and thick. Jim could hardly think of one thing to say, not one that was worth what his best friend had just told him. All he could say was: "You shouldn't give credit to your father for all those things you say, George. They're good sayings. They're your sayings and they're good all on their own."

Jim and George threw their arms over each other's shoulders, slapping each other hard on the back. After that, they coughed and sniffed and slapped at their faces as though they had never even thought of shedding a tear in the first place.

"I'm going to go back for them, George," Jim said hoarsely. "Not really sure I can explain how I know they're still alive, but I do. I'm going to go back and make it right. Even if I have to turn to stone to do it. I promise."

"You don't have to explain how you know, Jim. ' Cause the person who told me they was all still alive is probably the same person who told you." George looked over Jim's shoulder. When Jim turned from the river, he had to shield his eyes with his arm. A great, gold light nearly blinded him. The golden glow spilled onto the grass and glittered on the river, warmer than a summer morning. Floating at the light's heart, at its very source, was a young girl. When Jim dared to meet the girl's eyes, they glimmered with wisdom as ancient as the gypsy witch's who had once cursed Jim's box. Dragonfly wings hummed behind her shoulders. Her hair, yellow as the sun, fluttered behind her, held in place by a silver circlet that must have been her crown.

"Who are you?" Jim finally managed.

"I am Tanaquill," said the glowing girl. "Queen of the Faeries."

"It was your voice," Jim said, feeling the need to bow his head to the Queen. "It was your voice I heard in my dream. You saved us from the owls. You saved me from the poison."

"It was my voice that you heard," Tanaquill replied. "And indeed, it was my magic that pulled you back from the brink, and not a moment too soon! The poison had nearly reached your heart. Then you would have been lost forever. But it was not I who saved you from the owls." Tanaquill's eyes flitted past Jim to George. "Your friend carried you to me in his arms, some miles from where you fell. His strength was all but gone when I found him. I first thought his efforts in vain, for the poison within your blood ran deep." Tanaquill's light illuminated the blossoms drifting from the tree like tumbling stars to where Jim and George sat in the grass. "It was for the love your friend showed you, Jim Morgan, that I entered into your dream. Such love should never go unrewarded. But there are greater reasons I chose to save you. The first is that you now have a promise to keep." Tanaquill reached her finger to Jim's hand. Without touching, she unspooled the white bandages from his arm and sent them floating off beyond the tree like a swirling ribbon into the night.

From Jim's thumb, where he'd first drawn his own blood on the cursed thorn, a scar like a white leaf curled onto his palm. It unfolded there into the perfect image of a rose in bloom, the stem and leaves trailing down his arm. Jim knew without looking that the scar ran all the way up his shoulder and onto his chest, where the black poison had once twisted like a dreadful vine. Jim let his hand sink back down into his lap and his chin settled on his chest.

"Do not lose hope, Jim Morgan," Tanaquill said. She floated down to where Jim sat in the grass and lifted his chin with her finger, which was warm and kind as the dawn. "There is more to you than your scars, Son of Earth and Son of Sea. There is goodness in your heart." At that moment, another, golden light hovered over Tanaquill's shoulder. At first Jim thought it was another fairy. But it was only a firefly. The firefly bobbed once before Jim's face, and Jim knew then that it was the very firefly he'd freed from the spider's web. "To take pity on the smallest and most insignificant creatures is the sign of a great heart indeed."

"Your friends yet live. You are charged with saving them, as I saved you. The owls were summoned by the dark pirate, Splitbeard, who is no stranger to evil magic. Even now the Cromiers have them and draw near to the cave beneath the mountain. But Jim Morgan, there is one more task you must accomplish. There is one more reason I spared you from the poison in your veins." The faery queen's face grew solemn. She suddenly seemed thousands of years older than her child-like face belied. "You must not allow the Treasure of the Ocean to fall into Count Cromier's hands. The Treasure's power is as old as the faeries. It is the power of the seas and the winds and the clouds themselves. Only a Son of Earth and Son of Sea may harness this power. But of these rare children, there are only two. One is the son of Lindsay Morgan."

"The other is Bartholomew," Jim said. He was not sure how he knew, but somehow he was certain.

"Yes," Tanaquill said. "His heart has been blackened by his father."

"Can you help us?" Jim pleaded. "Can you use your magic against Splitbeard? Against the Cromiers?"

The Faerie Queen shook her head no.

"My power and the power of my people extend only as far as the edge of this field, to the river behind you. But there is a secret passage that leads to the Painted Cave beneath the mountain. It lies beyond a door lined in green and guarded by two white-blossomed trees. The passage may take you to the Hidden Chamber there within, masked behind a door of fangs, before the Cromiers and Splitbeard reach it. My people will take you there, but little time will you have to return before the fate of stone seals your doom. This you must do, Jim Morgan. Are you ready?"

"I suppose I have to be," Jim said. "Tanaquill, please take George back to the beach. If I'm able to free my friends, and if there's time, will you then take them all back to the Devil's Horns as well?"

"No, Jim!" said George. He jumped to his feet and crossed his arms over his chest. His eyes flashed with a passion that would have done Lacey proud. "You're not goin' into that cave alone. Not without me. Besides, if we are goin' to turn to stone, I've been savin' a special face to make at you when we go, just so everyone will know what a git you've been today!" A small smile flickered to life on Jim's face and George returned it.

"I suppose that will be two of us then," Jim said, standing up beside his friend.

"I have no further gift to give you, Jim Morgan, for I have already given you much. But take these at least from the river. Use them to right your wrong." Tanaquill pointed to the flowing waters behind Jim and George and two flames burst from the river and floated through the air toward Jim. Jim knew what they were. He reached out to take Lacey's book of stars and the compass. The Queen of the Faeries offered Jim a smile that brightened even the glow of her aura. She leaned forward in the air and kissed Jim gently on the forehead. From that place, warmth drifted down into Jim's fingers and toes.

"Take heart, Jim. There are few joys in the world greater than a broken bridge mended."

"Thank you, Tanaquill. Thank you for everything."

Tanaquill raised her hands and called out into the night with words that Jim would never learn. Bursts of light streaked into the night air from the long grass on the hill and flew into the darkened sky. They burned in nearly every color imaginable. In auras of blue and green and gold, they twirled and wound through the air. Embers of light trailed down behind them like sparks from a torch.

"That lizard," said George, his eyes staring through the display of light and color before him. " That blasted lizard, Twisttail, lied to us. He sent us away from this Field of Lights where the faeries woulda helped us. He said they were evil spirits! Almost got us killed! Why?"

"I don't know why, George. Maybe just for sport."

"He lied to us," George said again. A darkness fell over his face then, a darkness Jim had last seen when the King of Thieves had betrayed the Ratts in London.

"Do not give into anger, George Ratt," said Tanaquill, hovering before George. "Even in the face of great pain you have the gift of joy in times of hurt. That is a gift greater than any I could give you."

"Could you..." George began to ask. He swiped his hat from his head and twisted it in his hands, blushing fiercely. "Could you at least give me a kiss like Jim?" he asked, looking down at his feet. Tanaquill laughed, a laugh full of lightness and joy like chimes in the wind.

"You may have two kisses, George Ratt, and you deserve them both!" With that the Queen of the Faeries kissed George once on each cheek. Jim thought for a moment that his friend's feet were about to leave the ground and he would begin floating above the grass along with the faeries.

"Thank you, ma'am," George replied, slapping his hat back on his head all but staggering over beside Jim.

"Pull yourself together, mate," Jim whispered with a smile, elbowing his friend in the ribs.

"Now you must go, for there is little time." Tanaquill called again to her people. The glowing lights on the hill swirled together into a great river of light. They wound their way through the air toward Jim and George. The two of them were swept up in the tide, rolled over by a wave of light. The grass blurred beneath Jim like a rushing green carpet as the faeries whisked him and George over the fields and rolling hills toward the mountain. All the while the nighttime sky slowly turned from black to gray. The stars that Lacey so loved winked out one by one. Jim's friends were in terrible danger, and morning was coming. It loomed just over the horizon, and with it, a prison of stone.

TWELVE

THE PAINTED CAVE

The flying river of faeries raced to the edge of their land and crashed to a halt at the foot of the dark mountain, exploding like a wave against invisible rocks. Streaks of light splashed into the air and Jim and George went tumbling into the soft grass. Jim's body hummed from head to toe as he picked himself up from the ground. He and George were wind-blown and breathless from their flight over Queen Tanaquill's domain.

"Couldn't 'ave just set us down, could ya 'ave?" George said to the faeries as he readjusted his hat and his jacket. The army of pixies just laughed with a sound like soft rain on a pond. They pointed and waved at the boys - a sea of flickering candle flames. Jim could have watched them fly and play for hours and hours, mesmerized by the lights. But the dawn crept close behind them.

"Come on, George," Jim whispered. The two boys ran the rest of the way, to where the grass grew thin and the rocks slowly became the foot of the dark mountain. The black shape stood tall in the sky and masked what remained of the stars and the moon. Yet even in the shadow of the mountain, Jim and George quickly found the sign Tanaquill had promised.

Two trees, white blossoms bright even in the dark, stood in columns before the rock. Green ivy grew in an archway on the stone. Between the trees and beneath the ivy Jim found the hidden entrance to the cave. The door was carved from the rock itself. Beside it hung an unlit torch upon a grommet, the striking stone dangling there by a string. As it had been in the Pirate Vault of Treasures, a warning was carved deep into the face of the stone door.

"Another door, another warning." Jim said to himself.

"What does it say?" George asked, plucking the torch from the grommet and handing it to Jim.

"Magic, Monsters, and Doom Beyond this Door.
Ye Have Been Warned."

"Well, that sounds about right, don't it?" George said. He took a deep breath and swallowed hard, his face more than a bit pale.

"You don't have to go in, Georgie," Jim said as he struck the stone on the wall and lit the torch with the sparks. "I've done this sort of thing before, and it wasn't fun the first time, I promise you. So if you want to wait here—"

"People'll call you all sorts o' stuff, in this life, Jim, but don't ever let chicken be one of 'em." George said. "So my father always – well, so I always say." Jim smiled back at his friend.

"So, in we go?"

"In we go," said George.

Jim held the torch high and leaned against the stone door. It opened with the crunching grate of stone against stone. A gust of air rushed from the blackness beyond and the scent of ancient time swirled thick about them. The torch flame whispered and whipped in the wind. Jim summoned his courage and fixed his thoughts on Peter, Paul, and Lacey. He stepped into the darkness with George just behind.

The shadows on the cave walls swam about Jim and George as they followed the tunnel beneath the mountain. Darkness loomed on all sides, kept at bay only by the fire-lit reach of Jim's torch. Teeth of sharp stone jutted down over the boys' heads, and above the whisper of Jim's flame, the steady drip, drop of water echoed in the deep.

Jim and George stuck close together, tucking themselves in the center of the torchlight's sphere. But more than fear of the dark hastened their steps. The doom of sunrise followed close behind.

After a long while, the pair had gone so far that Jim feared they had missed a turn somewhere. He worried if they carried on much farther, they would descend to the very center of the earth. But he and George crept through an archway in the stone and the torchlight burst into the free space of a massive cavern. The ceiling above curved like a great dome, arching far over the boys' heads. Jim stared up at the high cavern roof, awed in spite of all his fears and worries. George whistled low and urgently tugged at Jim's tattered sleeve.

"Would you look at that?" George whispered. Jim raised the torch in his hand a little higher. His own eyes went wider still.

On the walls before them, polished smooth as glass and shining nearly like mirrors in the torchlight, enormous paintings lined the way from one entrance of the cavern to the other. Each drawing was taller than Jim and George and wider than their outstretched arms, a great mural from ancient times.

"It's the painted cave, George. We found it! Now we just need to find the entrance to the Hidden Chamber within."

"You know, Jim," George said. "Reminds me o' the stained glass back at St. Anne's, if you know what I mean. Like they're religious pictures that go in a story or somethin'." Jim ran the torch from the tunnel entrance to the other side of the cavern, where the tunnel resumed once more.

251

"I think you're right, George." A frightful story it was, too. The paintings told of a great city, peopled by giants - a city more vast and powerful than even London. But by the final image, the city had fallen into the sea. Only one building, a temple of some sort, remained. Over and over the symbol of the Treasure of the Ocean, the very same trident as was carved onto Jim's box, appeared amidst the calamitous tale. Death and destruction, Jim thought to himself. Those were the fates that surrounded the Treasure of the Ocean, Queen Melodia had warned him.

"That entire city was destroyed," Jim finally said. "I wonder how a whole city could be destroyed, George."

"Don't know about that, Jim, but maybe that giant snake over there had somethin' to do with it." Jim turned to find a serpent's face glaring at him from the far wall - mouth open, fangs bared, ready to devour any creature fool enough to tempt its wrath. The painting was so life like that it gave Jim a start, but he saw nearly at once that this drawing differed from the rest. Tanaquill's words from the riverbank came back to him, reminding him that the entrance to the Hidden Chamber lay behind a fanged doorway.

The two boys approached the hideous image with caution, for the open mouth was wide enough to swallow a handful of grown men whole.

"This must be the entrance to the hidden chamber," Jim said. But George ran his hand along the snake's fangs and found only solid rock behind the painting.

"Nothin' here but a big old' wall o' rock, Jim."

"That's why they call it a hidden chamber, George," Jim said. He stepped back a few paces from the serpent's mouth and stretched his torch toward the wall. "There must be some magic words or something." An idea stole into Jim's mind. Without wasting time he gave voice to the thought.

"Magic, monsters, and doom wait for me beyond this door.
I have been warned...but I'm not turning back."

The torch's whisper was the only reply. But just when George opened his mouth to say something smart, a slow grinding of stone cut through the quiet.

A dark hole broke through the cavern wall.

Jagged chunks of rock pulled away from one another like teeth in a beast's mouth. When the entrance fully opened, it appeared to Jim as though the painting had come to life in the rock – as though the great serpent bared its fangs for real. Jim and George looked at each other, then back at the newly formed hole in the wall. Their mouths hung open and the great spark of adventure caught fire once again in their hearts.

"Jim, if we ever do get to live in a house," George said, eyes sparkling in the torchlight. "This is the door I want to me room, 'cept with bigger fangs – definitely bigger fangs."

"I'm not sure Lacey would approve, Georgie. Not so sure how much I'd want to go in either, really."

"Yet in you must go, young Morgan," a voice said from behind them. "And in you shall go this very night!" The boys whirled around and found only darkness at their backs - until a second voice rasped from a black recess of the painted cave.

"Nara Lahaba!"

At those words three torches sparked to life. Beneath the flames, drenched in writhing shadows, the faces of Count Cromier, Bartholomew, and Splitbeard the Pirate leered at Jim and George. Lacey, Peter, and Paul struggled and squirmed in the villains' grasps, rough hands clamped over their mouths.

THIRTEEN

INTO THE SERPENT'S MOUTH

"Cromier!" Jim shouted. His angry voice echoed off the vaulted cavern walls. "Let them go, you coward!"

"You are in no position to demand anything, young Morgan," the Count snarled. His purple scar twisted and turned on his face. "Why do you persist in fighting the inevitable? You challenge death as haughtily and foolishly as your father. Yet you also bear in common with Lindsay his foolish courage, and even more of his dumb luck. Now you will use those cursed Morgan gifts to fetch for me the Hunter's Shell and lay it at my feet."

"Never!" Jim cried.

"Never?" the Count asked. He drew his sword and set the blade at Lacey's throat. Bartholomew took his sword in hand as well, resting the sharp edge on Peter's shoulder. "Never say never, Jim."

"I hoped you would say no, Morgan," Bartholomew seethed, his mouth twitching at the corners. "I want you to watch me do to every one of your friends what I should have done to you in your father's study. You can watch me run my blade through their hearts."

"Cowards!" Cornelius croaked weakly. He lifted his battered frame from Lacey's arms and raised a tattered wing to challenge Bartholomew. "To hide behind these young ones, to use them as your shields, marks you as curs and cheapens what traces of honor still cling to your name. You, who would claim the right to Lindsay Morgan's treasure, would hang another as bait upon a hook, out of fear for your own necks. You call yourself a captain of the sea? For shame, sir!"

Cornelius might have continued his barrage of insults at the Cromiers indefinitely, but the Count, a sneer upon his face, sheathed his sword and swatted Cornelius from Lacey's arms. The brave bird fell hard onto the rocky ground, where Cromier kicked him across the floor until he came to a rolling stop at Jim's feet. Broken feathers lay strewn across the rocks and the raven groaned in pain. Lacey shouted out and wrenched herself free of the Count's grasp. She ran to Cornelius and shielded him with her body. Gently, she stroked his feathers with her fingers and whispered that it would be all right. George had to hold Jim back from leaping across the cave and charging the Count, sword or no sword.

"Preach not to me of honor or chivalry or any of that rot, Darkfeather, you twit!" The Count raged. "You speak of good men and honor, but you know as well as I that Lindsay Morgan was nothing more than an arrogant thief. He was a man too frightened or too stupid to wield the power he had discovered. Nor speak to me of cowardice, for I am the one, the only Pirate of our order, willing to do what is necessary to unlock the greatest force of magic the world has ever known. If I must sacrifice some vagrant children to do so, then so be it."

"Perhaps we should skip straight to the sacrificing, Father," Bartholomew said. "Dawn is coming, Jim. So either stand here and watch your friends die by my blade or by stone, or bring my father his prize!"

"Speakin' o' dawn comin', you blackguard," George said, his fists balled up at his sides. "Maybe you should be just as worried about turnin' to stone as us!" It was Splitbeard who answered, a sly smile on his face and a curved dagger in his hand at Paul's throat.

"Have you not seen, oh callow thief? Splitbeard the Pirate has no fear of curses or death, nor has he need to flee with haste to the gate of the Devil's Horns. Thanks to Splitbeard's secret ways, the venerable Count Cromier and I have far more time than you think."

Jim rubbed his sweat-slicked palms against his breeches. One look at Peter and Paul, quivering with fear, and Lacey, tending to poor Cornelius, told Jim his hopes of beating the Cromiers were dashed. Once again, his friends' lives would hang in the balance as he risked a magical trial for his father's treasure – a magical trial that could easily end in his own death.

"Alright, Count," Jim said, his shoulders slumping in defeat. "I'll do it. But when I bring you the shell, swear to me that you will release my friends. Let them at least try for the Horns before dawn." George grabbed Jim by the arm and whispered harshly into his ear.

"Jim, are you sure about this? They may free us, mate, but you know that blighter, Bartholomew'll never let you go!"

"It's the only way, George. " But Jim knew in his heart George was right. Bartholomew would never let him live once the Count had the shell.

"Done," said the Count. He strode forward to stand over Lacey, who was still on her knees, cradling Cornelius. "But know this, young Morgan - if you attempt to deceive me as you did that petty criminal in London…" The Count pressed his blade beneath Lacey's chin until she gave a sharp gasp and a trickle of red ran down her neck. "Dawn will be the least of your friends' worries." The blackened rose's magic no longer held sway over Jim's heart or mind, but in that moment, he wanted nothing more than to knock the wicked smiles from the Cromiers' faces.

"Don't be afraid, Lacey," he said. He looked into her eyes with as much courage as he could find within himself. "I got the Amulet, remember? I'll get this shell as well." Jim reached into his pockets and withdrew the book of stars and the compass that had been lost in the river. He knelt down and set them on the ground beside Lacey. "I'm sorry," he said, his chin quivering. "I'm sorry for what I said and what I did. I'm going to make it right, I promise." Blade at her neck or no, Lacey threw an arm around Jim and pulled him close. Jim could feel her tears on his own cheek.

"Let me go with you, master Morgan," squawked a thin voice from the cradle of Lacey's arm. It was Cornelius, blinking open one bleary eye and stretching out one broken wing to touch Jim's face. "It will be just like old times, and I could always use a new story to tell, lad."

"Not this time," Jim said, patting the brave raven's head. "It looks like I'll need to walk into this vault on my own."

"You are your father's son, Jim Morgan," Cornelius said. When Jim frowned at this, the raven tapped him again with his wing. "That is a compliment, my son. Never believe otherwise."

"Thank you, Cornelius," Jim said. But the Count had seen enough. He took his blade from Lacey's throat and thrust the point to within an inch of Jim's nose.

"Enough! You will go into the cave and fetch me my prize now, Morgan. And do not delay, boy, for whether by my sword or a tomb of stone, doom lies just over the horizon."

"If I think for even a moment that you've hurt my friends," Jim growled in return. "I will lose the shell forever, and no one will have the Treasure of the Ocean. I swear it!" With that, Jim stood and turned on his heel to face the serpent's mouth - the entrance to the hidden chamber.

"Good luck, Jim," George managed.

"You make it back to us, Jim Morgan," Lacey added.

"I'll try." Jim stepped to the very lip of the gaping hole in the cavern wall. Looking down at the palm of his hand, he saw the white-scar rose plainly visible, even in the dim torchlight. "I must face another storm," he said to himself. "I would face ten thousand storms."

Jim put his head down, held his torch forth, and stepped into the blackness beyond the serpent's mouth.

FOURTEEN

UPON THE PATH OF RIDDLES

The darkness coiled about Jim. His torch flame choked to a dim flicker, as though suffocated by the thick black. Worse still, when Jim shone the torch at his feet, he discovered the rocky ground fell away steeply on either side, leaving only a narrow path to follow.

Jim's knees trembled and sweat slicked the palms of his hands. His toe caught a jagged rock at the path's edge and clattered down the cliff into the darkness. When the stone finally reached the bottom, only a splash echoed from some underground lake or river below.

It took all of Jim's will to move one foot forward and pull the second to join it. His legs were numb with fear. But, again and again, Jim repeated his deliberate steps until he was walking with some speed down the serpentine path of stone, deep into the heart of the cavern.

Jim's pace had quickened to nearly a jog when an unexpected splash sounded from the deep beneath the mountain.

Jim skidded to a halt. A gurgling came from below. Jim knew it then for certain – something had moved, something large in the waters.

Jim was not alone.

He wiped the sweat from his brow with the back of his hand and tightened his grip on the torch. Drawing once more on all his courage, he took another step.

A voice spoke in the dark.

"Who treads into the cavern of depths? Who has wandered into the cave of questions? Who walks upon the path of riddles?"

Jim froze again. His heartbeat thundered in his ears above the crackling torch flames. The voice in the dark rolled deep and large, like a great horn, echoing off the far-away walls of the hollow mountain. A growling lingered at the edges of the questions the voice asked Jim – an inhuman sound, Jim thought. An animal sound.

"I'm...I'm Jim Morgan, sir," Jim finally answered, not bothering to lie or even give a false name.

"Jim Morgan, will you stand still on the path forever?" the voice asked in reply. "If you have come here, to this place, then you have come for that which I protect. If you wish to possess the prize, then you must move forward, or our contest will stop before it begins. Go but a little further and I will ask you a riddle. Further still and I shall ask you another. Reach the end of the path, and I shall ask you but one more. There you must answer them all. Not one, or two, but all three riddles must be answered, and answered correctly."

"If I answer them all – the three riddles," Jim said, licking his lips and swallowing hard. "You'll let me have the Hunters Shell?"

"Yes."

"What if I get one wrong?" Jim asked. This time the voice answered with a laugh. The rumbling shook the chamber and rattled Jim to his bones. That laugh meant more than no. It meant something worse than no. Jim's torch trembled in his hand. Once the echoes of laughter finally faded away, the voice spoke again.

"So, Jim Morgan, will you step forward and face the challenge of the riddles? Or will you turn back?"

"I'm afraid, sir," Jim said.

"Then turn back."

"If I go back, the men waiting for me will see my friends to a bitter end. If morning comes before I get the shell, we will all turn to stone. If I hear your riddles and get them wrong, something worse than turning to stone will be my fate. Why does everything end so horribly on this wretched island?"

"On only this wretched island? Is it not so everywhere else, and for everyone else? I have seen no other shore but that of the Veiled Isle for some hundreds of years, Jim Morgan. But while I was still of the outside world, I knew that if one stands still his whole life, may he not as well turn to stone? If one runs back to the place from which he came, does he not surrender to whatever fate he fled at the first? If one steps forward, who knows what lies in store for him?"

Jim turned back toward the mouth of the cavern. It seemed miles and miles away in the dark, lit only by the Cromier's torches. He then faced the impenetrable black before him once more.

"You know," Jim said. "As a guardian of this place, shouldn't you try a bit harder to scare people away instead of encouraging them forward?"

"Perhaps I am simply bored," the voice replied. "Or perhaps I am hungry," it added. The voice laughed again. *Hungry*, Jim thought to himself, aghast. Now he knew what would happen if he guessed the riddles wrong. But in spite of even that horrible understanding, he had made his choice. He took another step along the rocky path.

"Excellent," said the voice. "Then we shall have our contest after all! Are you ready, Jim Morgan?"

"As I'll ever be, I suppose," Jim said. He was more focused on putting one foot after the other and not falling off the path than anything else. Far below, the sound of water churning and frothing passed from Jim's right to his left, crossing beneath him. Jim realized the path upon which he tread was some sort of bridge, spanning a great underground lake. He also knew, from the forceful clap of water, that whatever swam through the depths was massive and powerful.

"Then we shall begin!" The voice rumbled, sounding quite eager to get started. "I will present you with a riddle. You may answer that one by itself, or all three together. But in the end, questions and answers must equal three for the prize to be yours. This is the first of riddles three:"

The sun in day or the moon at night,
Not another of the same in sight,
That which is empty cannot be full,
Not by drink, nor by bread, not by gold, nor by jewels.
What am I?

Jim paused on the stone walkway for a long moment and turned the riddle's words over in his mind. The sun and moon were both lights, and there was something empty that needed to be filled up with something other than gold or food and drink. Was there something that light filled? Jim gritted his teeth and shook his head. He had no time to waste standing and puzzling over only the first riddle. He would at least hear the next one first.

"I'll just answer this one at the end," Jim said. He stepped forward once more, repeating the words of the first riddle silently to himself, hoping against hope that the clues would grow no more difficult the further he went.

"So be it, young one. I prefer to play the game this way regardless. So many times travelers attempt the first riddle straight away, only to fail. Then the contest ends too quickly, does it not? It is so long between games I am afraid. It is pleasant to hear the voice of another in this dark cave, I will admit."

"Then why stay?" Jim asked, curious in spite of his fear. "You could leave. I promise I wouldn't tell a soul."

"It is my duty," said the voice. "Those things I protect are worth protecting. But you have courage and good humor, Jim Morgan. I do like that. Now, hear the second of riddles three:"

Two roses together in the morning light,
A field of red by the coming of night,
One tree up on a hilltop high,
Soon a forest over the countryside.
Who are we?

Jim loosed a frustrated sigh and suddenly wanted to pitch the torch and himself off the path into the darkness. The second riddle was no easier than the first. In fact, it seemed that much more difficult to Jim. How could two roses fill up a whole field in just a day? How could a single tree turn into an entire forest? Success in the Vault of Treasures seemed so long ago, and doubts whispered in Jim's mind.

"I'll just answer all three together at the end," Jim said, trying to keep his voice from shaking like the trembling flame upon his torch. He swallowed hard. With great effort, he pushed the doubts aside and stepped forward again.

"All the same to me," said the voice amid the gurgling and roiling of water. "It is good to speak with one so young and strong. So many days and so many nights I have only the echoes of my own voice to keep me company. Those and the echoes of the past, of voices belonging to faces now all but forgotten."

"I know what you mean about not having anyone, I think," Jim said, trying to buy a bit more time to think about the riddles. "But it seems a shame to eat the only people you get a chance to talk to, wouldn't you say? That's what will happen if I answer wrong, right? You'll eat me?"

"You are correct on both counts, young Jim Morgan," replied the voice. "Answer wrong and you shall be devoured. And yes, that truly is a shame, for I can tell you have a good soul. But I am sworn to my duty – bound by honor and by powerful magic. Neither of those masters let me decide anything but the riddles by which I test those with the courage to attempt this path."

"You made these riddles?" Jim asked.

"Yes, and this is the third of three:"

Strength when weary, courage when none,
A strong knot makes two ropes one.
Many streams together form a flood,
Brother by choice and not by blood.
Who am I?

Jim paused on the path and worked to unlock the last of the riddles like a door with Peter's pins. Whatever creature swam down below, Jim thought, had created these riddles. Perhaps knowing that would help him find the answers. It seemed the creature had been here for a long, long time. Maybe that meant all the solutions were things very near to this place. The last riddle spoke of ropes and knots and streams and floods, so perhaps it referred to ships on the sea. But the more Jim thought the less confident he became.

"Maybe I'll just walk a little and think these over," Jim said. His mind was a whirlwind of guesses, questions, and doubts.

"I fear there is no room left for walking, or time for thinking, Jim Morgan," said the voice. "Cast your torch down and look at your feet." Jim paused his foot in mid-air and did as the voice commanded.

A startled cry escaped Jim's lips and echoed through the cavern. Jim's foot hung over nothing but black air. He now stood at the path's end. A sheer drop into dark nothingness was all that lay before him. Jim nearly fell over backward as he stepped away from the edge. When he finally summoned up the courage to peer back over the ledge, all he could see was a faint speck - the far-off reflection of his torch in the waters below.

"You have come at last to end of the Path of Riddles, and the end of the contest," said the voice. "Now is the time for answers. But before you speak, let us at least become better acquainted. Hold fast to what bravery you have left, Jim Morgan, for I am a fearsome sight to behold!"

A roar of ten ships cresting ten waves erupted from below Jim's feet as the creature burst through the surface of the waters. Jim fell even further back from the path's edge. He held his torch before him with two hands and fought hard to stifle the cries building up within in his chest. The waters parted and parted and parted, longer than Jim thought possible, until a dark shape rose above the pathway's end. Jim's heart froze in his chest as the great shadow took shape in the light of his torch.

The face of a giant sea serpent formed before him. It had a snout like a horse's, but long as a schooner and resting upon a scaled body as wide around as an oak trunk. The monster glared down on Jim with glowing gold eyes, bigger than wagon wheels. A row of spines like fence posts ran from the crest of the great head down its long, snaking body. Though his legs trembled beneath him, Jim stood his ground as he had seen Dread Steele do in the face of the Kraken.

"You did not cry out, nor did you run!" the sea serpent said, this time so close and so loud that the words enveloped Jim and nearly deafened him. "You have courage! Men call me Percival – keeper of the Path of Riddles and last of the great water dragons of the deep - sole survivor of a once great race."

"Pleased to meet you," Jim managed through clenched teeth, for it was all he could think to say.

"And you are well met also, Jim Morgan," said Percival, dipping his enormous head toward Jim in a bow. When the giant creature opened his mouth, fangs the length Jim's arm glinted in the torch-light. The massive eyes burned as molten gold. "Are you prepared now to answer? I admire your courage and your manners, and I hope for true you will answer correctly. It shall give me no pleasure to devour you whole should your answer prove false. But do so I must."

"Well...thanks, I suppose," Jim said, wondering if any of that was really supposed to make him feel any better.

"Morgan, Jim Morgan," said Percival suddenly, lowering his head to study Jim closer. "I knew your surname the moment I heard it, but now that you stand close, I see for certain what I only guessed to be true. The man who came before you lives in your face, and a hint of him also in your smell." Percival leaned in and breathed deeply of Jim, ruffling Jim's clothes and nearly extinguishing the torch in the process. "A hint anyway...for you do have the most fascinating smell, Jim Morgan."

"What do you mean when you say I smell different?" Jim asked.

"I am here to ask riddles, young adventurer, not to answer them. Why do you not ask your father yourself? For he seemed to me a very clever man, as far as humans go, anyway. Surely you know it was he who left the Shell in my care. In truth, I am surprised he sent you and did not come himself. We had a long and thoughtful conversation when I saw him last. Such conversations are so rare for me."

"You probably had a longer conversation with him than I ever did," Jim said. "He's not here because he's dead. He was murdered." Jim nearly choked on the words. Percival bowed his head even more and twisted it to one side, staring at Jim with one wide, yellow eye.

"And your mother?" Percival asked. To Jim, for half a moment, the water dragon seemed suddenly less dangerous, but far older and more sorrowful and wise, like a kind old man trapped in a monster's body.

"I never knew her."

"I see," said Percival, scrutinizing Jim with his one eye for a long moment. "There are questions I would ask you, Jim Morgan," the serpent finally said. But then he turned his head back and rose up over Jim, towering in the dark, yellow eyes flashing. "But I am bound by magic and honor. Three riddles you have been given and three answers you must return. Wrong or right, I must fulfill my duty." Percival finished his speech with a growl that reminded Jim this was no kindly man, but a magical beast of the deep with teeth long and sharp enough to gnash him to dust. Fear jumbled the riddles' words in Jim's mind. Panic all but drowned out any hopeful answers.

"Could you not at least give me a hint?" Jim pleaded. But the beast would not be swayed.

"I have already given you hints, Jim Morgan, if you were wise enough to hear them. From what you have told me, I thought you had no need of them, for the answers are as close to your heart as they are to mine. Now, give answer or face your fate!"

"That which is empty can never be full," Jim said to himself. "It could be something deep and dark," he ventured, trying to guess without answering. "Like a hole or a cave?" He tried to measure Percival's face, but the water dragon's eyes gave nothing away.

"Do not attempt to fool me with tricks or ply me with pleading eyes! I am an ancient guardian and have told my riddles for far too long to great kings and warriors and desperate thieves to be shamed in such a way. Stand tall like a man. Stand upright like your father and answer!"

Jim wracked his brain, but no matter how he tried, the answers would not come.

"Silence is an answer of its own kind, Jim Morgan!" Roared Percival. It was so loud that the stone bridge beneath Jim's feet shook and swayed. Dust and rocks fell from the cavern ceiling above. "And silence is as wrong an answer as any. I am sorry, son of Lindsay Morgan – but you have failed the test." The water dragon reared back, mouth opened wide, glistening teeth bared and ready to strike.

FIFTEEN

THE HUNTER'S SHELL

Jim watched the sea monster prepare to swallow him whole – but it hardly mattered to him any more. His thoughts dwelt on his friends – the Cromiers' sharp blades at their necks in the painted cave. His friends would look for him to come to their rescue from the tunnel. Knowing them, the Ratts, Lacey, and Cornelius, they would hold out hope to the very end, only to see it fail. The thought of Lacey's tears and George's failing smile tore a deep hole in Jim's chest.

It struck Jim then, from nowhere, a spark at the back of his mind. The hole in his chest – in his heart. Jim thought of the emptiness he felt ever since the death of his father and the loss of his home. It was an emptiness that only went away when he was with his friends. An emptiness that could never be full.

It was the answer to the first riddle.

"Alone!" Jim shouted at the last possible moment. "You're alone!"

Percival's open mouth was already careening toward Jim, tongue lashing and teeth like swords, ready to tear Jim to pieces. Jim threw his arms over his head as though that would make a difference. But the bite never came. When Jim peeked through a small gap between his arms, he found the water dragon's terrible maw shut, not inches from his trembling body. Percival turned his head to once more look upon Jim with one giant eye.

"What did you say?" the monster asked.

"You're alone," Jim repeated, trying to talk over the sound of his own heartbeat, which thundered like a drum in his ears. *The sun in the day, or the moon at night...*all alone in sky. You are the last of your people. I no longer have my mother and my father. We're the same, really. We're both alone."

Silence hung in the air between the dragon and the boy for what seemed like a very long time to Jim. Finally, Percival spoke in a voice more quiet than Jim imagined a great beast would possess.

"You have answered the first riddle correctly."

Jim's heart leapt, but his mind had already raced to the second riddle. The moment he had answered the first, he realized all three were bound by a common thread.

"*One tree up on a hilltop high, soon a forest over the countryside.* The answer to the second riddle is a family," Jim said. "They might start with only one or two...but before long they can be hundreds and hundreds."

"You are correct again! And the last, lad? Are you able to answer the last?" Percival asked. It seemed to Jim that the monster was cheering him on, whether against the magical rules of guardianship or not.

Jim smiled. He should have guessed this one from the beginning. The answer had been in the words shared between he and George on the riverbank in the field of the faeries that very night.

"*A strong knot makes two ropes one.* It's a friend," Jim said. His eyes stung and his throat tightened. "*Brother by choice and not by blood...*a friend."

"Indeed it is," whispered the sea serpent. "Long has it been since I have had one of those." A smile, rowed with razor-sharp teeth, broke over the water dragon's face. Percival the sea serpent rose up high above the path of stone and roared with his loudest voice, like a blasting of trumpets. The mighty call made Jim want to jump into the air and shout for joy.

"You have passed the test, Jim Morgan! What greater victory is there than that? Now you shall have your prize!" Percival lowered his head so that his spiked crown fell level with the pathway's end.

"Come, young adventurer. Have you ever ridden a great beast of the deep? There may be none alive and few who ever lived who have. But I believe you have earned the right. Come now and I shall carry you to your prize, and quickly we must go, for dawn approaches. I can smell it through the walls of rock that cage me in."

Jim took two deep breaths to steady his legs, which were all but shivering beneath him. With a running start, he leapt from the edge of the cliff onto Percival's head. When he landed, he grabbed hold of one the spines on the dragon's head as a handle, to keep from slipping on the wet scales and tumbling into the darkness beyond.

"Is that alright?" Jim asked suddenly, wondering if it hurt to grab the great beast so. But Percival just laughed. He laughed so hard that the cavern shook and Jim trembled from head to toe.

"But you do have impeccable manners don't you, master Morgan? Do not insult an ancient beast of the deep, my boy, to think that your tiny hands and feet could hurt me. I could carry a hundred men upon my back for a day and a night and not grow tired. In the glory of my youth I could battle a hundred sharks and have no fear of pain or defeat! And besides all that, our trip together will be very short indeed."

Percival swung about and Jim heard the water rush and roil far below as the dragon ripped through the underground lake. The light from Jim's torch was hardly enough to illuminate the way, but the blast of air whipping at Jim's hair and tugging at his clothes told him the sea serpent moved with incredible speed. As they rounded a corner in the dark, a new light came into view. Early morning's gray poured through a hole in the eastern side of the mountain. It lit upon a lone spire of stone that climbed from the dark waters. Atop the spire, the Hunter's Shell glimmered upon a pedestal of coral.

Percival glided to a halt at the stone tower, sending a large wave crashing into its base. Jim gripped the water dragon's spines as tight as he dared to keep from being thrown from his perch. All the while, Percival laughed and snorted, splashing his huge tail in the water, somewhere far, far behind where Jim stood on the monster's head.

"Apologies, Master Morgan, but it has been so, so long since I stretched myself out in the waters. The beast's heart within me is stirred by your adventure and I forget myself and the confines of this place."

"Confines?" Jim asked, hesitating only a moment before jumping down onto the flat surface of the stone tower. "I've never even heard of a cave this big before, Percival."

"Big?" Percival growled. "This cave is but a divot in the earth with a small puddle formed at the bottom. Surely you travelled upon the sea to arrive at the Veiled Isle, did you not? Does the ocean not take your breath away? It's breadth and depth awe even me, boy. It is too large to be owned by any one creature, too deep to belong to even any nation. The sea is large enough for one to lose himself and all that haunts him, and yet vast enough to find himself again on the other side - to rediscover joys thought lost forever. Would that you came faster to this cave, young Morgan, for I would speak more of such things to you. You listen with no rush to speak. That is a rare thing. Take your prize. You have won it."

Jim paused for a moment atop the beast's head. Beneath all of Percival's growls and threats, the monster's riddles had revealed a heart with a hole in it - a hole Jim knew well. But time was short, so Jim stepped to the stone spire. Light danced upon the shell's polished surface. It so dazzled Jim's eyes that he could not be sure whether the glow came from the morning light's reflection or from the magic within the shell itself. When Jim touched the conch, warmth tingled his fingers and heat tickled the palms of his hands. The power within the talisman thrummed through his arms all the way into his chest. Surely, Jim thought, there was more than enough magic in the shell to find anything in the world – including the Treasure of the Ocean. But even with his friends in danger of death, Jim feared the thought of this enchanted tool falling into the hands of the Cromiers. He lifted it from the coral and a silent flash pulsed into the cave. It blew Jim's hair back from his face and sent a sphere of purple light running along the underground lake.

Jim took off the tattered remains of his jacket and wrapped the shell within them, the heat and tingles leaving his arms the moment it was covered. With the shell's glow concealed beneath his dirty coat, however, he noticed the light shining through the hole in the mountain wall was no longer a dull gray, but the bright yellow of a morning sun. Dawn had come. Jim hung his head. The shell felt heavy in his arms. The white rose scar ached on his palm.

"I'm too late," Jim said. "Even if the Cromiers let my friends go, they won't make it back to the faeries in time. After all this, we're still going to turn to stone on this island."

"I am truly sorry, Jim Morgan," said Percival. "Of all the adventurers to test my riddles in this cave, I wished success most for you. At least have this small comfort. You have won the game of riddles, so you may now command me to protect something of your choosing until the next traveler comes. It was so with your father, now it shall be so with you. Shall I protect the shell, or something else?" Jim was about to ask what this mysterious object was that his father had won all those years ago, when suddenly, clear as a bell, a thought only a young man with boundless imagination might dare to hope.

"Percival," Jim said, rushing to the very edge of the stone tower. "The rules that bind you, they state simply that you must guard whatever the winner of the game of riddles commands you to?"

"That is true, young Morgan."

"*Anything?*"

The water dragon, who had once, hundreds of years ago, been a young and wily sea creature himself, prone to leaping and splashing in the waves, caught a whiff of salty air and ocean wind now emanating from Jim. Percival leaned his huge head down to look at Jim, eye to monstrous, yellow eye.

"Yes, young Master Morgan," the dragon said, smiling with rows upon rows of glistening teeth. "Anything!"

SIXTEEN

WHILE JIM WAS IN THE CHAMBER

J ust beyond the stone-fanged mouth to the cavern of riddles, the Ratts and Lacey, with poor Cornelius tucked in the folds of her arms, huddled together. Jim had been gone for far too long. The little clan was beginning to fear for not only his life, but for their own as well. Dawn neared. Even the Cromiers knew their time on the island had grown short, which made them more desperate and violent than even before.

"I say we send one of these other whelps in after him," Bartholomew snarled to his father, jabbing a furious finger in George's face. "The boy may already be dead, and we waste time just standing here! Morning is nearly upon us!"

"There is yet time, Bartholomew," replied the Count. He cast a questioning glance to Splitbeard. The pirate was still leaned against

275

one of the stone fangs at the mouth of the black cavern, amusing himself by walking a silver coin back and forth over his knuckles.

"Have no fear, oh son of the most venerable Count," said the pirate. He palmed the coin in his fist and held it up beside his toothy smile. "When the time comes, Splitbeard shall remove us from these most unfortunate shores. It shall be as though we were never here at all." He unfurled his hand one finger at a time to reveal the coin disappeared from his calloused palm, laughing at his own trick. The Ratts, of course, were hardly impressed.

"Amateur," Paul whispered to Peter, rolling his eyes.

"Switched it to his other hand almost five minutes ago," Peter agreed with a snort.

"The only real way to do that trick is to make a gold coin appear in your hand instead of silver'n," George said, sneering with his brothers.

"Quiet!" Lacey whisper-snapped at the brothers. Her blue eyes flashed and her auburn curls whipped about as she spun on them, doing her best to keep the boastful brothers from making matters worse. "This is serious!" But she was already too late. Splitbeard had stepped away from where he leaned and was sauntering slowly toward the clan.

"Right you are, oh sweet little girl. Tis a most serious matter indeed. But when Splitbeard the Pirate has his back against the wall, he has greater tricks to call upon than vanishing coins, no?" Splitbeard leaned toward Lacey and reached behind his back. From some hidden pocket, he withdrew a long black and silver feather - the feather of a giant owl. Lacey flinched from the smirking pirate.

"Leave off of her, you jackanapes!" George challenged. He pulled Lacey behind him and defiantly set his jaw at Splitbeard and the Cromiers. "If you lot are in such a blasted 'urry to get whatever it is waitin' in that cave, why don't you just go in after it yourself?" Then George, who often had no idea when to quit, and even less so when seized by his passions, crossed the line with Bartholomew Cromier. "I heard you whinin' and cryin' at how much better you are than Jim, about how you should kill 'im cause you don't need 'im. So 'ow 'bout you prove it, Bartholomew!" George added the *Bartholomew* as nastily as he could, throwing the captain his most hateful glare.

Yet the moment the words left his mouth, George realized too late that he'd made a dreadful mistake.

A terrible change crawled over Bartholomew's deathly-white face. A thin line of blood-red color ran through his cheeks. His ice-cold eyes narrowed in frosty hatred. His chin twitched and quivered, smoke rising from a volcano on the verge of eruption.

"Oh dear," Lacey said.

Bartholomew stalked toward George and his brothers, hand on the sword at his side. "Perhaps you're right, little street trash. Perhaps now is the time I put to rest all doubt and vanquish any remaining hope in the son of Lindsay Morgan once and for all. But, consider this: if I enter the cave on my own, what need have I for any of you?" Bartholomew's sword flashed from his scabbard, a glimmer of steel in the torchlight. He sliced one of the buttons from George's coat and swung the blade back around to rest at George's check. The sharp point drew a teardrop of blood from the eldest Ratt's face.

The Count came to stand by Bartholomew, eyeing his son, then the Ratts and Lacey. More than once Cromier had stayed Bartholomew's murderous anger. But now, as Lacey and George watched the villain trace his scar with a firm, gloved finger, they realized the time for such mercies had ended.

"So be it, my son. If you wish to test yourself and earn my trust once more, it shall be so. But for now, dawn has come. Splitbeard shall return us through the Devil's Horns. Naught but a moment will have passed on the other side. We shall rejoin the battle against Dread Steele, drive him off, or finally see him from this world. Then, in one night and one day, we shall try our hand again."

"Dread Steele will flee or fall beneath my blade," vowed Bartholomew. His face gleamed with sweat and more than a hint of madness.

"Splitbeard," Cromier said. "I believe the time for our departure has arrived."

"As you say, oh honorable Count. But oh great, red one," he added, mocking Lacey and the Ratts with a false, sad frown upon his swarthy face. "Two men, and perhaps three, I might be able to whisk to the gates called the Devil's Horns before the sun rises. But no more than that. Oh what, what, what shall become of our youthful comrades?"

Count Cromier's gaze passed over the small huddle of friends. A cruel smile slipped onto his lips.

"Take the girl as a prisoner," the Count pronounced. "As for the boys and the bird, kill them all."

Bartholomew drew his sword over his shoulder, his attention fixed with glee on George, who was trying to be as brave as possible in his last moments.

"Finally," was all Bartholomew said. But as he moved to strike, Splitbeard interrupted with a rasping shout.

"Wait!" he said. "Listen!"

Bartholomew rolled his eyes with furious impatience. He was seemingly ready to ignore the pirate and finish poor George off anyway, when suddenly, his own face twitched. Only then did George, Lacey, Peter, and Paul catch a hint of the sound that startled the villains before them.

It came from within the hidden chamber.

It reminded George of the first time he heard waves crashing against the shore at old MacGuffy's lighthouse. Splitbeard the Pirate slowly retreated from the mouth of the cave. For the first time since any of the children had laid eyes on the wizardly pirate, a tumbling wave of fear swept over his face.

The rushing sound grew louder and louder until it broke against the cavern wall. The chamber mouth exploded in a rain of rock shards and dust clouds. A real serpent's head, eyes aglow and teeth snapping, burst from the rubble into the painted cave. The Ratts and Lacey fell on their seats in the middle of the cavern, mouths hanging open and eyes all but springing from their heads.

The sea serpent opened its mouth wide and roared with primeval might. The Ratt Clan threw their hands over their ears and the cave trembled beneath the monster's cry. The water dragon focused the brunt of its cry on Bartholomew Cromier. The force of the roar sent the black-haired captain tumbling head over heels until he struck the far wall of the great cave, where he crashed with a loud smack. Count Cromier had managed to dive aside, and Splitbeard - swagger long forgotten - scrambled on all fours like a mouse scurrying to escape a cat.

With the pirates scattered, the beast turned its yellow eyes on George, Lacey, Peter, Paul, and Cornelius. Surprised that the end would come this way, they threw their arms about each other and began to say their goodbyes. But the creature opened his toothy maw once more and, of all things, spoke.

"Good morning, friends of Jim Morgan," the sea serpent said, and in a rather deep and charming voice, Lacey thought. "I am Percival, last of the water dragons of the deep. As of this moment, you are under my protection."

Out from behind one of the spines atop Percival's scaly head, waving his hat and a rogue's grin stretched across his face, popped none other than Jim Morgan. For the first time in many days, he was obviously having the time of his life.

SEVENTEEN

ESCAPE BY MONSTER

When Jim saw his friends alive and well, surprise draped across their faces, a spring of joy burst inside his heart and a smile flashed across his lips.

"Hullo!" he cried, poking his head out from behind Percival's spine, his hat in his hand. "Don't just sit there, you lot! Don't you recognize a getaway when you see one?"

The shocked looks on the Ratt Clan's faces lasted only the blink of an eye. When grown-ups might have wasted time asking questions or trying understand a completely fantastic situation, the Ratts and Lacey leapt to their feet and scampered atop Percival's enormous head without so much as a second thought.

"All aboard then, friends of Jim Morgan," Percival said, laughing between his growls. "Hang on tight, all of you. For long has it been since Percival the Great has gone for a swim. And he is ready to move fast!"

"Grab on!" Jim shouted. Fortunately his friends had no need to be told twice. No sooner had they taken hold of a spine each than the water dragon ducked back into the cave and launched himself and his passengers into the darkness. If Jim thought Percival had swum with speed before, he found himself magnificently mistaken. The wind whipped at his face, his eyes watered, and his heart raced like a jack-rabbit within his chest.

The roar of churning water drowned out the startled cries of the clan. Jim held tight to his spine with one arm and squeezed the shell close to him with the other as Percival twisted and turned over the surface of the dark lake. The stone column and the eastward hole in the mountainside flew past in an instant. Percival dove into a hidden tunnel. He careered right and left through labyrinthine turns and around sharp corners Jim never saw coming.

Jim looked back to ensure his friends were all accounted for, and that none had been sent flying into the lake. They were all still there, with eyes wide as saucers and faces white as waves' foam. A light appeared at the end of the tunnel, and a roaring even louder than Percival's swimming awaited them ahead.

"I hope none of you minds getting wet!" Percival shouted, laughing his dragon's laugh.

"What do you mean?" Jim asked. The answer came faster than Percival's reply. The enormous waterfall that cascaded down the side of the dark mountain was the entrance to the tunnel. Percival aimed to blow right through it.

"Hang on!" Jim cried. He pressed himself against the spine and gripped the shell even tighter. The water smacked Jim like a blast of cold air as Percival burst through the waterfall. He coughed and sputtered in the torrential flood raining down on his head. But when Percival cleared the fall, and Jim felt the warmth of morning upon his face, he opened his eyes with a smile.

The sea serpent flew through the air, his long body stretched out over the river called the Mountain's Tears. The waterfall roared behind and the whole of the island, from the dark forest to the crags, and from the field of the faeries to the beach, stretched out before. With the shell in his hands and his friends at his back, all that had frightened Jim and caused him dread disappeared. Water droplets danced in the air and caught the rising sun's light, exploding it into a hundred rainbows. Jim loosed the wild cry of a boy with the taste of victory on his lips and the exultation of life upon his tongue.

Percival splashed down into the river. When he rose again to resume his tear to the ocean, the Brothers Ratt and Lacey joined in Jim's whooping, crowing, and calling, heads held back and fists raised in the air.

"Jim!" cried George, shaking his head and splashing water from his long, dark locks. "How exactly did you come by your own sea monster, mate? It's the most brilliant thing ever!"

"Yeah, Jim, that was fairly mad," added Paul, smiling in the sunlight and nodding his head like a wide-eyed chipmunk. "Can't be sure cause of all the water, of course, but I'm pretty sure Peter just peed himself."

"I did NOT, Paul!"

"All of you, look," cried Lacey. She pointed with great urgency out toward the eastern edge of the island, to the horizon. "Look at the sun. It's almost up!" When Jim and the Ratts followed Lacey's gaze, the bright yellow disc was indeed nearly two-thirds risen over the sea. But Percival, still roaring with joy, put Lacey's fears to rest.

"Have no fear, milads and milady. Percival the Mighty shall not fail you! We will break through the Devil's Horns with yet a quarter of the sun to spare." Jim breathed a sigh of relief and patted the water dragon on the spine. But there was one more surprise when a sputtering, coughing squawk erupted from Lacey's arms.

"I say, I say!" cawed Cornelius Darkfeather, coming to, for he had been passed out since his injuries in the cave. "I was only resting my eyes. There was no need to douse me, sweet Lacey, I'm awake, I'm awake!"

"Oh, Cornelius!" Lacey shouted, hugging the raven close to her chest. "I was so worried we were going to lose you. And we didn't splash you, we just swam through a waterfall, that's all."

"Swam through a waterfall?" said Cornelius, black eyes darting about in utter confusion. "Where are we? Back on the *Spectre*? Have you five managed to confiscate a ship of some sort?"

"Actually," said George, grinning obnoxiously. "We're just ridin' on the back of a giant sea serpent if you must know."

"Riding on a sea serpent?" cawed Cornelius. The raven took such a start that he nearly fell from Lacey's arms. But after looking about and finding George's description true, the bird had but one thing to say. "Well, I do believe that this is a first." Jim and the Ratts burst into laughter and Lacey kissed Cornelius on the top of his head.

"Look at that!" said Peter, pointing with his free hand to the green field rushing beside them. Through the trees and over the rolling hills, a swarm of lights flitted and danced like a flock of glowing birds, racing to keep pace with the furiously swimming water dragon.

"It's the faeries," cried Jim, waving wildly. The flitting lights in the great pack blinked and bobbed, waving back as they flew.

"Faeries?" asked Lacey. George then began to babble, nearly incoherently, about everything that had happened to him and Jim since they were separated by the owls at the dark forest. While George was yammering, mostly focused on how he had carried Jim with one arm for what was now ten miles while fighting off the giant owls all by himself, Cornelius squawked urgently to Jim.

"And the shell, my boy? For all we have suffered and bled, have we at least come away with the shell?" Jim answered with only a smile. He gave Cornelius a peek at the shell, glowing bright from between the folds of his drenched coat.

"What about your hand, Jim?" asked Lacey, trying to block out George, Peter, and Paul, who were now proclaiming themselves the greatest adventurers of all time. "What happened to your hand? How did you get rid of the poison?" Jim tucked the shell back beneath his arm and showed his open palm and wrist. His new white rose scar shone in the morning light. Lacey reached out to touch Jim's hand. A hint of sadness lingered in her eyes, but a smile lit her face.

"It's good to have you back, Jim," she said, her auburn curls flying back from her face in the wind.

"Thanks," said Jim. "Glad to be back."

"Hold on tight one last time, friends of Jim Morgan!" Percival bellowed over the roar of the water. "The ocean approaches. And just beyond the shore, the Devil's Horns, and home!"

"Percival!" Jim shouted. He suddenly remembered that though the adventure on the island was nearly behind him, danger still lurked through the magic gates ahead. "When we cross back into our world, you should probably know that there's a battle going on. I think you might just surprise two boatfuls of pirates in the middle of it all."

"Fear not, lad," said Percival. "Must I remind you again that I am an ancient water dragon of the deep? I have no fear of pirates or battles or dangers, in this world or any world. Now on we go!"

The beach came up quickly, and the ocean a moment after. As Percival reached the Devil's Horns, Jim took one last glance at the rising sun and found it three-quarters of the way over the horizon. But when Jim blinked, it seemed to him as though a great candle in the sky had been blown out. What had been a bright yellow, rising sun, suddenly became one blood red, setting beneath the sea. What had been a warm morning breeze turned into a cold evening wind. On the back of that wind carried the sounds of pistols and swords and shouting men. Jim and his friends had rejoined the battle upon the sea.

EIGHTEEN

BACK ABOARD THE *SPECTRE*

The fighting raged across the decks. The green-hulled *Spectre* sat knifed into the *Sea Spider's* flank. A mist of pistol smoke hovered over the ships. Cutlasses and knives glimmered like lightning flashes within the gray cloud. Beyond the touch of the setting red sun, both sky and sea were growing black. In the deepening dusk, Jim saw that Dread Steele and his men were hopelessly outnumbered. The Corsair pirates were gaining the upper hand. They would soon have victory within their grasp. Jim leaned on one of Percival's foremost spines, stepping so far forward he nearly stood on the sea serpent's scaly brow, and shouted over the din of the battle

"Percival, the green ship and all her men are with us. It looks like they're in a spot of trouble!"

"Well then, my new friend," growled Percival. "Let us announce your arrival and turn the tide!" Percival surged forth. He twisted and turned around the jagged rocks until he spiraled up along the *Spectre's* starboard side. He raised his great head over the railing, teeth bared.

There was a sudden, startled silence at the sight of the monster. The battle came to stunned pause - until screams and shouts of terror broke the quiet. The Corsairs and Dread Steele's men split apart like oil and water. Each crew fell back into the frightened clutches of their mates. All swords, pikes, and pistols were now held toward Percival, as though such weapons offered any protection at all from the strength of a water dragon. Percival turned his molten gold eyes upon the Corsairs. He let his long teeth glisten blood red in the dying sunlight. He then roared with such force at the *Sea Spider's* men that they fell over backwards or dropped to their knees. At once they threw down their weapons and covered their faces with their arms in fear for their lives. From atop the sea serpent's head, Jim and the Brothers Ratt shook their fists at the fallen Corsairs, hopelessly trying to match Percival roar for roar.

When Percival stopped rumbling, a more lasting hush fell over the ships. The shaken Corsairs held up their hands, as if surrender might stop the sea monster from tearing them to bits. With the enemy humbled, Percival lowered his head to the deck. Down jumped the Clan of the Ratt. They were absolutely covered from top to bottom in dirt and grime. Holes and tears split the tattered remains of what had been, only a few days ago, their nicest clothes. MacGuffy burst through the ranks of pirates, a cutlass and rapier held one in each hand. His thin white hair stuck in all directions, mussed and matted from the heat of battle.

"Jim! Lacey dear! Even ye sea Ratts! How in the devil...and... and what manner of malevolent beastie is that which ye have brought along?" Giant Mufwalme, Murdoch, and Wang-Chi all stood dumbstruck beside the old salt, their weapons held tremulously toward the unexpected monster.

"Have no fear, old MacGuffy," assured George. He strutted forward beside his brothers with his thumbs stuck through two holes in his shirt as though they were suspenders. "Percival there in't malleable at all!"

"That's malevolent, Georgie," said Peter, still supporting Paul under one arm.

"Exactly what I said, Peter," said George. He nodded smartly at MacGuffy and then tossed his head back toward Percival. The water dragon still hovered over the deck, poised to strike at the cowering Corsairs. "He's a bit of a personal of friend of ours, you see. I was even considerin' inductin' 'im into the Clan of the Ratt, as an official member."

"Oh you were?" said Lacey with a roll of her eyes.

"Yeah we were," said George, looking to his brothers. "Weren't we boys?"

"I dunno, Georgie. " Paul looked back and forth between his older brother and the scaly beast behind them. "I mean, he's fairly handy in a pinch, I'll give him that. But somethin' tells me sneakin' about and pickin' pockets might come as a struggle."

"What are ye sayin', ye blasted sea mice?" MacGuffy finally snapped, waving his swords about excitedly. "That ye rode that beastie here? And from where exactly did ye pups acquire this new friend?"

"It's sort of a long story, MacGuffy," said Jim. He stepped forward with his bundle held tightly in his arms and a rascal's grin splitting his face. "But maybe for now I might just skip to this."

Jim pulled aside the folds of his ruined coat.

The pirates gathered about. They murmured and whistled and made oaths to the sea and the sky when Jim produced the shell. Even MacGuffy, who had seen more treasure and magic than most in his long life, took a step back, growling some unintelligible curse.

Dread Steele himself braced at the sight of the gleaming shell. He stepped quickly through the ranks of his men to cover it again with Jim's coat, some whispered incantation on his lips. But before the Captain could fully conceal the talisman, one last ray of fading daylight struck the shell's polished surface. The shell thrummed to life in Jim's hands. A violet glow swam over the smooth surface, until it coiled up and leapt into the sky. The pulse of magic streaked through the darkening air and disappeared far away into the night. The pirates of the *Spectre* fell back from the shell. Even from a distance, the Corsairs murmured amongst themselves, whimpering and moaning of magic and ancient curses.

"Beware, Jim Morgan," Percival warned. "Like me, the shell has not tasted the air of this world for many years. And like me, it is not entirely tame, nor entirely safe."

"Your scaled ally speaks true, Jim," Steele said, casting a wary glance in Percival's direction as he finally managed to cover the shell completely. A shadow passed over the pirate lord's face. Jim could hear concern at the edges of Steele's voice. "Keep the shell hidden for now, Jim. Magic draws magic. We must beware the attention of such forces." Jim hardly knew what to make of such dire tidings, but he caught Steele's eyes glanced skyward, as though some dark power might be lurking just overhead.

"And what became o' those curs, the Cromiers and Splitbeard, I wonder?" MacGuffy asked, spitting on the deck. Jim looked back at the Devil's Horns. The rocks were quiet and still, and the setting sun was about to wink out of existence below the horizon.

"I think we may have seen the last of them, MacGuffy," he said. "If you stay too long on the island, you turn to stone forever. And their time is nearly over." Jim's own words caught him by surprise as he considered what they might mean. The men who had taken everything from him, his father, his fortune, his home, they were gone - gone forever.

"You faced the Cromiers and Splitbeard upon the Veiled Isle?" Steele asked, raising a curious eyebrow.

"Oh, they was there, Cap'n," George chimed in. "Had us at the end of our ropes too if Jim and Percival hadn't come bustin' in at the last moment...well, between them and the giant owls...and the faeries..."

"And possibly being turned to stone," Lacey said.

"And the harpies!" Peter and Paul added together. The corners of Dread Steele's mouth finally twitched and pulled into a half grin on his dark and dangerous face. He looked down on Cornelius, his gray eyes laughing.

"Have you nothing to add, old friend, of such goings on? This seems a tale to rival even your own, exaggerated stories from the days of your youth." At this, Cornelius cleared his throat and would have flapped up into the air, full of indignation, if his wings were strong enough to do so.

"I hardly exaggerate, Captain. But this time, I have the scars to prove the tale true!"

"The scars will be worth it if we can at last have some peace," Jim said. He glanced down at his palm before looking up once more to the horizon. The last lip of the sun clung to the edge of the sea, a final finger of light losing its grip on the world.

"As long as I am able, I shall accompany you to the end of this journey, Jim. We may yet see more storms and bear more scars, but we shall also see the sun rise again on a happier day." The Captain put a hand on Jim's shoulder and let the smile linger on his face.

"Steele and Morgan, together again?" Jim asked.

"Morgan and Steele, to the end," Steele agreed. For one brief moment Jim saw an easier road stretched out before him. But that daydream was shattered by a piercing scream.

"Look!" Mufwalme bellowed in his deep voice, his eyes wide and staring at the Devil's Horns.

From the Devil's Horns, just as the last crescent of burning sun fell beneath the waves, a trio of great owls burst from the gate in a flash of green magic. The leader screeched a battle cry as he arched into the air, leading his flock over the head of Percival the water dragon. Percival roared in rage. Atop two of the owls sat Count Cromier and Bartholomew, hateful glares in their eyes. Jim felt the malicious eyes of the villains fall upon him alone.

The owls circled low. The Count and Bartholomew leapt down from their mounts, swords drawn. They beckoned their pirate thugs back to their feet. The winged hunters circled once over the decks and came to rest atop the *Spectre's* masts, taunting the water dragon below. But the third owl landed at Count Cromier's side. A pale-yellow light burned amongst its feathers. The giant owl shrank and twisted into the form of a man, smiling darkly as he stood in the dim light of evening.

Splitbeard the Pirate, sorcerer of the seas, had returned.

"I don't believe it!" Jim sputtered.

"He controlled the owls when he took us, Jim," said, Lacey, shrinking back into the small huddle of friends. "But I never thought he could become one!"

Splitbeard laughed with delight at Lacey's revulsion.

"It is said upon the seas that Dread Steele is Lord of the Pirates, a master of the arcane arts. But it is I, Splitbeard of the Corsairs, who has plunged deepest into the depths of the black arts. I cannot be so easily undone."

"You have something that belongs to me, Morgan!" Count Cromier cried, mad rage swimming in his eyes. "Fifteen years have I searched and waited – fifteen years since your father took from me what was mine. I shall have it, boy, even if it costs me everything. Even if I must bathe in blood to take it back. The Treasure shall be mine again!"

Bartholomew screamed then, beckoning the Corsairs behind him with his naked blade. "Charge!"

The battle before the Devil's Horns began again.

Dread Steele and his men rushed into the fray, clashing with the Cromiers in the center of the *Spectre's* deck. Jim and his friends fled to the safety of the quarterdeck. They watched as the remaining owls launched themselves into the sky to attack Percival with outstretched talons. Percival fought back, but the crafty owls flitted just beyond the reach of his snapping jaws.

Jim gaped at the battle before him. Pirates, sea monsters, and great owls were locked in combat. Who could believe such a thing that had not seen it with his own eyes? He was sure that nothing could surpass such madness on the *Spectre,* until he looked back over the ocean, where the last of the evening light was fading away.

A shadow darker than night moved across the sky. It crawled through the air with purpose, a stalking animal hunting its prey. At the first flash of lightning Jim's heart dropped into his stomach. His arms and legs went weak. A storm was coming. But this was no ordinary storm. The clouds churned pitch black, but the edges glowed blood red.

The Crimson Storm from Jim's nightmares had come.

NINETEEN

Jim Morgan and the Pirates of the Black Skull

The first drops of rain fell hard on the *Spectre's* deck. They splashed on the railings and spattered Jim and his friends. Whipping winds, monstrous waves, and thunder followed. The storm's fury quickly drowned out the sounds of the pirate battle. Jim huddled close together with Lacey and the Ratts, their backs pressed against the aft railing.

"Of all things," George growled. He pulling his ragged coat tightly around his shoulders and threw the sky a nasty glare. "A storm on top of this fight."

"The storm didn't come out of nowhere, George," Jim said, shouting now so that his friends could hear him over the thunder and fighting. "It came here on purpose. I think it came because of the shell." Jim nodded down to the bundle in his arms. He squeezed it to his chest as though afraid the storm might reach down with a hand of lightning and snatch it from his grasp.

"Storms don't decide to go anywhere, Jim," Lacey cried over the rain, her auburn hair dripping wet and slicked to the sides of her face.

"Magic storms, do," Jim said. He looked down at Cornelius, who was still cradled in Lacey's arms. "Don't they, Cornelius?"

"I'm afraid they do, my boy. They do indeed."

"Magic storms?" Lacey shook her head in dismay. "I don't understand!"

"It's the treasure, Lacey. The Treasure of the Ocean is more powerful magic than anything else in the world. I don't know how, but when my father, Dread Steele, and Count Cromier first tried to use the Treasure of the Ocean, they somehow brought about this storm. The storm is after the Treasure. But I think it might also be after me!"

"Only figuring this out now, my young friend?" a voice snarled from the quarterdeck's steps. Jim peered through the falling rain, but he already recognized that voice.

Count Cromier rose like a black wraith from the portside steps. In a flash of lightning, Jim saw his crimson wig darkened in the rain to the color of blood. The rainwater ran down his scar like a river pouring over a jagged cliff.

"I told you before that this was about more than silver and gold. The Treasure of the Ocean will yield unto me ultimate power. Kings? Armies? Those are but shadows of true power. Perhaps if you understood that you would join me, as your father once did."

"I would never join you!" Jim shouted. "You're a murderer!" Jim mustered all the defiance he had, even as he and the others inched away from the Count, looking for an escape. Yet escape would not be found. The way was blocked by a second shade, lurking on the starboard steps.

Bartholomew Cromier smiled in the blackness of the storm. His long hair whipped in the wind and his eyes burned at Jim. His red lips curled into a sneer on his pale face. His brandished sword gleamed in the lightning.

"It does my heart glad to hear you say that, Morgan," Bartholomew seethed. "For I would never have you with me. We don't need you! I shall find the Treasure for my father. I shall be the one to wield the power in his name. You will be nothing more than a memory!" Bartholomew lowered his sword toward Jim, the blade dripping with rainwater.

"Give me the shell, boy," Cromier held out a black-gloved hand and curled his fingers, beckoning Jim to obey. "No one else need bleed here tonight. No one else need die." Jim and his friends pressed themselves back against the rail as far as they could. But there was nowhere left to run. Percival was fighting the owls over the waves, and the *Spectre's* crew was battling the Corsairs on the ship's deck. Even if Jim and all his friends had swords, they would stand no chance against the Cromiers.

But the voice of the one who had time and again saved Jim's life called over the storm.

"Cromier!"

Dread Steele swung over the wheel on rigging from the main mast. He landed between the Count and his son, sword drawn. He spun to face both men, standing as a shield for Jim and his friends.

"Well, isn't this poetic?" said Cromier, laughing. The Count shook his head at the storm in the sky and then at Dread Steele. "Look at us. We are all that remains of the Pirates of the Black Skull. Our work is almost complete. So here we are, together again."

"I no longer call myself a member of that order," Steele spat. "The Treasure is Jim's by right. The shell is ours, and with it, the Treasure that was once Lindsay Morgan's. You lost your claim to it long ago."

"In my dreams, I have seen you fall beneath my sword, Steele," Cromier growled.

"I think you shall find the swords in your dream less sharp than those in my hands." Steele drew a second blade from his belt. "Now come to me!"

The two Cromiers fell upon Dread Steele as one. But Dread Steele showed once more why he was Lord of the Pirates. The Captain of the *Spectre* dove into a roll and the two Cromiers swung over top of him, clashing their own swords together. Steele was on his feet again in the blink of an eye. He danced across the deck and took the fight to his enemies.

"Two at once, Jim!" George cried, slapping Jim on the back. He and his brothers shouted encouragement to the Captain over the rain.

"Let's help!" Jim said. He and the Ratts ran to a stack of piled cannon balls. With mischievous gleams in their eyes, they rolled them across the deck, targeting the Cromiers' feet.

"Be careful!" Lacey shouted. But she was never content to sit still herself. She crept over to one of Mister Gilley's barrels and tipped it over. With all of her strength she kicked it hard toward the Count, who failed to see it and tripped over backward, crashing hard onto the deck.

"Well kicked, milady!" Squawked Cornelius.

Jim and George rolled a cannonball each over Bartholomew's toes at the very same moment. The pale captain erupted in a howling stream of curses as he staggered back in pain. Jim and the Ratts leapt up with a cheer, celebratory fists in the air. But a screech then tore over the rain and thunder. A giant owl swooped out of the dark, talons bared, reaching for the shell in Jim's arms.

"Look out, Jim!" Peter and Paul said together. The two younger Ratts tackled Jim out of the way just in time. The owl tore just over their heads. But Jim had no time to thank his friends, for Lacey screamed a second warning.

As the owl had hunted Jim, Percival hunted the owl. His great head crashed through the port railing. The monster's body, many boatlengths long, coiled about the *Spectre* as he fought the owl. His scaly bulk came to rest over the quarterdeck like an armored wall between the Ratt Clan and the battling pirates. Jim and his friends threw themselves against the aft railing as splinters and bits of shattered wood joined the water raining on their heads.

As Jim hit the deck, the shell was jarred loose from his arms. It tumbled across the wooden deck and nearly clattered over the starboard side and into the ocean.

"The shell!" Jim cried. He tore free of Peter and Paul's grasp to chase it down.

"Jim, be careful!" George shouted as Jim slid across the slick wood to retrieve the powerful talisman. But just as Jim's fingertips grazed the Shell's curled edge, a pair of swarthy hands swooped down and snatched up the polished artifact for their own. Jim scrambled back on his hands and knees. He looked up to find Splitbeard the pirate, the Hunter's Shell in his grasp.

TWENTY

THE MANY LIES OF SPLITBEARD THE PIRATE

"Ah, it burns!" Splitbeard gasped. No sooner than he had gained it, the pirate took a start and nearly dropped the shell. The shell's glow returned to life beneath his touch. The sorcerous captain stared deep into the magic flame, as though lost within it. "The shell burns with life. This is most powerful magic indeed, oh brave son of Lindsay Morgan." As the shell's aura strengthened in Splitbeard's hands, so the storm's thunder deepened. The wind slammed against the *Spectre* and the rain stung harder against Jim's skin.

"It's too powerful for you, Splitbeard," Jim yelled, casting his eyes fearfully at the crimson clouds above the ship. "It brought this storm here, can't you see that?"

Splitbeard threw back his head, howling with laughter. The pouring rain splashed in his face and fell into his open mouth. It slicked long strands of greasy locks to his face until he seemed more animal than man.

"Too much magic for Splitbeard the Pirate? There is no such thing, oh young son of Morgan. Do you think that I, master of the black arts, fear this cloud, with its pesky rain? Have you not seen what I can do? Or, perhaps, oh young and foolish one, did you see and not realize that you saw?"

Splitbeard put two fingers to his mouth and loosed a shrill whistle. It was so high and loud that it carried even above the battle and the storm. But there was something in the whistle, Jim thought, something familiar to the rising and falling tune. With a green flash, the pirate's form warped and grew and burst into feathers. Splitbeard transformed his body again into a great owl. He spread his fearsome wings wide and clutched the shell in his claws.

"I know you bore witness to this form, young Morgan, but do you recall this one?" Splitbeard whistled again. His frame twisted and shrunk. The feathers molted down to scaly skin until all that remained was a lizard…a lizard with a twisted tail.

"Hmmm, good to see you took my advice and travelled through the crags, good sirs and lady," the lizard said with a dry, cackling laugh. Jim felt his face grow hot, even in the cold rain. George leapt to his feet behind him, fists clenched at his sides.

"You lied to us!" George raged. He lunged forward as though to charge the lizard and tear him apart with his bare hands. But his younger brothers and Lacey held him back, though it took all three of them to do so. "You lied to us and almost got us killed! You almost got me brothers and me best friends killed! Why do they all keep doing that to us?"

"Almost killed, oh little Ratt child," the lizard said. "If Splitbeard wanted all-the-way killed, I could have done so with ease. Your good friend, Master Morgan, would have been dead long before this adventure even began, before he even left the beach near the pile of ash that had once been his home." The lizard whistled once more. The creature's body writhed and curled until it stood in Splitbeard the Pirate's shape. But just when the pirate had reached full height, he changed again. He shrank shorter and shorter. His smooth, swarthy skin paled and wrinkled. His long black hair retreated into his skull, turning frail and gray. Lastly, his twin-braided beard took solid form and fell from his chin into his hand – a wooden pipe with two necks.

"Philus Philonius!" Jim cried.

"That's the man who took your necklace, Jim?" Lacey gasped. She still held tight to George's arm, though she too seemed more than ready to attack the little wizard who had hurt so many of her friends. "You liar! You should be ashamed of yourself!"

"Indeed I am, little lady," said Philus, though he was smiling gleefully and twittling a little tune on his flute. He reached beneath his shirt and revealed Jim's mother's necklace, dangling it before his eyes. "A good thing I did, too. This little lovely protected me from all the evil enchantments of the island - even from the faeries themselves. I never even would have turned to stone with this around my neck. It is powerful magic, boy. And you gave it to me of your own free will! But nevertheless, you should not be angry. If anything, you should be thanking me."

"Thanking you?" Jim seethed. "For what? Stealing my mother's necklace from me? Sending us into the harpy's nest? Snatching my friends up with your owls? Poisoning me with your cursed rose? You tried to murder me!"

"Murder you?" Philus said, an overly dramatic look of hurt on his face. "Believe me boy, I would have done nothing of the sort. I could have killed you there on the beach, could I not? And think of all the ways I helped you on your journey. If I had not sent you through the crags, the harpies would not have followed you out into the Sea of Grass and saved you from the Cromiers. When my owls captured your friends, they whisked them over the entire dark forest, full of deadly creatures and hidden pitfalls. Your trials were painful, yes, but murdering you? Oh no, Jim, oh no."

Almost at once Jim understood. Philus Philonius wanted the Treasure of the Ocean for himself. But he was no Son of Earth and Son of Sea. He could not wield the Treasure's power on his own. The truth of the rose thorn's poison was more horrifying than Jim could have ever guessed.

"The poison would not have killed my body," Jim said. "But it would have killed me...my soul. That's why I couldn't do what I wanted. I was doing what you wanted. I would have become your slave!"

"Slave?" Philus said, the false incredulity dripping from his face. "Partners, Jim. Partners! All those challenges on the Isle were but tests. Now I know what you're made of, boy. And as for the rose, it fulfilled its purpose, just as I promised it would."

"Fulfilled its purpose?" Jim said, desperately thinking of a way to catch Philus by surprise and win back the shell. "If you mean turning me into your puppet, then you're wrong!"

"Oh no, young Morgan," replied the little sorcerer. He tapped his flute against his chin as a slow, sly grin spread over his rain-slicked face. "The rose has given you the chance to strike revenge. It has given it to you now." Philus stepped to the side, revealing the smashed timbers of the *Spectre* where Percival had broken through. There, dangling by the collar of his red coat, pierced with a splintered board, hung the unconscious Bartholomew Cromier. With a loud snap, the board holding Bartholomew splintered almost to the breaking point, and nearly dumped the angry, young captain into the sea.

"Oh-ho!" Philus said. He danced up and down as the board groaned under the strain of the weather and the weight of Bartholomew's body. "Come with me, Jim. Think of all we can do with the Treasure in our grasp. We can turn the tables on your foes, just as I promised. You need not even strike. In truth, you need not even lift a finger. All you have to do is watch."

The board cracked again, closer and closer to tumbling into the ocean and taking Bartholomew with it. A small ache pulsed from the palm of Jim's hand. He held the hand up, the white rose bloom clearly visible in the lightning's flash. The stem ran all the way to Jim's heart, where the poison of the blackened rose had nearly killed him. Jim looked from his hand to Bartholomew. The pale captain once again seemed so young, not much older than Jim himself. The raindrops were falling down his face like tears.

The board finally snapped in two and Philus Philonius gave a whoop of joy. He threw one hand behind his ear and waited with gleeful anticipation for the loud splash to follow.

But no splash came, for Bartholomew Cromier never fell into the sea.

Jim caught him by the collar of his red coat.

Bartholomew's weight nearly dragged Jim across the wet deck and into the ocean, but Lacey and the Ratts came to the rescue. Together, they pulled with all their might to bring both Jim and the raven-haired Cromier back on deck.

"You fool!" Philus raged. "Do you think he, Bartholomew Cromier, would have spared you? No, no, no! He would have run his blade through your little heart before watching you fall into the sea! It could have been ours, Jim. All the power in the world was yours for the taking!"

"I don't want any power," Jim shouted back over the wind. The storm was growing ever more violent. It tossed the ship back and forth on the waves amongst the rocks. "I just want to go home. But I won't let someone like you or the Cromiers have it either."

"Someone like me?" Philus sneered at Jim. "Look at me, boy! This is the real me. This is the me as I was over one hundred years ago. Do you think a man like this could stand up for himself in this world? I was a victim of all those bigger, stronger, and more powerful than myself." Philus held up the flute, his eyes, half-mad and glazed with fury, fixed upon it. "Magic gave me power. It is that power alone that has kept me safe. Think of all that has been taken from you, Jim. With the power of the very ocean itself at your command, you could be safe from all your enemies for as long as you live. You need never fear again!"

Jim and George went silent. Jim looked to the eldest Ratt Brother, his best friend, and saw that he too considered all the sadness and loss that had befallen them. He too wondered what it might be worth to be so strong that one would never suffer again. Lacey, however, never paused at all. She stepped forward with her fists clenched, glaring at the small sorcerer. Her eyes blazed nearly as bright as the lightning in the air.

"You all try and make it sound like magic will just fix everything, don't you? But every time we've crossed magic, every time, it has almost killed us!" Jim had only to remember the tortuous ache of his poisoned hand to know that Lacey spoke the truth.

"Lacey's right. You talk about protecting us from liars, but you're just another liar yourself." Philus's narrowed his eyes at Jim and his friends. His frail shoulders and hands shook with rage. He jabbed the flute toward Jim's face, his teeth clenched in an animal snarl.

"So be it, Morgan," Philus growled. "But mark my words, child. The day will come when you regret passing this one chance by. You will curse yourself a fool for your weakness!"

Philus Philonius backed away from Jim and his friends and dropped his angry eyes to the shell in his hands. Its glow brightened and cast deep shadows on Philus's aged face. Entranced by the magic, Philus put the flute in his pocket so that he might place both hands on the shell. Its power coursed into his arms.

"As for me," Philus said, his voice high and shrill with ecstasy, "I shall have no such regrets."

The violet light pulsed and shimmered. It threw magic arcs of purple and blue into the sky. The shell's thrum grew louder and louder, and Philus Philonius cackled higher and higher with it. Above Jim's head, the red clouds of the crimson storm began to swirl tight and fast. Purple flashes bloomed within the billows, and thunder rolled over the ocean.

"Lacey, George!" Jim shouted. "Get to Peter and Paul!" He pointed to the two younger Ratt Brothers, clinging tight to the railing at the back of the ship. The swirling storm clouds lowered themselves toward the deck, drawn to the shell's power. Jim had seen this storm before in his dreams. Somehow, in a way he did not fully understand, he knew the storm. He knew it would show no mercy.

"Philus!" Jim screamed as Lacey and George fought through the wind and rain to help Peter and Paul. "The storm! The storm is growing more powerful! Stop using the shell or you'll destroy us all!"

"I cannot be destroyed, Jim Morgan," Philus said, laughing as the shell's power burned like a violet fire in his hands. "I am a master of magic. The shell will lead me to even greater power - the Treasure of the Ocean! Whether through you or Bartholomew Cromier, I shall—" But the last words of the magician's boast were lost in a shuddering boom that shook Jim to his bones. The thunder clapped so sharply in the night that Jim was sure the sky had been split it two.

The truth was worse.

Jim's hands dropped hopelessly to his sides as he stared into the storm. The swirling clouds spiraled down to the *Spectre* in a cyclone of fury. In the center of the funnel, a face formed of lightning like molten steel – the face of the skull from Jim's dreams.

"Philus!" Jim tried one last time. "Stop this!"

But it was too late. Lightning bolts began to fall like arrows.

TWENTY–ONE

THE CRIMSON STORM'S REVENGE

The first barrage of bolts struck the sea around the stalwart *Spectre*. The onslaught was so sudden and ferocious that the pirate battle came to a sudden halt on the ship's deck. The Corsairs and Steele's crew stared in horror at the impossible power descending upon them. Even Percival gave up chasing the owls. He drew his long body from the deck of the *Spectre* and held himself upright and stared into the clouds. The two giant birds fled for their lives into the night.

Another bolt came closer. Then another found its mark. A flash of sizzling heat and blue light blew open a hole in the center of the quarterdeck. The explosion tossed Jim into a heap by the *Spectre's* wheel.

Jim's ears rang as he struggled to sit back up. Lightning bolts were now pouring from the storm's eyes. Before him, on the quarterdeck, a perfect ring of orange fire burned around the hole where the lightning had struck. Jim saw Philus sprawled on the deck. The sorcerer was on all fours and reaching for the shell, which had fallen from his grasp.

Jim staggered to his feet. Not far from him, his tattered jacket still lay on the deck, soaked from the rain. A plan took shape in Jim's mind. If he could beat Philus to the shell and cover it with his jacket, even hurl it into the sea – he might be able to stave off this magic storm and save the lives of his friends. But it was only then that Jim realized he no longer saw either the Ratts or Lacey on the deck.

Where were they? Jim's heart pounded. For a moment he thought the worst, that they had been struck by the great bolt and thrown into the angry sea, or burned into nothing. Then Jim spied two small hands desperately gripping a frayed rope, which hung from the singed aft railing.

Philus had nearly reached the shell, still aglow in purple flame, but for Jim, there was now no choice. He stepped back against Mister Gilly's wheel and took a deep breath, then ran and launched himself over the flaming hole in the ship. He landed hard and slid into the railing. Jim grabbed on to whoever's hands held the rope and peered over the edge of the ship to find that those particular hands belonged to George Ratt. Below him hung, Lacey, Peter, Paul, and Cornelius in a chain of wide-eyed and terrified faces.

"You've all been eatin' spare meals behind me back, 'aven't you?" George screamed, straining against the rope. "You feel like four great rocks tied to me legs!"

"George Ratt, we are no heavier than your big head!" Lacey screamed. But though Jim had arrived in time to help his friends, there was no one to help him. The rope snapped under the weight of the Ratts and Lacey. As they fell, they dragged Jim overboard behind them. A scream started in Jim's chest, but when he hit the water the air was jarred from his lungs. The waves churned over Jim's head and threatened to drag him into the deep. Jim blindly reached for his friends' hands. If they were going to sink, he wanted to be together.

But two lights lit the darkness beneath the surface – two orbs like molten globes. Percival the water dragon had not abandoned his new friends. The great sea serpent brought his head beneath the children and lifted them up from the waves in one swoop. The entire clan plus one half-drowned raven broke the surface, all of them coughing and spitting seawater from their mouths.

"Thank you, Percival!" Jim shouted, patting the water dragon's snout.

"You are still under my protection, are you not?" Percival growled. "I am bound by honor to uphold my duty!"

"Well, you're doing marvelously!" Jim said. Then he turned to his friends. "Are you all alright?"

"Don't worry about us, boy!" Cornelius squawked. "Get the shell, lad, the shell!"

"I'm after it, Cornelius," Jim said. "Percival, take the others out of the storm's reach!" Before his friends had a chance to protest, Jim leapt from Percival's snout over the *Spectre's* railings, as the water dragon swam back from the ship. But by the time Jim dove within reach of the shell, he found he was again too late. Philus was already on his feet. He held the shell in his hands. The purple magic burned bright and the old sorcerer wore a sneer upon his lips.

"How many times will you choose so poorly, young Morgan? You truly are a fool. You don't deserve this magic." Philus glanced up at the face in the clouds. It still bore down on the ship, eyes flashing with yet another burst of lightning. "Goodbye, Jim Morgan," Philus said. "When I see you again, you shall kneel at my feet."

Philus pulled his flute from his pocket, placing it to his lips to transform himself into some manner of beast, no doubt. But yet again, as he had so many times before, Dread Steele appeared from nowhere to fight for Jim and his friends. The Captain leapt over the burning hole and landed on his feet. With one slash of his cutlass he struck the enchanted flute with the flat of his blade and sent it clattering to the deck. Philus Philonius howled as he fell back from Dread Steele.

"Enough!" shouted Steele. "You have given us too much grief for one day, magician. You shall trouble us no more."

"Stay back, dark shadow!" Philus squealed. "The shell is mine! And the Treasure of the Ocean shall be mine as well!"

Steele raised his sword to strike down the quailing wizard, but just before his doom, Philus Philonius burst into tears. Without his magic flute and the power to transform, he was lost. The little sorcerer fell to his knees, trembling shamelessly before the pirate captain. At the pitiful sight of a grown man groveling, much less one that had for so long masqueraded as a pirate of the sea, Dread Steele's gray eyes softened. He lowered his blade, and like a father taking a toy from a disobedient child, the pirate captain contented himself to pry the shell from Philus's grasp. Yet even in light of this mercy, Philus refused to relinquish his prize. He choked back his tears, screaming and cursing, and clung to the shell with both hands.

As Jim watched Steele and Philus wrestle for the shell, the magic talisman burned hotter and hotter. Violet flames washed over the deck and the railings. Jim looked to the sky and caught a startled scream in his throat. The lightning eyes of the storm's face blazed to strike again.

"Steele!" Jim cried above the gale's roar. "The storm!"

The crack of burning air and the rumble of shattered sky tossed Jim's warning to the waves. With all its might, the storm lashed the deck of the *Spectre* with a crooked blade of lightning. A twisting tongue of blue fire raced down from the crimson face in the clouds and at last found its target. It struck the shell with a blow so powerful it swept Jim and his friends from their feet and sent them tumbling across the deck. The taunting, thunderous laugh of the storm rumbled above it all.

Silence followed.

The rain stopped falling and the wind ceased blowing.

In the stillness, Jim lifted his head, slowly, painfully. He saw Steele and Philus, thrown to the deck like scattered leaves in the wind. The shell lay between them, split perfectly in two halves, the shorn edges aglow like molten steel.

TWENTY–TWO

COUNT CROMIER'S ESCAPE

The crimson face in the black clouds melted away and the funnel withdrew. The storm, as if satisfied at last, gathered into itself and crawled across the sky. The last claps of thunder echoed off the ocean waves in its wake.

Stars appeared again. The ocean stilled. A quiet, thick as fog, fell over the deck. All pirates, both Corsair and Buccaneer alike, stared blankly at each other or into the sky, as though they had all woken from the same dream at the same time.

Count Cromier's enraged scream shattered the silence.

"Impossible!" The Red Count cried, picking himself up from the deck where Dread Steele had thrown him down in defeat. "This cannot be!"

Cromier stormed up the stairs and over the burnt remains of the quarterdeck to where the two halves of the shell now lay, lightless, dull, and bereft of all magic. "Lost! All lost!" Cromier screamed again. He collected one of the shell's halves and turned it over in trembling hands. His purple scar quivered violently upon his face.

While Cromier stood stunned, Jim gathered his wits and leapt to his feet. He ran across the deck and seized the other half of the shell before Cromier could take it as well. The Count lifted his eyes, wide and crazed.

"Give that to me, *now*, you cursed son of Morgan!" Cromier spat. He clenched his teeth so tight Jim thought they would break into pieces in the Count's mouth.

"It's broken," Jim said. His heart beat wildly as he looked into the Count's mad eyes, but he refused to back away. "As you said, it's lost. The way to the Treasure is lost. Perhaps it is better that way. It's over."

"Over?" said the Count, scoffing. A grotesque smile twisted his face. "No, no, no, my boy." Cromier squeezed one gloved hand into a fist. "It will never be over, not as long as I draw breath! But for you... for you, young Morgan, it is over. I was a fool to keep my son from cutting out your heart on that island. Now I shall amend my lone mistake."

"At last, father," Bartholomew said, conscious again and appearing at his father's side. A nasty cut bled on his head from where Dread Steele had struck him, but Bartholomew's sword was in his hand. "I am by your side, father. Together we shall yet complete our quest, until we alone hold the power of the Treasure in our grasp. Then the world will tremble beneath our feet!"

"Yes, my son." Cromier flicked his pitiless eyes only for a moment to the fallen form of Philus Philonius, who had not moved. Then he called out to the remaining pirates of the *Sea Spider*. "Men! What share was once meant for your captain, shall now be divided amongst you. Take no prisoners and show no mercy."

The Corsairs shouted their fierce acceptance of this new deal, more loyal to gold, it seemed, than their defeated captain. The men of the *Spectre*, however, bruised and battered and bleeding, from old MacGuffy to sleepy Mister Gilly, hardly raised a sword to their defense. The mighty Dread Steele lay as still as Philus Philonius on the deck. He did not rise to lead them or call out to give them hope. Jim's heart pumped fear into his blood as the Corsairs closed in on the quarterdeck, pushing back the *Spectre's* men. Jim clutched his half of the shell close to his chest, though he held little hope that his strength would be enough to keep it from the Count or his pirates.

Jim closed his eyes and waited for the cold sensation of steel to touch his skin, when a shrill cry pierced the air as Bartholomew shrieked in pain. Jim's eyes flew open to find an arrow quivering in Bartholomew Cromier's arm. The pale captain dropped his sword and it clattered to the deck. The bolt in his shoulder was a white arrow — fashioned from coral of the sea.

The Queen of the Sea, Melodia, and her people had returned. Fulkern and his warriors loosed arrow after arrow and spear after spear at the Cromiers and their men. The merpeople burst from the water and unleashed their attack on the Corsairs, who fled from even the sight of the sea-folk. They all but trampled one another beneath their own boots to escape to the deck of the *Sea Spider*. But flight would not come easily for the Count's thugs.

A fountain of seawater exploded into the sky as Percival returned, the Ratts and Lacey upon his back. He rose up over the decks. The water dragon unleashed his roar with such fury that it sent Corsairs tumbling overboard and into the waves, where the merpeople dragged them into the depths.

Count Cromier turned about in a circle. He watched hopelessly as his hired army was chased by the sea-folk's spears from the left, and swept into the sea by a water dragon of the deep to the right.

"Do not think this means you have won, Jim Morgan!" The Count vowed, stabbing a black-gloved finger in Jim's face. "A pirate does not live so long as I have lived without learning how to survive a single defeat. No, this is not the end, boy. Do not sleep with both eyes closed. Do not rest with your windows open. Do not sit with your back to a door. When you least expect it, I shall return. I shall take what is mine! When I finally possess the power of the Treasure of the Ocean, I shall bend all of its might toward your unending suffering!"

The Count seized Bartholomew by his wounded shoulder, drawing a pained yelp from his son. He then withdrew a small pouch from his pocket. Tipping the pouch over in his hand, the Count poured black powder in a ring on the deck. No sooner did the Cromiers step into the ring than the black powder began to swirl. Faster and faster it turned until it became a black cyclone of smoke that blew away on the ocean wind, leaving not even a trace of the Count or Bartholomew behind.

When the two villains had vanished in the night, Jim ran across the deck and threw himself down at Dread Steele's side. Soot smudged the Captain's face. His shirt and waistcoat were singed black from the lightning bolt that had cleaved the Hunter's Shell in two. Jim gently shook the Captain's shoulder.

"Captain," Jim whispered. "Captain Steele?" The pirate crew of the *Spectre*, MacGuffy and Mufwalme at their head, now gathered around their fallen leader. Just when Jim had given up all hope that Steele would ever stir again, the pirate's eyes quivered and his lids opened half way. His chapped, burnt lips parted just enough for a few hushed words to sneak through.

"Cromiers gone? Crew safe?"

"Yes," said Jim. A hot fire burned in his throat and stung his eyes. "The storm is gone. Queen Melodia came. She and Percival drove the corsairs away. The Count and Bartholomew escaped in a black cloud."

"The shell?" Steele asked. Even his whisper began to fail.

"It's shorn in two, Captain." Jim's words shook and his tears brimmed. "I have one half of it. Cromier has the other. But the magic in the shell is dead, I think. I don't believe anyone will find the Treasure of the Ocean now, Captain. Maybe it's better that way."

Steele weakly shook his head. "There is always a way. The sea is a million roads...full of...storms..."

"I know," Jim said. "I won't let them get me lost again." His chin quivered uncontrollably.

"I'm sorry, Jim. I'm sorry."

"Sorry for what, sir?" Jim leaned closer to the Captain, for his words grew softer with each breath.

"I will not finish this adventure with you." Steele lifted one hand and pointed to Jim's chest. "Though there be ten thousand storms, sail on, Jim. I sail on." Then Dread Steele, shadow of the sea, smiled. It was a quivering grin on his lips that remembered a younger man from brighter days long gone. Then he breathed his last.

Only gently crackling flames and a whispering wind in the slack sails of the great ship *Spectre* marked the passing of Dread Steele, Lord of the Pirates. Two great tears spilt from Jim's eyes. They rolled down his face to drop onto the pirate's cheeks above his smile, like tears of joy on a sea-worn face.

TWENTY-THREE

Sailing On For Distant Shores

Some miles from the Devil's Horns, across the sea, a lonely atoll rose from the waves. It was not much more than a hill of sand and a circle of palm trees at its crest. In the dim morning gray, Jim, the Ratts, Lacey, and all the crew of the *Spectre* stood on the beach, heads down and hats in their hands. Melodia, Queen of the Merpeople, and her folk treaded nearby in the shallow waters. Even Percival, last of the water dragons, looked on from the deeper sea beyond the anchored ship.

In the bottom of a small dinghy, resting on a bed of palms from the island's trees, Dread Steele lay with his eyes closed and face toward the sky. Jim had laid Dread Steele's cutlass and his pistol beside the Captain when the pirates had put him in the boat, and Lacey had kissed his forehead. The Ratts placed one of the toy soldiers Jim had gifted them for Christmas into the boat, for it was all they had to give.

A cool, ocean wind blew across the waves, ruffling cloaks and stinging tear-stained faces. MacGuffy, who was holding the little boat against the tide, opened his mouth to speak some words, but they caught in the old man's throat and refused to come. The aged pirate shook his scarred head and his old chin trembled. Finally, Queen Melodia swam from her people to the side of the boat. Her golden hair shone even before the dawn and her voice rang like a choir of bells.

"There are those in this world who live in the shadows. Sometimes, only when they are gone, do we see they did so to bring light to the darkness. Goodbye, Dread Steele, last Friend of the Sea. Your light will shine on the shores of the country to where you now sail. May it show the way for we who shall one day follow."

Melodia bent down and kissed Dread Steele on the forehead. Then she whispered a few words in her own tongue. At her touch, the small dinghy began to glow. A magic flame spread across every board and nail until it shone the brightest gold. Without so much as a push or pull the little boat glided out on the waters, sailing toward the horizon.

"Sail on, me Cap'n!" MacGuffy cried, great rolling tears falling from his one good eye. "Nothin' can stop the man of the sea from sailin' home, not even death."

"Sail on," said the crew of the *Spectre*, and even Lacey and the Ratts.

"Sail on, Dread Steele," Jim whispered. Quite unexpectedly, in spite of his own tears, a smile found its way on Jim's face. He imagined that perhaps Dread Steele would not be alone when he came to the shores of the next world. Perhaps Lindsay Morgan would be waiting there for him. "Morgan and Steele, together again," Jim said.

Before the boat disappeared from sight, the sun rose over the west and painted a golden path upon the waves. It seemed to Jim that the little boat traveled that shining road to some place beyond where the ocean met the sky.

That same morning, the ocean breeze blew warm and drove the clouds away. The *Spectre's* crew readied to hoist anchor and set sail for home. Jim, Lacey, George, Peter, and Paul stood at the prow to say their goodbyes. Percival swam up alongside the *Spectre*. The spines along his head and his curved teeth flashed in the sun. Jim reached over the railing and petted Percival on his scaly nose.

"Goodbye, Percival," Jim said. "Thank you. Thank you for everything."

"You are most welcome, young Jim Morgan," the sea serpent replied in the softest growl he could manage. "I am sorry for all that you have lost. For the shell yes, which was a powerful talisman left by your father. But more so for the loss of your friend."

"Thank you, Percival," Jim said. "But I did make a new one at least, didn't I?"

"That you have, Jim Morgan. That you have indeed."

"Where will you go now, Percival?" Lacey asked, coming up to stand beside Jim at the railing and pet the dragon a few times herself. "What will you do now that you don't live in that cave under the mountain?"

"Ah, young lady, I will do that which my heart as longed to do for over a hundred years. I will swim into the deep depths, deeper and darker than even the merpeople dare dive. There will I search and search, for I still hold hope that somewhere there is one of my kind yet swimming free."

"I hope you find them, Percival," Lacey said. She leaned as far out as she could and kissed the dragon on the nose.

"We hope so too, Percival," said George, swaggering up with his thumbs stuck through the holes in his jacket again. "Of course, if worse comes to worst, you could always join our gang, right? Don't know what your other plans are after you go and find your mates and all that, but I still think you could have a real future in thievin'. Trust me, I've got an eye for talent."

"We'd have to change our cheer around a bit, Georgie," said Peter, hand on his chin as though trying to think up a new verse.

"We could definitely work it in," added Paul, hands on hips.

"You are all absolutely ridiculous," said Lacey. She shook her head at first, but then suddenly paused with a thought. "Wait, change the cheer? Why didn't you ever change it for me or Jim?"

"Are you a water dragon?" asked Peter.

"Of course not," Lacey replied.

"Well then there you have it, don't you?" said Paul, as though it were obvious. Lacey stomped her foot, but Percival laughed his monstrous laugh and turned with a great rush of water toward the sea.

"Goodbye for now, my friends," he called. "But surely not forever. Until we meet again!" The great sea serpent dove beneath the waves with a splash that clapped over his scaled back. He flicked his tail at the last and sprayed the crew, the bravest of which were waving their hats in salute to the last of the water dragons. No sooner had Percival disappeared beneath the depths than Melodia's sea chariot appeared beside the *Spectre*, drawn by her sharks.

"Goodbye, Queen Melodia," said Jim, bowing his head politely. Lacey managed a proper courtesy herself, but the Ratts, who had never, and would never, Jim thought, grow used to such things, bent over like broken hinges. Peter struck his head soundly on the railing and nearly fell over backward, holding his forehead in both hands while his brothers snickered at him most indiscreetly. Lacey's face pinked horribly, but the Queen smiled nevertheless, the curves of her face as smooth and gentle as crystal glass.

"Farewell, Jim Morgan, son of Lindsay Morgan. Though perhaps we also shall meet again one day soon," said the Queen. Her smile drifted away, though, and she looked upon Jim and his friends with fearful eyes. "I hope with all my heart that you are kept safe until that time. Dangerous days lie ahead. If Count Cromier and his son claim the Treasure of the Ocean, all creatures of good that walk the earth and swim the sea will know unending sorrow."

"I don't know if he will be able to find it, your majesty," said Jim. He played with the silver shell necklace that now hung about his neck, as his father once had when his thoughts grew deep. "The Crimson

Storm destroyed the shell. But even if Cromier discovered a way to repair it, I promise I'll keep my half safe from him. I won't let him have the Treasure of the Ocean."

"You have great courage, Jim," whispered the queen. Her gaze drifted down to the silver shell at Jim's neck, and for a moment, Jim thought he saw the Queen's eyes brighten. "Courage like your parents had. Perhaps there is hope after all. If a day of darkness comes, and you find yourself in need of aid, sail to the island called the Tower's Top. You will find it drawn on Dread Steele's map. Dip the opened shell you wear about your neck into the white foam of the waves at dawn, and we shall come to you. Until that day, I bid you farewell, Son of Earth and Son of Sea."

Before Jim could even return her goodbye, the Queen flicked the seaweed reins of her chariot and the hammerhead sharks pulled the carriage beneath the waves. All the Queen's people followed her with white splashes in the water. They drifted like so many shadows beneath the blue waves until they disappeared from sight, into the depths below.

"Come on now, ye scurvy sons o' squids!" MacGuffy shouted. He stood with Mister Gilly by the wheel, along with giant Mufwalme. "Bend every sail to the wind and set course for the coast o' Spain. May a strong gust and the warmth o' the sun be at our backs 'til we make that port our home!" The crew wasted no time. They dashed back and forth across the deck, scaled the nets to the masts, loosed the sails, and pulled tight the riggings to reach out and grab hold of the wind.

"Spain?" said Lacey in surprise. "Are we not going back to the lighthouse?"

"No," said Jim, as the *Spectre's* canvas sails snapped taut. The stalwart ship crested the first wave of a new journey in an ocean spray. The mist floated through the air, and Jim stared off through it, toward the eastern horizon where the morning sun still lit a golden path upon the sea. "MacGuffy says the Cromiers will have spies waiting there for us, all over England, really. He says that they'll try for the other half of the shell. He says that they may never stop trying for it. So we have to stay on the run."

"Spain, eh?" said George, clicking his teeth with his tongue. "Bet they never even heard of thieves as good as us in Spain." George tried to flash Jim and his brothers his winning smile, but it faltered slightly on his face. He followed Jim's eyes out over the sea, where the boat carrying Dread Steele was still somewhere, floating away.

"What are you going to do, Jim?" Lacey asked, coming to stand between Jim and George. Jim said nothing for a moment, only stood there watching the waves whisk by and breathing in the salty scent of the ocean air.

"Dread Steele said that the ocean was a sea of roads," Jim finally said. "Just a few days ago, we started a journey for home. Surely one of those roads leads to a home for us. Maybe to get there we'll have to face that Crimson Storm again, or fight off the Cromiers from getting the shell. Or maybe we'll have to mend the shell ourselves. But no matter what, I'm still dreaming of a home for us."

"I don't know, Jim," said Peter, leaning on the railing and looking down into the running water below. "Facing those Cromiers again won't exactly be much fun, will it?"

"Or that storm," said Paul, sidling up next to his older brothers. "That was like nothin' I ever even heard of before."

Just then, Cornelius flapped on his healing wing and landed on Jim's shoulder, patting Jim on the back of his head with an outstretched, bandaged wing.

"Shall we sail on then, my boy?" said the raven. "On toward distant shores?"

"On toward home, Cornelius," Jim said, smiling at Peter and Paul with all the hope in his heart. "And I promise you all this – if home is out there, I'll weather ten thousand storms to find it for us."

Epilogue

What Came Through
the Magic Tear

As Jim Morgan and his friends sailed away upon the *Spectre*, an unnatural shadow passed over the rocks and the waves around the Devil's Horns.

The moment the Crimson Storm shattered the Hunter's Shell with a fiery bolt, a small, unseen tear in the fabric between this world and the world of magic ripped open in the air above the rocks. The balance between the two began to come undone.

The fish and the birds sensed this tear and fled. The wild beasts felt things no man knew.

Something, or someone, was coming.

It began with a pop and a flash over one of the rocks. Bursts of light like small fireworks crackled. Green bolts lanced from that unseen tear in the sky. The magic lightning struck the stones and the sea and filled the air with a burning stench. A dark cloud swirled into being in the sky above the rocks. Finally, the force behind the veil broke through in a fountain of green fire and magic flames. Like glowing water poured into a glass, the flame took shape upon one of the boulders. It molded itself into the form of a man.

A column of steam rose from the place where the green flames had burned. The razor edge of the rock had melted like candle wax. When the wind blew the column of smoke away, all that remained was the man. He was tall and thin. He wore silk breeches and a silk split tail coat. A long, hooked nose stabbed from his face beneath dark eyes, and a sly smile spread across his pallid cheeks. Before him, the man tapped his long, spidery fingertips together in eager anticipation.

"At last," said the man to nobody but himself. He took a long breath of free air and smiled with delight at the sound of his own voice. "Free at last, free at last. Did you think you had escaped me, Jim Morgan? Did you really think you had seen the last of me? Silly boy, silly, silly boy. There is no prison that can hold me. There is no escape from me...not before, and certainly not now. For I am the King of Thieves."

The man, the King of Thieves, laughed a cackling howl of glee that echoed over the waters. Bright green flames lit in his eyes and, with the crackle of magic, he disappeared into nowhere, as though he had never even been there at all.

TO BE CONTINUED...

ACKNOWLEDGMENTS

Sometime in the summer of 2008, I wrote the first words of *Jim Morgan and the King of Thieves*. It's strange to think back to that time, before Jim and his story constantly took up all my nights and weekends. It's even stranger to think back to that younger version of myself, just feeling his way along his writer's journey. That summer I only intended to write a single book, which would encompass young Jim's entire adventure. In fact, the original title of the first novel was simply *The Adventures of Jim Morgan*.

Before I ever wrote the very first sentence that summer, I had already been pursuing creative writing for several years. I'd written a handful of screenplays, two or three of which I'm actually still quite fond. I'd also written two science fiction novels and several short stories that gained a small readership online. Along the way, I read a pile of books on story structure, plot, character development, and all those other tedious, essential things. But what changed for me that summer was that I finally stumbled upon a story I needed to tell. It is still the story I love telling now.

Something else began to change for me that year. When I first set out to write – to *really* write – with the hope that others would read my work and possibly even walk away better for it, I thought a book was the work of the author alone. After all, it is the author's name alone beneath the title on the cover, right? I've been mistaken about many things in my life. About this I was hopelessly wrong.

A great deal is made of the need for persistence in the creative world, and rightfully so. Rejection is the pits, and the will to stand back up after being slapped down is essential to surviving the writing life. But more than even that, I believe what any adventurer needs to reach the end of his or her personal quest, whether creative or not, is learning. Learning is being challenged with failure, over and over again. Learning is coming to grips with the fact that we don't know it all, and never will. Learning is change, even when we don't want to. Learning is growth, even when we think we're already grown. To learn, we need teachers and friends and family. We need those courageous enough to look us in the eye and tell us that what we've done isn't good enough – that we're capable of doing better. I've been blessed with many of these wonderful people upon my journey. Though my thanks is just a few words on a page, I hope it conveys to them the depths of my gratitude for walking even a part of the way down this path beside me.

To Prof. Bill Campbell, Prof. David Bradley, Julie Gray, and Tamson Weston, you've all taught me more about writing that you may ever realize.

To Prof. Jean-Marie Rouhier-Willoughby, thank you for introducing me to the language of myth and storytelling. You may not know it, but your class on folklore was what truly sparked my love of story.

To Lora Lee, thank you for bringing the gift of your beautiful artwork to the world of Jim Morgan.

To Steve Martinez, Richard Smith, Sam Winokur, Eric "Che" Lopez, Bridget Fredstrom, Jenny Minniti, Nikki Katz, Cassandra Brown, and Ty King, thank you for being my brain trust and my readers. But most of all, thank you for being my friends.

To the Cottinghams, the Smiths, the Johnsons, Chad Perkins, the Phams, Ditter Kellen, and David Berger, thank you for your love and encouragement.

Acknowledgments

To my Mom, Heather, Mickey, Oma, Opa, and all my family, thank you for your faith in me. Thank you for telling me that I can do anything – and for believing it.

Finally, thank you to anyone and everyone who has taken the time to read my books. I hope the stories stay with you, and perhaps provide you with at least a smile when one is needed.

Made in the USA
San Bernardino, CA
25 May 2014